The Brothers Grimm
Volume 2:
110 Grimmer Fairy Tales

Word Cloud Classics

A Christmas Carol
and Other Holiday Treasures

Adventures of
Huckleberry Finn

The Adventures of
Sherlock Holmes

Aesop's Fables

The Age of Innocence

Anna Karenina

Anne of Green Gables

The Art of War

The Brothers Grimm:
101 Fairy Tales

Common Sense and Selected
Works of Thomas Paine

The Count of Monte Cristo

Don Quixote

Dracula

Emma

Frankenstein

Great Expectations

Inferno

Jane Eyre

Lady Chatterley's Lover

Les Misérables

Little Women

Madame Bovary

Moby-Dick

Narrative of the Life of
Frederick Douglass and
Other Works

Persuasion

The Picture of Dorian Gray

Pride and Prejudice

The Prince and Other Writings

The Red Badge of Courage
and Other Stories

The Scarlet Letter

The Secret Garden

Sense and Sensibility

The Three Musketeers

Twenty Thousand Leagues
Under the Sea

Uncle Tom's Cabin

Walden and Civil
Disobedience

The Wizard of Oz

The Brothers Grimm
Volume 2:
110 Grimmer Fairy Tales

Translation by Margaret Hunt

Word Cloud Classics

San Diego

Canterbury Classics
An imprint of Printers Row Publishing Group
10350 Barnes Canyon Road, Suite 100, San Diego, CA 92121
www.thunderbaybooks.com

Printers Row Publishing Group is a division of Readerlink Distribution Services, LLC. The Canterbury Classics and Word Cloud Classics names and logos are trademarks of Readerlink Distribution Services, LLC.

All correspondence concerning the content of this book should be addressed to Canterbury Classics, Editorial Department, at the above address.

Publisher: Peter Norton
Publishing Team: Lori Asbury, Ana Parker, Laura Vignale, Kathryn Chipinka
Editorial Team: JoAnn Padgett, Melinda Allman
Production Team: Jonathan Lopes, Rusty von Dyl

Library of Congress Cataloging-in-Publication Data

Kinder- und Hausmärchen. English. Selections.
  The Brothers Grimm. Volume II, 110 Grimmer Fairy Tales.
    pages cm
  ISBN-13: 978-1-60710-730-9 (alk. paper)
  ISBN-10: 1-60710-730-9 (alk. paper)
1. Fairy tales--Germany. I. Grimm, Jacob, 1785-1863. II. Grimm,
Wilhelm, 1786-1859. III. Title: 110 Grimmer Fairy Tales.

GR166.K53213 2013
398.20943--dc23

                        2012041469

              PRINTED IN CHINA

          20 19 18 17 16 6 7 8 9 10

CONTENTS

1. The Willow Wren and the Bear

Once in summertime the bear and the wolf were walking in the forest, and the bear heard a bird singing so beautifully that he said, "Brother wolf, what bird is it that sings so well?"

"That is the King of birds," said the wolf, "before whom we must bow down." It was, however, in reality the willow wren (Zaunkönig).

"If that's the case," said the bear, "I should very much like to see his royal palace; come, take me there."

"That is not done quite as you seem to think," said the wolf; "you must wait until the Queen comes."

Soon afterward, the Queen arrived with some food in her beak, and the lord King came too, and they began to feed their young ones. The bear would have liked to go at once, but the wolf held him back by the sleeve, and said, "No, you must wait until the lord and lady Queen have gone away again." So they observed the hole in which was the nest, and trotted away.

The bear, however, could not rest until he had seen the royal palace, and when a short time had passed, again went to it. The King and Queen had just flown out, so he peeped in and saw five or six young ones lying in it. "Is that the royal palace?" cried the bear. "It is a wretched palace, and you are not King's children, you are disreputable children!"

When the young wrens heard that, they were frightfully angry, and screamed, "No, that we are not! Our parents are honest people! Bear, you will have to pay for that!"

The bear and the wolf grew uneasy, and turned back and went into their holes. The young willow wrens, however, continued to cry and scream, and when their parents again brought food they said, "We will not so much as touch one fly's leg, no, not if we were dying of hunger, until you have settled whether we are respectable children or not; the bear has been here and has insulted us!"

Then the old King said, "Be easy, he shall be punished," and he at once flew with the Queen to the bear's cave, and called in, "Old Growler, why have you insulted my children? You shall suffer for it—we will punish you by a bloody war." Thus war was announced to the Bear, and all four-footed animals were summoned to take part in it, oxen, asses, cows, deer, and every other animal the earth contained. And the willow wren summoned everything which flew in the air, not only birds, large and small, but midges, and hornets, bees and flies had to come.

When the time came for the war to begin, the willow wren sent out spies to discover who was the enemy's commander-in-chief. The gnat, who was the most crafty, flew into the forest where the enemy was assembled, and hid herself beneath a leaf of the tree where the watchword was to be given. There stood the bear, and he called the fox before him and said, "Fox, you are the most cunning of all animals, you shall be general and lead us."

"Good," said the fox, "but what signal shall we agree upon?" No one knew that, so the fox said, "I have a fine long bushy tail, which almost looks like a plume of red feathers. When I lift my tail up quite high, all is going well, and you must charge; but if I let it hang down, run away as fast as you can." When the gnat had heard that, she flew away again, and revealed everything, with the greatest minuteness, to the willow wren. When day broke, and the battle was to begin, all the four-footed animals came running up with such a noise that the earth trembled. The willow wren also came flying through the air with his army with such a humming, and whirring, and swarming that everyone was uneasy and afraid, and on both sides they advanced against each other. But the willow wren sent down the hornet, with orders to get beneath the fox's tail, and sting with all his might. When the fox felt the first sting, he started so that he drew up one leg, in pain, but he bore it, and still kept his tail high in the air; at the second sting, he was forced to put it down for a moment; at the third, he could hold out no longer, and screamed out and put his tail between his legs. When the animals saw that, they thought all was lost, and began to fly, each into his hole and the birds had won the battle.

Then the King and Queen flew home to their children and cried, "Children, rejoice, eat and drink to your heart's content, we have won the battle!"

But the young wrens said, "We will not eat yet, the bear must come to the nest, and beg for pardon and say that we are honorable children, before we will do that."

Then the willow wren flew to the bear's hole and cried, "Growler, you are to come to the nest to my children, and beg their pardon, or else every rib of your body shall be broken." So the bear crept there in the greatest fear, and begged their pardon. And now at last the young wrens were satisfied, and sat down together and ate and drank, and made merry till quite late into the night.

2. *Sweet Porridge*

There was a poor but good little girl who lived alone with her mother, and they no longer had anything to eat. So the child went into the forest, and there an aged woman met her who was aware of her sorrow, and presented her with a little pot, which when she said, "Cook, little pot, cook," would cook good, sweet porridge, and when she said, "Stop, little pot," it ceased to cook. The girl took the pot home to her mother, and now they were freed from their poverty and hunger, and ate sweet porridge as often as they chose.

Once on a time when the girl had gone out, her mother said, "Cook, little pot, cook." And it did cook and she ate till she was satisfied, and then she wanted the pot to stop cooking, but did not know the word. So it went on cooking and the porridge rose over the edge, and still it cooked on until the kitchen and whole house were full, and then the next house, and then the whole street, just as if it wanted to satisfy the hunger of the whole world, and there was the greatest distress, but no one knew how to stop it. At last when only one single house remained, the child came home and just said, "Stop, little pot," and it stopped and gave up cooking, and whoever wished to return to the town had to eat his way back.

3. *Wise Folks*

One day a peasant took his good hazel stick out of the corner and said to his wife, "Trina, I am going across country, and shall not return for three days. If during that time the cattle dealer should happen to call and want to buy our three cows, you may strike a bargain at once, but not unless you can get two hundred thalers for them; nothing less, do you hear?"

"For heaven's sake just go in peace," answered the woman, "I will manage that."

"You, indeed," said the man. "You once fell on your head when you were a little child, and that affects you even now; but let me tell you this, if you do anything foolish, I will make your back black and blue, and not with paint, I assure you, but with the stick that I have in my hand, and the coloring shall last a whole year, you may rely on that." And having said that, the man went on his way.

Next morning the cattle dealer came, and the woman had no need to say many words to him. When he had seen the cows and heard the price, he said, "I am quite willing to give that, honestly speaking, they are worth it. I will take the beasts away with me at once."

He unfastened their chains and drove them out of the barn, but just as he was going out of the door, the woman clutched him by the sleeve and said, "You must give me the two hundred thalers now, or I cannot let the cows go."

"True," answered the man, "but I have forgotten to buckle on my money belt. Have no fear, however, you shall have security for my paying. I will take two cows with me and leave one, and then you will have a good pledge."

The woman saw the force of this, and let the man go away with the cows, and thought to herself, "How pleased Hans will be when he finds how cleverly I have managed it!"

The peasant came home on the third day as he had said he would, and at once inquired if the cows were sold. "Yes, indeed, dear Hans," answered the woman, "and as you said, for two hundred thalers. They are scarcely worth so much, but the man took them without making any objection."

"Where is the money?" asked the peasant.

"Oh, I have not got the money," replied the woman; "he had happened to forget his money belt, but he will soon bring it, and he left good security behind him."

"What kind of security?" asked the man.

"One of the three cows, which he shall not have until he has paid for the other two. I have managed very cunningly, for I have kept the smallest, which eats the least."

The man was enraged and lifted up his stick, and was just going to give her the beating he had promised her. Suddenly he let the stick fall and said, "You are the stupidest goose that ever waddled on God's earth, but I am sorry for you. I will go out into the highways and wait for three days to see if I find anyone who is still stupider than you. If I succeed in doing so, you shall go scot-free, but if I do not find him, you shall receive your well-deserved reward without any discount."

He went out into the great highways, sat down on a stone, and waited for what would happen. Then he saw a peasant's wagon coming toward him, and a woman was standing upright in the middle of it, instead of sitting on the bundle of straw which was lying beside her, or walking near the oxen and leading them. The man thought to himself, "That is certainly one of the kind I am in search of," and jumped up and ran backward and forward in front of the wagon like one who is not very wise.

"What do you want, my friend?" said the woman to him; "I don't know you, where do you come from?"

"I have fallen down from heaven," replied the man, "and don't know how to get back again, couldn't you drive me up?"

"No," said the woman, "I don't know the way, but if you come from heaven you can surely tell me how my husband, who has been there these three years, is. You must have seen him?"

"Oh, yes, I have seen him, but all men can't get on well. He keeps sheep, and the sheep give him a great deal to do. They run up the mountains and lose their way in the wilderness, and he has to run after them and drive them together again. His clothes are all torn to pieces too, and will soon fall off his body. There is no tailor there, for Saint Peter won't let any of them in, as you know by the story."

"Who would have thought it?" cried the woman. "I tell you what, I will fetch his Sunday coat that is still hanging at home in the cupboard, he can wear that and look respectable. You will be so kind as to take it with you."

"That won't do very well," answered the peasant; "people are not allowed to take clothes into heaven, they are taken away from one at the gate."

"Then listen," said the woman, "I sold my fine wheat yesterday and got a good lot of money for it, I will send that to him. If you hide the purse in your pocket, no one will know that you have it."

"If you can't manage it any other way," said the peasant, "I will do you that favor."

"Just sit still where you are," said she, "and I will drive home and fetch the purse, I shall soon be back again. I do not sit down on the bundle of straw, but stand up in the wagon, because it makes it lighter for the cattle."

She drove her oxen away, and the peasant thought, "That woman has a perfect talent for folly, if she really brings the money, my wife may think herself fortunate, for she will get no beating." It was not long before she came in a great hurry with the money, and with her own hands put it in his pocket. Before she went away, she thanked him again a thousand times for his courtesy.

When the woman got home again, she found her son who had come in from the field. She told him what unlooked-for things had befallen her, and then added, "I am truly delighted at having found an opportunity of sending something to my poor husband. Who would ever have imagined that he could be suffering for want of anything up in heaven?"

The son was full of astonishment. "Mother," said he, "it is not every day that a man comes from heaven in this way, I will go out immediately, and see if he is still to be found; he must tell me what it is like up there, and how the work is done." He saddled the horse and rode off with all speed. He found the peasant who was sitting under a willow tree, and was just going to count the money in the purse. "Have you seen the man who has fallen down from heaven?" cried the youth to him.

"Yes," answered the peasant, "he has set out on his way back there, and has gone up that hill, from which it will be rather nearer; you could still catch him up, if you were to ride fast."

"Alas," said the youth, "I have been doing tiring work all day, and the ride here has completely worn me out; you know the man, be so kind as to get on my horse, and go and persuade him to come here."

"Aha!" thought the peasant, "here is another who has no wick in his lamp!" But he said, "Why should I not do you this favor?" and mounted the horse and rode off in a quick trot.

The youth remained sitting there till night fell, but the peasant never came back. "The man from heaven must certainly have been in a great hurry, and would not turn back," thought he, "and the peasant has no doubt given him the horse to take to my father." He went home and told his mother what had happened, and that he had sent his father the horse so that he might not have to be always running about. "You have done well," answered she. "Your legs are younger than his, and you can go on foot."

When the peasant got home, he put the horse in the stable beside the cow that he had as a pledge, and then went to his wife and said, "Trina, as your luck would have it, I have found two who are still sillier fools than you; this time you escape without a beating, I will store it up for another occasion." Then he lighted his pipe, sat down in his grandfather's chair, and said, "It was a good stroke of business to get a sleek horse and a great purse full of money into the bargain, for two lean cows. If stupidity always brought in as much as that, I would be quite willing to hold it in honor." So thought the peasant, but you no doubt prefer the simple folks.

4. Stories about Snakes

FIRST STORY.

There was once a little child whose mother gave her every afternoon a small bowl of milk and bread, and the child seated herself in the yard with it. When she began to eat, however, a snake came creeping out of a crevice in the wall, dipped its little head in the dish, and ate with her. The child had pleasure in this, and when she was sitting there with her little dish and the snake did not come at once, she cried,

> "Snake, snake, come swiftly
> Here come, you tiny thing,
> You shall have your crumbs of bread,
> You shall refresh yourself with milk."

Then the snake came in haste, and enjoyed its food. Moreover it showed gratitude, for it brought the child all kinds of pretty things from its hidden treasures, bright stones, pearls, and golden playthings. The snake, however, only drank the milk, and left the breadcrumbs alone. Then one day the child took its little spoon and struck the snake gently on its head with it, and said, "Eat the breadcrumbs as well, little thing." The mother, who was standing in the kitchen, heard the child talking to someone, and when she saw that she was striking a snake with her spoon, ran out with a log of wood, and killed the good little creature.

From that time forth, a change came over the child. As long as the snake had eaten with her, she had grown tall and strong, but now she lost her pretty rosy cheeks and wasted away. It was not long before the funeral bird began to cry in the night, and the redbreast to collect little branches and leaves for a funeral garland, and soon afterward the child lay on her bier.

SECOND STORY.

An orphan child was sitting on the town walls spinning, when she saw a snake coming out of a hole low down in the wall. Swiftly she spread out beside this one of the blue silk handkerchiefs that snakes have such a strong liking for, and which are the only things they will creep on. As soon as the snake saw it, it went back, then returned, bringing with it a small golden crown, laid it on the handkerchief, and then went away again. The girl took up the crown, it glittered and was of delicate golden filigree work. It was not long before the snake came back for the second time, but when it no longer saw the crown, it crept up to the wall, and in its grief smote its little head against it as long as it had strength to do so, until at last it lay there dead. If the girl had but left the crown where it was, the snake would certainly have brought still more of its treasures out of the hole.

THIRD STORY.

A snake cries, "Huhu, huhu."
A child says, "Come out." The snake comes out, then the child inquires about her little sister: "Have you not seen little Red Stockings?"

The snake says, "No."
"Neither have I."
"Then I am like you. Huhu, huhu, huhu."

5. *The Poor Miller's Boy and the Cat*

In a certain mill lived an old miller who had neither wife nor child, and three apprentices served under him. As they had been with him several years, he one day said to them, "I am old, and want to sit in the chimney corner, go out, and whoever brings me the best horse home, to him I will give the mill, and in return for it he shall take care of me till my death." The third of the boys was, however, the drudge, who was looked on as foolish by the others; they could not imagine what he would do with a mill, and in any case, he would not have it. All three went out together, and when they came to the village, the two said to stupid Hans, "You may just as well stay here, as long as you live you will never get a horse."

Hans, however, went with them, and when it was night they came to a cave in which they lay down to sleep. The two sharp ones waited until Hans had fallen asleep, then they got up, and went away leaving him where he was. And they thought they had done a very clever thing, but it was certain to turn out ill for them. When the sun arose, and Hans woke up, he was lying in a deep cavern. He looked around on every side and exclaimed, "Oh, heavens, where am I?" Then he got up and clambered out of the cave, went into the forest, and thought, "Here I am quite alone and deserted, how shall I obtain a horse now?"

While he was thus walking full of thought, he met a small tabby cat, which said quite kindly, "Hans, where are you going?"

"Alas, you cannot help me."

"I well know your desire," said the cat. "You wish to have a beautiful horse. Come with me, and be my faithful servant for seven years long, and then I will give you one more beautiful than any you have ever seen in your whole life."

"Well, this is a wonderful cat!" thought Hans, "but I am determined to see if she is telling the truth." So she took him with her into her enchanted castle, where there were nothing but cats who were her servants. They leapt nimbly upstairs and downstairs, and were merry and happy. In the evening when they sat down to dinner, three of them had to make music. One played the bassoon, the other the fiddle, and the third put the trumpet to his lips, and blew out his cheeks as much as he possibly could. When they had dined, the table was carried away, and the cat said, "Now, Hans, come and dance with me."

"No," said he, "I won't dance with a pussycat. I have never done that yet."

"Then take him to bed," said she to the cats. So one of them lighted his way to his bedroom, one pulled his shoes off, one his stockings, and at last one of them blew out the candle.

Next morning they returned and helped him out of bed, one put his stockings on for him, one tied his garters, one brought his shoes, one washed him, and one dried his face with her tail. "That feels very soft!" said Hans. He, however, had to serve the cat, and chop some wood every day, and to do that, he had an ax of silver, and the wedge and saw were of silver and the mallet of copper. So he chopped the wood small; stayed there in the house and had good meat and drink, but never saw anyone but the tabby cat and her servants.

One day she said to him, "Go and mow my meadow, and dry the grass," and gave him a scythe of silver, and a whetstone of gold, but bade him deliver them up again carefully. So Hans went there, and did what he was bidden, and when he had finished the work, he carried the scythe, whetstone, and hay to the house, and asked if it was not yet time for her to give him his reward. "No," said the cat, "you must first do something more for me of the same kind. There is timber of silver, carpenter's ax, square, and everything that is needful, all of silver— with these build me a small house."

Then Hans built the small house, and said that he had now done everything, and still he had no horse. Nevertheless the seven years had gone by with him as if they were six months. The cat asked him if he would like to see her horses? "Yes," said Hans. Then she opened the door of the small house, and when she had opened it, there stood twelve horses, such horses, so bright and shining, that his heart rejoiced at the sight of them.

And now she gave him food and drink, and said, "Go home, I will not give you your horse away with you; but in three days' time I will follow you and bring it." So Hans set out, and she showed him the way to the mill. She had, however, never once given him a new coat, and he had been obliged to keep on his dirty old smock frock, which he had brought with him, and which during the seven years had everywhere become too small for him.

When he reached home, the two other apprentices were there again as well, and each of them certainly had brought a horse with him, but one of them was a blind one, and the other lame. They asked Hans where his horse was. "It will follow me in three days' time."

Then they laughed and said, "Indeed, stupid Hans, where will you get a horse?"

"It will be a fine one!"

Hans went into the parlor, but the miller said he should not sit down to table, for he was so ragged and torn, that they would all be ashamed of him if anyone came in. So they gave him a mouthful of food outside, and at night, when they went to rest, the two others would not let him have a bed, and at last he was forced to creep into the goose-house, and lie down on a little hard straw.

In the morning when he awoke, the three days had passed, and a coach came with six horses and they shone so bright that it was delightful to see them! And a servant brought a seventh as well, which was for the poor miller's boy. And a magnificent princess alighted from the coach and went into the mill, and this princess was the little tabby cat whom poor Hans had served for seven years. She asked the miller where the miller's boy and drudge was?

Then the miller said, "We cannot have him here in the mill, for he is so ragged; he is lying in the goose-house." Then the King's daughter said that they were to bring him immediately. So they brought him out, and he had to hold his little smock frock together to cover himself. The servants unpacked splendid garments, and washed him and dressed him, and when that was done, no King could have looked more handsome.

Then the maiden desired to see the horses that the other apprentices had brought home with them, and one of them was blind and the other lame. So she ordered the servant to bring the seventh horse, and when the miller saw it, he said that such a horse as that had never yet entered his yard. "And that is for the miller's third boy," said she.

"Then he must have the mill," said the miller, but the King's daughter said that the horse was there, and that he was to keep his mill as well, and took her faithful Hans and set him in the coach, and drove away with him. They first drove to the little house that he had built with the silver tools, and behold it was a great castle, and everything inside it was of silver and gold; and then she married him, and he was rich, so rich that he had enough for all the rest of his life. After this, let no one ever say that anyone who is silly can never become a person of importance.

6. *The Two Travelers*

Hill and vale do not come together, but the children of men do, good and bad. In this way a shoemaker and a tailor once met with each other in their travels. The tailor was a handsome little fellow who was always merry and full of enjoyment. He saw the shoemaker coming toward him from the other side, and as he observed by his bag what kind of a trade he plied, he sang a little mocking song to him,

> "Sew me the seam,
> Draw me the thread,
> Spread it over with pitch,
> Knock the nail on the head."

The shoemaker, however, could not endure a joke; he made a face as if he had drunk vinegar, and gestured as if he were about to seize the tailor by the throat. But the little fellow began to laugh, reached him his bottle, and said, "No harm was meant, take a drink, and swallow your anger down."

The shoemaker took a very hearty drink, and the storm on his face began to clear away. He gave the bottle back to the tailor, and said, "I spoke civilly to you; one speaks well after much drinking, but not after much thirst. Shall we travel together?"

"All right," answered the tailor, "if only it suits you to go into a big town where there is no lack of work."

"That is just where I want to go," answered the shoemaker. "In a small nest there is nothing to earn, and in the country, people like to go barefoot." They traveled therefore onward together, and always set one foot before the other like a weasel in the snow.

Both of them had time enough, but little to bite and to break. When they reached a town they went about and paid their respects to the tradesmen, and because the tailor looked so lively and merry, and had such pretty red cheeks, everyone gave him work willingly, and when luck was good the master's daughters gave him a kiss beneath the porch, as well. When he again fell in with the shoemaker, the tailor had always the most in his bundle. The ill-tempered shoemaker made a wry face, and thought, "The greater the rascal the more the luck," but the tailor began to laugh and to sing, and shared all he got with his comrade. If a couple of pence jingled in his pockets, he ordered good cheer, and thumped the table in his joy till the glasses danced, and it was lightly come, lightly go, with him.

When they had traveled for some time, they came to a great forest through which passed the road to the capital. Two footpaths, however, led through it, one of which was a seven days' journey, and the other only two, but neither of the travelers knew which way was the short one. They seated themselves beneath an oak tree, and took counsel together how they should forecast, and for how many days they should provide themselves with bread. The shoemaker said, "One must look before one leaps, I will take with me bread for a week."

"What!" said the tailor, "drag bread for seven days on one's back like a beast of burden, and not be able to look about. I shall trust in God, and not trouble myself about anything! The money I have in my pocket is as good in summer as in winter, but in hot weather bread gets dry, and moldy into the bargain; even my coat does not go as far as it might. Besides, why should we not find the right way? Bread for two days, and that's enough." Each, therefore, bought his own bread, and then they tried their luck in the forest.

It was as quiet there as in a church. No wind stirred, no brook murmured, no bird sang, and through the thickly-leaved branches no sunbeam forced its way. The shoemaker never spoke a word, the heavy bread weighed down his back until the perspiration streamed down his cross and gloomy face. The tailor, however, was quite merry, he jumped about, whistled on a leaf, or sang a song, and thought to himself, "God in heaven must be pleased to see me so happy."

This lasted two days, but on the third the forest would not come to an end, and the tailor had eaten up all his bread, so after all his heart sank down a yard deeper. In the meantime he did not lose courage, but relied on God and on his luck. On the third day he lay down in the evening hungry under a tree, and rose again next morning hungry still; so also passed the fourth day, and when the shoemaker seated himself on a fallen tree and devoured his dinner, the tailor was only a looker-on. If he begged for a little piece of bread the other laughed mockingly, and said, "You have always been so merry, now you can try for once what it is to be sad: the birds which sing too early in the morning are struck by the hawk in the evening." In short he was pitiless. But on the fifth morning the poor tailor could no longer stand up, and was hardly able to utter one word for weakness; his cheeks were white, and his eyes red. Then the shoemaker said to him, "I will give you a bit of bread today, but in return for it, I will put out your right eye." The unhappy tailor who still wished to save his life, could not do it in any other way; he wept once more with both eyes, and then held them open, and the shoemaker, who had a heart of stone, put out his right eye with a sharp knife.

The tailor called to remembrance what his mother had formerly said to him when he had been eating secretly in the pantry. "Eat what one can, and suffer what one must." When he had consumed his dearly-bought bread, he got on his legs again, forgot his misery and comforted himself with the thought that he could always see enough with one eye. But on the sixth day, hunger made itself felt again, and gnawed him almost to the heart. In the evening he fell down by a tree, and on the seventh morning he could not raise himself up for faintness, and death was close at hand.

Then said the shoemaker, "I will show mercy and give you bread once more, but you shall not have it for nothing, I shall put out your other eye for it."

And now the tailor felt how thoughtless his life had been, prayed to God for forgiveness, and said, "Do what you will, I will bear what I must, but remember that our Lord God does not always look on passively, and that an hour will come when the evil deed that you have done to me, and which I have not deserved of you, will be requited. When times were good with me, I shared what I had with you. My trade is of that kind that each stitch must always be exactly like the other. If I no longer have my eyes and can sew no more I must go a-begging. At any rate do not leave me here alone when I am blind, or I shall die of hunger." The shoemaker, however, who had driven God out of his heart, took the knife and put out his left eye. Then he gave him a bit of bread to eat, held out a stick to him, and drew him on behind him.

When the sun went down, they got out of the forest, and before them in the open country stood the gallows. There the shoemaker guided the blind tailor, and then left him alone and went his way. Weariness, pain, and hunger made the wretched man fall asleep, and he slept the whole night. When day dawned he awoke, but knew not where he lay. Two poor sinners were hanging on the gallows, and a crow sat on the head of each of them. Then one of the men who had been hanged began to speak, and said, "Brother, are you awake?"

"Yes, I am awake," answered the second.

"Then I will tell you something," said the first; "the dew that this night has fallen down over us from the gallows gives everyone who washes himself with it his eyes again. If blind people did but know this, how many would regain their sight who do not believe that to be possible."

When the tailor heard that, he took his handkerchief, pressed it on the grass, and when it was moist with dew, washed the sockets of his eyes with it. Immediately what the man on the gallows had said was fulfilled, and a couple of healthy new eyes filled the sockets. It was not long before the tailor saw the sun rise behind the mountains; in the plain before him lay the great royal city with its magnificent gates and hundred towers, and the golden balls and crosses that were on the spires began to shine. He could distinguish every leaf on the trees, saw the birds that flew past, and the midges that danced in the air. He took a needle out of his pocket, and as he could thread it as well as ever he had done, his heart danced with delight. He threw himself on his knees, thanked God for the mercy he had shown him, and said his morning prayer. He did not forget also to pray for the poor sinners who were hanging there swinging against each other in the wind like the pendulums of clocks. Then he took his bundle on his back and soon forgot the pain of heart he had endured, and went on his way singing and whistling.

The first thing he met was a brown foal running about the fields at large. He caught it by the mane, and wanted to spring on it and ride into the town. The foal, however, begged to be set free. "I am still too young," it said. "Even a light tailor such as you are would break my back in two, let me go till I have grown strong. A time may perhaps come when I may reward you for it."

"Run off," said the tailor, "I see you are still a giddy thing." He gave it a touch with a switch over its back, whereupon it kicked up its hind legs for joy, leapt over hedges and ditches, and galloped away into the open country.

But the little tailor had eaten nothing since the day before. "The sun to be sure fills my eyes," said he, "but the bread does not fill my mouth. The first thing that comes across me and is even half edible will have to suffer for it." In the meantime a stork stepped solemnly over the meadow toward him. "Halt, halt!" cried the tailor, and seized him by the leg. "I don't know if you are good to eat or not, but my hunger leaves me no great choice. I must cut your head off, and roast you."

"Don't do that," replied the stork; "I am a sacred bird that brings mankind great profit, and no one does me an injury. Leave me my life, and I may do you good in some other way."

"Well, be off, Cousin Longlegs," said the tailor. The stork rose up, let its long legs hang down, and flew gently away.

"What's to be the end of this?" said the tailor to himself at last, "My hunger grows greater and greater, and my stomach more and more empty. Whatever comes in my way now is lost." At this moment he saw a couple of young ducks come swimming toward him across a pond. "You come just at the right moment," said he, and laid hold of one of them and was about to wring its neck.

At this an old duck that was hidden among the reeds began to scream loudly, and swam to him with open beak, and begged him urgently to spare her dear children. "Can you not imagine," said she, "how your mother would mourn if anyone wanted to carry you off, and give you your finishing stroke?"

"Only be quiet," said the good-tempered tailor, "you shall keep your children," and put the prisoner back into the water.

When he turned around, he was standing in front of an old tree that was partly hollow, and saw some wild bees flying in and out of it. "There I shall at once find the reward of my good deed," said the tailor. "The honey will refresh me." But the Queen bee came out, threatened him and said, "If you touch my people, and destroy my nest, our stings shall pierce your skin like ten thousand red-hot needles. But if you will leave us in peace and go your way, we will do you a service for it another time."

The little tailor saw that here also nothing was to be done. "Three dishes empty and nothing on the fourth is a bad dinner!" He dragged himself therefore with his starved-out stomach into the town, and as it was just striking twelve, all was ready-cooked for him in the inn, and he was able to sit down at once to dinner. When he was satisfied he said, "Now I will get to work." He went around the town, sought a master, and soon found a good situation. As, however, he had thoroughly learned his trade, it was not long before he became famous, and everyone wanted to have his new coat made by the little tailor, whose importance increased daily. "I can go no further in skill," said he, "and yet things improve every day." At last the King appointed him court tailor.

But how things do happen in the world! On the very same day his former comrade the shoemaker also became court shoemaker. When the latter caught sight of the tailor, and saw that he had once more two healthy eyes, his conscience troubled him. "Before he takes revenge on me," thought he to himself, "I must dig a pit for him." He, however, who digs a pit for another, falls into it himself.

In the evening when work was over and it had grown dusk, he stole to the King and said, "Lord King, the tailor is an arrogant fellow and has boasted that he will get the gold crown back again that was lost in ancient times."

"That would please me very much," said the King, and he had the tailor brought before him next morning, and ordered him to get the crown back again, or to leave the town forever.

"Oho!" thought the tailor, "a rogue gives more than he has got. If the surly King wants me to do what can be done by no one, I will not wait till morning, but will go out of the town at once, today." He packed up his bundle, therefore, but when he was outside the gate he could not help being sorry to give up his good fortune, and turn his back on the town in which all had gone so well with him. He came to the pond where he had made the acquaintance of the ducks; at that very moment the old one whose young ones he had spared was sitting there by the shore, pluming herself with her beak. She knew him again instantly, and asked why he was hanging his head so?

"You will not be surprised when you hear what has befallen me," replied the tailor, and told her his fate.

"If that be all," said the duck, "we can help you. The crown fell into the water, and lies down below at the bottom; we will soon bring it up again for you. In the meantime just spread out your handkerchief on the bank." She dived down with her twelve young ones, and in five minutes she was up again and sat with the crown resting on her wings, and the twelve young ones were swimming around about and had put their beaks under it, and were helping to carry it. They swam to the shore and put the crown on the handkerchief. No one can imagine how magnificent the crown was; when the sun shone on it, it gleamed like a hundred thousand carbuncles. The tailor tied his handkerchief together by the four corners, and carried it to the King, who was full of joy, and put a gold chain around the tailor's neck.

When the shoemaker saw that one stroke had failed, he contrived a second, and went to the King and said, "Lord King, the tailor has become insolent again; he boasts that he will copy in wax the whole of the royal palace, with everything that pertains to it, loose or fast, inside and out." The King sent for the tailor and ordered him to copy in wax the whole of the royal palace, with everything that pertained to it, movable or immovable, within and without, and if he did not succeed in doing this, or if so much as one nail on the wall were wanting, he should be imprisoned for his whole life underground.

The tailor thought, "It gets worse and worse! No one can endure that!" and threw his bundle on his back, and went forth. When he came to the hollow tree, he sat down and hung his head. The bees came flying out, and the Queen bee asked him if he had a stiff neck, since he held his head so awry? "Alas, no," answered the tailor, "something quite different weighs me down," and he told her what the King had demanded of him.

The bees began to buzz and hum amongst themselves, and the Queen bee said, "Just go home again, but come back tomorrow at this time, and bring a large sheet with you, and then all will be well." So he turned back again, but the bees flew to the royal palace and straight into it through the open windows, crept around about into every corner, and inspected everything most carefully. Then they hurried back and modeled the palace in wax with such rapidity that anyone looking on would have thought it was growing before his eyes. By the evening all was ready, and when the tailor came next morning, the whole of the splendid building was there, and not one nail in the wall or tile of the roof was wanting, and it was delicate, and white as snow, and smelled sweet as honey. The tailor wrapped it carefully in his cloth and took it to the King, who could not admire it enough, placed it in his largest hall, and in return for it presented the tailor with a large stone house.

The shoemaker, however, did not give up, but went for the third time to the King and said, "Lord King, it has come to the tailor's ears that no water will spring up in the courtyard of the castle, and he has boasted that it shall rise up in the middle of the courtyard to a man's height and be clear as crystal."

Then the King ordered the tailor to be brought before him and said, "If a stream of water does not rise in my courtyard by tomorrow as you have promised, the executioner shall in that very place make you shorter by the head." The poor tailor did not take long to think about it, but hurried out to the gate, and because this time it was a matter of life and death to him, tears rolled down his face.

While he was thus going forth full of sorrow, the foal to which he had formerly given its liberty, and which had now become a beautiful chestnut horse, came leaping toward him. "The time has come," it said to the tailor, "when I can repay you for your good deed. I know already what is needful to you, but you shall soon have help; get on me, my back can carry two such as you." The tailor's courage came back to him; he jumped up in one bound, and the horse went full speed into the town, and right up to the courtyard of the castle. It galloped as quick as lightning thrice around it, and at the third time it fell violently down. At the same instant, however, there was a terrific clap of thunder, a fragment of earth in the middle of the courtyard sprang like a cannonball into the air, and over the castle, and directly after it a jet of water rose as high as a man on horseback, and the water was as pure as crystal, and the sunbeams began to dance on it. When the King saw that, he arose in amazement, and went and embraced the tailor in the sight of all men.

But good fortune did not last long. The King had daughters in plenty, one still prettier than the other, but he had no son. So the malicious shoemaker betook himself for the fourth time to the King, and said, "Lord King, the tailor has not given up his arrogance. He has now boasted that if he liked, he could cause a son to be brought to the Lord king through the air."

The King commanded the tailor to be summoned, and said, "If you cause a son to be brought to me within nine days, you shall have my eldest daughter as wife."

"The reward is indeed great," thought the little tailor; "one would willingly do something for it, but the cherries grow too high for me, if I climb for them, the bough will break beneath me, and I shall fall."

He went home, seated himself cross-legged on his worktable, and thought over what was to be done. "It can't be managed," cried he at last, "I will go away; after all I can't live in peace here." He tied up his bundle and hurried away to the gate. When he got to the meadow, he perceived his old friend the stork, who was walking backward and forward like a philosopher. Sometimes he stood still, took a frog into close consideration, and at length swallowed it down.

The stork came to him and greeted him. "I see," he began, "that you have your pack on your back. Why are you leaving the town?" The tailor told him what the King had required of him, and how he could not perform it, and lamented his misfortune. "Don't let your hair grow grey about that," said the stork. "I will help you out of your difficulty. For a long time now, I have carried the children in swaddling clothes into the town, so for once I can fetch a little prince out of the well. Go home and be easy. In nine days from this time repair to the royal palace, and there I will come."

The little tailor went home, and at the appointed time was at the castle. It was not long before the stork came flying there and tapped at the window. The tailor opened it, and cousin Longlegs came carefully in, and walked with solemn steps over the smooth marble pavement. He had, moreover, a baby in his beak that was as lovely as an angel, and stretched out its little hands to the Queen. The stork laid it in her lap, and she caressed it and kissed it, and was beside herself with delight. Before the stork flew away, he took his traveling bag off his back and handed it over to the Queen. In it there were little paper parcels with colored sweetmeats, and they were divided amongst the little princesses. The eldest, however, had none of them, but got the merry tailor for a husband. "It seems to me," said he, "just as if I had won the highest prize. My mother was right after all, she always said that whoever trusts in God and only has good luck, can never fail."

The shoemaker had to make the shoes in which the little tailor danced at the wedding festival, after which he was commanded to quit the town forever. The road to the forest led him to the gallows. Worn out with anger, rage, and the heat of the day, he threw himself down. When he had closed his eyes and was about to sleep, the two crows flew down from the heads of the men who were hanging there, and pecked his eyes out. In his madness he ran into the forest and must have died there of hunger, for no one has ever either seen him or heard of him again.

7. *Hans the Hedgehog*

There was once a countryman who had money and land in plenty, but no matter how rich he was, one thing was still wanting in his happiness—he had no children. Often when he went into the town with the other peasants they mocked him and asked why he had no children. At last he became angry, and when he got home he said, "I will have a child, even if it be a hedgehog."

Then his wife had a child, which was a hedgehog in the upper part of his body, and a boy in the lower, and when she saw the child, she was terrified, and said, "See, there you have brought ill luck on us."

Then said the man, "What can be done now? The boy must be christened, but we shall not be able to get a godfather for him."

The woman said, "And we cannot call him anything else but Hans the Hedgehog."

When he was christened, the parson said, "He cannot go into any ordinary bed because of his spikes." So a little straw was put behind the stove, and Hans the Hedgehog was laid on it. His mother could not suckle him, for he would have pricked her with his quills. So he lay there behind the stove for eight years, and his father was tired of him and thought, "If he would but die!" He did not die, however, but remained lying there.

Now it happened that there was a fair in the town, and the peasant was about to go to it, and asked his wife what he should bring back with him for her. "A little meat and a couple of white rolls, which are wanted for the house," said she.

Then he asked the servant, and she wanted a pair of slippers and some stockings with designs. At last he said also, "And what will you have, Hans my Hedgehog?"

"Dear father," he said, "do bring me bagpipes." When, therefore, the father came home again, he gave his wife what he had bought for her; meat and white rolls, and then he gave the maid the slippers, and the stockings with designs; and, lastly, he went behind the stove, and gave Hans the Hedgehog the bagpipes. And when Hans the Hedgehog had the bagpipes, he said, "Dear father, do go to the forge and get the cock shod, and then I will ride away, and never come back again." At this, the father was delighted to think that he was going to get rid of him, and had the cock shod for him, and when it was done, Hans the Hedgehog got on it, and rode away, but took swine and asses with him, which he intended to keep in the forest.

When they got there he made the cock fly onto a high tree with him, and there he sat for many a long year, and watched his asses and swine until the herd was quite large, and his father knew nothing about him. While he was sitting in the tree, however, he played his bagpipes, and made music that was very beautiful. Once a King came traveling by who had lost his way and heard the music. He was astonished at it, and sent his servant forth to look all around and see from where this music came. He spied about, but saw nothing but a little animal sitting up aloft on the tree that looked like a cock with a hedgehog on it, which made this music. Then the King told the servant he was to ask why he sat there, and if he knew the road that led to his kingdom.

So Hans the Hedgehog descended from the tree, and said he would show the way if the King would write a bond and promise him whatever he first met in the royal courtyard as soon as he arrived at home. Then the King thought, "I can easily do that, Hans the Hedgehog understands nothing, and I can write what I like." So the King took pen and ink and wrote something, and when he had done it, Hans the Hedgehog showed him the way, and he got safely home. But his daughter, when she saw him from afar, was so overjoyed that she ran to meet him, and kissed him. Then he remembered Hans the Hedgehog, and told her what had happened, and that he had been forced to promise whatever first met him when he got home, to a very strange animal which sat on a cock as if it were a horse, and made beautiful music, but that instead of writing that he should have what he wanted, he had written that he should not have it. Thereupon the princess was glad, and said he had done well, for she never would have gone away with the Hedgehog.

Hans the Hedgehog, however, looked after his asses and pigs, and was always merry and sat on the tree and played his bagpipes.

Now it came to pass that another King came journeying by with his attendants and runners, and he also had lost his way, and did not know how to get home again because the forest was so large. He likewise heard the beautiful music from a distance, and asked his runner what that could be, and told him to go and see. Then the runner went under the tree, and saw the cock sitting at the top of it, and Hans the Hedgehog on the cock. The runner asked him what he was about up there? "I am keeping my asses and my pigs; but what is your desire?" The messenger said that they had lost their way, and could not get back into their own kingdom, and asked if he would not show them the way. Then Hans the Hedgehog got down the tree with the cock, and told the aged King that he would show him the way, if he would give him for his own whatever first met him in front of his royal palace. The King said, "Yes," and wrote a promise to Hans the Hedgehog that he should have this. That done, Hans rode on before him on the cock, and pointed out the way, and the King reached his kingdom again in safety.

When he got to the courtyard, there were great rejoicings. Now he had an only daughter who was very beautiful; she ran to meet him, threw her arms around his neck, and was delighted to have her old father back again. She asked him where in the world he had been so long. So he told her how he had lost his way, and had very nearly not come back at all, but that as he was traveling through a great forest, a creature, half hedgehog, half man, who was sitting astride a cock in a high tree, and making music, had shown him the way and helped him to get out, but that in return he had promised him whatever first met him in the royal courtyard, and how that was she herself, which made him unhappy now. But at this she promised that, for love of her father, she would willingly go with this Hans if he came.

Hans the Hedgehog, however, took care of his pigs, and the pigs multiplied until they became so many in number that the whole forest was filled with them. Then Hans the Hedgehog resolved not to live in the forest any longer, and sent word to his father to have every sty in the village emptied, for he was coming with such a great herd that anyone who wished to kill could do so. When his father heard that, he was troubled, for he thought Hans the Hedgehog had died long ago. Hans the Hedgehog, however, seated himself on the cock, and drove the pigs before him into the village, and ordered the slaughter to begin. Ha! but there was a killing and a chopping that might have been heard two miles off! After this Hans the Hedgehog said, "Father, let me have the cock shod once more at the forge, and then I will ride away and never come back as long as I live." Then the father had the cock shod once more, and was pleased that Hans the Hedgehog would never return again.

Hans the Hedgehog rode away to the first kingdom. There the King had commanded that whoever came mounted on a cock and had bagpipes with him should be shot at, cut down, or stabbed by everyone, so that he might not enter the palace. When, therefore, Hans the Hedgehog came riding over, they all pressed forward against him with their pikes, but he spurred the cock and it flew up over the gate in front of the King's window and lighted there, and Hans cried that the King must give him what he had promised, or he would take both his life and his daughter's. Then the King began to speak his daughter fair, and to beg her to go away with Hans in order to save her own life and her father's. So she dressed herself in white, and her father gave her a carriage with six horses and magnificent attendants together with gold and possessions. She seated herself in the carriage, and placed Hans the Hedgehog beside her with the cock and the bagpipes, and then they took leave and drove away, and the King thought he should never see her again. He was, however, deceived in his expectation, for when they were at a short distance from the town, Hans the Hedgehog took her pretty clothes off, and pierced her with his hedgehog's skin until she bled all over. "That is the reward of your falseness," said he. "Go your way, I will not have you!" and on that he chased her home again, and she was disgraced for the rest of her life.

Hans the Hedgehog, however, rode on further on the cock, with his bagpipes, to the dominions of the second King to whom he had shown the way. This one, however, had arranged that if anyone resembling Hans the Hedgehog should come, they were to present arms, give him safe conduct, cry long life to him, and lead him to the royal palace.

But when the King's daughter saw him she was terrified, for he looked quite too strange. She remembered however, that she could not change her mind, for she had given her promise to her father. So Hans the Hedgehog was welcomed by her, and married to her, and had to go with her to the royal table, and she seated herself by his side, and they ate and drank. When the evening came and they wanted to go to sleep, she was afraid of his quills, but he told her she was not to fear, for no harm would befall her, and he told the old King that he was to appoint four men to watch by the door of the chamber, and light a great fire, and when he entered the room and was about to get into bed, he would creep out of his hedgehog's skin and leave it lying there by the bedside, and that the men were to run nimbly to it, throw it in the fire, and stay by it until it was consumed. When the clock struck eleven, he went into the chamber, stripped off the hedgehog's skin, and left it lying by the bed. Then came the men and fetched it swiftly, and threw it in the fire; and when the fire had consumed it, he was delivered, and lay there in bed in human form, but he was coal-black as if he had been burned. The King sent for his physician who washed him with precious salves, and anointed him, and he became white, and was a handsome young man. When the King's daughter saw that, she was glad, and the next morning they arose joyfully, ate and drank, and then the marriage was properly solemnized, and Hans the Hedgehog received the kingdom from the aged King.

When several years had passed he went with his wife to his father, and said that he was his son. The father, however, declared he had no son—he had never had but one, and he had been born like a hedgehog with spikes, and had gone forth into the world. Then Hans made himself known, and the old father rejoiced and went with him to his kingdom.

> My tale is done,
> And away it has run
> To little August's house.

8. *The Shroud*

There was once a mother who had a little boy of seven years old, who was so handsome and lovable that no one could look at him without liking him, and she herself worshipped him above everything in the world. Now it so happened that he suddenly became ill, and God took him to himself; and for this the mother could not be comforted, and wept both day and night. But soon afterward, when the child had been buried, it appeared by night in the places where it had sat and played during its life, and if the mother wept, it wept also, and when morning came it disappeared. As, however, the mother would not stop crying, it came one night, in the little white shroud in which it had been laid in its coffin, and with its wreath of flowers around its head, and stood on the bed at her feet, and said, "Oh, mother, do stop crying, or I shall never fall asleep in my coffin, for my shroud will not dry because of all your tears, which fall upon it." The mother was afraid when she heard that, and wept no more.

The next night the child came again, and held a little light in its hand, and said, "Look, mother, my shroud is nearly dry, and I can rest in my grave." Then the mother gave her sorrow into God's keeping, and bore it quietly and patiently, and the child came no more, but slept in its little bed beneath the earth.

9. *The Jew Among Thorns*

There was once a rich man, who had a servant who served him diligently and honestly: He was every morning the first out of bed, and the last to go to rest at night; and, whenever there was a difficult job to be done, which nobody cared to undertake, he was always the first to set himself to it. Moreover, he never complained, but was contented with everything, and always merry.

When a year was ended, his master gave him no wages, for he said to himself, "That is the cleverest way; for I shall save something, and he will not go away, but stay quietly in my service." The servant said nothing, but did his work the second year as he had done it the first; and when at the end of this, likewise, he received no wages, he made himself happy, and still stayed on.

When the third year also was past, the master considered, put his hand in his pocket, but pulled nothing out. Then at last the servant said, "Master, for three years I have served you honestly, be so good as to give me what I ought to have, for I wish to leave, and look about me a little more in the world."

"Yes, my good fellow," answered the old miser; "you have served me industriously, and, therefore, you shall be cheerfully rewarded." And he put his hand into his pocket, but counted out only three farthings, saying, "There, you have a farthing for each year; that is large and liberal pay, such as you would have received from few masters."

The honest servant, who understood little about money, put his fortune into his pocket, and thought, "Ah! now that I have my purse full, why need I trouble and plague myself any longer with hard work!" So on he went, up hill and down dale; and sang and jumped to his heart's content.

Now it came to pass that as he was going by a thicket a little man stepped out, and called to him, "Where away, merry brother? I see you do not carry many cares."

"Why should I be sad?" answered the servant; "I have enough; three years' wages are jingling in my pocket."

"How much is your treasure?" the dwarf asked him.

"How much? Three farthings sterling, all told."

"Look here," said the dwarf, "I am a poor needy man, give me your three farthings; I can work no longer, but you are young, and can easily earn your bread."

And as the servant had a good heart, and felt pity for the old man, he gave him the three farthings, saying, "Take them in the name of heaven, I shall not be any the worse for it."

Then the little man said, "As I see you have a good heart I grant you three wishes, one for each farthing, they shall all be fulfilled."

"Aha," said the servant, "you are one of those who can work wonders! Well, then, if it is to be so, I wish, first, for a gun, which shall hit everything that I aim at; secondly, for a fiddle, which when I play on it, shall compel all who hear it to dance; thirdly, that if I ask a favor of anyone he shall not be able to refuse it."

"All that you shall have," said the dwarf; and put his hand into the bush, and only think, there lay a fiddle and gun, all ready, just as if they had been ordered. These he gave to the servant, and then said to him, "Whatever you may ask at any time, no man in the world shall be able to deny you."

"Heart alive! What can one desire more?" said the servant to himself, and went merrily onward.

Soon afterward he met a Jew with a long goatee, who was standing listening to the song of a bird that was sitting up at the top of a tree. "Good heavens," he was exclaiming, "that such a small creature should have such a fearfully loud voice! If it were but mine! If only someone would sprinkle some salt upon its tail!"

"If that is all," said the servant, "the bird shall soon be down here;" and taking aim he pulled the trigger, and down fell the bird into the thornbushes. "Go, you rogue," he said to the Jew, "and fetch the bird out for yourself!"

"Oh!" said the Jew, "leave out the rogue, my master, and I will do it at once. I will get the bird out for myself, as you really have hit it." Then he lay down on the ground, and began to crawl into the thicket.

When he was fast among the thorns, the good servant's humor so tempted him that he took up his fiddle and began to play. In a moment the Jew's legs began to move, and to jump into the air, and the more the servant fiddled the better went the dance. But the thorns tore his shabby coat from him, combed his beard, and pricked and plucked him all over the body. "Oh dear," cried the Jew, "what do I want with your fiddling? Leave the fiddle alone, master; I do not want to dance."

But the servant did not listen to him, and thought, "You have fleeced people often enough, now the thornbushes shall do the same to you;" and he began to play over again, so that the Jew had to jump higher than ever, and scraps of his coat were left hanging on the thorns.

"Oh, woe's me!" cried the Jew; "I will give the gentleman whatever he asks if only he leaves off fiddling—a purse full of gold."

"If you are so liberal," said the servant, "I will stop my music; but this I must say to your credit, that you dance to it so well that it is quite an art;" and having taken the purse he went his way.

The Jew stood still and watched the servant quietly until he was far off and out of sight, and then he screamed out with all his might, "You miserable musician, you beer-hall fiddler! Wait till I catch you alone, I will hunt you till the soles of your shoes fall off! You ragamuffin! Just put five farthings in your mouth, and then you may be worth a halfpence!" and went on abusing him as fast as he could speak. As soon as he had refreshed himself a little in this way, and got his breath again, he ran into the town to the justice.

"My lord judge," he said, "I have come to make a complaint; see how a rascal has robbed and ill-treated me on the public highway! A stone on the ground might pity me; my clothes all torn, my body pricked and scratched, my little all gone with my purse, good ducats, each piece better than the last; for God's sake let the man be thrown into prison!"

"Was it a soldier," said the judge, "who cut you thus with his saber?"

"Nothing of the sort!" said the Jew; "it was no sword that he had, but a gun hanging at his back, and a fiddle at his neck; the wretch may easily be known."

So the judge sent his people out after the man, and they found the good servant, who had been going quite slowly along, and they found, too, the purse with the money upon him. As soon as he was taken before the judge he said, "I did not touch the Jew, nor take his money; he gave it to me of his own free will, that I might leave off fiddling because he could not bear my music."

"Heaven defend us!" cried the Jew. "His lies are as thick as flies upon the wall."

But the judge also did not believe his tale, and said, "This is a bad defense, no Jew would do that." And because he had committed robbery on the public highway, he sentenced the good servant to be hanged. As he was being led away the Jew again screamed after him, "You vagabond! you dog of a fiddler! Now you are going to receive your well-earned reward!"

The servant walked quietly with the hangman up the ladder, but upon the last step he turned around and said to the judge, "Grant me just one request before I die."

"Yes, if you do not ask your life," said the judge.

"I do not ask for life," answered the servant, "but as a last favor let me play once more upon my fiddle."

The Jew raised a great cry of "Murder! Murder! For goodness' sake do not allow it! Do not allow it!"

But the judge said, "Why should I not let him have this short pleasure? It has been granted to him, and he shall have it." However, he could not have refused on account of the gift that had been bestowed on the servant.

Then the Jew cried, "Oh! Woe's me! Tie me, tie me fast!" while the good servant took his fiddle from his neck, and made ready. As he gave the first scrape of the bow, they all began to quiver and shake, the judge, his clerk, and the hangman and his men, and the cord fell out of the hand of the one who was going to tie the Jew fast. At the second scrape all raised their legs, and the hangman let go his hold of the good servant, and made himself ready to dance. At the third scrape they all leaped up and began to dance; the judge and the Jew being the best at jumping. Soon all who had gathered in the marketplace out of curiosity were dancing with them; old and young, fat and lean, one with another. The dogs, likewise, which had run there got up on their hind legs and capered about; and the longer he played, the higher sprang the dancers, so that they knocked against each other's heads, and began to shriek terribly.

At length the judge cried, quite out of breath, "I will give you your life if you will only stop fiddling."

The good servant thereupon had compassion, took his fiddle and hung it around his neck again, and stepped down the ladder. Then he went up to the Jew, who was lying upon the ground panting for breath, and said, "You rascal, now confess, from where you got the money, or I will take my fiddle and begin to play again."

"I stole it, I stole it!" cried he; "but you have honestly earned it." So the judge had the Jew taken to the gallows and hanged as a thief.

10. The Skillful Hunter

There was once a young fellow who had learned the trade of locksmith, and told his father he would now go out into the world and seek his fortune. "Very well," said the father, "I am quite content with that," and gave him some money for his journey. So he traveled about and looked for work.

After a time he resolved not to follow the trade of locksmith any more, for he no longer liked it, but he took a fancy for hunting. Then he met in his rambles a hunter dressed in green, who asked from where he came and where he was going? The youth said he was a locksmith's apprentice, but that the trade no longer pleased him, and he had a liking for hunting, would he teach it to him? "Oh, yes," said the hunter, "if you will go with me."

Then the young fellow went with him, bound himself to him for some years, and learned the art of hunting. After this he wished to try his luck elsewhere, and the hunter gave him nothing in the way of payment but an air gun, which had, however, this property, that it hit its mark without fail whenever he shot with it. Then he set out and found himself in a very large forest, which he could not get to the end of in one day. When evening came he seated himself in a high tree in order to escape from the wild beasts. Toward midnight, it seemed to him as if a tiny little light glimmered in the distance. Then he looked down through the branches toward it, and kept well in his mind where it was. But in the first place he took off his hat and threw it down in the direction of the light, so that he might go to the hat as a mark when he had descended. Then he got down and went to his hat, put it on again and went straight forward.

The farther he went, the larger the light grew, and when he got close to it he saw that it was an enormous fire, and that three giants were sitting by it, who had an ox on the spit, and were roasting it. Presently one of them said, "I must just taste if the meat will soon be fit to eat," and pulled a piece off, and was about to put it in his mouth when the hunter shot it out of his hand. "Well, really," said the giant, "if the wind has not blown the bit out of my hand!" and helped himself to another. But when he was just about to bite into it, the hunter again shot it away from him. At this the giant gave the one who was sitting next to him a box on the ear, and cried angrily, "Why are you snatching my piece away from me?"

"I have not snatched it away," said the other. "A sharpshooter must have shot it away from you."

The giant took another piece, but could not, however, keep it in his hand, for the hunter shot it out. Then the giant said, "That must be a good shot to shoot the bit out of one's very mouth, one that would be useful to us." And he cried aloud, "Come here, you sharpshooter, seat yourself at the fire beside us and eat your fill, we will not hurt you; but if you will not come, and we have to bring you by force, you are a lost man!"

At this the youth went up to them and told them he was a skilled hunter, and that whatever he aimed at with his gun, he was certain to hit. Then they said if he would go with them he should be well treated, and they told him that outside the forest there was a great lake, behind which stood a tower, and in the tower was imprisoned a lovely princess, whom they wished very much to carry off. "Yes," said he, "I will soon get her for you."

Then they added, "But there is still something else, there is a tiny little dog, which begins to bark when anyone goes near, and as soon as it barks everyone in the royal palace wakes up, and for this reason we cannot get there; can you undertake to shoot it dead?"

"Yes," said he, "that will be a little bit of fun for me." After this he got into a boat and rowed over the lake, and as soon as he landed, the little dog came running out, and was about to bark, but the hunter took his air gun and shot it dead. When the giants saw that, they rejoiced, and thought they already had the King's daughter safe, but the hunter wished first to see how matters stood, and told them that they must stay outside until he called them. Then he went into the castle, and all was perfectly quiet within, and everyone was asleep.

When he opened the door of the first room, a sword was hanging on the wall that was made of pure silver, and there was a golden star on it, and the name of the King, and on a table near it lay a sealed letter which he broke open, and inside it was written that whoever had the sword could kill everything which opposed him. So he took the sword from the wall, hung it at his side and went onward: then he entered the room where the King's daughter was lying sleeping, and she was so beautiful that he stood still and, holding his breath, looked at her. He thought to himself, "How can I give an innocent maiden into the power of the wild giants, who have evil in their minds?" He looked about further, and under the bed stood a pair of slippers, on the right one was her father's name with a star, and on the left her own name with a star. She wore also a great neck-kerchief of silk embroidered with gold, and on the right side was her father's name, and on the left her own, all in golden letters. Then the hunter took a pair of scissors and cut the right corner off, and put it in his knapsack, and then he also took the right slipper with the King's name, and thrust that in. Now the maiden still lay sleeping, and she was quite sewn into her nightgown, and he cut a morsel from this also, and thrust it in with the rest, but he did all without touching her.

Then he went forth and left her lying asleep undisturbed, and when he came to the gate again, the giants were still standing outside waiting for him, and expecting that he was bringing the princess. But he cried to them that they were to come in, for the maiden was already in their power, that he could not open the gate for them, but there was a hole through which they must creep. Then the first approached, and the hunter wound the giant's hair around his hand, pulled the head in, and cut it off at one stroke with his sword, and then drew the rest of him in. He called to the second and cut his head off likewise, and then he killed the third also, and he was well pleased that he had freed the beautiful maiden from her enemies, and he cut out their tongues and put them in his knapsack. Then thought he, "I will go home to my father and let him see what I have already done, and afterward I will travel about the world; the luck which God is pleased to grant me will easily find me."

But when the King in the castle awoke, he saw the three giants lying there dead. So he went into the bedroom of his daughter, awoke her, and asked who could have killed the giants? Then said she, "Dear father, I know not, I have been asleep." But when she arose and would have put on her slippers, the right one was gone, and when she looked at her neck-kerchief it was cut, and the right corner was missing, and when she looked at her nightgown a piece was cut out of it. The King summoned his whole court together, soldiers and everyone else who was there, and asked who had set his daughter at liberty, and killed the giants?

Now it happened that he had a captain, who was one-eyed and a hideous man, and he said that he had done it. Then the old King said that as he had accomplished this, he should marry his daughter. But the maiden said, "Rather than marry him, dear father, I will go away into the world as far as my legs can carry me." But the King said that if she would not marry him she should take off her royal garments and wear peasant's clothing, and go forth, and that she should go to a potter, and begin a trade in earthen vessels. So she put off her royal apparel, and went to a potter and borrowed crockery enough for a stall, and she promised him also that if she had sold it by the evening, she would pay for it. Then the King said she was to seat herself in a corner with it and sell it, and he arranged with some peasants to drive over it with their carts, so that everything should be broken into a thousand pieces. When therefore the King's daughter had placed her stall in the street, the carts came by, and broke all she had into tiny fragments. She began to weep and said, "Alas, how shall I ever pay for the pots now?"

The King had, however, wished by this to force her to marry the captain; but instead of that, she again went to the potter, and asked him if he would lend to her once more. He said, "No," she must first pay for the things she had already had.

Then she went to her father and cried and lamented, and said she would go forth into the world. Then said he, "I will have a little hut built for you in the forest outside, and in it you shall stay all your life long and cook for everyone, but you shall take no money for it." When the hut was ready, a sign was hung on the door on which was written, "Today given, tomorrow sold." There she remained a long time, and it was rumored about the world that a maiden was there who cooked without asking for payment, and that this was set forth on a sign outside her door.

The hunter heard it likewise, and thought to himself, "That would suit you. You are poor, and have no money." So he took his air gun and his knapsack, wherein all the things that he had formerly carried away with him from the castle as tokens of his truthfulness were still lying, and went into the forest, and found the hut with the sign, "Today given, tomorrow sold." He had put on the sword with which he had cut off the heads of the three giants, and thus entered the hut, and ordered something to eat to be given to him. He was charmed with the beautiful maiden, who was indeed as lovely as any picture. She asked him where he came from and where he was going, and he said, "I am roaming about the world."

Then she asked him where he had got the sword, for her father's name was on it. He asked her if she were the King's daughter. "Yes," she answered.

"With this sword," said he, "did I cut off the heads of three giants." And he took their tongues out of his knapsack in proof. Then he also showed her the slipper, and the corner of the neck-kerchief, and the bit of the nightgown. Hereupon she was overjoyed, and said that he was the one who had delivered her.

At this they went together to the old King, and fetched him to the hut, and she led him into her room, and told him that the hunter was the man who had really set her free from the giants. And when the aged King saw all the proof of this, he could no longer doubt, and said that he was very glad he knew how everything had happened, and that the hunter should have her to wed, on which the maiden was glad at heart. Then she dressed the hunter as if he were a foreign lord, and the King ordered a feast to be prepared. When they went to table, the captain sat on the left side of the King's daughter, but the hunter was on the right, and the captain thought he was a foreign lord who had come on a visit.

When they had eaten and drunk, the old King said to the captain that he would set before him something that he must guess. "Supposing anyone said that he had killed the three giants and he were asked where the giants' tongues were, and he were forced to go and look, and there were none in their heads, how could that happen?"

The captain said, "Then they cannot have had any."

"Not so," said the King. "Every animal has a tongue," and then he likewise asked what anyone would deserve who made such an answer?

The captain replied, "He ought to be torn in pieces." Then the King said he had pronounced his own sentence, and the captain was put in prison and then torn in four pieces; but the King's daughter was married to the hunter. After this he brought his father and mother, and they lived with their son in happiness, and after the death of the old King he received the kingdom.

11. *The Flail From Heaven*

A countryman was once going out to plow with a pair of oxen. When he got to the field, both the animals' horns began to grow, and went on growing, and when he wanted to go home they were so big that the oxen could not get through the gateway for them. By good luck a butcher came by just then, and he delivered them over to him, and made the bargain in this way, that he should take the butcher a measure of turnip seed, and then the butcher was to count him out a thaler for every seed. I call that well sold! The peasant now went home, and carried the measure of turnip seed to him on his back. On the way, however, he lost one seed out of the bag. The butcher paid him justly as agreed on, and if the peasant had not lost the seed, he would have had one thaler the more.

In the meantime, when he went on his way back, the seed had grown into a tree that reached up to the sky. Then thought the peasant, "As you have the chance, you must just see what the angels are doing up there above, and for once have them before your eyes." So he climbed up, and saw that the angels above were threshing oats, and he looked on. While he was thus watching them, he observed that the tree on which he was standing, was beginning to totter; he peeped down, and saw that someone was just going to cut it down. "If I were to fall down from here it would be a bad thing," thought he, and in his necessity he did not know how to save himself better than by taking the chaff of the oats that lay there in heaps, and twisting a rope of it. He likewise snatched a hoe and a flail that were lying about in heaven, and let himself down by the rope. But he came down on the earth exactly in the middle of a deep, deep hole. So it was a real piece of luck that he had brought the hoe, for he hoed himself a flight of steps with it, and mounted up, and took the flail with him as a token of his truth, so that no one could have any doubt of his story.

12. The Two Kings' Children

There was once on a time a King who had a little boy of whom it had been foretold that he should be killed by a stag when he was sixteen years of age, and when he had reached that age the hunters once went hunting with him. In the forest, the King's son was separated from the others, and all at once he saw a great stag that he wanted to shoot, but could not hit. At length he chased the stag so far that they were quite out of the forest, and then suddenly a great tall man was standing there instead of the stag, and said, "It is well that I have you. I have already ruined six pairs of glass skates with running after you, and have not been able to get you." Then he took the King's son with him, and dragged him through a great lake to a great palace, and then he had to sit down to table with him and eat something. When they had eaten something together the King said, "I have three daughters, you must keep watch over the eldest for one night, from nine in the evening till six in the morning, and every time the clock strikes, I will come myself and call, and if you then give me no answer, tomorrow morning you shall be put to death, but if you always give me an answer, you shall have her as wife."

When the young folks went to the bedroom there stood a stone image of St. Christopher, and the King's daughter said to it, "My father will come at nine o'clock, and every hour till it strikes three; when he calls, give him an answer instead of the King's son." Then the stone image of St. Christopher nodded its head quite quickly, and then more and more slowly till at last it stood still. The next morning the King said to him, "You have done the business well, but I cannot give my daughter away. You must now watch a night by my second daughter, and then I will consider with myself, whether you can have my eldest daughter to wed, but I shall come every hour myself, and when I call you, answer me, and if I call you and you do not reply, your blood shall flow." Then they both went into the bedroom, and there stood a still larger stone image of St. Christopher, and the King's daughter said to it, "If my father calls, do answer him." Then the great stone image of St. Christopher again nodded its head quite quickly and then more and more slowly, until at last it stood still again. And the King's son lay down on the threshold, put his hand under his head and slept.

The next morning the King said to him, "You have done the business really well, but I cannot give my daughter away; you must now watch a night by the youngest princess, and then I will consider with myself whether you can have my second daughter to wife, but I shall come every hour myself, and when I call you answer me, and if I call you and you answer not, your blood shall flow for me."

Then they once more went to the bedroom together, and there was a much greater and much taller image of St. Christopher than the first two had been. The King's daughter said to it, "When my father calls, do answer." Then the great tall stone image of St. Christopher nodded quite half an hour with its head, until at length the head stood still again. And the King's son laid himself down on the threshold of the door and slept.

The next morning the King said, "You have indeed watched well, but I cannot give you my daughter now; I have a great forest, if you cut it down for me between six o'clock this morning and six at night, I will think about it." Then he gave him a glass ax, a glass wedge, and a glass mallet. When he got into the wood, he began at once to cut, but the ax broke in two, then he took the wedge, and struck it once with the mallet, and it became as short and as small as sand. Then he was much troubled and believed he would have to die, and sat down and wept.

Now when it was noon the King said, "One of you girls must take him something to eat."

"No," said the two eldest, "we will not take it to him; the one by whom he last watched, can take him something."

Then the youngest was forced to go and take him something to eat. When she got into the forest, she asked him how he was getting on? "Oh," said he, "I am getting on very badly." Then she said he was to come and just eat a little. "Nay," said he, "I cannot do that, I shall still have to die, so I will eat no more."

Then she spoke so kindly to him and begged him just to try, that he came and ate something. When he had eaten something she said, "I will comb your hair a while, and then you will feel happier."

So she combed his hair, and he became weary and fell asleep, and then she took her handkerchief and made a knot in it, and struck it three times on the earth, and said, "Earth-workers, come forth." In a moment, numbers of little earth-men came forth, and asked what the

King's daughter commanded? Then said she, "In three hours' time the great forest must be cut down, and the whole of the wood laid in heaps." So the little earth-men went about and got together the whole of their kindred to help them with the work. They began at once, and when the three hours were over, all was done, and they came back to the King's daughter and told her so. Then she took her white handkerchief again and said, "Earth-workers, go home." At this they all disappeared.

When the King's son awoke, he was delighted, and she said, "Come home when it has struck six o'clock."

He did as she told him, and then the King asked, "Have you made away with the forest?"

"Yes," said the King's son.

When they were sitting at table, the King said, "I cannot yet give you my daughter to marry, you must still do something more for her sake." So he asked what it was to be, then? "I have a great fishpond," said the King. "You must go to it tomorrow morning and clear it of all mud until it is as bright as a mirror, and fill it with every kind of fish." The next morning the King gave him a glass shovel and said, "The fishpond must be done by six o'clock." So he went away, and when he came to the fishpond he stuck his shovel in the mud and it broke in two, then he stuck his hoe in the mud, and broke it also. Then he was much troubled.

At noon the youngest daughter brought him something to eat, and asked him how he was getting on? So the King's son said everything was going very ill with him, and he would certainly have to lose his head. "My tools have broken to pieces again."

"Oh," said she, "you must just come and eat something, and then you will be in another frame of mind."

"No," said he, "I cannot eat, I am far too unhappy for that!"

Then she gave him many good words until at last he came and ate something. Then she combed his hair again, and he fell asleep, so once more she took her handkerchief, tied a knot in it, and struck the ground thrice with the knot, and said, "Earth-workers, come forth." In a moment a great many little earth-men came and asked what she desired, and she told them that in three hours' time, they must have the fishpond entirely cleaned out, and it must be so clear that people could see themselves reflected in it, and every kind of fish must be in it.

The little earth-men went away and summoned all their kindred to help them, and in two hours it was done. Then they returned to her and said, "We have done as you have commanded."

The King's daughter took the handkerchief and once more struck thrice on the ground with it, and said, "Earth-workers, go home again." Then they all went away.

When the King's son awoke the fishpond was done. Then the King's daughter went away also, and told him that when it was six he was to come to the house. When he arrived at the house the King asked, "Have you got the fishpond done?"

"Yes," said the King's son. That was very good.

When they were again sitting at table the King said, "You have certainly done the fishpond, but I cannot give you my daughter yet; you must just do one more thing."

"What is that, then?" asked the King's son. The King said he had a great mountain on which there was nothing but briars, which must all be cut down, and at the top of it the youth must build up a great castle, which must be as strong as could be conceived, and all the furniture and fittings belonging to a castle must be inside it. And when he arose next morning the King gave him a glass ax and a glass gimlet with him, and he was to have all done by six o'clock.

As he was cutting down the first briar with the ax, it broke off short, and so small that the pieces flew all around about, and he could not use the gimlet either. Then he was quite miserable, and waited for his dearest to see if she would not come and help him in his need. When it was midday she came and brought him something to eat. He went to meet her and told her all, and ate something, and let her comb his hair and fell asleep.

Then she once more took the knot and struck the earth with it, and said, "Earth-workers, come forth!" Then came once again numbers of earth-men, and asked what her desire was. Then said she, "In the space of three hours they must cut down the whole of the briars, and a castle must be built on the top of the mountain that must be as strong as anyone could conceive, and all the furniture that pertains to a castle must be inside it." They went away, and summoned their kindred to help them and when the time came, all was ready. Then they came to the King's daughter and told her so, and the King's daughter took her handkerchief and struck thrice on the earth with it, and said, "Earth-workers, go home," at which they all disappeared. When therefore the

King's son awoke and saw everything done, he was as happy as a bird in air.

When it had struck six, they went home together. Then said the King, "Is the castle ready?"

"Yes," said the King's son.

When they sat down to table, the King said, "I cannot give away my youngest daughter until the two eldest are married."

Then the King's son and the King's daughter were quite troubled, and the King's son had no idea what to do. But he went by night to the King's daughter and ran away with her. When they had got a little distance away, the King's daughter peeped around and saw her father behind her. "Oh," said she, "what are we to do? My father is behind us, and will take us back with him. I will at once change you into a briar, and myself into a rose, and I will shelter myself in the middle of the bush." When the father reached the place, there stood a briar with one rose on it, then he was about to gather the rose, when the thorn came and pricked his finger so that he was forced to go home again. His wife asked why he had not brought their daughter back with him? So he said he had nearly got up to her, but that all at once he had lost sight of her, and a briar with one rose was growing on the spot.

Then said the Queen, "If you had but gathered the rose, the briar would have been forced to come too." So he went back again to fetch the rose, but in the meantime the two were already far over the plain, and the King ran after them. Then the daughter once more looked around and saw her father coming, and said, "Oh, what shall we do now? I will instantly change you into a church and myself into a priest, and I will stand up in the pulpit, and preach." When the King got to the place, there stood a church, and in the pulpit was a priest preaching. So he listened to the sermon, and then went home again.

Then the Queen asked why he had not brought their daughter with him, and he said, "Nay, I ran a long time after her, and just as I thought I should soon overtake her, a church was standing there and a priest was in the pulpit preaching."

"You should just have brought the priest," said his wife, "and then the church would soon have come. It is no use to send you, I must go there myself."

When she had walked for some time, and could see the two in the distance, the King's daughter peeped around and saw her mother coming, and said, "Now we are undone, for my mother is coming herself: I will immediately change you into a fishpond and myself into a fish."

When the mother came to the place, there was a large fishpond, and in the middle of it a fish was leaping about and peeping out of the water, and it was quite merry. She wanted to catch the fish, but she could not. Then she was very angry, and drank up the whole pond in order to catch the fish, but it made her so ill that she was forced to vomit, and vomited the whole pond out again. Then she cried, "I see very well that nothing can be done now," and asked them now to come back to her. Then the King's daughter went back again, and the Queen gave her daughter three walnuts, and said, "With these you can help yourself when you are in your greatest need."

So the young folks went away together once more. And when they had walked quite ten miles, they arrived at the castle from where the King's son came, and close by it was a village. When they reached it, the King's son said, "Stay here, my dearest, I will just go to the castle, and then I will come with a carriage and with attendants to fetch you."

When he got to the castle they all rejoiced greatly at having the King's son back again, and he told them he had a bride who was now in the village, and they must go with the carriage to fetch her. Then they harnessed the horses at once, and many attendants seated themselves outside the carriage. When the King's son was about to get in, his mother gave him a kiss, and he forgot everything that had happened, and also what he was about to do. At this his mother ordered the horses to be taken out of the carriage again, and everyone went back into the house. But the maiden sat in the village and watched and watched, and thought he would come and fetch her, but no one came. Then the King's daughter took service in the mill that belonged to the castle, and was obliged to sit by the pond every afternoon and clean the tubs.

And the Queen came one day on foot from the castle, and went walking by the pond, and saw the well-grown maiden sitting there, and said, "What a fine strong girl that is! She pleases me well!" Then she and all with her looked at the maid, but no one knew her. So a long time passed by during which the maiden served the miller honorably and faithfully. In the meantime, the Queen had sought a wife for her son, who came from quite a distant part of the world.

When the bride came, they were at once to be married. And many people hurried together, all of whom wanted to see everything. Then the girl said to the miller that he might be so good as to give her leave to go also. So the miller said, "Yes, do go there."

When she was about to go, she opened one of the three walnuts, and a beautiful dress lay inside it. She put it on, and went into the church and stood by the altar. Suddenly came the bride and bridegroom, and seated themselves before the altar, and when the priest was just going to bless them, the bride peeped half around and saw the maiden standing there. Then she stood up again, and said she would not be given away until she also had as beautiful a dress as that lady there. So they went back to the house again, and sent to ask the lady if she would sell that dress. No, she would not sell it, but the bride might perhaps earn it. Then the bride asked her how she was to do this? Then the maiden said if she might sleep one night outside the King's son's door, the bride might have what she wanted. So the bride said, "Yes," she was willing to do that. But the servants were ordered to give the King's son a sleeping potion, and then the maiden laid herself down on the threshold and lamented all night long. She had had the forest cut down for him, she had had the fishpond cleaned out for him, she had had the castle built for him, she had changed him into a briar, and then into a church, and at last into a fishpond, and yet he had forgotten her so quickly. The King's son did not hear one word of it, but the servants had been awakened, and had listened to it, and had not known what it could mean.

The next morning when they were all up, the bride put on the dress, and went away to the church with the bridegroom. In the meantime the maiden opened the second walnut, and a still more beautiful dress was inside it. She put it on, and went and stood by the altar in the church, and everything happened as it had happened the time before. And the maiden again lay all night on the threshold that led to the chamber of the King's son, and the servant was once more to give him a sleeping potion. The servant, however, went to him and gave him something to keep him awake, and then the King's son went to bed, and the miller's maiden bemoaned herself as before on the threshold of the door, and told of all that she had done. All this the King's son heard, and was sore troubled, and what was past came back to him. Then he wanted to go to her, but his mother had locked the door.

The next morning, however, he went at once to his beloved, and told her everything which had happened to him, and prayed her not to be angry with him for having forgotten her. Then the King's daughter opened the third walnut, and within it was a still more magnificent dress, which she put on, and went with her bridegroom to church, and numbers of children came who gave them flowers, and offered them gay ribbons to bind about their feet, and they were blessed by the priest, and had a merry wedding. But the false mother and the bride she had chosen had to depart. And the mouth of the person who last told all this is still warm.

13. *The Cunning Little Tailor*

There was once on a time a princess who was extremely proud. If a wooer came she gave him some riddle to guess, and if he could not find it out, he was sent contemptuously away. She let it be made known also that whoever solved her riddle should marry her, let him be who he might. At length, therefore, three tailors fell in with each other, the two eldest of whom thought they had done so many dexterous bits of work successfully that they could not fail to succeed in this also; the third was a little useless scamp who did not even know his trade, but thought he must have some luck in this venture, for where else was it to come from? Then the two others said to him, "Just stay at home; you cannot do much with your little bit of understanding." The little tailor, however, did not let himself be discouraged, and said he had set his head to work about this for once, and he would manage well enough, and he went forth as if the whole world were his.

They all three announced themselves to the princess, and said she was to propound her riddle to them, and that the right persons had now come, who had understandings so fine that they could be threaded in a needle. Then said the princess, "I have two kinds of hair on my head, of what color is it?"

"If that be all," said the first, "it must be black and white, like the cloth that is called pepper and salt."

The princess said, "Wrongly guessed; let the second answer."

Then said the second, "If it be not black and white, then it is brown and red, like my father's company coat."

"Wrongly guessed," said the princess, "let the third give the answer, for I see very well he knows it for certain."

Then the little tailor stepped boldly forth and said, "The princess has a silver and a golden hair on her head, and those are the two different colors."

When the princess heard that, she turned pale and nearly fell down with terror, for the little tailor had guessed her riddle, and she had firmly believed that no man on earth could discover it. When her courage returned she said, "You have not won me yet by that; there is still something else that you must do. Below in the stable is a bear with which you shall pass the night, and when I get up in the morning if you are still alive, you shall marry me."

She expected, however, she should thus get rid of the tailor, for the bear had never yet left anyone alive who had fallen into his clutches. The little tailor did not let himself be frightened away, but was quite delighted, and said, "Boldly ventured is half won."

When therefore the evening came, our little tailor was taken down to the bear. The bear was about to set at the little fellow at once, and give him a hearty welcome with his paws: "Softly, softly," said the little tailor, "I will soon make you quiet." Then quite composedly, and as if he had not an anxiety in the world, he took some nuts out of his pocket, cracked them, and ate the kernels.

When the bear saw that, he was seized with a desire to have some nuts too. The tailor felt in his pockets, and reached him a handful; they were, however, not nuts, but pebbles. The bear put them in his mouth, but could get nothing out of them, let him bite as he would. "Eh!" thought he, "what a stupid blockhead I am! I cannot even crack a nut!" and then he said to the tailor, "Here, crack me the nuts."

"There, see what a stupid fellow you are!" said the little tailor. "To have such a great mouth, and not be able to crack a small nut!" Then he took the pebble and nimbly put a nut in his mouth in the place of it, and crack, it was in two!

"I must try the thing again," said the bear; "when I watch you, I then think I ought to be able to do it too." So the tailor once more gave him a pebble, and the bear tried and tried to bite into it with all the strength of his body. But no one will imagine that he accomplished it. When that was over, the tailor took out a violin from beneath his coat, and played a piece on it to himself.

When the bear heard the music, he could not help beginning to dance, and when he had danced a while, the thing pleased him so well that he said to the little tailor, "Is the fiddle heavy?"

"Light enough for a child. Look, with the left hand I lay my fingers on it, and with the right I stroke it with the bow, and then it goes merrily, hop sa sa vivallalera!"

"So," said the bear, "fiddling is a thing I should like to understand too, that I might dance whenever I had a fancy. What do you think of that? Will you give me lessons?"

"With all my heart," said the tailor, "if you have a talent for it. But just let me see your claws, they are terribly long, I must cut your nails a little." Then a vise was brought, and the bear put his claws in it, and the little tailor screwed it tight, and said, "Now wait until I come with the scissors," and he let the bear growl as he liked, and lay down in the corner on a bundle of straw, and fell asleep.

When the princess heard the bear growling so fiercely during the night, she believed nothing else but that he was growling for joy, and had made an end of the tailor. In the morning she arose careless and happy, but when she peeped into the stable, the tailor stood gaily before her, and was as healthy as a fish in water. Now she could not say another word against the wedding because she had given a promise before everyone, and the King ordered a carriage to be brought in which she was to drive to church with the tailor, and there she was to be married. When they had got into the carriage, the two other tailors, who had false hearts and envied him his good fortune, went into the stable and unscrewed the bear again. The bear in great fury ran after the carriage.

The princess heard him snorting and growling; she was terrified, and she cried, "Ah, the bear is behind us and wants to get you!"

The tailor was quick and stood on his head, stuck his legs out of the window, and cried, "Do you see the vise? If you do not be off you shall be put into it again." When the bear saw that, he turned around and ran away. The tailor drove quietly to church, and the princess was married to him at once, and he lived with her as happy as a woodlark. Whoever does not believe this, must pay a thaler.

14. The Bright Sun Brings It to Light

A tailor's apprentice was traveling about the world in search of work, and at one time he could find none, and his poverty was so great that he had not a farthing to live on. Presently he met a Jew on the road, and as he thought he would have a great deal of money about him, the tailor thrust God out of his heart, fell on the Jew, and said, "Give me your money, or I will strike you dead."

Then said the Jew, "Grant me my life, I have no money but eight farthings."

But the tailor said, "Money you have; and it shall be produced," and used violence and beat him until he was near death.

And when the Jew was dying, the last words he said were, "The bright sun will bring it to light," and thereupon he died.

The tailor's apprentice felt in his pockets and sought for money, but he found nothing but eight farthings, as the Jew had said. Then he took him up and carried him behind a clump of trees, and went onward to seek work. After he had traveled about a long while, he got work in a town with a master who had a pretty daughter, with whom he fell in love, and he married her, and lived in good and happy wedlock.

After a long time when he and his wife had two children, the wife's father and mother died, and the young people kept house alone. One morning, when the husband was sitting at the table before the window, his wife brought him his coffee, and when he had poured it out into the saucer, and was just going to drink, the sun shone on it and the reflection gleamed here and there on the wall above, and made circles on it. Then the tailor looked up and said, "Yes, it would like very much to bring it to light, and cannot!"

The woman said, "Oh, dear husband, what is that, then? What do you mean by that?"

He answered, "I must not tell you."

But she said, "If you love me, you must tell me," and used her most affectionate words, and said that no one should ever know it, and left him no rest.

Then he told her how years ago, when he was traveling about seeking work and quite worn out and penniless, he had killed a Jew, and that in the last agonies of death, the Jew had spoken the words, "The bright sun will bring it to light." And now, the sun had just wanted to bring it to light, and had gleamed and made circles on the wall, but had not been able to do it. After this, he again charged her particularly never to tell this, or he would lose his life, and she did promise. When, however, he had sat down to work again, she went to her great friend and confided the story to her, but she was never to repeat it to any human being, but before two days were over, the whole town knew it, and the tailor was brought to trial, and condemned. And thus, after all, the bright sun did bring it to light.

15. *The Blue Light*

There was once on a time a soldier who for many years had served the King faithfully, but when the war came to an end could serve no longer because of the many wounds that he had received. The King said to him, "You may return to your home, I need you no longer, and you will not receive any more money, for he only receives wages who renders me service for them."

Then the soldier did not know how to earn a living, went away greatly troubled, and walked the whole day, until in the evening he entered a forest. When darkness came on, he saw a light, which he went up to, and came to a house where a witch lived. "Do give me one night's lodging, and a little to eat and drink," said he to her, "or I shall starve."

"Oho!" she answered, "who gives anything to a runaway soldier? Yet I will be compassionate, and take you in, if you will do what I wish."

"What do you wish?" said the soldier.

"That you should dig all around my garden for me, tomorrow."

The soldier consented, and next day labored with all his strength, but could not finish it by the evening.

"I see well enough," said the witch, "that you can do no more today, but I will keep you yet another night, in payment for which you must tomorrow chop me a load of wood, and make it small." The soldier spent the whole day in doing it, and in the evening the witch proposed that he should stay one night more. "Tomorrow, you shall only do me a very trifling piece of work. Behind my house, there is an old dry well, into which my light has fallen. It burns blue, and never goes out, and you shall bring it up again for me."

Next day the old woman took him to the well, and let him down in a basket. He found the blue light, and made her a signal to draw him up again. She did draw him up, but when he came near the edge, she stretched down her hand and wanted to take the blue light away from him. "No," said he, perceiving her evil intention, "I will not give you the light until I am standing with both feet upon the ground." The witch fell into a passion, let him down again into the well, and went away.

The poor soldier fell without injury on the moist ground, and the blue light went on burning, but of what use was that to him? He saw very well that he could not escape death. He sat for a while very sorrowfully, then suddenly he felt in his pocket and found his tobacco pipe, which was still half full. "This shall be my last pleasure," thought he, pulled it out, lit it at the blue light and began to smoke. When the smoke had circled about the cavern, suddenly a little black dwarf stood before him, and said, "Lord, what are your commands?"

"What commands have I to give you?" replied the soldier, quite astonished.

"I must do everything you bid me," said the dwarf.

"Good," said the soldier; "then in the first place help me out of this well." The dwarf took him by the hand, and led him through an underground passage, but he did not forget to take the blue light with him. On the way the dwarf showed him the treasures that the witch had collected and hidden there, and the soldier took as much gold as he could carry. When he was above, he said to the dwarf, "Now go and bind the old witch, and carry her before the judge." In a short time she, with frightful cries, came riding by, as swift as the wind on a wild tomcat, and not long after that the dwarf reappeared.

"It is all done," said he, "and the witch is already hanging on the gallows. What further commands does my lord have?" inquired the dwarf.

"At this moment, none," answered the soldier; "You can return home, only be at hand immediately, if I summon you."

"Nothing more is needed than that you should light your pipe at the blue light, and I will appear before you at once." Thereupon he vanished from his sight.

The soldier returned to the town from which he had come. He went to the best inn, ordered himself handsome clothes, and then bade the landlord furnish him a room as handsomely as possible. When it was ready and the soldier had taken possession of it, he summoned the little black dwarf and said, "I have served the King faithfully, but he has dismissed me, and left me to hunger, and now I want to take my revenge."

"What am I to do?" asked the dwarf.

"Late at night, when the King's daughter is in bed, bring her here in her sleep, she shall do servant's work for me."

The dwarf said, "That is an easy thing for me to do, but a very dangerous thing for you, for if it is discovered, you will fare ill."

When twelve o'clock had struck, the door sprang open, and the dwarf carried in the princess. "Aha! are you there?" cried the soldier. "Get to your work at once! Fetch the broom and sweep the chamber." When she had done this, he ordered her to come to his chair, and then he stretched out his feet and said, "Pull off my boots for me," and then he threw them in her face, and made her pick them up again, and clean and brighten them. She, however, did everything he bade her, without opposition, silently and with half-shut eyes. When the first cock crowed, the dwarf carried her back to the royal palace, and laid her in her bed.

Next morning when the princess arose, she went to her father, and told him that she had had a very strange dream. "I was carried through the streets with the rapidity of lightning," said she, "and taken into a soldier's room, and I had to wait upon him like a servant, sweep his room, clean his boots, and do all kinds of menial work. It was only a dream, and yet I am just as tired as if I really had done everything."

"The dream may have been true," said the King. "I will give you a piece of advice. Fill your pocket full of peas, and make a small hole in it, and then if you are carried away again, they will fall out and leave a track in the streets." But unseen by the King, the dwarf was standing beside him when he said that, and heard all. At night when the sleeping princess was again carried through the streets, some peas certainly did fall out of her pocket, but they made no track, for the crafty dwarf had just before scattered peas in every street there was. And again the princess was compelled to do servant's work until the cock crowed.

Next morning the King sent his people out to seek the track, but it was all in vain, for in every street poor children were sitting, picking up peas, and saying, "It must have rained peas, last night."

"We must think of something else," said the King; "keep your shoes on when you go to bed, and before you come back from the place where you are taken, hide one of them there, I will soon contrive to find it." The black dwarf heard this plot, and at night when the soldier again ordered him to bring the princess, revealed it to him, and told him that he knew of no expedient to counteract this stratagem, and that if the shoe were found in the soldier's house it would go badly with him. "Do what I bid you," replied the soldier, and again this third night the princess was obliged to work like a servant, but before she went away, she hid her shoe under the bed.

Next morning the King had the entire town searched for his

daughter's shoe. It was found at the soldier's, and the soldier himself, who at the entreaty of the dwarf had gone outside the gate, was soon brought back, and thrown into prison. In his flight he had forgotten the most valuable things he had, the blue light and the gold, and had only one ducat in his pocket. And now loaded with chains, he was standing at the window of his dungeon, when he chanced to see one of his comrades passing by. The soldier tapped at the pane of glass, and when this man came up, said to him, "Be so kind as to fetch me the small bundle I have left lying in the inn, and I will give you a ducat for doing it."

His comrade ran there and brought him what he wanted. As soon as the soldier was alone again, he lighted his pipe and summoned the black dwarf. "Have no fear," said the latter to his master. "Go wherever they take you, and let them do what they will, only take the blue light with you."

The next day the soldier was tried, and though he had done nothing wicked, the judge condemned him to death. When he was led forth to die, he begged a last favor of the King. "What is it?" asked the King.

"That I may smoke one more pipe on my way."

"You may smoke three," answered the King, "but do not imagine that I will spare your life."

Then the soldier pulled out his pipe and lighted it at the blue light, and as soon as a few wreaths of smoke had ascended, the dwarf was there with a small cudgel in his hand, and said, "What does my lord command?"

"Strike down to earth that false judge there, and his constable, and spare not the King who has treated me so ill."

Then the dwarf fell on them like lightning, darting this way and that way, and whoever was so much as touched by his cudgel fell to earth, and did not venture to stir again. The King was terrified; he threw himself on the soldier's mercy, and merely to be allowed to live at all, gave him his kingdom for his own, and the princess to marry.

16. *The Willful Child*

Once upon a time there was a child who was willful, and would not do as her mother wished. For this reason God had no pleasure in her, and let her become ill, and no doctor could do her any good, and in a short time she lay on her deathbed. When she had been lowered into her grave, and the earth was spread over her, all at once her arm came out again, and stretched upward, and when they had put it in and spread fresh earth over it, it was all to no purpose, for the arm always came out again. Then the mother herself was obliged to go to the grave, and strike the arm with a rod, and when she had done that, it was drawn in, and then at last the child had rest beneath the ground.

17. The Three Army Surgeons

Three army surgeons who thought they knew their art perfectly, were traveling about the world, and they came to an inn where they wanted to pass the night. The host asked where they came from, and where they were going?

"We are roaming about the world and practicing our art."

"Just show me for once what you can do," said the host.

Then the first said he would cut off his own hand, and put it on again early next morning; the second said he would tear out his heart, and replace it next morning; the third said he would cut out his eyes and heal them again next morning. "If you can do that," said the innkeeper, "you have learned everything." They, however, had a salve, with which they rubbed themselves, which joined parts together, and they carried the little bottle in which it was, constantly with them. Then they cut the hand, heart, and eyes from their bodies as they had said they would, and laid them all together on a plate, and gave it to the innkeeper. The innkeeper gave it to a servant who was to set it in the cupboard, and take good care of it.

The girl, however, had a lover in secret, who was a soldier. When therefore the innkeeper, the three army surgeons, and everyone else in the house were asleep, the soldier came and wanted something to eat. The girl opened the cupboard and brought him some food, and in her love forgot to shut the cupboard door again. She seated herself at the table by her lover, and they chattered away together. While she sat so contentedly there, thinking of no ill luck, the cat came creeping in, found the cupboard open, took the hand and heart and eyes of the three army surgeons, and ran off with them.

When the soldier had done eating, and the girl was taking away the things and going to shut the cupboard she saw that the plate that the innkeeper had given her to take care of, was empty. Then she said in a fright to her lover, "Ah, miserable girl, what shall I do? The hand is gone, the heart and the eyes are gone too, what will become of me in the morning?"

"Be easy," said he, "I will help you out of your trouble—there is a thief hanging outside on the gallows, I will cut off his hand. Which hand was it?"

"The right one."

Then the girl gave him a sharp knife, and he went and cut the poor sinner's right hand off, and brought it to her. After this he caught the cat and cut its eyes out, and now nothing but the heart was wanting. "Have you not been slaughtering, and are not the dead pigs in the cellar?" said he.

"Yes," said the girl.

"That's well," said the soldier, and he went down and fetched a pig's heart. The girl placed all together on the plate, and put it in the cupboard, and when after this her lover took leave of her, she went quietly to bed.

In the morning when the three army surgeons got up, they told the girl she was to bring them the plate on which the hand, heart, and eyes were lying. Then she brought it out of the cupboard, and the first fixed the thief's hand on and smeared it with his salve, and it grew to his arm directly. The second took the cat's eyes and put them in his own head. The third fixed the pig's heart firm in the place where his own had been, and the innkeeper stood by, admired their skill, and said he had never yet seen such a thing as that done, and would sing their praises and recommend them to everyone. Then they paid their bill, and traveled farther.

As they were on their way, the one with the pig's heart did not stay with them at all, but wherever there was a corner he ran to it, and rooted about in it with his nose as pigs do. The others wanted to hold him back by the tail of his coat, but that did no good; he tore himself loose, and ran wherever the dirt was thickest. The second also behaved very strangely; he rubbed his eyes, and said to the others, "Comrades, what is the matter? I don't see at all. Will one of you lead me, so that I do not fall."

Then with difficulty they traveled on till evening, when they reached another inn. They went into the bar together, and there at a table in the corner sat a rich man counting money. The one with the thief's hand walked around about him, made a sudden movement twice with his arm, and at last when the stranger turned away, he snatched at the pile of money, and took a handful from it. One of them saw this, and said, "Comrade, what are you about? You must not steal—shame on you!"

"Eh," said he, "but how can I stop myself? My hand twitches, and I am forced to snatch things whether I want to or not."

After this, they lay down to sleep, and while they were lying there it was so dark that no one could see his own hand. All at once the one with the cat's eyes awoke, aroused the others, and said, "Brothers, just look up, do you see the white mice running about there?" The two sat up, but could see nothing. Then said he, "Things are not right with us, we have not got back again what is ours. We must return to the innkeeper, he has deceived us."

They went back therefore, the next morning, and told the host they had not got what was their own again; that the first had a thief's hand, the second cat's eyes, and the third a pig's heart. The innkeeper said that the girl must be to blame for that, and was going to call her, but when she had seen the three coming, she had run out by the backdoor, and not come back. Then the three said he must give them a great deal of money, or they would set his house on fire. He gave them what he had, and whatever he could get together, and the three went away with it. It was enough for the rest of their lives, but they would rather have had their own proper organs.

18. The Seven Swabians

Seven Swabians were once together. The first was Master Schulz; the second, Jackli; the third, Marli; the fourth, Jergli; the fifth, Michal; the sixth, Hans; the seventh, Veitli. All seven had made up their minds to travel about the world to seek adventures, and perform great deeds. But in order that they might go in security and with arms in their hands, they thought it would be advisable that they should have one solitary, but very strong, and very long spear made for them. This spear all seven of them took in their hands at once; in front walked the boldest and bravest, and that was Master Schulz; all the others followed in a row, and Veitli was the last.

Then it came to pass one day in the haymaking month (July), when they had walked a long distance, and still had a long way to go before they reached the village where they were to pass the night, that as they were in a meadow in the twilight a great beetle or hornet flew by them from behind a bush, and hummed in a menacing manner. Master Schulz was so terrified that he all but dropped the spear, and a cold perspiration broke out over his whole body. "Listen! listen!" cried he to his comrades. "Good heavens! I hear a drum."

Jackli, who was behind him holding the spear, and who perceived some kind of a smell, said, "Something is most certainly going on, for I taste powder and matches."

At these words Master Schulz began to take to flight, and in a moment jumped over a hedge, but as he just happened to jump onto the teeth of a rake, which had been left lying there after the haymaking, the handle of it struck against his face and gave him a tremendous blow. "Oh dear! Oh dear!" screamed Master Schulz. "Take me prisoner; I surrender! I surrender!"

The other six all leapt over, one on the top of the other, crying, "If you surrender, I surrender too! If you surrender, I surrender too!" At length, as no enemy was there to bind and take them away, they saw that they had been mistaken, and in order that the story might not be known, and they be treated as fools and ridiculed, they all swore to each other to hold their peace about it until one of them accidentally spoke of it.

Then they journeyed onward. The second danger which they survived cannot be compared with the first. Some days afterward, their path led them through a fallow field where a hare was sitting sleeping in the sun. Her ears were standing straight up, and her great glassy eyes were wide open. All of them were alarmed at the sight of the horrible wild beast, and they consulted together as to what would be the least dangerous thing to do. For if they were to run away, they knew that the monster would pursue and swallow them whole. So they said, "We must go through a great and dangerous struggle. Boldly ventured, is half won," and all seven grasped the spear, Master Schulz in front, and Veitli behind.

Master Schulz was always trying to keep the spear back, but Veitli had become quite brave while behind, and wanted to dash forward and cried,

> "Strike home, in every Swabian's name,
> Or else I wish you may be lame."

But Hans knew how to meet this, and said,

> "Thunder and lightning, it's fine to prate,
> But for dragon-hunting you're too late."

Michal cried,

> "Nothing is wanting, not even a hair,
> Be sure the Devil himself is there."

Then it was Jergli's turn to speak,

> "If it be not, it's at least his mother,
> Or else it's the Devil's own stepbrother."

And now Marli had a bright thought, and said to Veitli,

> "Advance, Veitli, advance, advance,
> And I behind will hold the lance."

Veitli, however, did not attend to that, and Jackli said,

> "Tis Schulz's place the first to be,
> No one deserves that honor but he."

Then Master Schulz plucked up his courage, and said, gravely,

> "Then let us boldly advance to the fight,
> And thus we shall show our valor and might."

Then they all together set on the dragon. Master Schulz crossed himself and prayed for God's assistance, but as all this was of no avail, and he was getting nearer and nearer to the enemy, he screamed, "Oho! oho! ho! ho! ho!" in the greatest anguish. This awakened the hare, which in great alarm darted swiftly away. When Master Schulz saw her thus flying from the field of battle, he cried in his joy.

> "Quick, Veitli, quick, look there, look there,
> The monster's nothing but a hare!"

But the Swabian allies went in search of further adventures, and came to the Moselle, a mossy, quiet, deep river, over which there are few bridges, and which in many places people have to cross in boats. As the seven Swabians did not know this, they called to a man who was working on the opposite side of the river, to know how people contrived to get across. The distance and their way of speaking made the man unable to understand what they wanted, and he said, "What? what?" in the way people speak in the neighborhood of Treves. Master Schulz thought he was saying, "Wade, wade through the water," and as he was the first, began to set out and went into the Moselle. It was not long before he sank in the mud and the deep waves that drove against him, but his hat was blown on the opposite shore by the wind, and a frog sat down beside it, and croaked, "Wat, wat, wat." The other six on the opposite side heard that, and said, "Oho, comrades, Master Schulz is calling us; if he can wade across, why cannot we?" So they all jumped into the water together in a great hurry, and were drowned, and thus one frog took the lives of all six of them, and not one of the Swabian allies ever reached home again.

19. The Three Apprentices

There were once three apprentices, who had agreed to keep always together while traveling, and always to work in the same town. At one time, however, their masters had no more work to give them, so that at last they were in rags, and had nothing to live on. Then one of them said, "What shall we do? We cannot stay here any longer. We will travel once more, and if we do not find any work in the town we go to, we will arrange with the innkeeper there, that we are to write and tell him where we are staying, so that we can always have news of each other, and then we will separate." And that seemed best to the others also.

They went forth, and met on the way a richly-dressed man who asked who they were. "We are apprentices looking for work; up to this time we have kept together, but if we cannot find anything to do we are going to separate."

"There is no need for that," said the man, "if you will do what I tell you, you shall not want for gold or for work; nay, you shall become great lords, and drive in your carriages!"

One of them said, "If our souls and salvation are not endangered, we will certainly do it."

"They are not," replied the man. "I have no claim on you."

One of the others had, however, looked at his feet, and when he saw a horse's foot and a man's foot, he did not want to have anything to do with him. The Devil, however, said, "Be easy, I have no designs on you, but on another soul, which is half my own already, and will be all mine soon." As they were now secure, they consented, and the Devil told them what he wanted. The first was to answer, "All three of us," to every question; the second was to say, "For money," and the third, "And quite right too!" They were always to say this, one after the other, but they were not to say one word more, and if they disobeyed this order, all their money would disappear at once, but so long as they observed it, their pockets would always be full.

As a beginning, he at once gave them as much as they could carry, and told them to go to such and such an inn when they got to the town. They went to it, and the innkeeper came to meet them, and asked if they wished for anything to eat? The first replied, "All three of us."

"Yes," said the host, "that is what I mean."

The second said, "For money."

"Of course," said the host.

The third said, "And quite right too!"

"Certainly it is right," said the host.

Good meat and drink were now brought to them, and they were well waited on. After the dinner came the payment, and the innkeeper gave the bill to the one who said, "All three of us," the second said, "For money," and the third, "And quite right too!"

"Indeed it is right," said the host, "all three pay, and without money I can give nothing."

They, however, paid still more than he had asked. The lodgers, who were looking on, said, "These people must be mad."

"Yes, indeed they are," said the host. "They are not very wise."

So they stayed some time in the inn, and said nothing else but, "All three of us," "For money," and "And quite right too!" But they saw and knew all that was going on. It so happened that a great merchant came with a large sum of money, and said, "Sir host, take care of my money for me, here are three crazy apprentices who might steal it from me." The host did as he was asked. As he was carrying the trunk into his room, he felt that it was heavy with gold. Thereupon he gave the three apprentices a lodging below, but the merchant came upstairs into a separate apartment. When it was midnight, and the host thought that all were asleep, he came with his wife, and they had an ax and struck the rich merchant dead; and after they had murdered him they went to bed again.

When it was day there was a great outcry; the merchant lay dead in bed bathed in blood. All the guests ran at once but the host said, "The three crazy apprentices have done this;" the lodgers confirmed it, and said, "It can have been no one else."

The innkeeper, however, had them called, and said to them, "Have you killed the merchant?"

"All three of us," said the first, "For money," said the second; and the third added, "And quite right too!"

"There now, you hear," said the host, "they confess it themselves."

They were taken to prison, therefore, and were to be tried. When they saw that things were going so seriously, they were after all afraid, but at night the Devil came and said, "Bear it just one day longer, and do not play away your luck, not one hair of your head shall be hurt."

The next morning they were led to the bar, and the judge said, "Are you the murderers?"

"All three of us."

"Why did you kill the merchant?"

"For money."

"You wicked wretches, you have no horror of your sins?"

"And quite right too!"

"They have confessed, and are still stubborn," said the judge. "Lead them to death instantly." So they were taken out, and the host had to go with them into the circle. When they were taken hold of by the executioner's men, and were just going to be led up to the scaffold where the headsman was standing with naked sword, a coach drawn by four blood-red chestnut horses came up suddenly, driving so fast that fire flashed from the stones, and someone made signs from the window with a white handkerchief.

Then said the headsman, "It is a pardon coming," and "Pardon! pardon!" was called from the carriage also.

Then the Devil stepped out as a very noble gentleman, beautifully dressed, and said, "You three are innocent; you may now speak, make known what you have seen and heard."

Then said the eldest, "We did not kill the merchant, the murderer is standing there in the circle," and he pointed to the innkeeper. "In proof of this, go into his cellar, where many others whom he has killed are still hanging."

Then the judge sent the executioner's men there, and they found it was as the apprentices said, and when they had informed the judge of this, he caused the innkeeper to be led up, and his head was cut off. Then said the Devil to the three, "Now I have got the soul that I wanted to have, and you are free, and have money for the rest of your lives."

20. *The King's Son Who Feared Nothing*

There was once a King's son, who was no longer content to stay at home in his father's house, and as he had no fear of anything, he thought, "I will go forth into the wide world, there the time will not seem long to me, and I shall see wonders enough." So he took leave of his parents, and went forth, and on and on from morning till night, and whichever way his path led it was the same to him. It came to pass that he got to the house of a giant, and as he was so tired he sat down by the door and rested. And as he let his eyes roam here and there, he saw the giant's playthings lying in the yard. These were a couple of enormous balls, and nine pins as tall as a man. After a while he had a fancy to set the nine pins up and then rolled the balls at them, and screamed and cried out when the nine pins fell, and had a merry time of it.

The giant heard the noise, stretched his head out of the window, and saw a man who was not taller than other men, and yet played with his nine pins. "Little worm," cried he, "why are you playing with my balls? Who gave you strength to do it?"

The King's son looked up, saw the giant, and said, "Oh, you blockhead, you think indeed that only you have strong arms, I can do everything I want to do."

The giant came down and watched the bowling with great admiration, and said, "Child of man, if you are one of that kind, go and bring me an apple of the tree of life."

"What do you want with it?" said the King's son.

"I do not want the apple for myself," answered the giant, "but I have a betrothed bride who wishes for it. I have traveled far about the world and cannot find the tree."

"I will soon find it," said the King's son, "and I do not know what is to prevent me from getting the apple down."

The giant said, "You really believe it to be so easy! The garden in which the tree stands is surrounded by an iron railing, and in front of the railing lie wild beasts, each close to the other, and they keep watch and let no man go in."

"They will be sure to let me in," said the King's son.

"Yes, but even if you do get into the garden, and see the apple hanging to the tree, it is still not yours; a ring hangs in front of it, through which anyone who wants to reach the apple and break it off, must put his hand, and no one has yet had the luck to do it."

"That luck will be mine," said the King's son.

Then he took leave of the giant, and went forth over mountain and valley, and through plains and forests, until at length he came to the wondrous garden.

The beasts lay around about it, but they had put their heads down and were asleep. Moreover, they did not awake when he went up to them, so he stepped over them, climbed the fence, and got safely into the garden. There, in the very middle of it, stood the tree of life, and the red apples were shining upon the branches. He climbed up the trunk to the top, and as he was about to reach out for an apple, he saw a ring hanging before it; but he thrust his hand through that without any difficulty, and gathered the apple. The ring closed tightly on his arm, and all at once he felt a prodigious strength flowing through his veins. When he had come down again from the tree with the apple, he would not climb over the fence, but grasped the great gate, and had no need to shake it more than once before it sprang open with a loud crash. Then he went out, and the lion, which had been lying down before, was awake and sprang after him, not in rage and fierceness, but following him humbly as its master.

The King's son took the giant the apple he had promised him, and said, "See, I have brought it without difficulty." The giant was glad that his desire had been so soon satisfied, hastened to his bride, and gave her the apple for which she had wished.

She was a beautiful and wise maiden, and as she did not see the ring on his arm, she said, "I shall never believe that you have brought the apple, until I see the ring on your arm."

The giant said, "I have nothing to do but go home and fetch it," and thought it would be easy to take away by force from the weak man, what he would not give of his own free will. He therefore demanded the ring from him, but the King's son refused it. "Where the apple is, the ring must be also," said the giant; "if you will not give it of your own accord, you must fight with me for it."

They wrestled with each other for a long time, but the giant could not get the better of the King's son, who was strengthened by the magical power of the ring. Then the giant thought of a stratagem, and said, "I have got warm with fighting, and so have you. We will bathe in the river, and cool ourselves before we begin again." The King's son, who knew nothing of falsehood, went with him to the water, and pulled off with his clothes the ring also from his arm, and sprang into the river. The giant instantly snatched the ring, and ran away with it, but the lion, which had observed the theft, pursued the giant, tore the ring out of his hand, and brought it back to its master. Then the giant placed himself behind an oak tree, and while the King's son was busy putting on his clothes again, surprised him, and put both his eyes out.

And now the unhappy King's son stood there, and was blind and knew not how to help himself. Then the giant came back to him, took him by the hand as if he were someone who wanted to guide him, and led him to the top of a high rock. There he left him standing, and thought, "Just two steps more, and he will fall down and kill himself, and I can take the ring from him." But the faithful lion had not deserted its master; it held him fast by the clothes, and drew him gradually back again.

When the giant came and wanted to rob the dead man, he saw that his cunning had been in vain. "Is there no way, then, of destroying a weak child of man like that?" said he angrily to himself, and seized the King's son and led him back again to the precipice by another way, but the lion, which saw his evil design, helped its master out of danger here also. When they had got close to the edge, the giant let the blind man's hand drop, and was going to leave him behind alone, but the lion pushed the giant so that he was thrown down and fell, dashed to pieces, on the ground.

The faithful animal again drew its master back from the precipice, and guided him to a tree by which flowed a clear brook. The King's son sat down there, but the lion lay down, and sprinkled the water in his face with its paws. Scarcely had a couple of drops wetted the sockets of his eyes, than he was once more able to see something, and observed a little bird flying quite close by, which wounded itself against the trunk of a tree. On this it went down to the water and bathed itself, and then it soared upward and swept between the trees without touching them, as if it had recovered its sight again. Then the King's son recognized a sign from God and stooped down to the water, and washed and bathed his face in it. And when he arose he had his eyes once more, brighter and clearer than they had ever been.

The King's son thanked God for his great mercy, and traveled with his lion onward through the world. And it came to pass that he arrived before a castle that was enchanted. In the gateway stood a maiden of beautiful form and fine face, but she was quite black. She spoke to him and said, "Ah, if you could but deliver me from the evil spell that is thrown over me."

"What shall I do?" said the King's son.

The maiden answered, "You must pass three nights in the great hall of this enchanted castle, but you must let no fear enter your heart. When they are doing their worst to torment you, if you bear it without letting a sound escape you, I shall be free. Your life they dare not take."

Then said the King's son, "I have no fear; with God's help I will try it." So he went gaily into the castle, and when it grew dark he seated himself in the large hall and waited. Everything was quiet, however, till midnight, when all at once a great tumult began, and out of every hole and corner came little devils. They behaved as if they did not see him, seated themselves in the middle of the room, lighted a fire, and began to gamble.

When one of them lost, he said, "It is not right; someone is here who does not belong to us; it is his fault that I am losing."

"Wait, you fellow behind the stove, I am coming," said another. The screaming became still louder, so that no one could have heard it without terror. The King's son stayed sitting quite quietly, and was not afraid; but at last the devils jumped up from the ground, and fell on him, and there were so many of them that he could not defend himself from them. They dragged him about on the floor, pinched him, pricked him, beat him, and tormented him, but no sound escaped from him.

Toward morning they disappeared, and he was so exhausted that he could scarcely move his limbs, but when day dawned the black maiden came to him. She bore in her hand a little bottle that held the water of life with which she washed him, and he at once felt all pain depart and new strength flow through his veins. She said, "You have held out successfully for one night, but two more lie before you." Then she went away again, and as she was going, he observed that her feet had become white.

The next night the devils came and began their gambling anew. They fell on the King's son, and beat him much more severely than the night before, until his body was covered with wounds. But as he bore all quietly, they were forced to leave him, and when dawn appeared, the maiden came and healed him with the water of life. And when she went away, he saw with joy that she had already become white to the tips of her fingers.

And now he had only one more night to go through, but it was the worst. The hobgoblins came again: "Are you there still?" cried they. "You shall be tormented till your breath stops." They pricked him and beat him, and threw him here and there, and pulled him by the arms and legs as if they wanted to tear him to pieces, but he bore everything, and never uttered a cry. At last the devils vanished, but he lay fainting there, and did not stir, nor could he raise his eyes to look at the maiden who came in, and sprinkled and bathed him with the water of life. But suddenly he was freed from all pain, and felt fresh and healthy as if he had awakened from sleep, and when he opened his eyes he saw the maiden standing by him, snow-white, and fair as day.

"Rise," said she, "and swing your sword three times over the stairs, and then all will be delivered." And when he had done that, the whole castle was released from enchantment, and the maiden was a rich King's daughter. The servants came and said that the table was already set in the great hall, and dinner served up. Then they sat down and ate and drank together, and in the evening the wedding was solemnized with great rejoicings.

21. *Donkey Cabbages*

There was once a young hunter who went into the forest to lie in wait. He had a fresh and joyous heart, and as he was going there, whistling upon a leaf, an ugly old crone came up, who spoke to him and said, "Good day, dear hunter, truly you are merry and contented, but I am suffering from hunger and thirst, do give me an alms." The hunter had compassion on the poor old creature, felt in his pocket, and gave her what he could afford. He was then about to go further, but the old woman stopped him and said, "Listen, dear hunter, to what I tell you; I will make you a present in return for your kindness. Go on your way now, but in a little while you will come to a tree, where nine birds are sitting that have a cloak in their claws, and are plucking at it; take your gun and shoot into the middle of them, they will let the cloak fall down to you, but one of the birds will be hurt, and will drop down dead. Carry away the cloak, it is a wishing cloak; when you throw it over your shoulders, you only have to wish to be in a certain place, and you will be there in the twinkling of an eye. Take out the heart of the dead bird and swallow it whole, and every morning early, when you get up, you will find a gold piece under your pillow."

The hunter thanked the wise woman, and thought to himself, "Those are fine things that she has promised me, if all does but come true." And verily when he had walked about a hundred paces, he heard in the branches above him such a screaming and twittering that he looked up and saw there a crowd of birds who were tearing a piece of cloth about with their beaks and claws, and tugging and fighting as if each wanted to have it all to himself. "Well," said the hunter, "this is wonderful, it has really come to pass just as the old wife foretold!" and he took the gun from his shoulder, aimed and fired right into the middle of them, so that the feathers flew about. The birds instantly took to flight with loud outcries, but one dropped down dead, and the cloak fell at the same time. Then the hunter did as the old woman had directed him, cut open the bird, sought the heart, swallowed it down, and took the cloak home with him.

Next morning, when he awoke, the promise occurred to him, and he wished to see if it also had been fulfilled. When he lifted up the pillow, the gold piece shone in his eyes, and next day he found another, and so it went on, every time he got up. He gathered together a heap of gold, but at last he thought, "Of what use is all my gold to me if I stay at home? I will go forth and see the world."

He then took leave of his parents, buckled on his hunter's pouch and gun, and went out into the world. It came to pass, that one day he traveled through a dense forest, and when he came to the end of it, in the plain before him stood a fine castle. An old woman was standing with a wonderfully beautiful maiden, looking out of one of the windows. The old woman, however, was a witch and said to the maiden, "There comes one out of the forest, who has a wonderful treasure, we must filch it from him, my dear daughter, it is more suitable for us than for him. He has a bird's heart about him, by means of which a gold piece lies every morning under his pillow." She told her what she was to do to get it, and what part she had to play, and finally threatened her, and said with angry eyes, "And if you do not attend to what I say, it will be the worse for you."

Now when the hunter came nearer he spied the maiden, and said to himself, "I have traveled about for such a long time, I will take a rest for once, and enter that beautiful castle. I have certainly money enough." Nevertheless, the real reason was that he had caught sight of the pretty girl.

He entered the house, and was well received and courteously entertained. Before long he was so much in love with the young witch that he no longer thought of anything else, and only saw things as she saw them, and did what she desired. The old woman then said, "Now we must have the bird's heart, he will never miss it."

She prepared a drink, and when it was ready, poured it into a cup and gave it to the maiden, who was to present it to the hunter. She did so, saying, "Now, my dearest, drink to me." So he took the cup, and when he had swallowed the drink, he brought up the heart of the bird. The girl had to take it away secretly and swallow it herself, for the old woman would have it so. From then on he found no more gold under his pillow, but it lay instead under that of the maiden, from where the old woman fetched it away every morning; but he was so much in love and so befooled, that he thought of nothing else but of passing his time with the girl.

Then the old witch said, "We have the bird's heart, but we must also take the wishing cloak away from him."

The girl answered, "We will leave him that, he has lost his wealth."

The old woman was angry and said, "Such a mantle is a wonderful thing, and is seldom to be found in this world. I must and will have it!" She gave the girl several blows, and said that if she did not obey, it should fare ill with her.

So she did the old woman's bidding, placed herself at the window and looked on the distant country, as if she were very sorrowful. The hunter asked, "Why do you stand there so sorrowfully?"

"Ah, my beloved," was her answer, "over yonder lies the Garnet Mountain, where the precious stones grow. I long for them so much that when I think of them, I feel quite sad, but who can get them? Only the birds; they fly and can reach them, but a man never."

"Have you nothing else to complain of?" said the hunter. "I will soon remove that burden from your heart."

With that he drew her under his mantle, wished himself on the Garnet Mountain, and in the twinkling of an eye they were sitting on it together. Precious stones were glistening on every side so that it was a joy to see them, and together they gathered the finest and costliest of them. Now, the old woman had, through her sorceries, contrived that the eyes of the hunter should become heavy. He said to the maiden, "We will sit down and rest awhile, I am so tired that I can no longer stand on my feet." Then they sat down, and he laid his head in her lap, and fell asleep. When he was asleep, she unfastened the mantle from his shoulders, and wrapped herself in it, picked up the garnets and stones, and wished herself back at home with them.

But when the hunter had had his sleep out and awoke, and perceived that his sweetheart had betrayed him, and left him alone on the wild mountain, he said, "Oh, what treachery there is in the world!" and sat down there in care and sorrow, not knowing what to do. But the mountain belonged to some wild and monstrous giants who dwelt on it and lived their lives there, and he had not sat long before he saw three of them coming toward him, so he lay down as if he were sunk in a deep sleep.

Then the giants came up, and the first kicked him with his foot and said, "What sort of an earth-worm is lying curled up here?"

The second said, "Step upon him and kill him."

But the third said, "That would indeed be worth your while; just let him live, he cannot remain here; and when he climbs higher, toward the summit of the mountain, the clouds will lay hold of him and bear him away." So saying they passed by. But the hunter had paid heed to their words, and as soon as they were gone, he rose and climbed up to the summit of the mountain, and when he had sat there a while, a cloud floated toward him, caught him up, carried him away, and traveled about for a long time in the heavens. Then it sank lower, and let itself down on a great cabbage garden, girt around by walls, so that he came softly to the ground on cabbages and vegetables.

Then the hunter looked about him and said, "If I had but something to eat! I am so hungry, and my hunger will increase in course of time; but I see here neither apples nor pears, nor any other sort of fruit, everywhere nothing but cabbages," but at length he thought, "At a pinch I can eat some of the leaves, they do not taste particularly good, but they will refresh me." With that he picked himself out a fine head of cabbage, and ate it, but scarcely had he swallowed a couple of mouthfuls than he felt very strange and quite different.

Four legs grew on him, a large head and two thick ears, and he saw with horror that he was changed into an ass. Still as his hunger increased every minute, and as the juicy leaves were suitable to his present nature, he went on eating with great zest. At last he arrived at a different kind of cabbage, but as soon as he had swallowed it, he again felt a change, and reassumed his former human shape.

Then the hunter lay down and slept off his fatigue. When he awoke next morning, he broke off one head of the bad cabbages and another of the good ones, and thought to himself, "This shall help me to get my own belongings again and punish treachery." Then he took the cabbages with him, climbed over the wall, and went forth to seek for the castle of his sweetheart.

After wandering about for a couple of days he was lucky enough to find it again. He dyed his face brown, so that his own mother would not have known him; and begged for shelter: "I am so tired," said he, "that I can go no further."

The witch asked, "Who are you, countryman, and what is your business?"

"I am a King's messenger, and was sent out to seek the most delicious salad that grows beneath the sun. I have even been so fortunate as to find it, and am carrying it about with me; but the heat of the sun is so intense that the delicate cabbage threatens to wither, and I do not know if I can carry it any further."

When the old woman heard of the exquisite salad, she was greedy, and said, "Dear countryman, let me just taste this wonderful salad."

"Why not?" answered he. "I have brought two heads with me, and will give you one of them," and he opened his pouch and handed her the bad cabbage. The witch suspected nothing amiss, and her mouth watered so for this new dish that she herself went into the kitchen and dressed it. When it was prepared she could not wait until it was set on the table, but took a couple of leaves at once, and put them in her mouth, but hardly had she swallowed them than she was deprived of her human shape, and she ran out into the courtyard in the form of an ass. Presently the servant entered the kitchen, saw the salad standing there ready prepared, and was about to carry it up; but on the way, according to habit, she was seized by the desire to taste, and she ate a couple of leaves. Instantly the magic power showed itself, and she likewise became an ass and ran out to the old woman, and the dish of salad fell to the ground.

Meantime the messenger sat beside the beautiful girl, and as no one came with the salad and she also was longing for it, she said, "I don't know what has become of the salad."

The hunter thought, "The salad must have already taken effect," and said, "I will go to the kitchen and inquire about it." As he went down he saw the two asses running about in the courtyard; the salad, however, was lying on the ground. "All right," said he, "the two have taken their portion," and he picked up the other leaves, laid them on the dish, and carried them to the maiden. "I bring you the delicate food myself," said he, "in order that you may not have to wait longer." Then she ate of it, and was, like the others, immediately deprived of her human form, and ran out into the courtyard in the shape of an ass.

After the hunter had washed his face, so that the transformed ones could recognize him, he went down into the courtyard, and said, "Now you shall receive the wages of your treachery," and bound them together, all three with one rope, and drove them along until he came to a mill. He knocked at the window, the miller put out his head, and asked what he wanted. "I have three unmanageable beasts," answered he, "which I don't want to keep any longer. Will you take them in, and give them food and stable room, and manage them as I tell you, and then I will pay you what you ask."

The miller said, "Why not? But how am I to manage them?" The hunter then said that he was to give three beatings and one meal daily to the old donkey, and that was the witch; one beating and three meals to the younger one, which was the servant girl; and to the youngest, which was the maiden, no beatings and three meals, for he could not bring himself to have the maiden beaten. After that he went back into the castle, and found inside everything he needed.

After a couple of days, the miller came and said he must inform him that the old ass that had received three beatings and only one meal daily was dead; "the two others," he continued, "are certainly not dead, and are fed three times daily, but they are so sad that they cannot last much longer." The hunter was moved to pity, put away his anger, and told the miller to drive them back again to him. And when they came, he gave them some of the good salad, so that they became human again.

The beautiful girl fell on her knees before him, and said, "Ah, my beloved, forgive me for the evil I have done you; my mother drove me to it; it was done against my will, for I love you dearly. Your wishing cloak hangs in a cupboard, and as for the bird's heart I will take a vomiting potion."

But he thought otherwise, and said, "Keep it; it is all the same, for I will take you for my true wife." So the wedding was celebrated, and they lived happily together until their death.

22. *The Old Woman in the Wood*

A poor servant girl was once traveling with the family with which she was in service, through a great forest, and when they were in the middle of it, robbers came out of the thicket, and murdered all they found. All perished together except the girl, who had jumped out of the carriage in a fright, and hidden herself behind a tree. When the robbers had gone away with their booty, she came out and beheld the great disaster. Then she began to weep bitterly, and said, "What can a poor girl like me do now? I do not know how to get out of the forest, no human being lives in it, so I must certainly starve." She walked about and looked for a road, but could find none. When it was evening she seated herself under a tree, gave herself into God's keeping, and resolved to sit waiting there and not go away, no matter what might happen.

When, however, she had sat there for a while, a white dove came flying to her with a little golden key in its mouth. It put the little key in her hand, and said, "Do you see that great tree, therein is a little lock, it opens with the tiny key, and there you will find food enough, and suffer no more hunger."

Then she went to the tree and opened it, and found milk in a little dish, and white bread to break into it, so that she could eat her fill. When she was satisfied, she said, "It is now the time when the hens at home go to roost, I am so tired I could go to bed too."

Then the dove flew to her again, and brought another golden key in its bill, and said, "Open that tree there, and you will find a bed." So she opened it, and found a beautiful white bed, and she prayed God to protect her during the night, and lay down and slept.

In the morning the dove came for the third time, and again brought a little key, and said, "Open that tree there, and you will find clothes." And when she opened it, she found garments beset with gold and with jewels, more splendid than those of any king's daughter. So she lived there for some time, and the dove came every day and provided her with all she needed, and it was a quiet good life.

Once, however, the dove came and said, "Will you do something for my sake?"

"With all my heart," said the girl.

Then said the little dove, "I will guide you to a small house; enter it, and inside it, an old woman will be sitting by the fire and will say, 'Good day.' But on your life give her no answer, let her do what she will, but pass by her on the right side; further on, there is a door, which you will open, and you will enter into a room where a quantity of rings of all kinds are lying, amongst which are some magnificent ones with shining stones; leave them, however, where they are, and seek out a plain one, which must likewise be amongst them, and bring it here to me as quickly as you can."

The girl went to the little house, and came to the door. There sat an old woman who stared when she saw her, and said, "Good day, my child." The girl gave her no answer, and opened the door. "Where away," cried the old woman, and seized her by the gown, and wanted to hold her fast, saying, "That is my house; no one can go in there if I choose not to allow it." But the girl was silent, got away from her, and went straight into the room.

Now there lay on the table an enormous quantity of rings, which gleamed and glittered before her eyes. She turned them over and looked for the plain one, but could not find it. While she was seeking, she saw the old woman and how she was stealing away, and wanting to get off with a birdcage that she had in her hand. So she went after her and took the cage out of her hand, and when she raised it up and looked into it, a bird was inside that had the plain ring in its bill. Then she took the ring, and ran quite joyously home with it, and thought the little white dove would come and get the ring, but it did not. Then she leaned against a tree and determined to wait for the dove, and, as she thus stood, it seemed just as if the tree was soft and pliant, and was letting its branches down. And suddenly the branches twined around her, and were two arms, and when she looked around, the tree was a handsome man, who embraced and kissed her heartily, and said, "You have delivered me from the power of the old woman, who is a wicked witch. She had changed me into a tree, and every day for two hours I was a white dove, and so long as she possessed the ring I could not regain my human form."

Then his servants and his horses, who had likewise been changed into trees, were freed from the enchantment also, and stood beside him. And he led them forth to his kingdom, for he was a King's son, and they married, and lived happily.

23. *The Three Brothers*

There was once a man who had three sons, and nothing else in the world but the house in which he lived. Now each of the sons wished to have the house after his father's death; but the father loved them all alike, and did not know what to do; he did not wish to sell the house, because it had belonged to his forefathers, else he might have divided the money amongst them. At last a plan came into his head, and he said to his sons, "Go into the world, and try each of you to learn a trade, and, when you all come back, he who makes the best masterpiece shall have the house."

The sons were well content with this, and the eldest determined to be a blacksmith, the second a barber, and the third a fencing master. They fixed a time when they should all come home again, and then each went his way.

It chanced that they all found skillful masters, who taught them their trades well. The blacksmith had to shoe the King's horses, and he thought to himself, "The house is mine, without doubt." The barber only shaved great people, and he too already looked upon the house as his own. The fencing master got many a blow, but he only bit his lip, and let nothing vex him; "for," said he to himself, "if you are afraid of a blow, you'll never win the house."

When the appointed time had gone by, the three brothers came back home to their father; but they did not know how to find the best opportunity for showing their skill, so they sat down and consulted together. As they were sitting thus, all at once a hare came running across the field. "Ah, ha, just in time!" said the barber. So he took his basin and soap, and lathered away until the hare came up; then he soaped and shaved off the hare's whiskers while he was running at the top of his speed, and did not even cut his skin or injure a hair on his body.

"Well done!" said the old man. "Your brothers will have to exert themselves wonderfully, or the house will be yours."

Soon after, up came a nobleman in his coach, dashing along at full speed. "Now you shall see what I can do, Father," said the blacksmith;

so away he ran after the coach, took all four shoes off the feet of one of the horses while he was galloping, and put on him four new shoes without stopping him.

"You are a fine fellow, and as clever as your brother," said his father; "I do not know to which I ought to give the house."

Then the third son said, "Father, let me have my turn, if you please;" and, as it was beginning to rain, he drew his sword, and flourished it backward and forward above his head so fast that not a drop fell upon him. It rained still harder and harder, till at last it came down in torrents; but he only flourished his sword faster and faster, and remained as dry as if he were sitting in a house.

When his father saw this he was amazed, and said, "This is the masterpiece, the house is yours!"

His brothers were satisfied with this, as was agreed beforehand; and, as they loved one another very much, they all three stayed together in the house, followed their trades, and, as they had learned them so well and were so clever, they earned a great deal of money. Thus they lived together happily until they grew old; and at last, when one of them fell sick and died, the two others grieved so sorely about it that they also fell ill, and soon after died. And because they had been so clever, and had loved one another so much, they were all laid in the same grave.

24. *The Devil and His Grandmother*

There was a great war, and the King had many soldiers, but gave them small pay, so small that they could not live upon it, so three of them agreed among themselves to desert. One of them said to the others, "If we are caught we shall be hanged on the gallows; how shall we manage it?"

Another said, "Look at that great cornfield, if we were to hide ourselves there, no one could find us; the troops are not allowed to enter it, and tomorrow they are to march away."

They crept into the corn, only the troops did not march away, but remained lying all around about it. They stayed in the corn for two days and two nights, and were so hungry that they all but died, but if they had come out, their death would have been certain.

Then said they, "What is the use of our deserting if we have to perish miserably here?" But now a fiery dragon came flying through the air, and it came down to them, and asked why they had concealed themselves there. They answered, "We are three soldiers who have deserted because the pay was so bad, and now we shall have to die of hunger if we stay here, or to dangle on the gallows if we go out."

"If you will serve me for seven years," said the dragon, "I will convey you through the army so that no one shall seize you."

"We have no choice and are compelled to accept," they replied.

Then the dragon caught hold of them with his claws, and carried them away through the air over the army, and put them down again on the earth far from it; but the dragon was no other than the Devil. He gave them a small whip and said, "Whip with it and crack it, and then as much gold will spring up around about as you can wish for; then you can live like great lords, keep horses, and drive your carriages, but when the seven years have come to an end, you are my property." Then he put before them a book, which they were all three forced to sign. "I will, however, then set you a riddle," said he, "and if you can guess that, you shall be free, and released from my power."

Then the dragon flew away from them, and they went away with their whip, had gold in plenty, ordered themselves rich apparel, and traveled about the world. Wherever they were they lived in pleasure and magnificence, rode on horseback, drove in carriages, ate and drank, but did nothing wicked. The time slipped quickly away, and when the seven years were coming to an end, two of them were terribly anxious and alarmed; but the third took the affair easily, and said, "Brothers, fear nothing, my head is sharp enough, I shall guess the riddle." They went out into the open country and sat down, and the two made sorrowful faces.

Then an aged woman came up to them who inquired why they were so sad. "Alas!" said they, "how can that concern you? After all, you cannot help us."

"Who knows?" said she. "Confide your trouble to me." So they told her that they had been the Devil's servants for nearly seven years, and that he had provided them with gold as plentifully as if it had been blackberries, but that they had sold themselves to him, and were forfeited to him, if at the end of the seven years they could not guess a riddle. The old woman said, "If you are to be saved, one of you must go into the forest, there he will come to a fallen rock that looks like a little house, he must enter that, and then he will obtain help."

The two melancholy ones thought to themselves, "That will still not save us," and stayed where they were, but the third, the merry one, got up and walked on in the forest until he found the rock house. In the little house, however, a very aged woman was sitting, who was the Devil's grandmother, and asked the soldier where he came from, and what he wanted there. He told her everything that had happened, and as he pleased her well, she had pity on him, and said she would help him.

She lifted up a great stone that lay above a cellar, and said, "Conceal yourself there, you can hear everything that is said here; only sit still, and do not stir. When the dragon comes, I will question him about the riddle, he tells everything to me, so listen carefully to his answer."

At twelve o'clock at night, the dragon came flying there, and asked for his dinner. The grandmother laid the table, and served up food and drink, so that he was pleased, and they ate and drank together. In the course of conversation, she asked him what kind of a day he had had, and how many souls he had got? "Nothing went very well today," he answered, "but I have laid hold of three soldiers, I have them safe."

"Indeed! three soldiers, that's something to like, but they may escape you yet."

The Devil said mockingly, "They are mine! I will set them a riddle, which they will never in this world be able to guess!"

"What riddle is that?" she inquired.

"I will tell you. In the great North Sea lies a dead dogfish, that shall be your roast meat, and the rib of a whale shall be your silver spoon, and a hollow old horse's hoof shall be your wineglass."

When the Devil had gone to bed, the old grandmother raised up the stone, and let out the soldier. "Have you paid particular attention to everything?"

"Yes," said he, "I know enough, and will contrive to save myself." Then he had to go back another way, through the window, secretly and with all speed to his companions. He told them how the Devil had been overreached by the old grandmother, and how he had learned the answer to the riddle from him. Then they were all joyous, and of good cheer, and took the whip and whipped so much gold for themselves that it ran all over the ground.

When the seven years had fully gone by, the Devil came with the book, showed the signatures, and said, "I will take you with me to hell. There you shall have a meal! If you can guess what kind of roast meat you will have to eat, you shall be free and released from your bargain, and may keep the whip as well."

Then the first soldier began and said, "In the great North Sea lies a dead dogfish, that no doubt is the roast meat."

The Devil was angry, and began to mutter, "Hm! hm! hm!" and asked the second, "But what will your spoon be?"

"The rib of a whale, that is to be our silver spoon."

The Devil made a wry face, again growled, "Hm! hm! hm!" and said to the third, "And do you also know what your wineglass is to be?"

"An old horse's hoof is to be our wineglass." Then the Devil flew away with a loud cry, and had no more power over them, but the three kept the whip, whipped as much money for themselves with it as they wanted, and lived happily to their end.

25. *Ferdinand the Faithful*

Once on a time lived a man and a woman who so long as they were rich had no children, but when they were poor they had a little boy. They could, however, find no godfather for him, so the man said he would just go to another place to see if he could get one there. As he went, a poor man met him, who asked him where he was going. He said he was going to see if he could get a godfather, that he was poor, so no one would stand as godfather for him. "Oh," said the poor man, "you are poor, and I am poor; I will be godfather for you, but I am so ill off I can give the child nothing. Go home and tell the nurse that she is to come to the church with the child."

When they all got to the church together, the beggar was already there, and he gave the child the name of Ferdinand the Faithful.

When he was going out of the church, the beggar said, "Now go home, I can give you nothing, and you likewise ought to give me nothing." But he gave a key to the nurse, and told her when she got home she was to give it to the father, who was to take care of it until the child was fourteen years old, and then he was to go on the heath where there was a castle, which the key would fit, and that all that was inside should belong to him.

Now when the child was seven years old and had grown very big, he once went to play with some other boys, and each of them boasted that he had got more from his godfather than the other; but the child could say nothing, and was vexed, and went home and said to his father, "Did I get nothing at all, then, from my godfather?"

"Oh, yes," said the father, "you had a key. If there is a castle standing on the heath, just go to it and open it." Then the boy went there, but no castle was to be seen, or heard of.

After seven years more, when he was fourteen years old, he again went there, and there stood the castle. When he had opened it, there was nothing within but a horse, a white one. Then the boy was so full of joy because he had a horse, that he mounted on it and galloped back to his father. "Now I have a white horse, and I will travel," said he.

So he set out, and as he was on his way, a pen was lying on the road. At first he thought he would pick it up, but then again he thought to himself, "You should leave it lying there; you will easily find a pen where you are going, if you have need of one."

As he was thus riding away, a voice called after him, "Ferdinand the Faithful, take it with you." He looked around, but saw no one, then he went back again and picked it up.

When he had ridden a little way farther, he passed by a lake, and a fish was lying on the bank, gasping and panting for breath, so he said, "Wait, my dear fish, I will help you get into the water," and he took hold of it by the tail, and threw it into the lake.

Then the fish put its head out of the water and said, "As you have helped me out of the mud I will give you a flute; when you are in any need, play on it, and then I will help you, and if ever you let anything fall in the water, just play and I will reach it out to you." Then he rode away, and there came to him a man who asked him where he was going.

"Oh, to the next place." Then he asked what his name was. "Ferdinand the Faithful."

"So! then we have got almost the same name, I am called Ferdinand the Unfaithful." And they both set out to the inn in the nearest place.

Now it was unfortunate that Ferdinand the Unfaithful knew everything that the other had ever thought and everything he was about to do; he knew it by means of all kinds of wicked arts. There was, however, in the inn an honest girl, who had a bright face and behaved very prettily. She fell in love with Ferdinand the Faithful because he was a handsome man, and she asked him where he was going. "Oh, I am just traveling around about," said he. Then she said he ought to stay there, for the King of that country wanted an attendant or an outrider, and he ought to enter his service. He answered he could not very well go to anyone like that and offer himself.

Then said the maiden, "Oh, but I will soon do that for you." And so she went straight to the King, and told him that she knew of an excellent servant for him. He was well pleased with that, and had Ferdinand the Faithful brought to him, and wanted to make him his servant. He, however, liked better to be an outrider, for where his horse was, there he also wanted to be, so the King made him an outrider.

When Ferdinand the Unfaithful learned that, he said to the girl, "What! Do you help him and not me?"

"Oh," said the girl, "I will help you too." She thought, "I must keep friends with that man, for he is not to be trusted." She went to the King, and offered him as a servant, and the King was willing.

Now when the King met his lords in the morning, he always lamented and said, "Oh, if I had but my love with me."

Ferdinand the Unfaithful was, however, always hostile to Ferdinand the Faithful. So once, when the King was complaining thus, he said, "You have the outrider, send him away to get her, and if he does not do it, his head must be struck off." Then the King sent for Ferdinand the Faithful, and told him that there was, in this place or in that place, a girl he loved, and that he was to bring her to him, and if he did not do it he should die.

Ferdinand the Faithful went into the stable to his white horse, and complained and lamented, "Oh, what an unhappy man I am!"

Then someone behind him cried, "Ferdinand the Faithful, why do you weep?"

He looked around but saw no one, and went on lamenting, "Oh, my dear little white horse, now must I leave you; now must I die."

Then someone cried once more, "Ferdinand the Faithful, why do you weep?"

Then for the first time he was aware that it was his little white horse who was putting that question. "Do you speak, my little white horse; can you do that?" And again, he said, "I am to go to this place and to that, and am to bring the bride; can you tell me how I am to set about it?"

Then answered the little white horse, "Go to the King, and say if he will give you what you must have, you will get her for him. If he will give you a ship full of meat, and a ship full of bread, it will succeed. Great giants dwell on the lake, and if you take no meat with you for them, they will tear you to pieces, and there are the large birds that would peck the eyes out of your head if you had no bread for them." Then the King made all the butchers in the land kill, and all the bakers bake, that the ships might be filled. When they were full, the little white horse said to Ferdinand the Faithful, "Now mount me, and go with me into the ship, and then when the giants come, say,

> "Peace, peace, my dear little giants,
> I have had thought of you,
> Something I have brought for you;"

and when the birds come, you shall again say,

> "Peace, peace, my dear little birds,
> I have had thought of you,
> Something I have brought for you;"

then they will do nothing to you, and when you come to the castle, the giants will help you. Then go up to the castle, and take a couple of giants with you. There the princess lies sleeping; you must, however, not awaken her, but the giants must lift her up, and carry her in her bed to the ship."

And now everything took place as the little white horse had said, and Ferdinand the Faithful gave the giants and the birds what he had brought with him for them, and that made the giants willing, and they carried the princess in her bed to the King. And when she came to the King, she said she could not live, she must have her writings, they had been left in her castle. Then by the instigation of Ferdinand the Unfaithful, Ferdinand the Faithful was called, and the King told him he must fetch the writings from the castle, or he should die.

Then he went once more into the stable, and bemoaned himself and said, "Oh, my dear little white horse, now I am to go away again, how am I to do it?" Then the little white horse said he was just to load the ships full again.

So it happened again as it had happened before, and the giants and the birds were satisfied, and made gentle by the meat. When they came to the castle, the white horse told Ferdinand the Faithful that he must go in, and that on the table in the princess's bedroom lay the writings. And Ferdinand the Faithful went in, and fetched them. When they were on the lake, he let his pen fall into the water; then said the white horse, "Now I cannot help you at all." But he remembered his flute, and began to play on it, and the fish came with the pen in its mouth, and gave it to him. So he took the writings to the castle, where the wedding was celebrated.

The Queen, however, did not love the King because he had no nose, but she would have much liked to love Ferdinand the Faithful. Once, therefore, when all the lords of the court were together, the Queen said she could do feats of magic, that she could cut off anyone's head and put it on again, and that one of them ought just to try it. But none of them would be the first, so Ferdinand the Faithful, again at the instigation of Ferdinand the Unfaithful, undertook it and she hewed off his head, and put it on again for him, and it healed together directly, so that it looked as if he had a red thread around his throat.

Then the King said to her, "My child, where have you learned that?"

"Yes," she said, "I understand the art; shall I just try it on you also?"

"Oh, yes," said he. But she cut off his head, and did not put it on again; but pretended that she could not get it on, and that it would not keep fixed. Then the King was buried, but she married Ferdinand the Faithful.

He, however, always rode on his white horse, and once when he was seated on it, it told him that he was to go on to the heath that he knew, and gallop three times around it. And when he had done that, the white horse stood up on its hind legs, and was changed into a King's son.

26. *The Iron Stove*

In the days when wishing was still of some use, a King's son was bewitched by an old witch, and shut up in an iron stove in a forest. There he passed many years, and no one could deliver him. Then a King's daughter came into the forest, who had lost herself, and could not find her father's kingdom again. After she had wandered about for nine days, she at length came to the iron stove. Then a voice came forth from it, and asked her, "From where do you come, and where are you going?"

She answered, "I have lost my father's kingdom, and cannot get home again."

Then a voice inside the iron stove said, "I will help you to get home again, and that indeed most swiftly, if you will promise to do what I desire of you. I am the son of a far greater King than your father, and I will marry you."

Then was she afraid, and thought, "Good heavens! What can I do with an iron stove?" But as she much wished to get home to her father, she promised to do as he desired.

But he said, "You shall return here, and bring a knife with you, and scrape a hole in the iron." Then he gave her a companion who walked near her, but did not speak, but in two hours he took her home; there was great joy in the castle when the King's daughter came home, and the old King fell on her neck and kissed her.

She, however, was sorely troubled, and said, "Dear father, what I have suffered! I should never have got home again from the great wild forest, if I had not come to an iron stove, but I have been forced to give my word that I will go back to it, set it free, and marry it." Then the old King was so terrified that he all but fainted, for he had but this one daughter. They therefore resolved they would send, in her place, the miller's daughter, who was very beautiful. They took her there, gave her a knife, and said she was to scrape at the iron stove. So she scraped at it for twenty-four hours, but could not bring off the least morsel of it.

When day dawned, a voice in the stove said, "It seems to me it is day outside."

Then she answered, "It seems so to me too; I fancy I hear the noise of my father's mill."

"So you are a miller's daughter! Then go your way at once, and let the King's daughter come here." Then she went away at once, and told the old King that the man outside there would have none of her, he wanted the King's daughter. They, however, still had a swineherd's daughter, who was even prettier than the miller's daughter, and they determined to give her a piece of gold to go to the iron stove instead of the King's daughter. So she was taken there, and she also had to scrape for twenty-four hours. She, however, made nothing of it.

When day broke, a voice inside the stove cried, "It seems to me it is day outside!"

Then answered she, "So it seems to me also; I fancy I hear my father's horn blowing."

"Then you are a swineherd's daughter! Go away at once, and tell the King's daughter to come, and tell her all must be done as promised, and if she does not come, everything in the kingdom shall be ruined and destroyed, and not one stone be left standing on another."

When the King's daughter heard that she began to weep, but now there was nothing for it but to keep her promise. So she took leave of her father, put a knife in her pocket, and went forth to the iron stove in the forest. When she got there, she began to scrape, and the iron gave way, and when two hours were over, she had already scraped a small hole. Then she peeped in, and saw a youth so handsome, and so brilliant with gold and with precious jewels, that her very soul was delighted. Now, therefore, she went on scraping, and made the hole so large that he was able to get out.

Then said he, "You are mine, and I am yours; you are my bride, and have released me." He wanted to take her away with him to his kingdom, but she entreated him to let her go once again to her father, and the King's son allowed her to do so, but she was not to say more to her father than three words, and then she was to come back again. So she went home, but she spoke more than three words, and instantly the iron stove disappeared, and was taken far away over glass mountains and piercing swords; but the King's son was set free, and no longer shut up in it.

After this she bade good-bye to her father, took some money with her, but not much, and went back to the great forest, and looked for the iron stove, but it was nowhere to be found. For nine days she sought it, and then her hunger grew so great that she did not know what to do, for she could no longer live. When it was evening, she seated herself in a small tree, and made up her mind to spend the night there, as she was afraid of wild beasts. When midnight drew near she saw in the distance a small light, and thought, "Ah, there I should be saved!" She got down from the tree, and went toward the light, but on the way she prayed.

Then she came to a little old house, and much grass had grown all about it, and a small heap of wood lay in front of it. She thought, "Ah, where have I come," and peeped in through the window, but she saw nothing inside but toads, big and little, except a table well covered with wine and roast meat, and the plates and glasses were of silver. Then she took courage, and knocked at the door. The fat toad cried,

> "Little green waiting maid,
> Waiting maid with the limping leg,
> Little dog of the limping leg,
> Hop here and over there,
> And quickly see who is outside;"

and a small toad came walking by and opened the door to her. When she entered, they all bade her welcome, and she was forced to sit down. They asked, "Where have you come from, and where are you going?" Then she related all that had befallen her, and how because she had transgressed the order that had been given her not to say more than three words, the stove, and the King's son also, had disappeared, and now she was about to seek him over hill and dale until she found him. Then the old fat one said,

> "Little green waiting maid,
> Waiting maid with the limping leg,
> Little dog of the limping leg,
> Hop here and over there,
> And bring me the great box."

Then the little one went and brought the box. After this they gave her meat and drink, and took her to a well-made bed, which felt like silk and velvet, and she laid herself in it, in God's name, and slept. When morning came she arose, and the old toad gave her three needles out of the great box that she was to take with her; they would be needed by her, for she had to cross a high glass mountain, and go over three piercing swords and a great lake. If she did all this she would get her lover back again. Then she gave her three things, which she was to take the greatest care of, namely, three large needles, a plow wheel, and three nuts.

With these she traveled onward, and when she came to the glass mountain that was so slippery, she stuck the three needles first behind her feet and then before them, and so got over it, and when she was over it, she hid them in a place that she marked carefully. After this she came to the three piercing swords, and then she seated herself on her plow wheel, and rolled over them. At last she arrived in front of a great lake, and when she had crossed it, she came to a large and beautiful castle. She went and asked for a place; she was a poor girl, she said, and would like to be hired. She knew, however, that the King's son whom she had released from the iron stove in the great forest was in the castle. Then she was taken as a kitchen maid at low wages. But, already the King's son had another maiden by his side whom he wanted to marry, for he thought that she had long been dead.

In the evening, when she had washed up and was done, she felt in her pocket and found the three nuts that the old toad had given her. She cracked one with her teeth, and was going to eat the kernel when lo and behold there was a stately royal garment in it! But when the bride heard of this she came and asked for the dress, and wanted to buy it, and said, "It is not a dress for a servant girl." But she said no, she would not sell it, but if the bride would grant her one thing she should have it, and that was, let her sleep one night in her bridegroom's chamber. The bride gave her permission because the dress was so pretty, and she had never had one like it. When it was evening she said to her bridegroom, "That silly girl will sleep in your room."

"If you are willing so am I," said he. She, however, gave him a glass of wine in which she had poured a sleeping potion. So the bridegroom and the kitchen maid went to sleep in the room, and he slept so soundly that she could not wake him.

She wept the whole night and cried, "I set you free when you were in an iron stove in the wild forest, I sought you, and walked over a glass mountain, and three sharp swords, and a great lake before I found you, and yet you will not hear me!"

The servants sat by the chamber door, and heard how she thus wept the whole night through, and in the morning they told it to their lord. And the next evening when she had washed up, she opened the second nut, and a far more beautiful dress was within it, and when the bride beheld it, she wished to buy that also. But the girl would not take money, and begged that she might once again sleep in the bridegroom's chamber. The bride, however, gave him a sleeping potion, and he slept so soundly that he could hear nothing.

But the kitchen maid wept the whole night long, and cried, "I set you free when you were in an iron stove in the wild forest, I sought you, and walked over a glass mountain, and over three sharp swords and a great lake before I found you, and yet you will not hear me!"

The servants sat by the chamber door and heard her weeping the whole night through, and in the morning informed their lord of it. And on the third evening, when she had washed up, she opened the third nut, and within it was a still more beautiful dress, which was stiff with pure gold. When the bride saw that she wanted to have it, but the maiden only gave it up on condition that she might for the third time sleep in the bridegroom's apartment. The King's son was, however, on his guard, and threw the sleeping potion away.

Now, therefore, when she began to weep and to cry, "Dearest love, I set you free when you were in the iron stove in the terrible wild forest," the King's son leapt up and said, "You are the true one, you are mine, and I am yours." Thereupon, while it was still night, he got into a carriage with her, and they took away the false bride's clothes so that she could not get up. When they came to the great lake, they sailed across it, and when they reached the three sharp-cutting swords they seated themselves on the plow wheel, and when they got to the glass mountain they thrust the three needles in it, and so at length they got to the little old house; but when they went inside that, it was a great castle, and the toads were all disenchanted, and were King's children, and full of happiness. Then the wedding was celebrated, and the King's son and the princess remained in the castle, which was much larger than the castles of their fathers. As, however, the old King grieved at being left alone, they fetched him away, and brought him to live with them, and they had two kingdoms, and lived in happy wedlock.

A mouse did run,
This story is done.

27. *The Lazy Spinner*

In a certain village there once lived a man and his wife, and the wife was so idle that she would never work at anything; whatever her husband gave her to spin, she did not get done, and what she did spin she did not wind, but let it all remain entangled in a heap. If the man scolded her, she was always ready with her tongue, and said, "Well, how should I wind it, when I have no reel? Just you go into the forest and get me one."

"If that is all," said the man, "then I will go into the forest, and get some wood for making reels." Then the woman was afraid that if he had the wood he would make her a reel of it, and she would have to wind her yarn off, and then begin to spin again. She thought a little, and then a lucky idea occurred to her, and she secretly followed the man into the forest, and when he had climbed into a tree to choose and cut the wood, she crept into the thicket below where he could not see her, and cried,

> "He who cuts wood for reels shall die,
> And he who winds, shall perish."

The man listened, laid down his ax for a moment, and began to consider what that could mean. "Hollo," he said at last, "what can that have been; my ears must have been singing, I won't alarm myself for nothing." So he again seized the ax, and began to hew, then again there came a cry from below:

> "He who cuts wood for reels shall die,
> And he who winds, shall perish."

He stopped, and felt afraid and alarmed, and pondered over the circumstance. But when a few moments had passed, he took heart again, and a third time he stretched out his hand for the ax, and began to cut. But someone called out a third time, and said loudly,

> "He who cuts wood for reels shall die,
> And he who winds, shall perish."

That was enough for him, and all inclination had departed from him, so he hastily descended the tree, and set out on his way home. The woman ran as fast as she could by byways so as to get home first. So when he entered the parlor, she put on an innocent look as if nothing had happened, and said, "Well, have you brought a nice piece of wood for reels?"

"No," said he, "I see very well that winding won't do," and told her what had happened to him in the forest, and from that time forth left her in peace about it. Nevertheless after some time, the man again began to complain of the disorder in the house. "Wife," said he, "it is really a shame that the spun yarn should lie there all entangled!"

"I'll tell you what," said she, "as we still don't come by any reel, go up into the loft, and I will stand down below, and will throw the yarn up to you, and you will throw it down to me, and so we shall get a skein after all."

"Yes, that will do," said the man. So they did that, and when it was done, he said, "The yarn is in skeins, now it must be boiled." The woman was again distressed; she certainly said, "Yes, we will boil it next morning early," but she was secretly contriving another trick.

Early in the morning she got up, lighted a fire, and put the kettle on, only instead of the yarn, she put in a lump of tow, and let it boil. After that she went to the man who was still lying in bed, and said to him, "I must just go out, you must get up and look after the yarn that is in the kettle on the fire, but you must be at hand at once; mind that, for if the cock should happen to crow, and you are not attending to the yarn, it will become tow." The man was willing and took good care not to loiter. He got up as quickly as he could, and went into the kitchen. But when he reached the kettle and peeped in, he saw, to his horror, nothing but a lump of tow. Then the poor man was as still as a mouse, thinking he had neglected it, and was to blame, and in future said no more about yarn and spinning. But you yourself must own she was an odious woman!

28. *The Four Skillful Brothers*

There was once a poor man who had four sons, and when they were grown up, he said to them, "My dear children, you must now go out into the world, for I have nothing to give you, so set out, and go to some distance and learn a trade, and see how you can make your way." So the four brothers took their sticks, bade their father farewell, and went through the town gate together. When they had traveled about for some time, they came to a crossroad that branched off in four different directions. Then said the eldest, "Here we must separate, but on this day in four years, we will meet each other again at this spot, and in the meantime we will seek our fortunes."

Then each of them went his way, and the eldest met a man who asked him where he was going, and what he was intending to do? "I want to learn a trade," he replied.

Then the other said, "Come with me, and be a thief."

"No," he answered, "that is no longer regarded as a reputable trade, and the end of it is that one has to swing on the gallows."

"Oh," said the man, "you need not be afraid of the gallows; I will only teach you to get such things as no other man could ever lay hold of, and no one will ever detect you." So he allowed himself to be talked into it, and while with the man became an accomplished thief, and so dexterous that nothing was safe from him, if he once desired to have it.

The second brother met a man who put the same question to him what he wanted to learn in the world. "I don't know yet," he replied.

"Then come with me, and be an astronomer; there is nothing better than that, for nothing is hid from you." He liked the idea, and became such a skillful astronomer that when he had learned everything, and was about to travel onward, his master gave him a telescope and said to him, "With that you can see whatever takes place either on Earth or in heaven, and nothing can remain concealed from you."

A hunter took the third brother into training, and gave him such excellent instruction in everything that related to hunting, that he became an experienced hunter. When he went away, his master gave him a gun and said, "It will never fail you; whatever you aim at, you are certain to hit."

The youngest brother also met a man who spoke to him, and inquired what his intentions were. "Would you not like to be a tailor?" said he.

"Not that I know of," said the youth; "sitting doubled up from morning till night, driving the needle and the goose backward and forward, is not to my taste."

"Oh, but you are speaking in ignorance," answered the man; "with me you would learn a very different kind of tailoring, which is respectable and proper, and for the most part very honorable." So he let himself be persuaded, and went with the man, and learned his art from the very beginning. When they parted, the man gave the youth a needle, and said, "With this you can sew together whatever is given you, whether it is as soft as an egg or as hard as steel; and it will all become one piece of stuff, so that no seam will be visible."

When the appointed four years were over, the four brothers arrived at the same time at the crossroads, embraced and kissed each other, and returned home to their father. "So now," said he, quite delighted, "the wind has blown you back again to me." They told him of all that had happened to them, and that each had learned his own trade. Now they were sitting just in front of the house under a large tree, and the father said, "I will put you all to the test, and see what you can do." Then he looked up and said to his second son, "Between two branches up at the top of this tree, there is a chaffinch's nest, tell me how many eggs there are in it?"

The astronomer took his glass, looked up, and said, "There are five."

Then the father said to the eldest, "Fetch the eggs down without disturbing the bird that is sitting hatching them." The skillful thief climbed up, and took the five eggs from beneath the bird, which never observed what he was doing, and remained quietly sitting where she was, and brought them down to his father.

The father took them, and put one of them on each corner of the table, and the fifth in the middle, and said to the hunter, "With one shot you shall shoot me the five eggs in two, through the middle." The hunter aimed, and shot the eggs, all five as the father had desired, and that at one shot. He certainly must have had some of the powder for shooting around corners.

"Now it's your turn," said the father to the fourth son; "you shall sew the eggs together again, and the young birds that are inside them as well, and you must do it so that they are not hurt by the shot." The tailor brought his needle, and sewed them as his father wished. When he had done this the thief had to climb up the tree again, and carry them to the nest, and put them back again under the bird without her being aware of it. The bird sat her full time, and after a few days the young ones crept out, and they had a red line around their necks where they had been sewn together by the tailor.

"Well," said the old man to his sons, "I begin to think you are worth more than green clover; you have used your time well, and learned something good. I can't say which of you deserves the most praise. That will be proved if you have but an early opportunity of using your talents." Not long after this, there was a great uproar in the country, for the King's daughter was carried off by a dragon. The King was full of trouble about it, both by day and night, and caused it to be proclaimed that whoever brought her back should have her to wed. The four brothers said to each other, "This would be a fine opportunity for us to show what we can do!" and resolved to go forth together and liberate the King's daughter.

"I will soon know where she is," said the astronomer, and looked through his telescope and said, "I see her already, she is far away from here on a rock in the sea, and the dragon is beside her watching her." Then he went to the King, and asked for a ship for himself and his brothers, and sailed with them over the sea until they came to the rock. There the King's daughter was sitting, and the dragon was lying asleep on her lap.

The hunter said, "I dare not fire, I should kill the beautiful maiden at the same time."

"Then I will try my art," said the thief, and he crept over and stole her away from under the dragon, so quietly and dexterously, that the monster never noticed it, but went on snoring. Full of joy, they hurried off with her onboard, and steered out into the open sea; but the dragon, who when he awoke had found no princess there, followed them, and came snorting angrily through the air. Just as he was circling above the ship, and about to descend on it, the hunter shouldered his gun, and shot him to the heart. The monster fell down dead, but was so large and powerful that his fall shattered the whole ship. Fortunately, however, they laid hold of a couple of planks, and swam about the wide sea. Then again they were in great peril, but the tailor, who was not idle, took his wondrous needle, and with a few stitches sewed the planks together, and they seated themselves upon them, and collected together all the fragments of the vessel. Then he sewed these so skillfully together, that in a very short time the ship was once more seaworthy, and they could go home again in safety.

When the King once more saw his daughter, there were great rejoicings. He said to the four brothers, "One of you shall have her as wife, but which of you it is to be you must settle among yourselves." Then a warm contest arose among them, for each of them preferred his own claim.

The astronomer said, "If I had not seen the princess, all your arts would have been useless, so she is mine."

The thief said, "What would have been the use of your seeing, if I had not got her away from the dragon? So she is mine."

The hunter said, "You and the princess, and all of you, would have been torn to pieces by the dragon if my ball had not hit him, so she is mine."

The tailor said, "And if I, by my art, had not sewn the ship together again, you would all of you have been miserably drowned, so she is mine."

Then the King uttered this saying, "Each of you has an equal right, and as all of you cannot have the maiden, none of you shall have her, but I will give to each of you, as a reward, half a kingdom."

The brothers were pleased with this decision, and said, "It is better thus than that we should be at variance with each other." Then each of them received half a kingdom, and they lived with their father in the greatest happiness as long as it pleased God.

29. One-eye, Two-eyes, and Three-eyes

There was once a woman who had three daughters, the eldest of whom was called One-eye, because she had only one eye in the middle of her forehead, and the second, Two-eyes, because she had two eyes like other folks, and the youngest, Three-eyes, because she had three eyes; and her third eye was also in the center of her forehead. However, as Two-eyes saw just as other human beings did, her sisters and her mother could not endure her. They said to her, "You, with your two eyes, are no better than the common people; you do not belong to us!" They pushed her about, and threw old clothes to her, and gave her nothing to eat but what they left, and did everything that they could to make her unhappy. It came to pass that Two-eyes had to go out into the fields and tend the goat, but she was still quite hungry, because her sisters had given her so little to eat. So she sat down on a ridge and began to weep, so bitterly that two streams ran down from her eyes.

And once when she looked up in her grief, a woman was standing beside her, who said, "Why are you weeping, little Two-eyes?"

Two-Eyes answered, "Have I not reason to weep, when I have two eyes like other people, and my sisters and mother hate me for it, and push me from one corner to another, throw old clothes at me, and give me nothing to eat but the scraps they leave? Today they have given me so little that I am still quite hungry." Then the wise woman said, "Wipe away your tears, Two-eyes, and I will tell you something to stop you ever suffering from hunger again; just say to your goat,

> "Bleat, my little goat, bleat,
> Cover the table with something to eat,"

and then a clean well-spread little table will stand before you, with the most delicious food upon it of which you may eat as much as you like, and when you have had enough, and have no more need of the little table, just say,

> "Bleat, bleat, my little goat, I pray,
> And take the table quite away,"

and then it will vanish again from your sight." Then the wise woman departed. But Two-eyes thought, "I must instantly try, and see if what she said is true, for I am far too hungry," and she said,

> "Bleat, my little goat, bleat,
> Cover the table with something to eat,"

and scarcely had she spoken the words than a little table, covered with a white cloth, was standing there, and on it was a plate with a knife and fork, and a silver spoon; and the most delicious food was there also, warm and smoking as if it had just come out of the kitchen. Then Two-eyes said the shortest prayer she knew, "Lord God, be with us always, Amen," and helped herself to some food, and enjoyed it. And when she was satisfied, she said, as the wise woman had taught her,

> "Bleat, bleat, my little goat, I pray,
> And take the table quite away,"

and immediately the little table and everything on it was gone again. "That is a delightful way of keeping house!" thought Two-eyes, and was quite glad and happy.

In the evening, when she went home with her goat, she found a small earthenware dish with some food, which her sisters had set ready for her, but she did not touch it. Next day she again went out with her goat, and left the few bits of broken bread that had been handed to her lying untouched. The first and second time that she did this, her sisters did not remark it at all, but as it happened every time, they did observe it, and said, "There is something wrong about Two-eyes, she always leaves her food untasted, and she used to eat up everything that was given her; she must have discovered other ways of getting food." In order that they might learn the truth, they resolved to send One-eye with Two-eyes when she went to drive her goat to the pasture, to observe what Two-eyes did when she was there, and whether anyone brought her anything to eat and drink. So when Two-eyes set out the next time, One-eye went to her and said, "I will go with you to the pasture, and see that the goat is well taken care of, and driven where there is food." But Two-eyes knew what was in One-eye's mind, and drove the goat into high grass and said, "Come, One-eye, we will sit down, and I will sing something to you." One-eye sat down and was tired with the unaccustomed walk and the heat of the sun, and Two-eyes sang constantly,

> "One eye, are you awake?
> One eye, are you asleep?"

until One-eye shut her one eye, and fell asleep, and as soon as Two-eyes saw that One-eye was fast asleep, and could discover nothing, she said,

> "Bleat, my little goat, bleat,
> Cover the table with something to eat,"

and seated herself at her table, and ate and drank until she was satisfied, and then she again cried,

> "Bleat, bleat, my little goat, I pray,
> And take the table quite away,"

and in an instant all was gone.

Two-eyes now awakened One-eye, and said, "One-eye, you want to take care of the goat, and go to sleep while you are doing it, and in the meantime the goat might run all over the world. Come, let us go home again."

So they went home, and again Two-eyes let her little dish stand untouched, and One-eye could not tell her mother why she would not eat it, and to excuse herself said, "I fell asleep when I was out."

Next day the mother said to Three-eyes, "This time you shall go and observe if Two-eyes eats anything when she is out, and if anyone fetches her food and drink, for she must eat and drink in secret."

So Three-eyes went to Two-eyes, and said, "I will go with you and see if the goat is taken proper care of, and driven where there is food."

But Two-eyes knew what was in Three-eyes's mind, and drove the goat into high grass and said, "We will sit down, and I will sing something to you, Three-eyes." Three-eyes sat down and was tired with the walk and with the heat of the sun, and Two-eyes began the same song as before, and sang,

> "Three eyes, are you waking?"

but then, instead of singing,

> "Three eyes, are you sleeping?"

as she ought to have done, she thoughtlessly sang,

> "Two eyes, are you sleeping?"

and sang all the time,

> "Three eyes, are you waking?
> Two eyes, are you sleeping?"

Then two of the eyes that Three-eyes had, shut and fell asleep, but the third, as it had not been named in the song, did not sleep. It is true that Three-eyes shut it, but only in her cunning, to pretend it was asleep too, but it blinked, and could see everything very well. And when Two-eyes thought that Three-eyes was fast asleep, she used her little charm,

> "Bleat, my little goat, bleat,
> Cover the table with something to eat,"

and ate and drank as much as her heart desired, and then ordered the table to go away again,

> "Bleat, bleat, my little goat, I pray,
> And take the table quite away,"

and Three-eyes saw everything. Then Two-eyes came to her, waked her and said, "Have you been asleep, Three-eyes? You are a good caretaker! Come, we will go home."

And when they got home, Two-eyes again did not eat, and Three-eyes said to the mother, "Now, I know why that high-minded thing there does not eat. When she is out, she says to the goat,

> "Bleat, my little goat, bleat,
> Cover the table with something to eat,"

and then a little table appears before her covered with the best of food, much better than any we have here, and when she has eaten all she wants, she says,

"Bleat, bleat, my little goat, I pray,
And take the table quite away,"

and all disappears. I watched everything closely. She put two of my eyes to sleep by using a spell, but luckily the one in my forehead kept awake."

Then the envious mother cried, "Do you want to fare better than we do? The desire shall pass away," and she fetched a butcher's knife, and thrust it into the heart of the goat, which fell down dead.

When Two-eyes saw that, she went out full of trouble, seated herself on the ridge of grass at the edge of the field, and wept bitter tears. Suddenly the wise woman once more stood by her side, and said, "Two-eyes, why are you weeping?"

"Have I not reason to weep?" she answered. "The goat that covered the table for me every day when I spoke your charm, has been killed by my mother, and now I shall again have to bear hunger and want."

The wise woman said, "Two-eyes, I will give you a piece of good advice; ask your sisters to give you the entrails of the slaughtered goat, and bury them in the ground in front of the house, and your fortune will be made."

Then she vanished, and Two-eyes went home and said to her sisters, "Dear sisters, do give me some part of my goat; I don't wish for what is good, but give me the entrails."

Then they laughed and said, "If that's all you want, you can have it." So Two-eyes took the entrails and buried them quietly in the evening, in front of the housedoor, as the wise woman had counseled her to do.

Next morning, when they all awoke, and went to the housedoor, there stood a strangely magnificent tree with leaves of silver, and fruit of gold hanging among them, so that in all the wide world there was nothing more beautiful or precious. They did not know how the tree could have come there during the night, but Two-eyes saw that it had grown up out of the entrails of the goat, for it was standing on the exact spot where she had buried them.

Then the mother said to One-eye, "Climb up, my child, and gather some of the fruit of the tree for us." One-eye climbed up, but when she was about to get hold of one of the golden apples, the branch escaped from her hands, and that happened each time, so that she could not pluck a single apple, no matter how hard she tried. Then said the mother, "Three-eyes, you climb up; you with your three eyes can look about you better than One-eye." One-eye slipped down, and Three-eyes climbed up. Three-eyes was not more skillful, and though she tried, the golden apples always escaped her. At length the mother grew impatient, and climbed up herself, but could get hold of the fruit no better than One-eye and Three-eyes, for she always clutched empty air.

Then said Two-eyes, "I will just go up, perhaps I may succeed better."

The sisters cried, "You indeed, with your two eyes, what can you do?" But Two-eyes climbed up, and the golden apples did not get out of her way, but came into her hand of their own will, so that she could pluck them one after the other, and brought a whole apronful down with her. The mother took them away from her, and instead of treating poor Two-eyes any better for this, she and One-eye and Three-eyes were only envious, because Two-eyes alone had been able to get the fruit, and they treated her still more cruelly.

It so happened that once when they were all standing together by the tree, a young knight came up. "Quick, Two-eyes," cried the two sisters, "creep under this, and don't disgrace us!" and with all speed they turned an empty barrel, which was standing close by the tree, over poor Two-eyes, and they pushed the golden apples that she had been gathering, under it too. When the knight came nearer he was a handsome lord, who stopped and admired the magnificent gold and silver tree, and said to the two sisters, "To whom does this fine tree belong? Anyone who would bestow one branch of it on me might in return for it ask whatever he desired." Then One-eye and Three-eyes replied that the tree belonged to them, and that they would give him a branch. They both took great trouble, but they were not able to do it, for the branches and fruit both moved away from them every time.

Then said the knight, "It is very strange that the tree should belong to you, and that you should still not be able to break a piece off." They again asserted that the tree was their property. While they were saying so, Two-eyes rolled out a couple of golden apples from under the barrel to the feet of the knight, for she was vexed with One-eye and Three-eyes, for not speaking the truth. When the knight saw the apples he was astonished, and asked where they came from. One-eye and Three-eyes answered that they had another sister, who was not allowed to show herself, for she had only two eyes like any common person. The knight, however, desired to see her, and cried, "Two-eyes, come forth."

Then Two-eyes, quite comforted, came from beneath the barrel, and the knight was surprised at her great beauty, and said, "You, Two-eyes, can certainly break off a branch from the tree for me."

"Yes," replied Two-eyes, "that I certainly shall be able to do, for the tree belongs to me." And she climbed up, and with the greatest ease broke off a branch with beautiful silver leaves and golden fruit, and gave it to the knight.

Then said the knight, "Two-eyes, what shall I give you for it?"

"Alas!" answered Two-eyes, "I suffer from hunger and thirst, grief and want, from early morning till late night; if you would take me with you, and deliver me from these things, I should be happy."

So the knight lifted Two-eyes onto his horse, and took her home with him to his father's castle, and there he gave her beautiful clothes, and meat and drink to her heart's content, and as he loved her so much he married her, and the wedding was solemnized with great rejoicing.

When Two-eyes was thus carried away by the handsome knight, her two sisters grudged her good fortune in downright earnest. "The wonderful tree, however, still remains with us," thought they, "and even if we can gather no fruit from it, still everyone will stand still and look at it, and come to us and admire it. Who knows what good things may be in store for us?" But next morning, the tree had vanished, and all their hopes were at an end. And when Two-eyes looked out of the window of her own little room, to her great delight it was standing in front of it, and so it had followed her.

Two-eyes lived a long time in happiness. Once two poor women came to her in her castle, and begged for alms. She looked in their faces, and recognized her sisters, One-eye, and Three-eyes, who had fallen into such poverty that they had to wander about and beg their bread from door to door. Two-eyes, however, made them welcome, and was kind to them, and took care of them, so that they both with all their hearts repented the evil that they had done their sister in their youth.

30. *Fair Katrinelje and Pif-paf-poltrie*

Good day, Father Hollenthe." "Many thanks, Pif-paf-poltrie." "May I be allowed to have your daughter?" "Oh, yes, if Mother Malcho (Milk cow), Brother High-and-Mighty, Sister Käsetraut, and fair Katrinelje are willing, you can have her." "Where is Mother Malcho, then?" "She is in the cow-house, milking the cow."

"Good day, Mother Malcho." "Many thanks, Pif-paf-poltrie." "May I be allowed to have your daughter?" "Oh, yes, if Father Hollenthe, Brother High-and-Mighty, Sister Käsetraut, and fair Katrinelje are willing, you can have her." "Where is Brother High-and-Mighty, then?" "He is in the room chopping some wood."

"Good day, Brother High-and-Mighty." "Many thanks, Pif-paf-poltrie." "May I be allowed to have your sister?" "Oh, yes, if Father Hollenthe, Mother Malcho, Sister Käsetraut, and fair Katrinelje are willing, you can have her." "Where is Sister Käsetraut, then?" "She is in the garden cutting cabbages."

"Good day, sister Käsetraut." "Many thanks, Pif-paf-poltrie." "May I be allowed to have your sister?" "Oh, yes, if Father Hollenthe, Mother Malcho, Brother High-and-Mighty, and fair Katrinelje are willing, you may have her." "Where is fair Katrinelje, then?" "She is in the parlor counting out her farthings."

"Good day, fair Katrinelje." "Many thanks, Pif-paf-poltrie." "Will you be my bride?" "Oh, yes, if Father Hollenthe, Mother Malcho, Brother High-and-Mighty, and Sister Käsetraut are willing, I am ready."

"Fair Katrinelje, how much dowry do you have?" "Fourteen farthings in ready money, three and a half pennies owing to me, half a pound of dried apples, a handful of fried bread, and a handful of spices.

And many other things are mine,
Have I not a dowry fine?

"Pif-paf-poltrie, what is your trade? Are you a tailor?" "Something better." "A shoemaker?" "Something better." "A farmer?" "Something better." "A joiner?" "Something better." "A smith?" "Something better." "A miller?" "Something better." "Perhaps a broom-maker?" "Yes, that's what I am, is it not a fine trade?"

31. *The Fox and the Horse*

Apeasant had a faithful horse that had grown old and could do no more work, so his master would no longer give him anything to eat and said, "I can certainly make no more use of you, but still I mean well by you; if you prove yourself still strong enough to bring me a lion here, I will maintain you, but now take yourself away out of my stable," and with that he chased him into the open country. The horse was sad, and went to the forest to seek a little protection there from the weather.

There a fox met him and said, "Why do you hang your head so, and go about all alone?"

"Alas," replied the horse, "greed and fidelity do not dwell together in one house. My master has forgotten what services I have performed for him for so many years, and because I can no longer plow well, he will give me no more food, and has driven me out."

"Without giving you a chance?" asked the fox.

"The chance was a bad one. He said, if I were still strong enough to bring him a lion, he would keep me, but he well knows that I cannot do that."

The fox said, "I will help you, just lay yourself down, stretch yourself out, as if you were dead, and do not stir." The horse did as the fox desired, and the fox went to the lion, who had his den not far off, and said, "A dead horse is lying outside there, just come with me, you can have a rich meal." The lion went with him, and when they were both standing by the horse the fox said, "After all, it is not very comfortable for you here, I tell you what, I will fasten it to you by the tail, and then you can drag it into your cave, and devour it in peace."

This advice pleased the lion; he lay down, and in order that the fox might tie the horse fast to him, he kept quite quiet. But the fox tied the lion's legs together with the horse's tail, and twisted and fastened all so well and so strongly that no strength could break it. When he had finished his work, he tapped the horse on the shoulder and said, "Pull, white horse, pull." Then up sprang the horse at once, and drew the lion away with him. The lion began to roar so that all the birds in the forest flew out in terror, but the horse let him roar, and drew him and dragged him over the country to his master's door.

When the master saw the lion, he was of a better mind, and said to the horse, "You shall stay with me and fare well," and he gave him plenty to eat until he died.

32. *The Shoes That Were Danced to Pieces*

There was once upon a time a King who had twelve daughters, each one more beautiful than the other. They all slept together in one chamber, in which their beds stood side by side, and every night when they were in them the King locked the door, and bolted it. But in the morning when he unlocked the door, he saw that their shoes were worn out with dancing, and no one could find out how that had come to pass. Then the King caused it to be proclaimed that whoever could discover where they danced at night, should choose one of them for his wife and be King after his death, but that whoever came forward and had not discovered it within three days and nights, should have forfeited his life.

It was not long before a King's son presented himself, and offered to undertake the enterprise. He was well received, and in the evening was led into a room adjoining the princesses' sleeping-chamber. His bed was placed there, and he was to observe where they went and danced, and in order that they might do nothing secretly or go away to some other place, the door of their room was left open.

But the eyelids of the prince grew heavy as lead, and he fell asleep, and when he awoke in the morning, all twelve had been to the dance, for their shoes were standing there with holes in the soles. On the second and third nights it fell out just the same, and then his head was struck off without mercy. Many others came after this and undertook the enterprise, but all forfeited their lives.

Now it came to pass that a poor soldier, who had a wound, and could serve no longer, found himself on the road to the town where the King lived. There he met an old woman, who asked him where he was going. "I hardly know myself," answered he, and added in jest, "I had half a mind to discover where the princesses danced their shoes into holes, and thus become King."

"That is not so difficult," said the old woman, "you must not drink the wine that will be brought to you at night, and must pretend to be sound asleep." With that she gave him a little cloak, and said, "If you put that on, you will be invisible, and then you can follow the twelve."

When the soldier had received this good advice, he went into the thing in earnest, took heart, went to the King, and announced himself as a suitor. He was as well received as the others, and royal garments were put upon him. He was conducted that evening at bedtime into the antechamber, and as he was about to go to bed, the eldest came and brought him a cup of wine, but he had tied a sponge under his chin, and let the wine run down into it, without drinking a drop. Then he lay down and when he had lain a while, he began to snore, as if in the deepest sleep.

The twelve princesses heard that, and laughed, and the eldest said, "He, too, might as well have saved his life." With that they got up, opened wardrobes, presses, cupboards, and brought out pretty dresses; dressed themselves before the mirrors, sprang about, and rejoiced at the prospect of the dance.

Only the youngest said, "I know not how it is; you are very happy, but I feel very strange; some misfortune is certainly about to befall us."

"You are a goose, who is always frightened," said the eldest. "Have you forgotten how many Kings' sons have already come here in vain? I had hardly any need to give the soldier a sleeping potion, in any case the clown would not have awakened." When they were all ready they looked carefully at the soldier, but he had closed his eyes and did not move or stir, so they felt themselves quite secure. The eldest then went to her bed and tapped it; it immediately sank into the earth, and one after the other they descended through the opening, the eldest going first.

The soldier, who had watched everything, tarried no longer, put on his little cloak, and went down last with the youngest. Halfway down the steps, he just trod a little on her dress; she was terrified at that, and cried out, "What is that? Who is pulling my dress?"

"Don't be so silly!" said the eldest. "You have caught it on a nail."

Then they went all the way down, and when they were at the bottom, they were standing in a wonderfully pretty avenue of trees, all the leaves of which were of silver, and shone and glistened. The soldier thought, "I must carry a token away with me," and broke off a twig from one of them, on which the tree cracked with a loud report.

The youngest cried out again. "Something is wrong, did you hear the crack?"

But the eldest said, "It is a gun fired for joy, because we have got rid of our prince so quickly."

After that they came into an avenue where all the leaves were of gold, and lastly into a third where they were of bright diamonds; he broke off a twig from each, which made such a crack each time that the youngest started back in terror, but the eldest still maintained that they were salutes. They went on and came to a great lake on which stood twelve little boats, and in every boat sat a handsome prince, all of whom were waiting for the twelve, and each took one of them with him, but the soldier seated himself by the youngest. Then her prince said, "I can't tell why the boat is so much heavier today; I shall have to row with all my strength, if I am to get it across."

"What should cause that," said the youngest, "but the warm weather? I feel very warm too."

On the opposite side of the lake stood a splendid, brightly lit castle, from which resounded the joyous music of trumpets and kettle drums. They rowed over there, entered, and each prince danced with the girl he loved, but the soldier danced with them unseen, and when one of them had a cup of wine in her hand he drank it up, so that the cup was empty when she carried it to her mouth; the youngest was alarmed at this, but the eldest always made her be silent.

They danced there till three o'clock in the morning when all the shoes were danced into holes, and they were forced to leave off; the princes rowed them back again over the lake, and this time the soldier seated himself by the eldest. On the shore they took leave of their princes, and promised to return the following night. When they reached the stairs the soldier ran on in front and lay down in his bed, and when the twelve had come up slowly and wearily, he was already snoring so loudly that they could all hear him, and they said, "So far as he is concerned, we are safe." They took off their beautiful dresses, laid them away, put the worn-out shoes under the bed, and lay down. Next morning the soldier was resolved not to speak, but to watch the wonderful goings on, and again went with them.

Everything was done just as it had been done the first time, and each time they danced until their shoes were worn to pieces. But the third time he took a cup away with him as a token. When the hour had arrived for him to give his answer, he took the three twigs and the cup, and went to the King, but the twelve stood behind the door, and listened for what he was going to say. When the King put the question, "Where have my twelve daughters danced their shoes to pieces in the night?" he answered, "In an underground castle with twelve princes," and related how it had come to pass, and brought out the tokens. The King then summoned his daughters, and asked them if the soldier had told the truth, and when they saw that they were found out, and that lies would be of no use, they were obliged to confess all. Thereupon the King asked which of them he would have to wife? He answered, "I am no longer young, so give me the eldest." Then the wedding was celebrated on the same day, and the kingdom was promised him after the King's death. But the princes were bewitched for as many days as they had danced nights with the twelve.

33. *The Six Servants*

Long ago there lived an aged Queen who was a sorceress, and her daughter was the most beautiful maiden under the sun. The old woman, however, had no other thought than how to lure mankind to destruction, and when a wooer appeared, she said that whoever wished to have her daughter must first perform a task, or die. Many had been dazzled by the daughter's beauty, and had actually risked this, but they never could accomplish what the old woman required them to do, and so no mercy was shown; they had to kneel down, and their heads were struck off.

A certain King's son who had also heard of the maiden's beauty, said to his father, "Let me go there, I want to demand her in marriage."

"Never," answered the King; "if you were to go, it would be going to your death." On this the son lay down and was sick unto death, and for seven years he lay there, and no physician could heal him. When the father perceived that all hope was over, with a heavy heart he said to him, "Go there, and try your luck, for I know no other means of curing you." When the son heard that, he rose from his bed and was well again, and joyfully set out on his way.

And it came to pass that as he was riding across a pasture, he saw from afar something like a great heap of hay lying on the ground, and when he drew nearer, he could see that it was the stomach of a man, who had laid himself down there, but the stomach looked like a small mountain. When the fat man saw the traveler, he stood up and said, "If you are in need of anyone, take me into your service."

The prince answered, "What can I do with such a great big man?"

"Oh," said the Stout One, "this is nothing, when I stretch myself out well, I am three thousand times fatter."

"If that's the case," said the prince, "I can make use of you, come with me." So the Stout One followed the prince, and after a while they found another man who was lying on the ground with his ear laid to the turf.

"What are you doing there?" asked the King's son.

"I am listening," replied the man.

"What are you listening to so attentively?"

"I am listening to what is just going on in the world, for nothing escapes my ears; I even hear the grass growing."

"Tell me," said the prince, "what you hear at the court of the old Queen who has the beautiful daughter."

Then he answered, "I hear the whizzing of the sword that is striking off a wooer's head."

The King's son said, "I can make use of you, come with me."

They went onward, and then saw a pair of feet lying and part of a pair of legs, but could not see the rest of the body. When they had walked on for a great distance, they came to the body, and at last to the head also. "Why," said the prince, "what a tall rascal you are!"

"Oh," replied the Tall One, "that is nothing at all yet; when I really stretch out my limbs, I am three thousand times as tall, and taller than the highest mountain on earth. I will gladly enter your service, if you will take me."

"Come with me," said the prince, "I can make use of you."

They went onward and found a man sitting by the road who had bound up his eyes. The prince said to him, "Have you weak eyes, that you cannot look at the light?"

"No," replied the man, "but I must not remove the bandage, for whatever I look at with my eyes, splits to pieces, my glance is so powerful. If you can use that, I shall be glad to serve you."

"Come with me," replied the King's son, "I can make use of you."

They journeyed onward and found a man who was lying in the hot sunshine, trembling and shivering all over his body, so that not a limb was still. "How can you shiver when the sun is shining so warm?" said the King's son. "Alack," replied the man, "I am of quite a different nature. The hotter it is, the colder I am, and the frost pierces through all my bones; and the colder it is, the hotter I am. In the middle of ice, I cannot endure the heat, nor in the middle of fire, the cold."

"You are a strange fellow," said the prince, "but if you will enter my service, follow me."

They traveled onward, and saw a man standing who made a long neck and looked about him, and could see over all the mountains. "What are you looking at so eagerly?" said the King's son.

The man replied, "I have such sharp eyes that I can see into every forest and field, and hill and valley, all over the world."

The prince said, "Come with me if you will, for I am still in want of such a person."

And now the King's son and his six servants came to the town where the aged Queen dwelt. He did not tell her who he was, but said, "If you will give me your beautiful daughter, I will perform any task you set me."

The sorceress was delighted to get such a handsome youth as this into her net, and said, "I will set you three tasks, and if you are able to perform them all, you shall be husband and master of my daughter."

"What is the first to be?"

"You shall fetch me my ring which I have dropped into the Red Sea."

So the King's son went home to his servants and said, "The first task is not easy. A ring is to be got out of the Red Sea. Come, find some way of doing it."

Then the man with the sharp sight said, "I will see where it is lying," and looked down into the water and said, "It is sticking there, on a pointed stone."

The Tall One carried them there, and said, "I would soon get it out, if I could only see it."

"Oh, is that all!" cried the Stout One, and lay down and put his mouth to the water, on which all the waves fell into it just as if it had been a whirlpool, and he drank up the whole sea till it was as dry as a meadow. The Tall One stooped down a little, and brought out the ring with his hand. Then the King's son rejoiced when he had the ring, and took it to the old Queen. She was astonished, and said, "Yes, it is the right ring. You have safely performed the first task, but now comes the second. Do you see the meadow in front of my palace? Three hundred fat oxen are feeding there, and these must you eat—skin, hair, bones, horns and all—and down below in my cellar lie three hundred casks of wine, and these you must drink up as well, and if one hair of the oxen, or one little drop of the wine is left, your life will be forfeited to me."

"May I invite no guests to this repast?" inquired the prince. "No dinner is good without some company."

The old woman laughed maliciously, and replied, "You may invite one for the sake of companionship, but no more."

The King's son went to his servants and said to the Stout One, "You shall be my guest today, and shall eat your fill." Hereupon the Stout One stretched himself out and ate the three hundred oxen without leaving one single hair, and then he asked if he was to have nothing but his breakfast. He drank the wine straight from the casks without feeling any need of a glass, and he licked the last drop from his fingernails.

When the meal was over, the prince went to the old woman, and told her that the second task also was performed. She wondered at this and said, "No one has ever done so much before, but one task still remains," and she thought to herself, "You shall not escape me, and will not keep your head on your shoulders!" "This night," said she, "I will bring my daughter to you in your chamber, and you shall put your arms around her, but when you are sitting there together, beware of falling asleep. When twelve o'clock is striking, I will come, and if she is then no longer in your arms, you are lost."

The prince thought, "The task is easy, I will most certainly keep my eyes open." Nevertheless he called his servants, told them what the old woman had said, and remarked, "Who knows what treachery lurks behind this? Foresight is a good thing—keep watch, and take care that the maiden does not go out of my room again." When night fell, the old woman came with her daughter, and gave her into the prince's arms, and then the Tall One wound himself around the two in a circle, and the Stout One placed himself by the door, so that no living creature could enter. There the two sat, and the maiden spoke never a word, but the moon shone through the window on her face, and the prince could behold her wondrous beauty. He did nothing but gaze at her, and was filled with love and happiness, and his eyes never felt weary. This lasted until eleven o'clock, when the old woman cast such a spell over all of them that they fell asleep, and at the same moment the maiden was carried away.

Then they all slept soundly until a quarter to twelve, when the magic lost its power, and all awoke again. "Oh, misery and misfortune!" cried the prince. "Now I am lost!"

The faithful servants also began to lament, but the Listener said, "Be quiet, I want to listen." Then he listened for an instant and said, "She is on a rock, a thousand miles from here, bewailing her fate. You alone, Tall One, can help her; if you will stand up, you will be there in a couple of steps."

"Yes," answered the Tall One, "but the one with the sharp eyes must go with me, that we may destroy the rock."

Then the Tall One took the one with bandaged eyes on his back, and in the twinkling of an eye they were on the enchanted rock. The Tall

One immediately took the bandage from the other's eyes, and he did but look around, and the rock shivered into a thousand pieces. Then the Tall One took the maiden in his arms, carried her back in a second, then fetched his companion with the same rapidity, and before it struck twelve they were all sitting as they had sat before, quite merrily and happily. When twelve struck, the aged sorceress came stealing in with a malicious face, which seemed to say, "Now he is mine!" for she believed that her daughter was on the rock a thousand miles off. But when she saw her in the prince's arms, she was alarmed, and said, "Here is one who knows more than I do!" She dared not make any opposition, and was forced to give him her daughter. But she whispered in her ear, "It is a disgrace to you to have to obey common people, and that you are not allowed to choose a husband to your own liking."

On this the proud heart of the maiden was filled with anger, and she plotted revenge. Next morning she caused three hundred great bundles of wood to be tied together, and said to the prince that though the three tasks were performed, she would still not be his wife until someone was ready to seat himself in the middle of the wood, and bear the fire. She thought that none of his servants would let themselves be burned for him, and that out of love for her, he himself would place himself upon it, and then she would be free. But the servants said, "Every one of us has done something except the Frosty One; he must set to work," and they put him in the middle of the pile, and set fire to it. Then the fire began to burn, and burned for three days until all the wood was consumed, and when the flames had burned out, the Frosty One was standing amid the ashes, trembling like an aspen leaf, and saying, "I never felt such a frost during the whole course of my life; if it had lasted much longer, I should have been frostbitten!"

As no other pretext was to be found, the beautiful maiden was now forced to take the unknown youth as a husband. But when they drove away to church, the old woman said, "I cannot endure the disgrace," and sent her warriors after them with orders to cut down all who opposed them, and bring back her daughter. But the Listener had sharpened his ears, and heard the secret discourse of the old woman. "What shall we do?" said he to the Stout One. But he knew what to do, and spat out once or twice behind the carriage some of the seawater that he had drunk, and a great sea arose in which the warriors were caught and drowned. When the sorceress perceived that, she sent her mailed knights; but the Listener heard the rattling of their armor, and undid the bandage from one eye of Sharp-eyes, who looked for a while rather fixedly at the enemy's troops, on which they all shattered to pieces like glass. Then the youth and the maiden went on their way undisturbed, and when the two had been blessed in church, the six servants took leave, and said to their master, "Your wishes are now satisfied, you need us no longer, we will go our way and seek our fortunes."

A mile from the palace of the prince's father was a village near which a swineherd tended his herd, and when they arrived, the prince said to his wife, "Do you know who I really am? I am no prince, but a herder of swine, and the man who is there with that herd, is my father. We two shall have to set to work also, and help him."

Then he alighted with her at the inn, and secretly told the innkeepers to take away her royal apparel during the night. So when she awoke in the morning, she had nothing to put on, and the innkeeper's wife gave her an old gown and a pair of worsted stockings, and at the same time seemed to consider it a great present, and said, "If it were not for the sake of your husband I should have given you nothing at all!"

Then the princess believed that he really was a swineherd, and tended the herd with him, and thought to herself, "I have deserved this for my haughtiness and pride." This lasted for a week, and then she could endure it no longer, for she had sores on her feet. And now came a couple of people who asked if she knew who her husband was. "Yes," she answered, "he is a swineherd, and has just gone out with cords and ropes to try to drive a little bargain."

But they said, "Just come with us, and we will take you to him," and they took her up to the palace, and when she entered the hall, there stood her husband in kingly raiment. But she did not recognize him until he took her in his arms, kissed her, and said, "I suffered much for you and now you, too, have had to suffer for me."

Then the wedding was celebrated, and he who has told you all this, wishes that he, too, had been present at it.

34. *The White Bride and the Black Bride*

A woman was going about the countryside with her daughter and her stepdaughter, when the Lord came walking toward them in the form of a poor man, and asked, "Which is the way into the village?"

"If you want to know," said the mother, "seek it for yourself."

The daughter added, "If you are afraid you will not find it—take a guide with you."

But the stepdaughter said, "Poor man, I will take you there, come with me."

Then God was angry with the mother and daughter, and turned his back on them, and wished that they should become as black as night and as ugly as sin. To the poor stepdaughter, however, God was gracious, and went with her, and when they were near the village, he said a blessing over her, and said, "Choose three things for yourself, and I will grant them to you."

Then the maiden said, "I should like to be as beautiful and fair as the sun," and instantly she was white and fair as day. "Then I should like to have a purse of money that would never grow empty."

That the Lord gave her also, but he said, "Do not forget what is best of all."

Said she, "For my third wish, I desire, after my death, to inhabit the eternal kingdom of Heaven." That also was granted unto her, and then the Lord left her.

When the stepmother came home with her daughter, and they saw that they were both as black as coal and ugly, but that the stepdaughter was white and beautiful, wickedness increased still more in their hearts, and they thought of nothing else but how they could injure her. The stepdaughter, however, had a brother called Reginer, whom she loved much, and she told him all that had happened. A long time ago Reginer said to her, "Dear sister, I will paint your portrait, that I may continually see you before mine eyes, for my love for you is so great that I should like always to look at you."

Then she answered, "But, I pray you, let no one see the picture." So he painted his sister and hung up the picture in his room; he, however, dwelt in the King's palace, for he was his coachman.

Every day he went and stood before the picture, and thanked God for the happiness of having such a dear sister. Now it happened that the King whom he served, had just lost his wife, who had been so beautiful that no one could be found to compare with her, and on this account the King was in deep grief. The attendants about the court, however, remarked that the coachman stood daily before this beautiful picture, and they were jealous of him, so they informed the King. Then the latter ordered the picture to be brought to him, and when he saw that it was like his lost wife in every respect, except that it was still more beautiful, he fell mortally in love with it. He caused the coachman to be brought before him, and asked whom the portrait represented? The coachman said it was his sister, so the King resolved to take no one but her as his wife, and gave him a carriage and horses and splendid garments of cloth of gold, and sent him forth to fetch his chosen bride.

When Reginer came on this errand, his sister was glad, but the black maiden was jealous of her good fortune, and grew angry above all measure, and said to her mother, "Of what use are all your arts to us now when you cannot procure such a piece of luck for me?"

"Be quiet," said the old woman, "I will soon give it to you," and by her arts of witchcraft, she so troubled the eyes of the coachman that he was half-blind, and she stopped the ears of the white maiden so that she was half-deaf. Then they got into the carriage, first the bride in her noble royal apparel, then the stepmother with her daughter, and Reginer sat on the box to drive. When they had been on the way for some time the coachman cried,

> "Cover you well, my sister dear,
> That the rain may not wet you,
> That the wind may not load you with dust,
> That you may be fair and beautiful
> When you appear before the King."

The bride asked, "What is my dear brother saying?"

"Ah," said the old woman, "he says that you ought to take off your golden dress and give it to your sister." Then she took it off, and put it on the black maiden, who gave her in exchange for it a shabby grey gown. They drove onward, and a short time afterward, the brother again cried,

> "Cover you well, my sister dear,
> That the rain may not wet you,
> That the wind may not load you with dust,
> That you may be fair and beautiful
> When you appear before the King."

The bride asked, "What is my dear brother saying?"

"Ah," said the old woman, "he says that you ought to take off your golden hood and give it to your sister." So she took off the hood and put it on her sister, and sat with her own head uncovered. And they drove on farther. After a while, the brother once more cried,

> "Cover you well, my sister dear,
> That the rain may not wet you,
> That the wind may not load you with dust,
> That you may be fair and beautiful
> When you appear before the King."

The bride asked, "What is my dear brother saying?"

"Ah," said the old woman, "he says you must look out of the carriage." They were, however, just on a bridge, which crossed deep water. When the bride stood up and leaned forward out of the carriage, they both pushed her out, and she fell into the middle of the water. At the same moment that she sank, a snow-white duck arose out of the mirror-smooth water, and swam down the river. The brother had observed nothing, and drove the carriage on until they reached the court. Then he took the black maiden to the King as his sister, and thought she really was so, because his eyes were dim, and he saw the golden garments glittering. When the King saw the boundless ugliness of his intended bride, he was very angry, and ordered the coachman to be thrown into a pit that was full of adders and nests of snakes. The old witch, however, knew so well how to flatter the King and deceive his eyes by her arts, that he kept her and her daughter until she appeared quite endurable to him, and he really married her.

One evening when the black bride was sitting on the King's knee, a white duck came swimming up the gutter to the kitchen, and said to the kitchen boy, "Boy, light a fire, that I may warm my feathers." The kitchen boy did it, and lighted a fire on the hearth. Then came the duck and sat down by it, and shook herself and smoothed her feathers with her bill. While she was sitting and enjoying herself, she asked, "What is my brother Reginer doing?"

The scullery boy replied, "He is imprisoned in the pit with adders and with snakes."

Then she asked, "What is the black witch doing in the house?"

The boy answered, "She is loved by the King and happy."

"May God have mercy on him," said the duck, and swam forth by the sink.

The next night she came again and put the same questions, and the third night also. Then the kitchen boy could bear it no longer, and went to the King and discovered all to him. The King, however, wanted to see it for himself, and next evening went there, and when the duck thrust her head in through the sink, he took his sword and cut through her neck, and suddenly she changed into a most beautiful maiden, exactly like the picture that her brother had made of her. The King was full of joy, and as she stood there quite wet, he caused splendid apparel to be brought and had her clothed in it. Then she told how she had been betrayed by cunning and falsehood, and at last thrown down into the water, and her first request was that her brother should be brought forth from the pit of snakes, and when the King had fulfilled this request, he went into the chamber where the old witch was, and asked, "What does she deserve who does this and that?" and related what had happened. Then was she so blinded that she was aware of nothing and said, "She deserves to be stripped naked, and put into a barrel with nails, and that a horse should be harnessed to the barrel, and the horse sent all over the world." All of which was done to her, and to her black daughter. But the King married the white and beautiful bride, and rewarded her faithful brother, and made him a rich and distinguished man.

35. *Iron John*

There was once a King who had a great forest near his palace, full of all kinds of wild animals. One day he sent out a hunter to shoot him a deer, but he did not come back. "Perhaps he has been in an accident," said the King, and the next day he sent out two more hunters who were to search for him, but they too stayed away. Then on the third day, he sent for all his hunters, and said, "Scour the whole forest through, and do not give up until you have found all three." But of these also, none came home again, and of the pack of hounds that they had taken with them, none were seen again. From then on, no one would venture into the forest, and it lay there in deep stillness and solitude, and nothing was seen of it, except sometimes an eagle or a hawk flying over it.

This lasted for many years, when a strange hunter announced himself to the King as seeking employment, and offered to go into the dangerous forest. The King, however, would not give his consent, and said, "It is not safe in there; I fear it would fare with you no better than with the others, and you would never come out again." The hunter replied, "Lord, I will venture it at my own risk; I know nothing of fear."

The hunter therefore went with his dog to the forest. It was not long before the dog fell in with some game on the way, and wanted to pursue it; but the dog hardly had run two steps when it stood before a deep pool, could go no farther, and a naked arm stretched itself out of the water, seized it, and drew it under. When the hunter saw that, he went back and fetched three men to come with buckets and bale out the water. When they could see to the bottom there lay a wild man whose body was brown like rusty iron, and whose hair hung over his face down to his knees. They bound him with cords, and led him away to the castle. There was great astonishment over the wild man; the King, however, had him put in an iron cage in his courtyard, and forbade the door to be opened on pain of death, and the Queen herself was to take the key into her keeping. And from this time forth everyone could again go into the forest with safety.

The King had a son of eight years, who was once playing in the courtyard, and while he was playing, his golden ball fell into the cage. The boy ran there and said, "Give me my ball."

"Not till you have opened the door for me," answered the man.

"No," said the boy, "I will not do that; the King has forbidden it," and ran away.

The next day he again went and asked for his ball; the wild man said, "Open my door," but the boy would not. On the third day the King had ridden out hunting, and the boy went once more and said, "I cannot open the door even if I wished, for I have not the key."

Then the wild man said, "It lies under your mother's pillow, you can get it there."

The boy, who wanted to have his ball back, cast all thought to the wind, and brought the key. The door opened with difficulty, and the boy pinched his fingers. When it was open the wild man stepped out, gave him the golden ball, and hurried away. The boy had become afraid; he called and cried after him, "Oh, wild man, do not go away, or I shall be beaten!" The wild man turned back, took him up, set him on his shoulder, and went with hasty steps into the forest.

When the King came home, he observed the empty cage, and asked the Queen how that had happened. She knew nothing about it, and sought the key, but it was gone. She called the boy, but no one answered. The King sent out people to look for him in the fields, but they did not find him. Then he could easily guess what had happened, and much grief reigned in the royal court.

When the wild man had once more reached the dark forest, he took the boy down from his shoulder, and said to him, "You will never see your father and mother again, but I will keep you with me, for you have set me free, and I have compassion on you. If you do all I ask you, you shall fare well. Of treasure and gold have I enough, and more than anyone in the world." He made a bed of moss for the boy on which he slept, and the next morning the man took him to a well, and said, "Behold, the gold well is as bright and clear as crystal; you shall sit beside it, and take care that nothing falls into it, or it will be polluted. I will come every evening to see if you have obeyed my order." The boy placed himself by the edge of the well, and often saw a golden fish or a golden snake show itself inside, and took care that nothing fell in. As he was sitting, his finger hurt him so violently that he involuntarily put it in the water. He drew it quickly out again, but saw that it was quite gilded, and whatever pains he took to wash the gold off again, all was to no purpose.

In the evening Iron John came back, looked at the boy, and said, "What has happened to the well?"

"Nothing, nothing," he answered, and held his finger behind his back, that the man might not see it.

But he said, "You have dipped your finger into the water, this time it may pass, but take care you do not again let anything go in." By daybreak the boy was already sitting by the well and watching it. His finger hurt him again and he passed it over his head, and then unhappily a hair fell down into the well. He took it quickly out, but it was already quite gilded. Iron John came, and already knew what had happened. "You have let a hair fall into the well," he said. "I will allow you to watch by it once more, but if this happens for the third time then the well is polluted, and you can no longer remain with me."

On the third day, the boy sat by the well, and did not stir his finger, however much it hurt him. But the time was long to him, and he looked at the reflection of his face on the surface of the water. And as he still bent down more and more while he was doing so, and trying to look straight into the eyes, his long hair fell down from his shoulders into the water. He raised himself up quickly, but the whole of the hair of his head was already golden and shone like the sun. You may imagine how terrified the poor boy was! He took his pocket-handkerchief and tied it around his head, in order that the man might not see it. When he came he already knew everything, and said, "Take the handkerchief off." Then the golden hair streamed forth, and let the boy excuse himself as he might, it was of no use. "You have not stood the trial, and can stay here no longer. Go forth into the world, there you will learn what poverty is. But as you have not a bad heart, and as I mean well by you, there is one thing I will grant you; if you fall into any difficulty, come to the forest and cry, 'Iron John,' and then I will come and help you. My power is great, greater than you think, and I have gold and silver in abundance."

Then the King's son left the forest, and walked by beaten and unbeaten paths for a long time until at last he reached a great city. There he looked for work, but could find none, and he had learned nothing by which he could help himself. At length he went to the palace, and asked if they would take him in. The people about court did not at all know what use they could make of him, but they liked him, and told him to stay. The cook took him into his service, and said he might carry wood and water, and rake the cinders together. Once when it so happened that no one else was at hand, the cook ordered him to carry the food to the royal table, but as he did not like to let his golden hair be seen, he kept his little cap on. Such a thing as that had never yet come under the King's notice, and he said, "When you come to the royal table you must take your hat off."

He answered, "Ah, Lord, I cannot; I have a bad sore place on my head." Then the King had the cook called before him and scolded him, and asked how he could take such a boy as that into his service; and that he was to turn him away at once. The cook, however, had pity on him, and exchanged him for the gardener's boy.

And now the boy had to plant and water the garden, hoe and dig, and bear the wind and bad weather. Once in summer when he was working alone in the garden, the day was so warm he took his little cap off that the air might cool him. As the sun shone on his hair it glittered and flashed so that the rays fell into the bedroom of the King's daughter, and up she sprang to see what that could be. Then she saw the boy, and cried to him, "Boy, bring me a wreath of flowers." He put his cap on with all haste, and gathered wild field flowers and bound them together. When he was ascending the stairs with them, the gardener met him, and said, "How can you take the King's daughter a garland of such common flowers? Go quickly, and get another, and seek out the prettiest and rarest."

"Oh, no," replied the boy, "the wild ones have more scent, and will please her better."

When he got into the room, the King's daughter said, "Take your cap off, it is not seemly to keep it on in my presence."

He again said, "I may not, I have a sore head." She, however, caught at his cap and pulled it off, and then his golden hair rolled down on his shoulders, and it was splendid to behold. He wanted to run out, but she held him by the arm, and gave him a handful of gold coins. With these he departed, but he cared nothing for the gold pieces. He took them to the gardener, and said, "I present them to your children, they can play with them." The following day the King's daughter again called to him that he was to bring her a wreath of field flowers, and when he went in with it, she instantly snatched at his cap, and wanted to take it away from him, but he held it fast with both hands. She again gave him a handful of coins, but he would not keep them, and gave them to the gardener for playthings for his children. On the third day things went just the same; she could not get his cap away from him, and he would not have her money.

Not long afterward, the country was overrun by war. The King gathered together his people, and did not know whether or not he could offer any opposition to the enemy, who was superior in strength and had a mighty army. Then said the gardener's boy, "I am grown up, and will go to the wars also, only give me a horse."

The others laughed, and said, "Seek one for yourself when we are gone, we will leave one behind us in the stable for you."

When they had gone forth, he went into the stable, and got the horse out; it was lame of one foot, and limped hobblety jig, hobblety jig; nevertheless he mounted it, and rode away to the dark forest. When he came to the outskirts, he called, "Iron John," three times so loudly that it echoed through the trees.

Thereupon the wild man appeared immediately, and said, "What do you desire?"

"I want a strong steed, for I am going to the wars."

"That you shall have, and still more than you ask for." Then the wild man went back into the forest, and it was not long before a stable boy came out of it, who led a horse that snorted with its nostrils, and could hardly be restrained, and behind them followed a great troop of soldiers entirely equipped in iron, and their swords flashed in the sun. The youth made over his three-legged horse to the stable boy, mounted the other, and rode at the head of the soldiers. When he got near the battlefield a great part of the King's men had already fallen, and little was wanting to make the rest give way. Then the youth galloped there with his iron soldiers, broke like a hurricane over the enemy, and beat down all who opposed him. They began to fly, but the youth pursued, and never stopped, until there was not a single man left. Instead, however, of returning to the King, he conducted his troop through a path back to the forest, and called forth Iron John.

"What do you desire?" asked the wild man.

"Take back your horse and your troops, and give me my three-legged horse again." All that he asked was done, and soon he was riding on his three-legged horse. When the King returned to his palace, his daughter went to meet him, and wished him joy of his victory. "I am not the one who carried away the victory," said he, "but a stranger knight who came to my assistance with his soldiers." The daughter wanted to hear who the strange knight was, but the King did not know, and said, "He followed the enemy, and I did not see him again." She inquired of the gardener where his boy was, but he smiled, and said, "He has just come home on his three-legged horse, and the others have been mocking him, and crying, 'Here comes our hobblety jig back again!'"

They asked, too, "Under what hedge have you been lying sleeping all the time?"

He, however, said, "I did the best of all, and it would have gone badly without me." And then he was still more ridiculed.

The King said to his daughter, "I will proclaim a great feast that shall last for three days, and you shall throw a golden apple. Perhaps the unknown will come to it."

When the feast was announced, the youth went out to the forest, and called Iron John.

"What do you desire?" asked he.

"That I may catch the King's daughter's golden apple."

"It is as safe as if you had it already," said Iron John. "You shall likewise have a suit of red armor for the occasion, and ride on a spirited chestnut horse."

When the day came, the youth galloped to the spot, took his place among the knights, and was recognized by no one. The King's daughter came forward, and threw a golden apple to the knights, but none of them caught it but he, only as soon as he had it, he galloped away.

On the second day Iron John equipped him as a white knight, and gave him a white horse. Again he was the only one who caught the apple, and he did not linger an instant, but galloped off with it. The King grew angry, and said, "That is not allowed; he must appear before me and tell his name." He gave the order that if the knight who caught the apple should go away again they should pursue him, and if he would not come back willingly, they were to cut him down and stab him.

On the third day, he received from Iron John a suit of black armor and a black horse, and again he caught the apple. But when he was riding off with it, the King's attendants pursued him, and one of them got so near him that he wounded the youth's leg with the point of his sword. The youth nevertheless escaped from them, but his horse leapt so violently that the helmet fell from the youth's head, and they could see that he had golden hair. They rode back and announced this to the King.

The following day the King's daughter asked the gardener about his boy. "He is at work in the garden; the queer creature has been at the festival too, and only came home yesterday evening; he has likewise shown my children three golden apples that he has won."

The King had him summoned into his presence, and he came and again had his little cap on his head. But the King's daughter went up to him and took it off, and then his golden hair fell down over his shoulders, and he was so handsome that all were amazed. "Are you the knight who came every day to the festival, always in different colors, and who caught the three golden apples?" asked the King.

"Yes," he answered, "and here the apples are," and he took them out of his pocket, and returned them to the King. "If you desire further proof, you may see the wound that your people gave me when they followed me. But I am likewise the knight who helped you to your victory over your enemies."

"If you can perform such deeds as that, you are no gardener's boy; tell me, who is your father?"

"My father is a mighty King, and gold have I in plenty as great as I require."

"I well see," said the King, "that I owe thanks to you; can I do anything to please you?"

"Yes," answered he, "that indeed you can. Give me your daughter to marry."

The maiden laughed, and said, "He does not stand much on ceremony, but I have already seen by his golden hair that he was no gardener's boy," and then she went and kissed him. His father and mother came to the wedding, and were in great delight, for they had given up all hope of ever seeing their dear son again. And as they were sitting at the marriage feast, the music suddenly stopped, the doors opened, and a stately King came in with a great retinue. He went up to the youth, embraced him and said, "I am Iron John, and was by enchantment a wild man, but you have set me free; all the treasures that I possess, shall be your property."

36. *The Three Black Princesses*

East India was besieged by an enemy who would not retire until he had received six hundred dollars. Then the townsfolk caused it to be proclaimed by beat of drum that whoever was able to procure the money should be mayor. Now there was a poor fisherman who fished on the lake with his son, and the enemy came and took the son prisoner, and gave the father six hundred dollars for him. So the father went and gave them to the great men of the town, and the enemy departed, and the fisherman became mayor. Then it was proclaimed that whoever did not say, "Mr. Mayor," should be put to death on the gallows.

The son got away again from the enemy, and came to a great forest on a high mountain. The mountain opened, and he went into a great enchanted castle, wherein chairs, tables, and benches were all hung with black. Then came three young princesses who were entirely dressed in black, but had a little white on their faces; they told him he was not to be afraid, they would not hurt him, and that he could save them. He said he would gladly do that, if he did but know how. At this, they told him he must for a whole year not speak to them and also not look at them, and what he wanted to have he was just to ask for, and if they dared give him an answer they would do so. When he had been there for a long while he said he should like to go to his father, and they told him he might go. He was to take with him this purse with money, put on this coat, and in a week he must be back there again.

Then he was caught up, and was instantly in East India. He could no longer find his father in the fisherman's hut, and asked the people where the poor fisherman could be, and they told him he must not say that, or he would come to the gallows. Then he went to his father and said, "Fisherman, how have you got here?"

Then the father said, "You must not say that, if the great men of the town knew of that, you would come to the gallows." He, however, would not stop, and was brought to the gallows.

When he was there, he said, "O, my masters, just let me go to the old fisherman's hut." Then he put on his old smock frock, and came back to the great men, and said, "Do ye not now see? Am I not the son of the poor fisherman? Did I not earn bread for my father and mother in these clothes?" Hereupon his father knew him again, and begged his pardon, and took him home with him, and then he related all that had happened to him, and how he had got into a forest on a high mountain, and the mountain had opened and he had gone into an enchanted castle, where all was black, and three young princesses had come to him who were black except a little white on their faces. And they had told him not to fear, and that he could save them. Then his mother said that might very likely not be a good thing to do, and that he ought to take a holy water vessel with him, and drop some boiling water on their faces.

He went back again, and he was afraid, and he dropped the water on their faces as they were sleeping, and they all turned half-white. Then all the three princesses sprang up, and said, "You accursed dog, our blood shall cry for vengeance on you! Now there is no man born in the world, nor will any ever be born who can set us free! We have still three brothers who are bound by seven chains—they shall tear you to pieces." Then there was a loud shrieking all over the castle, and he sprang out of the window, and broke his leg, and the castle sank into the earth again, the mountain shut to again, and no one knew where the castle had stood.

37. *Knoist and His Three Sons*

Between Werrel and Soist there lived a man whose name was Knoist, and he had three sons. One was blind, the other lame, and the third stark-naked. One time they went into a field, and there they saw a hare. The blind one shot it, the lame one caught it, the naked one put it in his pocket. Then they came to a mighty big lake, on which there were three boats, one sailed, one sank, the third had no bottom to it. They all three got into the one with no bottom to it. Then they came to a mighty big forest in which there was a mighty big tree; in the tree was a mighty big chapel; in the chapel was a sexton made of beech wood and a boxwood parson, who dealt out holy water with clubs.

> "How truly happy is that one
> Who can from holy water run!"

38. *The Maid of Brakel*

A girl from Brakel once went to St. Anne's Chapel at the foot of the Hinnenberg, and as she wanted to have a husband, and thought there was no one else in the chapel, she sang,

> "Oh, holy Saint Anne!
> Help me soon to a man.
> You know him right well,
> By Suttmer gate does he dwell,
> His hair it is golden,
> You know him right well."

The clerk, however, was standing behind the altar and heard that, so he cried in a very gruff voice, "You shall not have him! You shall not have him!" The maiden thought that the child Mary who stood by her mother Anne had called that out to her, and was angry, and cried, "Fiddle de dee, conceited thing, hold your tongue, and let your mother speak!"

39. *Domestic Servants*

Where are you going?" "To Walpe." "I to Walpe, you to Walpe, so, so, together we'll go."

"Have you a man? What is his name?" "Cham." "My man Cham, your man Cham; I to Walpe, you to Walpe; so, so, together we'll go."

"Have you a child? What is he called?" "Wild." "My child Wild, your child Wild; my man Cham, your man Cham; I to Walpe, you to Walpe, so, so, together we'll go."

"Have you a maid? What's she called?" "Mabel." "My maid Mabel, your maid Mabel, my child Wild, your child Wild, my man Cham, your man Cham; I to Walpe, you to Walpe, so, so, together we'll go."

"Have you a farmhand? What do you call him?" "From-your-work-do-not-budge." "My farmhand, From-your-work-do-not-budge; my child Wild, your child Wild; my man Cham, your man Cham; I to Walpe, you to Walpe; so, so, together we'll go."

40. *The Lamb and the Little Fish*

There were once a little brother and a little sister, who loved each other with all their hearts. Their own mother was, however, dead, and they had a stepmother, who was not kind to them, and secretly did everything she could to hurt them. It so happened that the two were playing with other children in a meadow before the house, and there was a pond in the meadow that came up to one side of the house. The children ran about it, and caught each other, and played at counting out.

> "Eneke Beneke, let me live,
> And I to you my bird will give.
> The little bird, it straw shall seek,
> The straw I'll give to the cow to eat.
> The pretty cow shall give me milk,
> The milk I'll to the baker take.
> The baker he shall bake a cake,
> The cake I'll give unto the cat.
> The cat shall catch some mice for that,
> The mice I'll hang up in the smoke,
> And then you'll see the *snow*."

They stood in a circle while they played this, and the one to whom the word *snow* fell, had to run away and all the others ran after him and caught him. As they were running about so merrily the stepmother watched them from the window, and grew angry. And as she understood arts of witchcraft she bewitched them both, and changed the little brother into a fish, and the little sister into a lamb. Then the fish swam here and there about the pond and was very sad, and the lamb walked up and down the meadow, and was miserable, and could not eat or touch one blade of grass. Thus passed a long time, and then strangers came as visitors to the castle. The false stepmother thought, "This is a good opportunity," and called the cook and said to him, "Go and fetch the lamb from the meadow and kill it; we have nothing else for the visitors." Then the cook went away and got the lamb, and took it into the kitchen and tied its feet, and all this it bore patiently. When he had drawn out his knife and was sharpening it on the doorstep to kill the lamb, he noticed a little fish swimming backward and forward in the water, in front of the kitchen sink and looking up at him. This, however, was the brother, for when the fish saw the cook take the lamb away, it followed them and swam along the pond to the house; then the lamb cried down to it,

> "Ah, brother, in the pond so deep,
> How sad is my poor heart!
> Even now the cook he whets his knife
> To take away my tender life."

The little fish answered,

> "Ah, little sister, up on high
> How sad is my poor heart
> While in this pond I lie."

When the cook heard that the lamb could speak and said such sad words to the fish down below, he was terrified and thought this could be no common lamb, but must be bewitched by the wicked woman in the house. Then he said, "Be calm, I will not kill you," and took another sheep and made it ready for the guests, and gave the lamb to a good peasant woman, to whom he related all that he had seen and heard.

The peasant was, however, the very woman who had been foster-mother to the little sister, and she suspected at once who the lamb was, and took it to a wise woman. Then the wise woman pronounced a blessing over the lamb and the little fish, through which they regained their human forms, and after this she took them both into a little hut in a great forest, where they lived alone, but were contented and happy.

41. *Simeli Mountain*

There were once two brothers, the one rich, the other poor. The rich one, however, gave nothing to the poor one, who gained a scanty living by trading in corn, and often did so badly that he had no bread for his wife and children. Once when he was wheeling a barrow through the forest he saw, on one side of him, a great, bare, naked-looking mountain, and as he had never seen it before, he stood still and stared at it with amazement.

While he was thus standing he saw twelve great, wild men coming toward him, and as he believed they were robbers he pushed his barrow into the thicket, climbed up a tree, and waited to see what would happen. The twelve men, however, went to the mountain and cried, "Semsi mountain, Semsi mountain, open," and immediately the barren mountain opened down the middle, and the twelve went into it, and as soon as they were within, it shut. After a short time, however, it opened again, and the men came forth carrying heavy sacks on their shoulders, and when they were all once more in the daylight they said, "Semsi mountain, Semsi mountain, shut yourself;" then the mountain closed together, and there was no longer any entrance to be seen to it, and the twelve went away.

When they were well out of sight the poor man got down from the tree, and was curious to know what really was secretly hidden in the mountain. So he went up to it and said, "Semsi mountain, Semsi mountain, open," and the mountain opened to him also. Then he went inside, and the whole mountain was a cavern full of silver and gold, and behind lay great piles of pearls and sparkling jewels, heaped up like corn. The poor man hardly knew what to do, and whether he might take any of these treasures for himself or not; but at last he filled his pockets with gold, but he left the pearls and precious stones where they were. When he came out again he also said, "Semsi mountain, Semsi mountain, shut yourself;" and the mountain closed itself, and he went home with his barrow.

And now he had no more cause for anxiety, but could buy bread for his wife and children with his gold, and wine into the bargain. He lived joyously and uprightly, gave help to the poor, and did good to everyone. When, however, the money came to an end he went to his brother, borrowed a measure that held a bushel, and brought himself some more, but did not touch any of the most valuable things. When for the third time he wanted to fetch something, he again borrowed the measure of his brother. The rich man had, however, long been envious of his brother's possessions, and of the handsome way of living that he had set on foot, and could not understand from where the riches came, and what his brother wanted with the measure. Then he thought of a cunning trick, and covered the bottom of the measure with pitch, and when he got the measure back a piece of money was sticking in it. He at once went to his brother and asked him, "What have you been measuring in the bushel measure?"

"Corn and barley," said the other. Then he showed him the piece of money, and threatened that if he did not tell the truth he would accuse him before a court of justice. The poor man then told him everything, just as it happened. The rich man, however, ordered his carriage to be made ready, and drove away, resolved to use the opportunity better than his brother had done, and to bring back with him quite different treasures.

When he came to the mountain he cried, "Semsi mountain, Semsi mountain, open." The mountain opened, and he went inside it. There lay the treasures all before him, and for a long time he did not know which to clutch at first. At length he loaded himself with as many precious stones as he could carry. He wished to carry his load outside, but, as his heart and soul were entirely full of the treasures, he had forgotten the name of the mountain, and cried, "Simeli mountain, Simeli mountain, open." That, however, was not the right name, and the mountain never stirred, but remained shut. Then he was alarmed, but the longer he thought about it the more his thoughts confused themselves, and his treasures were no more of any use to him. In the evening the mountain opened, and the twelve robbers came in, and when they saw him they laughed, and cried out, "Bird, have we caught you at last! Did you think we had never noticed that you had been in here twice? We could not catch you then; this third time you shall not get out again!"

Then he cried, "It was not I, it was my brother," but let him beg for his life and say what he would, they cut his head off.

42. *Going A-Traveling*

There was once a poor woman who had a son, who much wished to travel, but his mother said, "How can you travel? We have no money at all for you to take away with you."

Then said the son, "I will manage very well for myself; I will always say, 'Not much, not much, not much.'"

So he walked for a long time and always said, "Not much, not much, not much." Then he passed by a company of fishermen and said, "God speed you! not much, not much, not much."

"What say you peasant, 'not much?'" And when the net was drawn out they had not caught much fish. So one of them fell on the youth with a stick and said, "Have you never seen me threshing?"

"What should I say, then?" asked the youth.

"You must say, 'Get it full, get it full.'"

After this he again walked a long time, and said, "Get it full, get it full," until he came to the gallows, where they had a poor sinner whom they were about to hang. Then said he, "Good morning; get it full, get it full."

"What say you, knave, 'get it full?' Do you want to make out that there are still more wicked people in the world—is not this enough?"

And he again got some blows on his back. "What am I to say, then?" said he.

"You must say, 'May God have pity on the poor soul.'"

Again the youth walked on for a long while and said, "May God have pity on the poor soul!" Then he came to a pit by which stood a knacker who was cutting up a horse. The youth said, "Good morning; God have pity on the poor soul!"

"What do you say, you ill-tempered knave?" and the knacker gave him such a box on the ear, that he could not see out of his eyes.

"What am I to say, then?"

"You must say, 'There lies the carrion in the pit!'"

So he walked on, and always said, "There lies the carrion in the pit, there lies the carrion in the pit." And he came to a cart full of people, so he said, "Good morning; there lies the carrion in the pit!" Then the cart pushed him into a hole, and the driver took his whip and cracked it upon the youth, till he was forced to crawl back to his mother, and as long as he lived he never went out traveling again.

43. *The Donkey*

Once upon a time there lived a King and a Queen, who were rich, and had everything they wanted, but no children. The Queen lamented over this day and night, and said, "I am like a field on which nothing grows." At last God gave her her wish, but when the child came into the world, it did not look like a human child, but was a little donkey. When the mother saw that, her sorrow and outcries grew; she said she would far rather have had no child at all than have a donkey, and that they were to throw it into the water that the fishes might devour it.

But the King said, "No, since God has sent him he shall be my son and heir, and after my death sit on the royal throne, and wear the kingly crown."

The donkey, therefore, was brought up and grew bigger, and his ears grew up beautifully high and straight. He was, however, of a merry disposition, jumped about, played and had especial pleasure in music, so that he went to a celebrated musician and said, "Teach me your art, that I may play the lute as well as you do."

"Ah, dear little master," answered the musician, "that would come very hard to you, your fingers are certainly not suited to it, and are far too big. I am afraid the strings would not last."

No excuses were of any use. The donkey was determined to play the lute; he was persevering and industrious, and at last learned to do it as well as the master himself. The young lordling once went out walking full of thought and came to a well, he looked into it and in the mirror-clear water saw his donkey's form. He was so distressed about it, that he went out into the wide world and only took with him one faithful companion. They traveled up and down, and at last they came into a kingdom where an old King reigned who had an only but wonderfully beautiful daughter. The donkey said, "Here we will stay," knocked at the gate, and cried, "A guest is without—open, that he may enter." As, however, the gate was not opened, he sat down, took his lute and played it in the most delightful manner with his two forefeet.

Then the doorkeeper opened his eyes most wonderfully wide, and ran to the King and said, "Outside by the gate sits a young donkey that plays the lute as well as an experienced master!"

"Then let the musician come to me," said the King.

When, however, a donkey came in, everyone began to laugh at the lute player. And now the donkey was asked to sit down and eat with the servants. He, however, was unwilling, and said, "I am no common stable ass, I am a noble one."

Then they said, "If that is what you are, seat yourself with the men of war."

"No," said he, "I will sit by the King."

The King smiled, and said good-humoredly, "Yes, it shall be as you say, little ass, come here to me." Then he asked, "Little ass, how does my daughter please you?"

The donkey turned his head toward her, looked at her, nodded and said, "I like her above measure, I have never yet seen anyone so beautiful as she is."

"Well, then, you shall sit next to her too," said the King.

"That is exactly what I wish," said the donkey, and he placed himself by her side, ate and drank, and knew how to behave himself daintily and cleanly.

When the noble beast had stayed a long time at the King's court, he thought, "What good does all this do me, I shall still have to go home again?" let his head hang sadly, and went to the King and asked for his dismissal.

But the King had grown fond of him, and said, "Little ass, what ails you? You look as sour as a jug of vinegar, I will give you what you want. Do you want gold?"

"No," said the donkey, and shook his head.

"Do you want jewels and expensive clothes?"

"No."

"Do you wish for half my kingdom?"

"Indeed, no."

Then said the King, "if only I knew what would make you happy. Will you have my pretty daughter to wife?"

"Ah, yes," said the ass, "I should indeed like her," and all at once he became quite merry and full of happiness, for that was exactly what he was wishing for.

So a great and splendid wedding was held. In the evening, when the bride and bridegroom were led into their bedroom, the King wanted to know if the ass would behave well, and ordered a servant to hide himself there. When they were both inside, the bridegroom bolted the door, looked around, and as he believed that they were quite alone, he suddenly threw off his ass's skin, and stood there in the form of a handsome royal youth.

"Now," said he, "you see who I am, and see also that I am not unworthy of you." Then the bride was glad, and kissed him, and loved him dearly. When morning came, he jumped up, put his animal's skin on again, and no one could have guessed what kind of a form was hidden beneath it.

Soon came the old King. "Ah," cried he, "is the little ass merry? But surely you are sad," said he to his daughter, "that you have not got a proper man for your husband?"

"Oh, no, dear father, I love him as well as if he were the handsomest in the world, and I will keep him as long as I live."

The King was surprised, but the servant who had concealed himself came and revealed everything to him. The King said, "That cannot be true."

"Then watch yourself the next night, and you will see it with your own eyes; and listen, lord King, if you were to take his skin away and throw it in the fire, he would be forced to show himself in his true shape."

"Your advice is good," said the King, and at night when they were asleep, he stole in, and when he got to the bed he saw by the light of the moon a noble-looking youth lying there, and the skin lay stretched on the ground. So he took it away, and had a great fire lighted outside, and threw the skin into it, and remained by it himself until it was all burned to ashes. As, however, he was anxious to know how the robbed man would behave himself, he stayed awake the whole night and watched. When the youth had slept his sleep out, he got up by the first light of morning, and wanted to put on the ass's skin, but it was not to be found. On this he was alarmed, and, full of grief and anxiety, said, "Now I shall have to contrive to escape."

But when he went out, there stood the King, who said, "My son, where away in such haste? what have you in mind? Stay here, you are such a handsome man, you shall not go away from me. I will now give you half my kingdom, and after my death you shall have the whole of it."

"Then I hope that what begins so well may end well, and I will stay with you," said the youth.

And the old man gave him half the kingdom, and in a year's time, when he died, the youth had the whole, and after the death of his father he had another kingdom as well, and lived in all magnificence.

44. *The Ungrateful Son*

A man and his wife were once sitting by the door of their house, and they had a roasted chicken set before them, and were about to eat it together. Then the man saw that his aged father was coming, and hastily took the chicken and hid it, for he would not permit him to have any of it. The old man came, took a drink, and went away. Now the son wanted to put the roasted chicken on the table again, but when he took it up, it had become a great toad, which jumped into his face and sat there and never went away again, and if anyone wanted to take it off, it looked venomously at him as if it would jump in his face, so that no one would venture to touch it. And the ungrateful son was forced to feed the toad every day, or else it fed on his face; and thus he went about the world without knowing peace.

45. *The Turnip*

There were once two brothers who both served as soldiers; one of them was rich, and the other poor. Then the poor one, to escape from his poverty, took off his soldier's coat, and became a farmer. He dug and hoed his bit of land, and sowed it with turnip seed. The seed came up, and one turnip grew there that became large and vigorous, and visibly grew bigger and bigger, and seemed as if it would never stop growing, so that it might have been called the princess of turnips, for never was such a one seen before, and never will such a one be seen again.

At length it was so enormous that by itself it filled a whole cart, and two oxen were required to draw it, and the farmer had not the least idea what he was to do with the turnip, or whether it would be a fortune to him or a misfortune. At last he thought, "If you sell it, what will you get for it that is of any importance, and if you eat it yourself, why, the small turnips would do you just as much good; it would be better to take it to the King, and make him a present of it."

So he placed it on a cart, harnessed two oxen, took it to the palace, and presented it to the King. "What strange thing is this?" said the King. "Many wonderful things have come before my eyes, but never such a monster as this! From what seed can this have sprung, or are you a luck-child and have met with it by chance?"

"Ah, no!" said the farmer, "no luck-child am I. I am a poor soldier, who because he could no longer support himself hung his soldier's coat on a nail and took to farming land. I have a brother who is rich and well known to you, Lord King, but I, because I have nothing, am forgotten by everyone."

Then the King felt compassion for him, and said, "You shall be raised from your poverty, and shall have such gifts from me that you shall be equal to your rich brother." Then he bestowed on him much gold, and lands, and meadows, and herds, and made him immensely rich, so that the wealth of the other brother could not be compared with his. When the rich brother heard what the poor one had gained for himself with one single turnip, he envied him, and thought in every way how he also could get hold of a similar piece of luck. He would, however, set about it in a much wiser way, and took gold and horses and carried them to the King, and made certain the King would give him a much larger present in return. If his brother had got so much for one turnip, what would he not carry away with him in return for such beautiful things as these? The King accepted his present, and said he had nothing to give him in return that was more rare and excellent than the great turnip.

So the rich man was obliged to put his brother's turnip in a cart and have it taken to his home. When there he did not know on whom to vent his rage and anger, until bad thoughts came to him, and he resolved to kill his brother. He hired murderers, who were to lie in ambush, and then he went to his brother and said, "Dear brother, I know of a hidden treasure, we will dig it up together, and divide it between us." The other agreed to this, and accompanied him without suspicion. While they were on their way, however, the murderers attacked him, bound him, and would have hanged him to a tree. But just as they were doing this, loud singing and the sound of a horse's feet were heard in the distance. On this their hearts were filled with terror, and they pushed their prisoner headfirst into the sack, hung it on a branch, and ran away. He, however, worked up there until he had made a hole in the sack through which he could put his head.

The man who was coming by was a traveling student, a young fellow who rode on his way through the wood joyously singing his song. When he who was aloft saw that someone was passing below him, he cried, "Good day! You have come at a lucky time."

The student looked around on every side, but did not know from where the voice came. At last he said, "Who calls me?"

Then an answer came from the top of the tree, "Raise your eyes; here I sit aloft in the Sack of Wisdom. In a short time have I learned great things; compared with this all schools are a jest; in a very short time I shall have learned everything, and shall descend wiser than all other men. I understand the stars, and the signs of the Zodiac, and the tracks of the winds, the sand of the sea, the healing of illness, and the virtues of all herbs, birds, and stones. If you were once within it you would feel what noble things issue forth from the Sack of Knowledge."

The student, when he heard all this, was astonished, and said, "Blessed be the hour in which I have found you! May not I also enter the sack for a while?"

He who was above replied as if unwillingly, "For a short time I will let you get into it, if you reward me and give me good words; but you must wait an hour longer, for one thing remains that I must learn before I do it." When the student had waited a while he became impatient, and begged to be allowed to get in at once, his thirst for knowledge was so very great. So he who was above pretended at last to give in, and said, "In order that I may come forth from the house of knowledge you must let it down by the rope, and then you shall enter it."

So the student let the sack down, untied it, and set him free, and then cried, "Now draw me up at once," and was about to get into the sack.

"Halt!" said the other, "that won't do," and took him by the head and put him upside down into the sack, fastened it, and drew the disciple of wisdom up the tree by the rope. Then he swung him in the air and said, "How goes it with you, my dear fellow? Behold, already you feel wisdom coming, and are gaining valuable experience. Keep perfectly quiet until you become wiser." Thereupon he mounted the student's horse and rode away, but in an hour's time sent someone to let the student out again.

46. *The Old Man Made Young Again*

In the time when our Lord still walked this earth, he and St. Peter stopped one evening at a smith's and received free quarters. Then it came to pass that a poor beggar, hardly pressed by age and infirmity, came to this house and begged alms of the smith. St. Peter had compassion on him and said, "Lord and master, if it please you, cure his torments that he may be able to win his own bread."

The Lord said kindly, "Smith, lend me your oven, and put on some coals for me, and then I will make this ailing old man young again."

The smith was quite willing, and St. Peter blew the bellows, and when the coal fire sparked up large and high our Lord took the little old man, pushed him in the oven in the midst of the red-hot fire, so that he glowed like a rosebush, and praised God with a loud voice. After that the Lord went to the quenching tub, put the glowing little man into it so that the water closed over him, and after he had carefully cooled him, gave him his blessing, when behold the little man sprang nimbly out, looking fresh, strong, healthy, and as if he were twenty.

The smith, who had watched everything closely and attentively, invited them all to supper. He, however, had an old half-blind, crooked mother-in-law who went to the youth, and with great earnestness asked if the fire had burned him much. He answered that he had never felt more comfortable, and that he had sat in the red heat as if he had been in cool dew. The youth's words echoed in the ears of the old woman all night long, and early next morning, when the Lord had gone on his way again and had heartily thanked the smith, the latter thought he might make his old mother-in-law young again the same way, as he had watched everything so carefully, and it lay in the province of his trade. So he called to ask her if she, too, would like to go bounding about like a girl of eighteen. She said, "With all my heart, as the youth has come out of it so well."

So the smith made a great fire, and thrust the old woman into it, and she writhed about this way and that, and uttered terrible cries of murder. "Sit still; why are you screaming and jumping about so?" cried he, and as he spoke he blew the bellows again until all her rags were burned. The old woman cried without ceasing, and the smith thought to himself, "I have not quite the right art," and took her out and threw her into the cooling tub. Then she screamed so loudly that the smith's wife upstairs and her daughter-in-law heard, and they both ran downstairs, and saw the old woman lying in a heap in the quenching tub, howling and screaming, with her face wrinkled and shriveled and all out of shape. Then the two, who were both with child, were so terrified that that very night two boys were born who were not made like men but apes, and they ran into the woods, and from them sprang the race of apes.

47. The Lord's Animals and the Devil's

The Lord God had created all animals, and had chosen out the wolf to be his dog, but he had forgotten the goat. Then the Devil made ready and began to create also, and created goats with fine long tails. Now when they went to pasture, they generally remained caught in the hedges by their tails, then the Devil had to go there and disentangle them, with a great deal of trouble. This enraged him at last, and he went and bit off the tail of every goat, as may be seen to this day by the stump. Then he let them go to pasture alone, but it came to pass that the Lord God perceived how at one time they gnawed away at a fruitful tree, at another injured the noble vines, or destroyed other tender plants. This distressed him, so that in his goodness and mercy he summoned his wolves, who soon tore in pieces the goats that went there. When the devil observed this, he went before the Lord and said, "Your creatures have destroyed mine."

The Lord answered, "Why did you create things to do harm?"

The Devil said, "I was compelled to do it: inasmuch as my thoughts run on evil, what I create can have no other nature, and you must pay me heavy damages."

"I will pay you as soon as the oak leaves fall; come then, your money will then be ready counted out."

When the oak leaves had fallen, the Devil came and demanded what was due to him. But the Lord said, "In the church of Constantinople stands a tall oak tree that still has all its leaves."

With raging and curses, the Devil departed, and went to seek the oak, wandered in the wilderness for six months before he found it, and when he returned, all the oaks had in the meantime covered themselves again with green leaves. Then he had to forfeit his indemnity, and in his rage he put out the eyes of all the remaining goats, and put his own in instead.

This is why all goats have devil's eyes, and their tails bitten off, and why he likes to assume their shape.

48. *The Beam*

There was once a magician who was standing in the midst of a great crowd of people performing his wonders. He had a rooster brought in, which lifted a heavy beam and carried it as if it were as light as a feather. But a girl was present who had just found a bit of four-leafed clover, and had therefore become so wise that no deception could stand out against her, and she saw that the beam was nothing but a straw. So she cried, "You people, do you not see that it is a straw that the rooster is carrying, and no beam?"

Immediately the spell vanished, and the people saw what it was, and drove the magician away in shame and disgrace. He, however, full of inward anger, said, "I will soon revenge myself."

After some time the girl's wedding day came, and she was decked out, and went in a great procession over the fields to the place where the church was. All at once she came to a stream, which was very much swollen, and there was no bridge and no plank to cross it. Then the bride nimbly lifted her dress, and wanted to wade through it. And just as she was thus standing in the water, a man, and it was the magician, cried mockingly close beside her, "Aha! Where are your eyes that you take that for water?" Then her eyes were opened, and she saw that she was standing with her clothes lifted up in the middle of a field that was blue with the flowers of blue flax. Then all the people saw it likewise, and chased her away with ridicule and laughter.

49. *The Old Beggar Woman*

There was once an old woman, but you have surely seen an old woman go begging before now? This woman begged the same way, and when she got anything she said, "May God reward you."

The beggar woman came to a door, and there by the fire a friendly rogue of a boy was standing warming himself. The boy said kindly to the poor old woman as she was standing shivering by the door, "Come, old mother, and warm yourself."

She came in, but stood too near the fire, so that her old rags began to burn, and she was not aware of it. The boy stood and saw that, but he did not put the flames out. Is it not true that he should have put them out? And if he had not any water, then should he have wept all the water in his body out of his eyes, and that would have supplied two pretty streams with which to extinguish them.

50. *The Three Sluggards*

A certain King had three sons who were all equally dear to him, and he did not know which of them to appoint as his successor after his own death. When the time came when he was about to die, he summoned them to his bedside and said, "Dear children, I have been thinking of something which I will declare unto you; whoever of you is the laziest shall have the kingdom."

The eldest said, "Then, father, the kingdom is mine, for I am so idle that if I lie down to rest, and a drop falls in my eye, I will not open it that I may sleep."

The second said, "Father, the kingdom belongs to me, for I am so idle that when I am sitting by the fire warming myself, I would rather let my heel be burned off than draw back my leg."

The third said, "Father, the kingdom is mine, for I am so idle that if I were going to be hanged, and had the rope already around my neck, and anyone put a sharp knife into my hand with which I might cut the rope, I would rather let myself be hanged than raise my hand to the rope."

When the father heard that, he said, "You have carried it the farthest, and shall be King."

51. *The Twelve Idle Servants*

Twelve servants who had done nothing all the day would not exert themselves at night either, but laid themselves on the grass and boasted of their idleness. The first said, "What is your laziness to me, I have to concern myself about my own? The care of my body is my principal work, I eat a lot and drink still more. When I have had four meals, I fast a short time until I feel hunger again, and that suits me best. To rise early is not for me; when it is getting near midday, I already seek out a resting place for myself. If the master calls, I do exactly as if I had not heard him, and if he calls for the second time, I wait awhile before I get up, and go to him very slowly. In this way life is endurable."

The second said, "I have a horse to look after, but I leave the bit in his mouth, and if I do not want to do it, I give him no food, and I say he has had it already. I, however, lay myself in the oat chest and sleep for four hours. After this I stretch out one foot and move it a couple of times over the horse's body, and then he is combed and cleaned. Who is going to make a great business of that? Nevertheless work is too tiring for me."

The third said, "Why plague oneself with work? Nothing comes of it! I laid myself in the sun, and fell asleep. It began to rain a little, but why should I get up? I let it rain on in God's name. At last came a splashing shower, so heavy indeed, that it pulled the hair out of my head and washed it away, and I got a hole in the skull; I put a plaster on it, and then it was all right. I have already had several injuries of that kind."

The fourth said, "If I am to undertake a piece of work, I first lay about for an hour that I may save up my strength. After that I begin quite slowly, and ask if someone could help me. Then I let him do the chief of the work, and in reality only look on; but that also is still too much for me."

The fifth said, "What does that matter? Just think, I am to take away the manure from the horse's stable, and load the cart with it. I let it go on slowly, and if I have taken anything on the fork, I only half-raise it up, and then I rest just a quarter of an hour until I throw it in. It is enough and to spare if I take out a cartful in the day. I have no fancy for killing myself with work."

The sixth said, "Shame on ye; I am afraid of no work, but I lie down for three weeks, and never once take my clothes off. What is the use of buckling your shoes on? For all I care they may fall off my feet, it is no matter. If I am going up some steps, I drag one foot slowly after the other onto the first step, and then I count the rest of them that I may know where I must rest."

The seventh said, "That will not do with me; my master looks after my work, only he is not at home the whole day. But I neglect nothing, I run as fast as it is possible to do when one crawls. If I am to move, four sturdy men must push me with all their might. I came where six men were lying sleeping on a bed beside each other. I lay down by them and slept too. There was no wakening me again, and when they wanted to have me home, they had to carry me."

The eighth said, "I see plainly that I am the only active fellow; if a stone lies before me, I do not give myself the trouble to raise my legs and step over it. I lay myself down on the ground, and if I am wet and covered with mud and dirt, I stay lying until the sun has dried me again. At the very most, I only turn myself so that it can shine on me."

The ninth said, "That is the right way! Today the bread was before me, but I was too lazy to take it, and nearly died of hunger! Moreover a jug stood by it, but it was so big and heavy that I did not like to lift it up, and preferred bearing thirst. Just to turn myself around was too much for me, I remained lying like a log the whole day."

The tenth said, "Laziness has brought misfortune on me, a broken leg and swollen calf. Three of us were lying in the road, and I had my legs stretched out. Someone came with a cart, and the wheels went over me. I might indeed have drawn my legs back, but I did not hear the cart coming, for the mosquitos were humming about my ears, and creeping in at my nose and out again at my mouth; who can take the trouble to drive the vermin away?"

The eleventh said, "I gave up my place yesterday. I had no fancy for carrying the heavy books to my master any longer or fetching them away again. There was no end of it all day long. But to tell the truth, he gave me my dismissal, and would not keep me any longer, for his clothes, which I had left lying in the dust, were all moth-eaten, and I am very glad of it."

The twelfth said, "Today I had to drive the cart into the country, and made myself a bed of straw on it, and had a good sleep. The reins slipped out of my hand, and when I awoke, the horse had nearly torn itself loose, the harness was gone, the strap that fastened the horse to the shafts was gone, and so were the collar, the bridle, and bit. Someone had come by, who had carried all off. Besides this, the cart had got into mud and stuck fast. I left it standing, and stretched myself on the straw again. At last the master came himself, and pushed the cart out, and if he had not come I should not be lying here but there, and sleeping in full tranquility."

52. *The Shepherd Boy*

There was once a shepherd boy whose fame spread far and wide because of the wise answers that he gave to every question. The King of the country heard of it likewise, but did not believe it, and sent for the boy. Then he said to him, "If you can give me an answer to three questions that I will ask you, I will look on you as my own child, and you shall live with me in my royal palace."

The boy said, "What are the three questions?"

The King said, "The first is, how many drops of water are there in the ocean?"

The shepherd boy answered, "Lord King, if you will have all the rivers on earth dammed up so that not a single drop runs from them into the sea until I have counted it, I will tell you how many drops there are in the sea."

The King said, "The next question is, how many stars are there in the sky?"

The shepherd boy said, "Give me a great sheet of white paper," and then he made so many fine points on it with a pen that they could scarcely be seen, and it was all but impossible to count them; anyone who looked at them would have lost his sight. Then he said, "There are as many stars in the sky as there are points on the paper; just count them." But no one was able to do it.

The King said, "The third question is, how many seconds of time are there in eternity?"

Then the shepherd boy said, "In Lower Pomerania is the Diamond Mountain, which is two miles and a half high, two miles and a half wide, and two miles and a half in depth; every hundred years a little bird comes and sharpens its beak on it, and when the whole mountain is worn away by this, then the first second of eternity will be over."

The King said, "You have answered the three questions like a wise man, and shall henceforth dwell with me in my royal palace, and I will regard you as my own child."

53. *The Star Money*

There was once upon a time a little girl whose father and mother were dead, and she was so poor that she no longer had any little room to live in, or bed to sleep in, and at last she had nothing else but the clothes she was wearing and a little bit of bread in her hand that some charitable soul had given her. She was, however, good and pious. And as she was thus forsaken by all the world, she went forth into the open country, trusting in the good God.

Then a poor man met her, who said, "Ah, give me something to eat, I am so hungry!"

She gave him the whole of her piece of bread, and said, "May God bless it to your use," and went onward.

Then came a child who moaned and said, "My head is so cold, give me something to cover it with." So she took off her hood and gave it to him; and when she had walked a little farther, she met another child who had no jacket and was frozen with cold. Then she gave it her own; and a little farther on one begged for a frock, and she gave away that also.

At length she got into a forest and it had already become dark, and there came yet another child, and asked for a little shirt, and the good little girl thought to herself, "It is a dark night and no one sees you, you can very well give your little shirt away," and took it off, and gave away that also.

And as she stood, and had not one single thing left, suddenly some stars from heaven fell down, and they were nothing else but hard smooth pieces of money, and although she had just given her little shirt away, she had a new one that was of the very finest linen. Then she gathered together the money into this, and was rich all the days of her life.

54. The Stolen Pennies

A father was one day sitting at dinner with his wife and his children, and a good friend who had come on a visit was with them. And as they thus sat, and it was striking twelve o'clock, the stranger saw the door open, and a very pale child dressed in snow-white clothes came in. It did not look around, and it did not speak; but went straight into the next room. Soon afterward it came back, and went out the door again in the same quiet manner. On the second and on the third day, it came also exactly in the same way. At last the stranger asked the father to whom the beautiful child that went into the next room every day at noon belonged. "I have never seen it," said he, neither did he know to whom it could belong. The next day when it again came, the stranger pointed it out to the father, who however did not see it, and the mother and the children also all saw nothing.

On this the stranger got up, went to the room door, opened it a little, and peeped in. Then he saw the child sitting on the ground, and digging and seeking about industriously amongst the crevices between the boards of the floor, but when it saw the stranger, it disappeared. He now told what he had seen and described the child exactly, and the mother recognized it, and said, "Ah, it is my dear child who died a month ago."

They took up the boards and found two pennies, which the child had once received from its mother that it might give them to a poor man; it, however, had thought, "You can buy yourself a biscuit for that," and had kept the pennies, and hidden them in the openings between the boards; and therefore it had had no rest in its grave, and had come every day at noon to seek for these pennies. The parents gave the money at once to a poor man, and after that the child was never seen again.

55. *Brides On Trial*

There was once a young shepherd who wished to marry, and was acquainted with three sisters who were all equally pretty, so that it was difficult for him to make a choice, and he could not decide to give the preference to anyone of them.

Then he asked his mother for advice, and she said, "Invite all three, and set some cheese before them, and watch how they eat it." The youth did so; the first, however, swallowed the cheese with the rind on; the second hastily cut the rind off the cheese, but she cut it so quickly that she left much good cheese with it, and threw that away also; the third peeled the rind off carefully, and cut neither too much nor too little.

The shepherd told all this to his mother, who said, "Take the third for your wife." This he did, and lived contentedly and happily with her.

56. *Odds And Ends*

There was once upon a time a maiden who was pretty, but idle and negligent. When she had to spin she was so bad-tempered that if there was a little knot in the flax, she at once pulled out a whole heap of it, and strewed it about on the ground beside her. Now she had a servant who was industrious, and gathered together the bits of flax that were thrown away, cleaned them, span them fine, and had a beautiful gown made out of them for herself.

A young man had wooed the lazy girl, and the wedding was to take place. On the eve of the wedding, the industrious one was dancing merrily about in her pretty dress, and the bride said, "Ah, how that girl does jump about, dressed in my odds and ends."

The bridegroom heard that, and asked the bride what she meant by it. Then she told him that the girl was wearing a dress made of the flax that she had thrown away. When the bridegroom heard that, and saw how idle she was, and how industrious the poor girl was, he gave her up and went to the other, and chose her as his wife.

57. *The Sparrow and His Four Children*

A sparrow had four young ones in a swallow's nest. When they were fledged, some naughty boys pulled out the nest, but fortunately all the birds got safely away in the high wind. Then the old bird was grieved that as his sons had all gone out into the world, he had not first warned them of every kind of danger, and given them good instruction how to deal with each. In the autumn a great many sparrows assembled together in a wheat field, and there the old bird met his four children again, and full of joy took them home with him. "Ah, my dear sons, what pain I have been in about you all through the summer, because you got away in the wind without my teaching; listen to my words, obey your father, and be well on your guard. Little birds have to encounter great dangers!"

And then he asked the eldest where he had spent the summer, and how he had supported himself? "I stayed in the gardens, and looked for caterpillars and small worms, until the cherries got ripe."

"Ah, my son," said the father, "tidbits are not bad, but there is great risk about them; on that account take great care of yourself, and particularly when people are going about the gardens who carry long green poles that are hollow inside and have a little hole at the top."

"Yes, father, but what if a little green leaf is stuck over the hole with wax?" said the son.

"Where have you seen that?"

"In a merchant's garden," said the youngster.

"Oh, my son, merchant folks are quick folks," said the father. "If you have been among the children of the world, you have learned worldly shiftiness enough, only see that you use it well, and do not be too confident." After this he asked the next, "Where have you passed your time?"

"At court," said the son.

"Sparrows and silly little birds are of no use in that place—there one finds much gold, velvet, silk, armor, harnesses, sparrowhawks, screech owls and hen harriers; keep to the horses' stable where they winnow oats, or thresh, and then fortune may give you your daily grain of corn in peace."

"Yes, father," said the son, "but when the stable boys make traps and fix their gins and snares in the straw, many a one is caught fast."

"Where have you seen that?" said the old bird.

"At court, among the stable boys."

"Oh, my son, court boys are bad boys! If you have been to court and among the lords, and have left no feathers there, you have learned a fair amount, and will know very well how to go about the world, but look around you and above you, for the wolves devour the wisest dogs." The father examined the third also: "Where did you seek your safety?"

"I have broken up tubs and ropes on the roads and highways, and sometimes met with a grain of corn or barley."

"That is indeed dainty fare," said the father, "but be careful and look around, especially when you see anyone stooping and about to pick up a stone, there is not much time to stay then."

"That is true," said the son, "but what if anyone should carry a bit of rock, or ore, ready beforehand in his breast or pocket?"

"Where have you seen that?"

"Among the mountaineers, dear father; when they go out, they generally take little bits of ore with them."

"Mountain folks are working folks, and clever folks. If you have been among mountain lads, you have seen and learned something, but when you go there beware, for many a sparrow has been brought to a bad end by a mountain boy."

At length the father came to the youngest son: "You, my dear chirping nestling, were always the silliest and weakest; stay with me, the world has many rough, wicked birds that have crooked beaks and long claws, and lie in wait for poor little birds and swallow them. Keep with those of your own kind, and pick up little spiders and caterpillars from the trees, or the house, and then you will live long in peace."

"My dear father, he who feeds himself without injury to other people fares well, and no sparrowhawk, eagle, or kite will hurt him if he specially commits himself and his lawful food, evening and morning, faithfully to God, who is the Creator and Preserver of all forest and village birds, who likewise hear the cry and prayer of the young ravens, for no sparrow or wren ever falls to the ground except by his will."

"Where have you learned this?"

The son answered, "When the great blast of wind tore me away from you I came to a church, and there during the summer I have picked up the flies and spiders from the windows, and heard this lesson preached. The Father of all sparrows fed me all the summer through, and kept me from all mischance and from ferocious birds."

"In truth, my dear son, if you take refuge in the churches and help to clear away spiders and buzzing flies, and cry unto God like the young ravens, and commend yourself to the eternal Creator, all will be well with you, even if the whole world were full of wild malicious birds."

"He who to God commits his ways,
In silence suffers, waits, and prays,
Preserves his faith and conscience pure,
He is of God's protection sure."

58. *The Tale of Cock-a-doodle*

In the time of Cock-a-doodle I went there, and saw Rome and the Lateran hanging by a small silken thread, and a man without feet who outran a swift horse, and a keen sharp sword that cut through a bridge. There I saw a young ass with a silver nose that pursued two fleet hares, and a lime tree that was very large, on which hot cakes were growing. There I saw a lean old goat that carried about a hundred cartloads of fat on his body, and sixty loads of salt. Have I not told enough lies? There I saw a plow plowing without horse or cow, and a child of one year threw four millstones from Ratisbon to Treves, and from Treves to Strasburg, and a hawk swam over the Rhine, which he had a perfect right to do. There I heard some fishes begin to make such a disturbance with each other, that it resounded as far as heaven, and sweet honey flowed like water from a deep valley at the top of a high mountain, and these were strange things. There were two crows that were mowing a meadow, and I saw two gnats building a bridge, and two doves tore a wolf to pieces; two children brought forth two kids, and two frogs threshed corn together. There I saw two mice consecrating a bishop, and two cats scratching out a bear's tongue. Then a snail came running up and killed two furious lions. There stood a barber and shaved a woman's beard off; and two infants told their mother to hold her tongue. There I saw two greyhounds that brought a mill out of the water; and a sorry old horse was beside it, and said it was right. And four horses were standing in the yard threshing corn with all their might, and two goats were heating the stove, and a red cow shot the bread into the oven. Then a cock crowed, Cock-a- doodle-doo! That's my story—Cock-a-doodle-doo!

59. *The Ditmars Tale of Lies*

I will tell you something. I saw two roasted fowls flying; they flew quickly and had their breasts turned to heaven and their backs to hell, and an anvil and a millstone swam across the Rhine prettily, slowly, and gently, and a frog sat on the ice at Whitsuntide and ate a plowshare. Three fellows who wanted to catch a hare, went on crutches and stilts; one of them was deaf, the second blind, the third dumb, and the fourth could not stir a step. Do you want to know how it was done? First, the blind man saw the hare running across the field, the dumb one called to the lame one, and the lame one seized it by the neck.

There were certain men who wished to sail on dry land, and they set their sails in the wind, and sailed away over great fields. Then they sailed over a high mountain, and there they were miserably drowned. A crab was chasing a hare, which was running away at full speed, and high up on the roof lay a cow that had climbed up there. In that country the flies are as big as the goats are here. Open the window, that the lies may fly out.

60. *A Riddling Tale*

Three women were changed into flowers that grew in the field, but one of them was allowed to be in her own home at night. Then once, when day was drawing near, and she was forced to go back to her companions in the field and become a flower again, she said to her husband, "If you will come this afternoon and gather me, I shall be set free and henceforth stay with you." And he did so. Now the question is, how did her husband know her, for the flowers were exactly alike, and without any difference? Answer: as she was at her home during the night and not in the field, no dew fell on her as it did on the others, and by this her husband knew her.

61. *Snow White and Rose Red*

There was once a poor widow who lived in a lonely cottage. In front of the cottage was a garden wherein stood two rose trees, one of which bore white and the other red roses. She had two children who were like the two rose trees, and one was called Snow White, and the other Rose Red. They were as good and happy, as busy and cheerful as ever two children in the world were, only Snow White was more quiet and gentle than Rose Red. Rose Red liked better to run about in the meadows and fields seeking flowers and catching butterflies; but Snow White sat at home with her mother, and helped her with her housework, or read to her when there was nothing to do.

The two children were so fond of each other that they always held each other by the hand when they went out together, and when Snow White said, "We will not leave each other," Rose Red answered, "Never so long as we live," and their mother would add, "What one has she must share with the other."

They often ran about the forest alone and gathered red berries, and no beasts did them any harm, but came close to them trustfully. The little hare would eat a cabbage leaf out of their hands, the deer grazed by their side, the stag leapt merrily by them, and the birds sat still upon the boughs, and sang whatever they knew.

No trouble found them; if they had stayed too late in the forest, and night came, they laid themselves down near one another upon the moss, and slept until morning came, and their mother knew this and had no distress on their account.

Once when they had spent the night in the woods and the dawn had wakened them, they saw a beautiful child in a shining white dress sitting near their bed. He got up and looked quite kindly at them, but said nothing and went away into the forest. And when they looked around they found that they had been sleeping quite close to a pit, and would certainly have fallen into it in the darkness if they had gone only a few paces further. And their mother told them that it must have been the angel who watches over good children.

Snow White and Rose Red kept their mother's little cottage so neat that it was a pleasure to look inside it. In the summer Rose Red took care of the house, and every morning laid a wreath of flowers by her mother's bed before she awoke, in which was a rose from each tree. In the winter Snow White lit the fire and hung the kettle on the hob. The kettle was of copper and shone like gold, so brightly was it polished. In the evening, when the snowflakes fell, the mother said, "Go, Snow White, and bolt the door," and then they sat around the hearth, and the mother took her spectacles and read aloud out of a large book, and the two girls listened as they sat and span. And close by them lay a lamb upon the floor, and behind them upon a perch sat a white dove with its head hidden beneath its wings.

One evening, as they were thus sitting comfortably together, someone knocked at the door as if he wished to be let in. The mother said, "Quick, Rose Red, open the door, it must be a traveler who is seeking shelter." Rose Red went and pushed back the bolt, thinking that it was a poor man, but it was not; it was a bear that stretched his broad, black head within the door.

Rose Red screamed and sprang back, the lamb bleated, the dove fluttered, and Snow White hid herself behind her mother's bed. But the bear began to speak and said, "Do not be afraid, I will do you no harm! I am half-frozen, and only want to warm myself a little beside you."

"Poor bear," said the mother, "lie down by the fire, only take care that you do not burn your coat." Then she cried, "Snow White, Rose Red, come out, the bear will do you no harm, he means well." So they both came out, and the lamb and dove came nearer, and were not afraid of him.

The bear said, "Here, children, knock the snow out of my coat a little." So they brought the broom and swept the bear's hide clean; and he stretched himself by the fire and growled contentedly and comfortably. It was not long before they grew quite at home, and played with their clumsy guest. They tugged his hair with their hands, put their feet upon his back and rolled him about, or they took a hazel-switch and beat him, and when he growled they laughed. But the bear took it all in good fun, only when they were too rough he called out,

> "Children, children, let me live,

> "Snowy-white, Rosy-red,
> Will you beat your lover dead?"

When it was bedtime, and the others went to bed, the mother said to the bear, "You can lie there by the hearth, and then you will be safe from the cold and the bad weather." As soon as day dawned the two children let him out, and he trotted across the snow into the forest.

From then on, the bear came every evening at the same time, laid himself down by the hearth, and let the children amuse themselves with him as much as they liked; and they got so used to him that the doors were never fastened until their black friend had arrived.

When spring had come and all outside was green, the bear said one morning to Snow White, "Now I must go away, and cannot come back for the whole summer."

"Where are you going, then, dear bear?" asked Snow White.

"I must go into the forest and guard my treasures from the wicked dwarfs. In the winter, when the earth is frozen hard, they are obliged to stay below and cannot work their way through; but now, when the sun has thawed and warmed the earth, they break through it, and come out to pry and steal; and what once gets into their hands, and in their caves, does not easily see daylight again."

Snow White was sad that he was going away, and as she unbolted the door for him, and the bear was hurrying out, he caught against the bolt and a piece of his hairy coat was torn off, and it seemed to Snow White as if she had seen gold shining through it, but she was not sure about it. The bear ran away quickly, and was soon out of sight behind the trees.

A short time afterward the mother sent her children into the forest to get firewood. There they found a big tree that lay felled on the ground, and close by the trunk something was jumping backward and forward in the grass, but they could not make out what it was. When they came nearer they saw a dwarf with an old withered face and a snow-white beard a yard long. The end of the beard was caught in a crevice of the tree, and the little fellow was jumping backward and forward like a dog tied to a rope, and did not know what to do.

He glared at the girls with his fiery red eyes and cried, "Why do you stand there? Can you not come here and help me?"

"What are you doing there, little man?" asked Rose Red.

"You stupid, prying goose!" answered the dwarf. "I was going to split the tree to get a little wood for cooking. The little bit of food that one of us wants gets burned up directly with thick logs; we do not swallow so much as you coarse, greedy folk. I had just driven the wedge safely in, and everything was going as I wished; but the wretched wood was too smooth and suddenly sprang apart, and the tree closed so quickly that I could not pull out my beautiful white beard; so now it is trapped in and I cannot get away, and the silly, sleek, milk-faced things laugh! Ugh! How hateful you are!"

The children tried very hard, but they could not pull the beard out, it was caught too tight. "I will run and fetch someone," said Rose Red.

"You senseless goose!" snarled the dwarf. "Why should you fetch someone? You are already two too many for me; can you not think of something better?"

"Don't be impatient," said Snow White, "I will help you," and she pulled her scissors out of her pocket, and cut off the end of the beard.

As soon as the dwarf felt himself free he laid hold of a bag, which lay among the roots of the tree, and which was full of gold, and lifted it up, grumbling to himself, "Rude people, to cut off a piece of my fine beard. Bad luck to you!" and then he swung the bag upon his back, and went off without even once looking at the children.

Some time after that Snow White and Rose Red went to catch a dish of fish. As they came near the brook they saw something like a large grasshopper jumping toward the water, as if it were going to leap in. They ran to it and found it was the dwarf. "Where are you going?" said Rose Red. "You surely don't want to go into the water."

"I am not such a fool!" cried the dwarf; "don't you see that the accursed fish wants to pull me in?" The little man had been sitting there fishing, and unluckily the wind had twisted his beard with the fishing line; just then a big fish bit, and the feeble creature had not strength to pull it out; the fish kept the upper hand and pulled the dwarf toward him. He held on to all the reeds and rushes, but it was of little good, he was forced to follow the movements of the fish, and was in urgent danger of being dragged into the water.

The girls came just in time; they held him fast and tried to free his beard from the line, but all in vain, beard and line were entangled fast together. Nothing was left but to bring out the scissors and cut the beard, whereby a small part of it was lost. When the dwarf saw that he screamed out, "Is that civil, you toadstool, to disfigure one's face? Was it not enough to clip off the end of my beard? Now you have cut off the best part of it. I cannot let myself be seen by my people. I wish you had been made to run the soles off your shoes!" Then he took out a sack of pearls that lay in the rushes, and without saying a word more he dragged it away and disappeared behind a stone.

It happened that soon afterward the mother sent the two children to the town to buy needles and thread, and laces and ribbons. The road led them across a pasture upon which huge pieces of rock lay strewn here and there. Now they noticed a large bird hovering in the air, flying slowly around and around above them; it sank lower and lower, and at last settled near a rock not far off. Directly afterward they heard a loud, piteous cry. They ran up and saw with horror that the eagle had seized their old acquaintance the dwarf, and was going to carry him off.

The children, full of pity, at once took tight hold of the little man, and pulled against the eagle so long that at last he let his treasure go. As soon as the dwarf had recovered from his first fright he cried with his shrill voice, "Could you not have done it more carefully! You dragged at my brown coat so that it is all torn and full of holes, you helpless clumsy creatures!" Then he took up a sack full of precious stones, and slipped away again under the rock into his hole. The girls, who by this time were used to his thanklessness, went on their way and did their business in the town.

As they crossed the pasture again on their way home they surprised the dwarf, who had emptied out his bag of precious stones in a clean spot, and had not thought that anyone would come there so late. The evening sun shone upon the brilliant stones; they glittered and sparkled with all colors so beautifully that the children stood still and looked at them. "Why do you stand gaping there?" cried the dwarf, and his ashen-gray face became copper-red with rage. He was going on with his bad words when a loud growling was heard, and a black bear came trotting toward them out of the forest. The dwarf sprang up in a fright, but he could not get to his cave, for the bear was already close. Then in the dread of his heart he cried, "Dear Mr. Bear, spare me, I will give you all my treasures; look, the beautiful jewels lying there! Grant me my life; what do you want with such a slender little fellow as I? You would not feel me between your teeth. Come, take these two wicked girls, they are tender morsels for you, fat as young quails; for mercy's sake eat them!" The bear took no heed of his words, but gave the wicked creature a single blow with his paw, and he did not move again.

The girls had run away, but the bear called to them, "Snow White and Rose Red, do not be afraid; wait, I will come with you." Then they knew his voice and waited, and when he came up to them suddenly his bearskin fell off, and he stood there, a handsome man, clothed all in gold. "I am a King's son," he said, "and I was bewitched by that wicked dwarf, who had stolen my treasures; I have had to run about the forest as a savage bear until I was freed by his death. Now he has got his well-deserved punishment."

Snow White was married to him, and Rose Red to his brother, and they divided between them the great treasure that the dwarf had gathered together in his cave. The old mother lived peacefully and happily with her children for many years. She took the two rose trees with her, and they stood before her window, and every year bore the most beautiful roses, white and red.

62. *The Wise Servant*

How fortunate is the master, and how well all goes in his house, when he has a wise servant who listens to his orders and does not obey them, but prefers following his own wisdom.

A clever John of this kind was once sent out by his master to seek a lost cow. He stayed away a long time, and the master thought, "Faithful John does not spare any pains over his work!" As, however, he did not come back at all, the master was afraid that some trouble had found him, and set out himself to look for him. He had to search a long time, but at last he perceived the boy who was running up and down a large field. "Now, dear John," said the master when he had got up to him, "have you found the cow that I sent you to seek?"

"No, master," he answered, "I have not found the cow, but then I have not looked for it."

"Then what have you looked for, John?"

"Something better, and that luckily I have found."

"What is that, John?"

"Three blackbirds," answered the boy.

"And where are they?" asked the master.

"I see one of them, I hear the other, and I am running after the third," answered the wise boy.

Take example by this, do not trouble yourselves about your masters or their orders, but rather do what comes into your head and pleases you, and then you will act just as wisely as prudent John.

63. *The Glass Coffin*

Let no one ever say that a poor tailor cannot do great things and win high honors; all that is needed is that he should go to the right blacksmith, and what is of most consequence, that he should have good luck. A civil, resourceful tailor's apprentice once went out traveling, and came into a great forest, and, as he did not know the way, he lost himself. Night fell, and nothing was left for him to do, but to seek a bed in this painful solitude. He might certainly have found a good bed on the soft moss, but the fear of wild beasts let him have no rest there, and at last he was forced to make up his mind to spend the night in a tree. He sought out a high oak, climbed up to the top of it, and thanked God that he had his goose with him, for otherwise the wind that blew over the top of the tree would have carried him away.

After he had spent some hours in the darkness, not without fear and trembling, he saw nearby the glimmer of a light, and as he thought that a human home might be there, where he would be better off than on the branches of a tree, he got carefully down and went toward the light. It guided him to a small hut that was woven together of reeds and rushes. He knocked boldly, the door opened, and by the light which came forth he saw a little hoary old man who wore a coat made of bits of colored stuff sewn together. "Who are you, and what do you want?" asked the man in a grumbling voice.

"I am a poor tailor," he answered, "whom night has surprised here in the wilderness, and I beg you to take me into your hut until morning."

"Go your way," replied the old man in a surly voice, "I will have nothing to do with runaways; seek for yourself a shelter elsewhere." After these words he was about to slip into his hut again, but the tailor held him so tightly by the corner of his coat, and pleaded so piteously, that the old man, who was not so ill-natured as he wished to appear, was at last softened, and took him into the hut with him where he gave him something to eat, and then pointed out to him a very good bed in a corner.

The weary tailor needed no rocking; but slept sweetly till morning, but even then would not have thought of getting up, if he had not been awakened by a great noise. A violent sound of screaming and roaring forced its way through the thin walls of the hut. The tailor, full of unusual courage, jumped up, put his clothes on in a hurry, and rushed out. Then close by the hut, he saw a great black bull and a beautiful stag, which were just preparing for a violent struggle. They rushed at each other with such extreme rage that the ground shook with their trampling, and the air resounded with their cries. For a long time it was uncertain which of the two would gain the victory; at length the stag thrust his horns into his adversary's body, when the bull fell to the earth with a terrific roar, and was thoroughly beaten by a few strokes from the stag.

The tailor, who had watched the fight with astonishment, was still standing there motionless, when the stag in full career bounded up to him, and before he could escape, caught him up on his great horns. He had not much time to collect his thoughts, for it went in a swift race over stock and stone, mountain and valley, wood and meadow. He held with both hands to the tops of the horns, and resigned himself to his fate. It seemed, however, to him just as if he were flying away. At length the stag stopped in front of a wall of rock, and gently let the tailor down. The tailor, more dead than alive, required a longer time than that to recoup. When he had in some degree recovered, the stag, which had remained standing by him, pushed its horns with such force against a door that was in the rock that it sprang open. Flames of fire shot forth, after which followed a great smoke, which hid the stag from his sight. The tailor did not know what to do, or where to turn, in order to get out of this desert and back to human beings again. While he was standing undecided, a voice sounded out of the rock, which cried to him, "Enter without fear, no evil shall befall you." He hesitated, but driven by a mysterious force, he obeyed the voice and went through the iron door into a large spacious hall, whose ceiling, walls and floor were made of shining polished square stones, on each of which were cut letters that were unknown to him. He looked at everything full of admiration, and was on the point of going out again, when he once more heard the voice, which said to him, "Step on the stone that lies in the middle of the hall, and great good fortune awaits you."

His courage had already grown so great that he obeyed the order. The stone began to give way under his feet, and sank slowly down into the depths. When it was once more firm, and the tailor looked around, he found himself in a hall that in size resembled the former. Here, however, there was more to look at and to admire. Hollow places were cut in the walls, in which stood vases of transparent glass that were filled with colored spirit or with a bluish vapor. On the floor of the hall two great glass chests stood opposite to each other, which at once excited his curiosity. When he went to one of them he saw inside it a handsome structure like a castle surrounded by farm buildings, stables and barns, and a quantity of other good things. Everything was small, but exceedingly carefully and delicately made, and seemed to be cut out by a dexterous hand with the greatest precision.

He might not have turned away his eyes from the consideration of this rare site for some time, if the voice had not once more made itself heard. It ordered him to turn around and look at the glass chest that was standing opposite. How his admiration increased when he saw therein a maiden of the greatest beauty! She lay as if asleep, and was wrapped in her long fair hair as in a precious coat. Her eyes were closely shut, but the brightness of her complexion and a ribbon that her breathing moved to and fro left no doubt that she was alive. The tailor was looking at the beauty with beating heart, when she suddenly opened her eyes, and sat up at the sight of him in joyful terror. "Just Heaven!" cried she, "my deliverance is at hand! Quick, quick, help me out of my prison; if you push back the bolt of this glass coffin, then I shall be free." The tailor obeyed without delay, and she immediately raised up the glass lid, came out and hurried into the corner of the hall, where she covered herself with a large cloak. Then she seated herself on a stone, ordered the young man to come to her, and after she had imprinted a friendly kiss on his lips, she said, "My long-desired deliverer, kind Heaven has guided you to me, and put an end to my sorrows. On the same day when they end, shall your happiness begin. You are the husband chosen for me by Heaven, and shall pass your life in unbroken joy, loved by me, and rich to overflowing in every earthly possession. Seat yourself, and listen to the story of my life:

"I am the daughter of a rich count. My parents died when I was still in my tender youth, and recommended me in their last will to my elder brother, by whom I was brought up. We loved each other so tenderly, and were so alike in our way of thinking and our inclinations, that we both embraced the resolution never to marry, but to stay together to the end of our lives. In our house there was no lack of company; neighbors and friends visited us often, and we showed the greatest hospitality to everyone. So it came to pass one evening that a stranger came riding to our castle, and, under pretext of not being able to get on to the next place, begged for shelter for the night. We granted his request with ready courtesy, and he entertained us in the most agreeable manner during supper by conversation intermingled with stories. My brother liked the stranger so much that he begged him to spend a couple of days with us, to which, after some hesitation, he consented. We did not rise from table until late in the night, the stranger was shown to room, and I hastened, as I was tired, to lay my limbs in my soft bed. Hardly had I slept for a short time, when the sound of faint and delightful music awoke me. As I could not conceive from where it came, I wanted to summon my servant who slept in the next room, but to my astonishment I found that speech was taken away from me by an unknown force. I felt as if a mountain were weighing down my breast, and was unable to make the very slightest sound. In the meantime, by the light of my nightlamp, I saw the stranger enter my room through two doors that were fast bolted. He came to me and said, that by magic arts that were at his command, he had caused the lovely music to sound in order to awaken me, and that he now forced his way through all fastenings with the intention of offering me his hand and heart. My repugnance to his magic arts was, however, so great, that I gave him no answer. He remained for a time standing without moving, apparently with the idea of waiting for a favorable decision, but as I continued to keep silence, he angrily declared he would revenge himself and find means to punish my pride, and left the room. I passed the night in the greatest turmoil, and only fell asleep toward morning. When I awoke, I hurried to my brother, but did not find him in his room, and the attendants told me that he had ridden forth with the stranger to the chase by daybreak.

"I at once suspected nothing good. I dressed myself quickly, ordered my horse to be saddled, and accompanied only by one servant, rode full gallop to the forest. The servant fell with his horse, and could not follow me, for the horse had broken its foot. I pursued my way without halting, and in a few minutes I saw the stranger coming toward me with a beautiful stag that he led by a cord. I asked him where he had left my brother, and how he had come by this stag, out of whose great eyes I saw tears flowing. Instead of answering me, he began to laugh loudly. I fell into a great rage at this, pulled out a pistol and discharged it at the monster; but the ball rebounded from his breast and went into my horse's head. I fell to the ground, and the stranger muttered some words that deprived me of consciousness.

"When I came to my senses again I found myself in this underground cave in a glass coffin. The magician appeared once again, and said he had changed my brother into a stag, my castle with all that belonged to it, diminished in size by his magic, he had shut up in the other glass chest, and my people, who were all turned into smoke, he had confined in glass bottles. He told me that if I would now comply with his wish, it was an easy thing for him to put everything back in its former state, as he had nothing to do but open the vessels, and everything would return once more to its natural form. I answered him as little as I had done the first time. He vanished and left me in my prison, in which a deep sleep came on me. Among the visions that passed before my eyes, that was the most comforting in which a young man came and set me free, and when I opened my eyes today I saw you, and beheld my dream fulfilled. Help me to accomplish the other things that happened in those visions. The first is that we lift the glass chest in which my castle is enclosed, onto that broad stone."

As soon as the stone was laden, it began to rise up on high with the maiden and the young man, and mounted through the opening of the ceiling into the upper hall, from where they then could easily reach the open air. Here the maiden opened the lid, and it was marvelous to behold how the castle, the houses, and the farm buildings that were enclosed, stretched themselves out and grew to their natural size with the greatest rapidity. After this, the maiden and the tailor returned to the cave beneath the earth, and had the vessels that were filled with smoke carried up by the stone. The maiden had scarcely opened the bottles when the blue smoke rushed out and changed itself into living men, in whom she recognized her servants and her people. Her joy was still more increased when her brother, who had killed the magician in the form of the bull, came out of the forest toward them in his human form, and on the same day the maiden, in accordance with her promise, gave her hand at the altar to the lucky tailor.

64. *Lazy Harry*

Harry was lazy, and although he had nothing else to do but drive his goat daily to pasture, he nevertheless groaned when he went home after his day's work was done. "It is indeed a heavy burden," said he, "and a wearisome employment to drive a goat into the field this way year after year, till late into the autumn! If one could but lie down and sleep, but no, one must have one's eyes open lest it hurts the young trees, or squeezes itself through the hedge into a garden, or runs away altogether. How can one have any rest, or peace of one's life?" He seated himself, collected his thoughts, and considered how he could set his shoulders free from this burden. For a long time all thinking was to no purpose, but suddenly it was as if scales fell from his eyes. "I know what I will do," he cried, "I will marry fat Trina who has also a goat, and can take mine out with hers, and then I shall have no more need to trouble myself."

So Harry got up, set his weary legs in motion, and went right across the street, for it was no farther, to where the parents of fat Trina lived, and asked for their industrious and virtuous daughter in marriage. The parents did not reflect long. "Birds of a feather, flock together," they thought, and consented.

So fat Trina became Harry's wife, and led out both the goats. Harry had a good time of it, and had no work that he required to rest from but his own idleness. He only went out with her now and then, and said, "I merely do it that I may afterward enjoy rest more, otherwise one loses all feeling for it."

But fat Trina was no less idle. "Dear Harry," said she one day, "why should we make our lives so toilsome when there is no need for it, and thus ruin the best days of our youth? Would it not be better for us to give the two goats, which disturb us every morning in our sweetest sleep with their bleating, to our neighbor, and he will give us a beehive for them. We will put the beehive in a sunny place behind the house, and trouble ourselves no more about it. Bees do not require to be taken care of, or driven into the field; they fly out and find the way home again for themselves, and collect honey without giving the very least trouble."

"You have spoken like a sensible woman," replied Harry. "We will carry out your proposal without delay, and besides all that, honey tastes better and nourishes one better than goat's milk, and it can be kept longer too."

The neighbor willingly gave a beehive for the two goats. The bees flew in and out from early morning till late evening without ever tiring, and filled the hive with the most beautiful honey, so that in autumn Harry was able to take a whole pitcher out of it.

They placed the jug on a board that was fixed to the wall of their bedroom, and as they were afraid that it might be stolen from them, or that the mice might find it, Trina brought in a stout hazel-stick and put it beside her bed, so that without unnecessary getting up she might reach it with her hand, and drive away the uninvited guests. Lazy Harry did not like to leave his bed before noon. "He who rises early," said he, "wastes his substance."

One morning when he was still lying among the feathers in broad daylight, resting after his long sleep, he said to his wife, "Women are fond of sweet things, and you are always tasting the honey in private; it will be better for us to exchange it for a goose with a young gosling, before you eat up the whole of it."

"But," answered Trina, "not before we have a child to take care of them! Am I to worry myself with the little geese, and spend all my strength on them to no purpose?"

"Do you think," said Harry, "that the youngster will look after geese? Nowadays children no longer obey, they do according to their own fancy, because they consider themselves cleverer than their parents, just like that lad who was sent to seek the cow and chased three blackbirds."

"Oh," replied Trina, "this one shall fare badly if he does not do what I say! I will take a stick and belabor his skin for him with more blows than I can count. Look, Harry," she cried in her zeal, and seized the stick that she had to drive the mice away with. "Look, this is the way I will fall on him!" She reached her arm out to strike, but unhappily hit the honey pitcher above the bed. The pitcher struck against the wall and fell down in fragments, and the fine honey streamed down on the ground.

"There lie the goose and the young gosling," said Harry, "and want no looking after. But it is lucky that the pitcher did not fall on my head.

We have all reason to be satisfied with our lot." And then as he saw that there was still some honey in one of the fragments he stretched out his hand for it, and said quite gaily, "The remains, my wife, we will still eat with a relish, and we will rest a little after the fright we have had. What matters if we do get up a little later, the day is always long enough."

"Yes," answered Trina, "we shall always get to the end of it at the proper time. Do you know that the snail was once asked to a wedding and set out to go, but arrived at the christening. In front of the house it fell over the fence, and said, 'Speed does no good.'"

65. *The Griffin*

There was once upon a time a King, but where he reigned and what he was called, I do not know. He had no son, but an only daughter who had always been ill, and no doctor had been able to cure her. Then it was foretold to the King that his daughter should eat herself well with an apple. So he ordered it to be proclaimed throughout the whole of his kingdom, that whoever brought his daughter an apple with which she could eat herself well, should have her to wife, and be King. This became known to a peasant who had three sons, and he said to the eldest, "Go out into the garden and take a basketful of those beautiful apples with the red cheeks and carry them to the court; perhaps the King's daughter will be able to eat herself well with them, and then you will marry her and be King." The lad did so, and set out.

When he had gone a short way he met a little iron man who asked him what he had there in the basket, to which replied Uele, for so was he named, "Frogs' legs." On this the little man said, "Well, so shall it be, and remain," and went away. Finally, Uele arrived at the palace, and made it known that he had brought apples that would cure the King's daughter if she ate them. This delighted the King hugely, and he caused Uele to be brought before him; but, alas! when he opened the basket, instead of having apples in it he had frogs' legs, which were still kicking about. On this the King grew angry, and had him driven out of the house. When he got home he told his father how it had fared with him. Then the father sent the next son, who was called Seame, but all went with him just as it had gone with Uele. He also met the little iron man, who asked what he had there in the basket. Seame said, "Hogs' bristles," and the iron man said, "well, so shall it be, and remain."

When Seame got to the King's palace and said he brought apples with which the King's daughter might eat herself well, they did not want to let him go in, and said that one fellow had already been there, and had treated them as if they were fools. Seame, however, maintained that he certainly had the apples, and that they ought to let him go in. At length they believed him, and led him to the King. But when he uncovered the basket, he had but hogs' bristles. This enraged the King most terribly, so he caused Seame to be whipped out of the house. When he got home he related all that had befallen him, then the youngest boy, whose name was Hans, but who was always called Stupid Hans, came and asked his father if he might go with some apples. "Oh!" said the father, "you would be just the right fellow for such a thing! If the clever ones can't manage it, what can you do?"

The boy, however, did not believe him, and said, "Indeed, father, I wish to go."

"Just get away, you stupid fellow, you must wait till you are wiser," said the father to that, and turned his back. Hans, however, pulled at the back of his smock frock and said, "Indeed, father, I wish to go."

"Well, then, so far as I am concerned you may go, but you will soon come home again!" replied the old man in a spiteful voice. The boy, however, was tremendously delighted and jumped for joy. "Well, act like a fool! you grow more stupid every day!" said the father again. Hans, however, did not care about that, and did not let it spoil his pleasure, but as it was then night, he thought he might as well wait until the morrow, for he could not get to court that day. All night long he could not sleep in his bed, and if he did doze for a moment, he dreamt of beautiful maidens, of palaces, of gold, and of silver, and all kinds of things of that sort. Early in the morning, he went forth on his way, and directly afterward the little shabby-looking man in his iron clothes, came to him and asked what he was carrying in the basket. Hans gave him the answer that he was carrying apples with which the King's daughter was to eat herself well.

"Then," said the little man, "so shall they be, and remain." But at the court they would none of them let Hans go in, for they said two had already been there who had told them that they were bringing apples, and one of them had frogs' legs, and the other hogs' bristles. Hans, however, resolutely maintained that he most certainly had no frogs' legs, but some of the most beautiful apples in the whole kingdom. As he spoke so pleasantly, the doorkeeper thought he could not be telling a lie, and asked him to go in, and he was right, for when Hans uncovered his basket in the King's presence, golden-yellow apples came tumbling out. The King was delighted, and caused some of them to be taken to his daughter, and then waited in anxious expectation until news should be brought to him of the effect they had. But before much time had passed by, news was brought to him: but who do you think it was who came? It was his daughter herself! As soon as she had eaten of those apples, she was cured, and sprang out of her bed. The joy the King felt cannot be described! But now he did not want to give his daughter in marriage to Hans, and said he must first make him a boat that would go quicker on dry land than on water. Hans agreed to the conditions, and went home, and related how it had fared with him. Then the father sent Uele into the forest to make a boat of that kind. He worked diligently, and whistled all the time. At midday, when the sun was at the highest, came the little iron man and asked what he was making? Uele gave him for answer, "Wooden bowls for the kitchen."

The iron man said, "So it shall be, and remain." By evening Uele thought he had now made the boat, but when he wanted to get into it, he had nothing but wooden bowls. The next day Seame went into the forest, but everything went with him just as it had done with Uele. On the third day Stupid Hans went. He worked away most industriously, so that the whole forest resounded with the heavy strokes, and all the while he sang and whistled right merrily. At midday, when it was the hottest, the little man came again, and asked what he was making? "A boat which will go quicker on dry land than on the water," replied Hans, "and when I have finished it, I am to have the King's daughter for my wife."

"Well," said the little man, "such a one shall it be, and remain." In the evening, when the sun had turned into gold, Hans finished his boat, and all that was wanted for it. He got into it and rowed to the palace. The boat went as swiftly as the wind. The King saw it from afar, but would not give his daughter to Hans yet, and said he must first take a hundred hares out to pasture from early morning until late evening, and if one of them got away, he should not have his daughter. Hans was contented with this, and the next day went with his flock to the pasture, and took great care that none of them ran away.

Before many hours had passed came a servant from the palace, and told Hans that he must give her a hare instantly, for some visitors had come unexpectedly. Hans, however, was very well aware what that meant, and said he would not give her one; the King might set some hare soup before his guest next day. The maid, however, would not believe in his refusal, and at last she began to get angry with him. Then Hans said that if the King's daughter came herself, he would give her a hare. The maid told this in the palace, and the daughter did go herself. In the meantime, however, the little man came again to Hans, and asked him what he was doing there? He said he had to watch over a hundred hares and see that none of them ran away, and then he might marry the King's daughter and be King. "Good," said the little man, "there is a whistle for you, and if one of them runs away, just whistle with it, and then it will come back again."

When the King's daughter came, Hans gave her a hare into her apron; but when she had gone about a hundred steps with it, he whistled, and the hare jumped out of the apron, and before she could turn around was back to the flock again. When the evening came the hare-herd whistled once more, and looked to see if all were there, and then drove them to the palace. The King wondered how Hans had been able to take a hundred hares to graze without losing any of them; he would, however, not give him his daughter yet, and said he must now bring him a feather from the Griffin's tail. Hans set out at once, and walked straight forward. In the evening he came to a castle, and there he asked for a night's lodging, for at that time there were no inns. The lord of the castle promised him that with much pleasure, and asked where he was going? Hans answered, "To the Griffin."

"Oh! To the Griffin! They tell me he knows everything, and I have lost the key of an iron money-chest; so you might be so good as to ask him where it is."

"Yes, indeed," said Hans, "I will do that."

Early the next morning he went onward, and on his way arrived at another castle in which he again stayed the night. When the people who lived there learned that he was going to the Griffin, they said they had in the house a daughter who was ill, and that they had already tried every means to cure her, but none of them had done her any good, and he might be so kind as to ask the Griffin what would make their daughter healthy again? Hans said he would willingly do that, and went onward. Then he came to a lake, and instead of a ferryboat, a tall, tall man was there who had to carry everybody across. The man asked Hans where he was journeying? "To the Griffin," said Hans.

"Then when you get to him," said the man, "just ask him why I am forced to carry everybody over the lake."

"Yes, indeed, most certainly I'll do that," said Hans. Then the man took him up on his shoulders, and carried him across. At length Hans arrived at the Griffin's house, but the wife only was at home, and not the Griffin himself. Then the woman asked him what he wanted?

Thereupon he told her everything—that he had to get a feather out of the Griffin's tail, and that there was a castle where they had lost the key of their money chest, and he was to ask the Griffin where it was, that in another castle the daughter was ill, and he was to learn what would cure her—and then not far from there, there was a lake and a man beside it, who was forced to carry people across it, and he was very anxious to learn why the man was obliged to do it.

Then said the woman, "But look here, my good friend, no Christian can speak to the Griffin; he devours them all; but if you like, you can lie down under his bed, and in the night, when he is quite fast asleep, you can reach out and pull a feather out of his tail, and as for those things that you are to learn, I will ask about them myself."

Hans was quite satisfied with this, and got under the bed. In the evening, the Griffin came home, and as soon as he entered the room, said, "Wife, I smell a Christian."

"Yes," said the woman, "one was here today, but he went away again;" and on that the Griffin said no more.

In the middle of the night when the Griffin was snoring loudly, Hans reached out and plucked a feather from his tail. The Griffin woke up instantly, and said, "Wife, I smell a Christian, and it seems to me that somebody was pulling at my tail."

His wife said, "You have certainly been dreaming, and I told you before that a Christian was here today, but that he went away again. He told me all kinds of things, that in one castle they had lost the key of their money-chest, and could find it nowhere."

"Oh! the fools!" said the Griffin; "the key lies in the woodshed under a log of wood behind the door."

"And then he said that in another castle the daughter was ill, and they knew no remedy that would cure her."

"Oh! the fools!" said the Griffin; "under the cellar steps a toad has made its nest of her hair, and if she got her hair back she would be well."

"And then he also said that there was a place where there was a lake and a man beside it who was forced to carry everybody across."

"Oh, the fool!" said the Griffin; "if he only put one man down in the middle, he would never have to carry another across."

Early the next morning the Griffin got up and went out. Then Hans came forth from under the bed, and he had a beautiful feather, and had heard what the Griffin had said about the key, and the daughter, and the ferryman. The Griffin's wife repeated it all once more to him that he might not forget it, and then he went home again. First he came to the man by the lake, who asked him what the Griffin had said, but Hans replied that he must first carry him across, and then he would tell him. So the man carried him across, and when he was over Hans told him that all he had to do was to set one person down in the middle of the lake, and then he would never have to carry over any more. The man was hugely delighted, and told Hans that out of gratitude he would take him once more across, and back again. But Hans said no, he would save him the trouble, he was quite satisfied already, and pursued his way. Then he came to the castle where the daughter was ill; he took her on his shoulders, for she could not walk, and carried her down the cellar steps and pulled out the toad's nest from beneath the lowest step and gave it into her hand, and she sprang off his shoulder and up the steps before him, and was quite cured. Then were the father and mother beyond measure rejoiced, and they gave Hans gifts of gold and of silver, and whatever else he wished for, that they gave him. And when he got to the other castle he went at once into the woodshed, and found the key under the log of wood behind the door, and took it to the lord of the castle. He also was not a little pleased, and gave Hans as a reward much of the gold that was in the chest, and all kinds of things besides, such as cows, and sheep, and goats. When Hans arrived before the King, with all these things—with the money, and the gold, and the silver and the cows, sheep, and goats, the King asked him how he had come by them. Then Hans told him that the Griffin gave everyone whatever he wanted. So the King thought he himself could make such things useful, and set out on his way to the Griffin; but when he got to the lake, it happened that he was the very first who arrived there after Hans, and the man put him down in the middle of it and went away, and the King was drowned. Hans, however, married the daughter, and became King.

66. *Strong Hans*

There were once a man and a woman who had an only child, and lived quite alone in a solitary valley. It came to pass that the mother once went into the wood to gather branches of fir, and took with her little Hans, who was just two years old. As it was springtime, and the child took pleasure in the many-colored flowers, she went still further onward with him into the forest. Suddenly two robbers sprang out of the thicket, seized the mother and child, and carried them far away into the black forest, where no one ever came from one year's end to another. The poor woman urgently begged the robbers to set her and her child free, but their hearts were made of stone, they would not listen to her prayers and entreaties, and drove her on farther by force. After they had worked their way through bushes and briars for about two miles, they came to a rock where there was a door, at which the robbers knocked and it opened at once. They had to go through a long dark passage, and at last came into a great cavern, which was lighted by a fire that burned on the hearth. On the wall hung swords, sabers, and other deadly weapons that gleamed in the light, and in the midst stood a black table at which four other robbers were sitting gambling, and the captain sat at the head of it. As soon as he saw the woman he came and spoke to her, and told her to be at ease and have no fear, they would do nothing to hurt her, but she must look after the housekeeping, and if she kept everything in order, she should not fare ill with them. Thereupon they gave her something to eat, and showed her a bed where she might sleep with her child.

The woman stayed many years with the robbers, and Hans grew tall and strong. His mother told him stories, and taught him to read an old book of tales about knights that she found in the cave. When Hans was nine years old, he made himself a strong club out of a branch of fir, hid it behind the bed, and then went to his mother and said, "Dear mother, pray tell me who is my father; I must and will know." His mother was silent and would not tell him, that he might not become homesick; moreover she knew that the godless robbers would not let him go away, but it almost broke her heart that Hans should not go to his father. In the night, when the robbers came home from their robbing expedition, Hans brought out his club, stood before the captain, and said, "I now wish to know who is my father, and if you do not at once tell me I will strike you down." Then the captain laughed, and gave Hans such a box on the ear that he rolled under the table.

Hans got up again, held his tongue, and thought, "I will wait another year and then try again, perhaps I shall do better then." When the year was over, he brought out his club again, rubbed the dust off it, looked at it well, and said, "It is a stout strong club." At night the robbers came home, drank one jug of wine after another, and their heads began to be heavy. Then Hans brought out his club, placed himself before the captain, and asked him who was his father. But the captain again gave him such a vigorous box on the ear that Hans rolled under the table, but it was not long before he was up again, and beat the captain and the robbers so with his club, that they could no longer move either their arms or their legs. His mother stood in a corner full of admiration of his bravery and strength.

When Hans had done his work, he went to his mother, and said, "Now I have shown myself to be in earnest, but now I must also know who is my father."

"Dear Hans," answered the mother, "come, we will go and seek him until we find him." She took from the captain the key to the entrance-door, and Hans fetched a great meal-sack and packed into it gold and silver, and whatever else he could find that was beautiful, until it was full, and then he took it on his back.

They left the cave, but how Hans did open his eyes when he came out of the darkness into daylight, and saw the green forest, and the flowers, and the birds, and the morning sun in the sky. He stood there and wondered at everything just as if he had not been very wise. His mother looked for the way home, and when they had walked for a couple of hours, they got safely into their lonely valley and to their little house. The father was sitting in the doorway. He wept for joy when he recognized his wife and heard that Hans was his son, for he had long regarded them both as dead. But Hans, although he was not twelve years old, was a head taller than his father. They went into the little room together, but Hans had scarcely put his sack on the bench by the stove, than the whole house began to crack, the bench broke down and then the floor, and the heavy sack fell through into the cellar.

"God save us!" cried the father, "what's that? Now you have broken our little house to pieces!"

"Don't grow any grey hairs about that, dear father," answered Hans; "there, in that sack, is more than is wanting for a new house."

The father and Hans at once began to build a new house, to buy cattle and land, and to keep a farm. Hans plowed the fields, and when he followed the plow and pushed it into the ground, the bullocks had scarcely any need to draw. The next spring, Hans said, "Keep all the money and get a walking stick that weighs a hundred pounds made for me that I may go traveling." When the wished-for stick was ready, he left his father's house, went forth, and came to a deep, dark forest. There he heard something crunching and cracking, looked around, and saw a fir tree that was wound around like a rope from the bottom to the top, and when he looked upward he saw a great fellow who had laid hold of the tree and was twisting it like a willow wand.

"Hello!" cried Hans, "what are you doing up there?"

The fellow replied, "I got some bundles of sticks together yesterday and am twisting a rope for them."

"That is what I like," thought Hans, "he has some strength," and he called to him, "Leave that alone, and come with me." The fellow came down, and he was taller by a whole head than Hans, and Hans was not little. "Your name is now Fir-twister," said Hans to him.

Then they went further and heard something knocking and hammering with such force that the ground shook at every stroke. Shortly afterward they came to a mighty rock, before which a giant was standing and striking great pieces of it away with his fist. When Hans asked what he was about, he answered, "At night, when I want to sleep, bears, wolves, and other vermin of that kind come, which sniff and snuffle about me and won't let me rest; so I want to build myself a house and lay myself inside it, so that I may have some peace."

"Oh, indeed," thought Hans, "I can make use of this one also;" and said to him, "Leave your house-building alone, and go with me; you shall be called Rock-splitter." The man consented, and they all three roamed through the forest, and wherever they went the wild beasts were terrified, and ran away from them. In the evening they came to an old deserted castle, went up into it, and laid themselves down in the hall to sleep. The next morning Hans went into the garden. It had run quite wild, and was full of thorns and bushes. And as he was thus walking around about, a wild boar rushed at him; he, however, gave it such a blow with his club that it fell directly. He took it on his shoulders and carried it in, and they put it on a spit, roasted it, and enjoyed themselves. Then they arranged that each day, in turn, two should go out hunting, and one should stay at home, and cook nine pounds of meat for each of them. Fir-twister stayed at home the first, and Hans and Rock-splitter went out hunting. When Fir-twister was busy cooking, a little shriveled-up old manikin came to him in the castle, and asked for some meat. "Be off, sly hypocrite," he answered, "you need no meat."

But how astonished Fir-twister was when the little insignificant dwarf sprang up at him, and belabored him so with his fists that he could not defend himself, but fell on the ground and gasped for breath! The dwarf did not go away until he had thoroughly vented his anger on him. When the two others came home from hunting, Fir-twister said nothing to them of the old manikin and of the blows that he himself had received, and thought, "When they stay at home, they may just try their chance with the little scrubbing-brush;" and the mere thought of that gave him pleasure already.

The next day Rock-splitter stayed at home, and he fared just as Fir-twister had done, he was very ill-treated by the dwarf because he was not willing to give him any meat. When the others came home in the evening, Fir-twister easily saw what he had suffered, but both kept silence, and thought, "Hans also must taste some of that soup."

Hans, who had to stay at home the next day, did his work in the kitchen as it had to be done, and as he was standing skimming the pan, the dwarf came and without more ado demanded a bit of meat. Then Hans thought, "He is a poor wretch, I will give him some of my share, that the others may not run short," and handed him a bit. When the dwarf had devoured it, he again asked for some meat, and good-natured Hans gave it to him, and told him it was a handsome piece, and that he was to be content with it. But the dwarf begged again for the third time. "You are shameless!" said Hans, and gave him none. Then the malicious dwarf wanted to spring on him and treat him as he had treated Fir-twister and Rock-splitter, but he had got to the wrong man. Hans, without exerting himself much, gave him a couple of blows, which made him jump down the castle steps. Hans was about to run after him, but fell right over him, for he was so tall. When he rose up again, the dwarf had got the start of him. Hans hurried after him as far as the forest, and saw him slip into a hole in the rock.

Hans now went home, but he had marked the spot. When the two others came back, they were surprised that Hans was so well. He told them what had happened, and then they no longer concealed how it had fared with them. Hans laughed and said, "It served you quite right; why were you so greedy with your meat? It is a disgrace that you who are so big should have let yourselves be beaten by the dwarf." Then they took a basket and a rope, and all three went to the hole in the rock into which the dwarf had slipped, and let Hans and his club down in the basket. When Hans had reached the bottom, he found a door, and when he opened it a maiden was sitting there who was lovely as any picture, nay, so beautiful that no words can express it, and by her side sat the dwarf and grinned at Hans like a sea otter! She, however, was bound with chains, and looked so mournfully at him that Hans felt great pity for her, and thought to himself, "You must deliver her out of the power of the wicked dwarf," and gave him such a blow with his club that he fell down dead. Immediately the chains fell from the maiden, and Hans was enraptured with her beauty.

She told him she was a King's daughter whom a savage count had stolen away from her home, and imprisoned there among the rocks, because she would have nothing to say to him. The count had, however, set the dwarf as a watchman, and he had made her bear misery and vexation enough. And now Hans placed the maiden in the basket and had her drawn up; the basket came down again, but Hans did not trust his two companions, and thought, "They have already shown themselves to be false, and told me nothing about the dwarf; who knows what design they may have against me?" So he put his club in the basket, and it was lucky he did; for when the basket was halfway up, they let it fall again, and if Hans had really been sitting in it he would have been killed. But now he did not know how he was to work his way out of the depths, and when he turned it over and over in his mind he found no counsel. "It is indeed sad," said he to himself, "that I have to waste away down here," and as he was thus walking backward and forward, he once more came to the little chamber where the maiden had been sitting, and saw that the dwarf had a ring on his finger that shone and sparkled. Then he drew it off and put it on, and when he turned it around on his finger, he suddenly heard something rustle over his head. He looked up and saw spirits of the air hovering above, who told him he was their master, and asked what his desire might be? Hans was at first struck dumb, but afterward he said that they were to carry him above again. They obeyed instantly, and it was just as if he had flown up himself. When, however, he was above again, he found no one in sight. Fir-twister and Rock-splitter had hurried away, and had taken the beautiful maiden with them. But Hans turned the ring, and the spirits of the air came and told him that the two were on the sea. Hans ran and ran without stopping, until he came to the seashore, and there far, far out on the water, he perceived a little boat in which his faithless comrades were sitting; and in fierce anger he leapt, without thinking what he was doing, club in hand into the water, and began to swim, but the club, which weighed a hundred pounds, dragged him deep down until he was all but drowned. Then in the very nick of time he turned his ring, and immediately the spirits of the air came and bore him as swift as lightning into the boat. He swung his club and gave his wicked comrades the reward they merited and threw them into the water, and then he sailed with the beautiful maiden, who had been in the greatest alarm, and whom he delivered for the second time, home to her father and mother, and married her, and all rejoiced exceedingly.

67. *The Peasant in Heaven*

Once upon a time a poor pious peasant died, and arrived before the gate of heaven. At the same time a very rich, rich lord came there who also wanted to get into heaven. Then Saint Peter came with the key, and opened the door, and let the great man in, but apparently did not see the peasant, and shut the door again. And now the peasant outside, heard how the great man was received in heaven with all kinds of rejoicing, and how they were making music, and singing within. At length all became quiet again, and Saint Peter came and opened the gate of heaven, and let the peasant in. The peasant, however, expected that they would make music and sing when he went in also, but all remained quite quiet; he was received with great affection, it is true, and the angels came to meet him, but no one sang. Then the peasant asked Saint Peter how it was that they did not sing for him as they had done when the rich man went in, and said that it seemed to him that there in heaven things were done with just as much partiality as on earth. Then said Saint Peter, "By no means, you are just as dear to us as anyone else, and will enjoy every heavenly delight that the rich man enjoys, but poor fellows like you come to heaven every day, but a rich man like this does not come more than once in a hundred years!"

68. *Lean Lisa*

Lean Lisa was of a very different way of thinking from lazy Harry and fat Trina, who never let anything disturb their peace. She scoured everything with ashes, from morning till evening, and burdened her husband, Long Laurence, with so much work that he had heavier weights to carry than an ass with three sacks. It was, however, all to no purpose, they had nothing and came to nothing. One night as she lay in bed, and could hardly move one limb for weariness, she still did not allow her thoughts to go to sleep. She thrust her elbows into her husband's side, and said, "Listen, Lenz, to what I have been thinking: if I were to find one gold coin and one was given to me, I would borrow another to put to them, and you too should give me another, and then as soon as I had got the four gold coins together, I would buy a young cow." This pleased the husband right well.

"It is true," said he, "that I do not know where I am to get the gold coin that you want as a gift from me; but, if you can get the money together, and can buy a cow with it, you will do well to carry out your project. I shall be glad," he added, "if the cow has a calf, and then I shall often get a drink of milk to refresh me."

"The milk is not for you," said the woman, "we must let the calf suckle that it may become big and fat, and we may be able to sell it well."

"Certainly," replied the man, "but still we will take a little milk; that will do no harm."

"Who has taught you to manage cows?" said the woman; "Whether it does harm or not, I will not allow it, and even if you were to stand on your head for it, you should not have a drop of the milk! Do you think, because there is no satisfying you, Long Laurence, that you are to eat up what I earn with so much difficulty?"

"Wife," said the man, "be quiet, or I will give you a blow on your mouth!"

"What!" cried she. "You threaten me, you glutton, you rascal, you lazy Harry!" She was just laying hold of his hair, but long Laurence got up, seized both Lean Lisa's withered arms in one hand, and with the other he pressed down her head into the pillow, let her scold, and held her until she fell asleep for very weariness. Whether she continued to wrangle when she awoke next morning, or whether she went out to look for the gold coin that she wanted to find, that I know not.

69. *The Hut in the Forest*

A poor lumberjack lived with his wife and three daughters in a little hut on the edge of a lonely forest. One morning as he was about to go to his work, he said to his wife, "Let my lunch be brought into the forest to me by my eldest daughter, or I shall never get my work done, and in order that she may not miss her way," he added, "I will take a bag of millet with me and strew the seeds on the path." When, therefore, the sun was just above the center of the forest, the girl set out on her way with a bowl of soup, but the field sparrows, and wood sparrows, larks and finches, blackbirds and siskins had picked up the millet long before, and the girl could not find the track. Then trusting to chance, she went on and on, until the sun sank and night began to fall. The trees rustled in the darkness, the owls hooted, and she began to be afraid. Then in the distance she perceived a light, which glimmered between the trees.

"There ought to be some people living there, who can take me in for the night," thought she, and went up to the light. It was not long before she came to a house the windows of which were all lighted up.

She knocked, and a rough voice from inside cried, "Come in." The girl stepped into the dark entrance, and knocked at the door of the room. "Just come in," cried the voice, and when she opened the door, an old gray-haired man was sitting at the table, supporting his face with both hands, and his white beard fell down over the table almost as far as the ground. By the stove lay three animals, a hen, a rooster, and a brindled cow. The girl told her story to the old man, and begged for shelter for the night. The man said,

> "Pretty little hen,
> Pretty little rooster,
> And pretty brindled cow,
> What say ye to that?"

"Duks," answered the animals, and that must have meant, "We are willing," for the old man said, "Here you shall have shelter and food, go to the fire, and cook us our supper." The girl found in the kitchen abundance of everything, and cooked a good supper, but had no thought of the animals. She carried the full dishes to the table, seated herself by the gray-haired man, ate and satisfied her hunger.

When she had had enough, she said, "But now I am tired, where is there a bed in which I can lie down, and sleep?" The animals replied,

> "You have eaten with him,
> You have drunk with him,
> You have had no thought for us,
> So find out for yourself where you can pass the night."

Then said the old man, "Just go upstairs, and you will find a room with two beds, shake them up, and put white linen on them, and then I, too, will come and lie down to sleep." The girl went up, and when she had shaken the beds and put clean sheets on, she lay down in one of them without waiting any longer for the old man. After some time, however, the gray-haired man came, took his candle, looked at the girl, and shook his head. When he saw that she had fallen into a sound sleep, he opened a trapdoor, and let her down into the cellar.

Late at night the lumberjack came home, and reproached his wife for leaving him to hunger all day. "It is not my fault," she replied, "the girl went out with your lunch, and must have lost herself, but she is sure to come back tomorrow."

The lumberjack, however, arose before dawn to go into the forest, and requested that the second daughter should take him his lunch that day. "I will take a bag with lentils," said he; "the seeds are larger than millet, the girl will see them better, and can't lose her way." At lunchtime, therefore, the girl took out the food, but the lentils had disappeared. The birds of the forest had picked them up as they had done the day before, and had left none. The girl wandered about in the forest until night, and then she too reached the house of the old man, was told to go in, and begged for food and a bed. The man with the white beard again asked the animals,

> "Pretty little hen,
> Pretty little rooster,
> And pretty brindled cow,
> What say ye to that?"

The animals again replied "Duks," and everything happened just as it had happened the day before. The girl cooked a good meal, ate and drank with the old man, and did not concern herself about the animals, and when she inquired about her bed they answered,

> "You have eaten with him,
> You have drunk with him,
> You have had no thought for us,
> So find out for yourself where you can pass the
> night."

When she was asleep the old man came, looked at her, shook his head, and let her down into the cellar.

On the third morning the lumberjack said to his wife, "Send our youngest child out with my lunch today, she has always been good and obedient, and will stay in the right path, and not run about after every wild bumblebee, as her sisters did."

The mother did not want to do it, and said, "Am I to lose my dearest child, as well?"

"Have no fear," he replied, "the girl will not go astray; she is too prudent and sensible; besides I will take some peas with me, and strew them about. They are still larger than lentils, and will show her the way." But when the girl went out with her basket on her arm, the wood pigeons had already got all the peas in their crops, and she did not know which way she was to turn. She was full of sorrow and never ceased to think how hungry her father would be, and how her good mother would grieve, if she did not go home. At length when it grew dark, she saw the light and came to the house in the forest. She begged quite prettily to be allowed to spend the night there, and the man with the white beard once more asked his animals,

> "Pretty little hen,
> Pretty little rooster,
> And beautiful brindled cow,
> What say ye to that?"

"Duks," said they. Then the girl went to the stove where the animals were lying, and petted the rooster and hen, and stroked their smooth feathers with her hand, and caressed the brindled cow between her horns, and when, in obedience to the old man's orders, she had made ready some good soup, and the bowl was placed upon the table, she said, "Am I to eat as much as I want, and the good animals to have nothing? Outside is food in plenty, I will look after them first." So she went and brought some barley and stewed it for the rooster and hen, and a whole armful of sweet-smelling hay for the cow.

"I hope you will like it, dear animals," said she, "and you shall have a refreshing draft in case you are thirsty." Then she fetched in a bucketful of water, and the rooster and hen jumped onto the edge of it and dipped their beaks in, and then held up their heads as the birds do when they drink, and the brindled cow also took a hearty draft. When the animals were fed, the girl seated herself at the table by the old man, and ate what he had left. It was not long before the rooster and the hen began to thrust their heads beneath their wings, and the eyes of the cow likewise began to blink. Then said the girl, "Ought we not to go to bed?"

> "Pretty little hen,
> Pretty little rooster,
> And pretty brindled cow,
> What say ye to that?"

The animals answered "Duks."

> "You have eaten with us,
> You have drunk with us,
> You have had kind thought for all of us,
> We wish you good-night."

Then the maiden went upstairs, shook the featherbeds, and laid clean sheets on them, and when she had done it the old man came and lay down on one of the beds, and his white beard reached down to his feet. The girl lay down on the other, said her prayers, and fell asleep.

She slept quietly till midnight, and then there was such a noise in the house that she awoke. There was a sound of cracking and splitting in every corner, and the doors sprang open, and beat against the walls. The beams groaned as if they were being torn out of their joints, it seemed as if the staircase were falling down, and at length there was a crash as if the entire roof had fallen in. As, however, all grew quiet once more, and the girl was not hurt, she stayed quietly lying where she was, and fell asleep again. But when she woke up in the morning with the brilliancy of the sunshine, what did her eyes behold? She was lying in a vast hall, and everything around her shone with royal splendor; on the walls, golden flowers grew up on a ground of green silk, the bed was of ivory, and the canopy of red velvet, and on a chair close by, was a pair of shoes embroidered with pearls. The girl believed that she was in a dream, but three richly clad attendants came in, and asked what orders she would like to give? "If you will go," she replied, "I will get up at once and make ready some soup for the old man, and then I will feed the pretty little hen, and the rooster, and the beautiful brindled cow." She thought the old man was up already, and looked around at his bed; he, however, was not lying in it, but a stranger.

And while she was looking at him, and becoming aware that he was young and handsome, he awoke, sat up in bed, and said, "I am a King's son, and was bewitched by a wicked witch, and made to live in this forest, as an old gray-haired man; no one was allowed to be with me but my three attendants in the form of a rooster, a hen, and a brindled cow. The spell was not to be broken until a girl came to us whose heart was so good that she showed herself full of love, not only toward mankind, but toward animals—and that you have done, and by you at midnight we were set free, and the old hut in the forest was changed back again into my royal palace." And when they had arisen, the King's son ordered the three attendants to set out and fetch the father and mother of the girl to the marriage feast.

"But where are my two sisters?" inquired the maiden.

"I have locked them in the cellar, and tomorrow they shall be led into the forest, and shall live as servants to a charcoal burner, until they have grown kinder, and do not leave poor animals to suffer hunger."

70. *Sharing Joy and Sorrow*

There was once a tailor, who was a quarrelsome fellow, and his wife, who was good, industrious, and pious, never could please him. Whatever she did, he was not satisfied, but grumbled and scolded, and knocked her about and beat her. As the authorities at last heard of it, they had him summoned, and put in prison in order to make him better. He was kept for a while on bread and water, and then set free again. He was forced, however, to promise not to beat his wife anymore, but to live with her in peace, and share joy and sorrow with her, as married people ought to do. All went on well for a time, but then he fell into his old ways, and was surly and quarrelsome. And because he dared not beat her, he would seize her by the hair and tear it out. The woman escaped from him, and sprang out into the yard, but he ran after her with his yardstick and scissors, and chased her about, and threw the yardstick and scissors at her, and whatever else came his way. When he hit her he laughed, and when he missed her, he stormed and swore. This went on so long that the neighbors came to the wife's assistance.

The tailor was again summoned before the magistrates, and reminded of his promise. "Dear gentlemen," said he, "I have kept my word, I have not beaten her, but have shared joy and sorrow with her."

"How can that be," said the judge, "when she continually brings such heavy complaints against you?"

"I have not beaten her, but just because she looked so strange I wanted to comb her hair with my hand; she, however, got away from me, and left me quite spitefully. Then I hurried after her, and in order to bring her back to her duty, I threw at her as a well-meant admonition whatever came readily to hand. I have shared joy and sorrow with her also, for whenever I hit her I was full of joy, and she of sorrow, and if I missed her, then she was joyful, and I sorry." The judges were not satisfied with this answer, but gave him the reward he deserved.

71. The Willow Wren

In former days every sound still had its meaning and application. When the smith's hammer resounded, it cried, "Strike away! Strike away."

When the carpenter's plane grated, it said, "Here goes! Here goes."

If the mill wheel began to clack, it said, "Help, Lord God! Help, Lord God!"

And if the miller was a cheat and happened to leave the mill, it spoke high German, and first asked slowly, "Who is there? Who is there?" and then answered quickly, "The miller! the miller!" and at last quite in a hurry, "He steals bravely! He steals bravely! Three pecks in a bushel."

At this time the birds also had their own language, which everyone understood; now it only sounds like chirping, screeching, and whistling, and to some like music without words. It came into the bird's mind, however, that they would no longer be without a ruler, and would choose one of themselves to be their King. One alone among them, the green plover, was opposed to this. He had lived free, and would die free, and anxiously flying hither and thither, he cried, "Where shall I go? Where shall I go?" He retired into a solitary and unfrequented marsh, and showed himself no more among his fellows.

The birds now wished to discuss the matter, and on a fine May morning they all gathered together from the woods and fields: eagles and chaffinches, owls and crows, larks and sparrows, how can I name them all? Even the cuckoo came, and the hoopoe, his clerk, who is so called because he is always heard a few days before him, and a very small bird that as yet had no name, mingled with the band. The hen, which by some accident had heard nothing of the whole matter, was astonished at the great assemblage.

"What, what, what is going to be done?" she cackled.

But the rooster calmed his beloved hen, and said, "Only a lot of rich people," and told her what they had on hand.

It was decided, however, that the one who could fly the highest should be King. A tree frog that was sitting among the bushes, when he heard that, cried a warning, "No, no, no! No!" because he thought that many tears would be shed because of this.

But the crow said, "Caw, caw," and that all would pass off peaceably.

It was now determined that on this fine morning they should at once begin to ascend, so that hereafter no one should be able to say, "I could easily have flown much higher, but the evening came on, and I could do no more." On a given signal, therefore, the whole troop rose up in the air. The dust ascended from the land, and there was tremendous fluttering and whirring and beating of wings, and it looked as if a black cloud was rising up. The little birds were, however, soon left behind. They could go no farther, and fell back to the ground. The larger birds held out longer, but none could equal the eagle, who mounted so high that he could have picked the eyes out of the sun.

And when he saw that the others could not get up to him, he thought, "Why should you fly still higher, you are the King?" and began to let himself down again.

The birds beneath him at once cried to him, "You must be our King, no one has flown so high as you."

"Except me," screamed the little fellow without a name, who had crept into the breast feathers of the eagle. And as he was not at all tired, he rose up and mounted so high that he reached heaven itself.

When, however, he had gone as far as this, he folded his wings together, and called down with clear and penetrating voice, "I am King! I am King."

"You, our King?" cried the birds angrily. "You have compassed it by trick and cunning!" So they made another condition. He should be King who could go down lowest in the ground. How the goose did flap about with its broad breast when it was once more on the land! How quickly the cock scratched a hole! The duck came off the worst of all, for she leapt into a ditch, but sprained her legs, and waddled away to a neighboring pond, crying, "Cheating, cheating!"

The little bird without a name, however, sought out a mouse-hole, slipped down into it, and cried out of it with his small voice, "I am King! I am King!"

"You, our King!" cried the birds still more angrily. "Do you think your cunning shall prevail?" They determined to keep him a prisoner in the hole and starve him out. The owl was placed as sentinel in front of it, and was not to let the rascal out if she had any value for her life. When evening was come all the birds were feeling very tired after exerting their wings so much, so they went to bed with their wives and children.

The owl alone remained standing by the mouse-hole, gazing steadfastly into it with her great eyes. In the meantime she, too, had grown tired and thought to herself, "You might certainly shut one eye, you will still watch with the other, and the little miscreant shall not come out of his hole." So she shut one eye, and with the other looked straight at the mouse-hole. The little fellow put his head out and peeped, and wanted to slip away, but the owl came forward immediately, and he drew his head back again. Then the owl opened the one eye again, and shut the other, intending to shut them in turn all through the night.

But when she next shut the one eye, she forgot to open the other, and as soon as both her eyes were shut she fell asleep. The little fellow soon observed that, and slipped away.

From that day forth, the owl has never dared to show herself by daylight, for if she does the other birds chase her and pluck her feathers out. She only flies out by night, but hates and pursues mice because they make such ugly holes. The little bird, too, is very unwilling to let himself be seen, because he is afraid it will cost him his life if he is caught. He steals about in the hedges, and when he is quite safe, he sometimes cries, "I am King," and for this reason, the other birds call him in mockery, 'King of the hedges' (Zaunkönig). No one, however, was so happy as the lark at not having to obey the little King. As soon as the sun appears, she ascends high in the air and cries, "Ah, how beautiful that is! Beautiful that is! Beautiful, beautiful! Ah, how beautiful that is!"

72. *The Flounder*

The fishes had for a long time been discontented because no order prevailed in their kingdom. None of them turned aside for the others, but all swam to the right or the left as they fancied, or darted between those who wanted to stay together, or got into their way; and a strong one gave a weak one a blow with its tail, which drove it away, or else swallowed it up without more ado. "How delightful it would be," said they, "if we had a king who enforced law and justice among us!" and they met together to choose for their ruler the one who could cleave through the water most quickly, and give help to the weak ones.

They placed themselves in rank and file by the shore, and the pike gave the signal with his tail, on which they all started. Like an arrow, the pike darted away, and with him the herring, the gudgeon, the perch, the carp, and all the rest of them. Even the flounder swam with them, and hoped to reach the winning place.

All at once, the cry was heard, "The herring is first!"

"Who is first?" screamed angrily the flat envious flounder, who had been left far behind. "Who is first?"

"The herring! The herring," was the answer.

"The naked herring?" cried the jealous creature. "The naked herring?" Since that time the flounder's mouth has been at one side for a punishment.

73. *The Bittern and the Hoopoe*

Where do you like best to feed your flocks?" said a man to an old cowherd.

"Here, sir, where the grass is neither too rich nor too poor, or else it is no use."

"Why not?" asked the man.

"Do you hear that melancholy cry from the meadow there?" answered the shepherd. "That is the bittern; he was once a shepherd, and so was the hoopoe also—I will tell you the story. The bittern pastured his flocks on rich green meadows where flowers grew in abundance, so his cows became wild and unmanageable. The hoopoe drove his cattle onto high barren hills, where the wind plays with the sand, and his cows became thin, and got no strength. When it was evening, and the shepherds wanted to drive their cows homewards, the bittern could not get his together again; they were too high-spirited, and ran away from him. He called, 'Come, cows, come,' but it was of no use; they took no notice of his calling. The hoopoe, however, could not even get his cows up on their legs, so faint and weak had they become. 'Up, up, up,' screamed he, but it was in vain, they remained lying on the sand. That is the way when one has no moderation. And to this day, though they have no flocks now to watch, the bittern cries, 'Come, cows, come,' and the hoopoe, 'Up, up, up.'"

74. *The Owl*

Two or three hundred years ago, when people were far from being so crafty and cunning as they are today, an extraordinary event took place in a little town. By some mischance one of the great owls, called horned owls, had come from the neighboring woods into the barn of one of the townsfolk in the nighttime, and when day broke did not dare to venture forth again from her retreat, for fear of the other birds, which raised a terrible outcry whenever she appeared. In the morning when the manservant went into the barn to fetch some straw, he was so mightily alarmed at the sight of the owl sitting there in a corner, that he ran away and announced to his master that a monster, the like of which he had never set eyes on in his life, and which could devour a man without the slightest difficulty, was sitting in the barn, rolling its eyes about in its head. "I know you already," said the master. "You have courage enough to chase a blackbird about the fields, but when you see a dead hen lying, you have to get a stick before you go near it. I must go and see for myself what kind of a monster it is," added the master, and went quite boldly into the granary and looked around him. When, however, he saw the strange grim creature with his own eyes, he was no less terrified than the servant had been. With two bounds he sprang out, ran to his neighbors, and begged them imploringly to lend him assistance against an unknown and dangerous beast, or else the whole town might be in danger if it were to break loose out of the barn, where it was shut up. A great noise and clamor arose in all the streets, the townsmen came armed with spears, hayforks, scythes, and axes, as if they were going out against an enemy; finally, the senators appeared with the mayor at their head. When they had drawn up in the marketplace, they marched to the barn, and surrounded it on all sides. Thereupon one of the most courageous of them stepped forth and entered with his spear lowered, but came running out immediately afterward with a shriek and as pale as death, and could not utter a single word. Yet two others ventured in, but they fared no better.

At last one stepped forth, a great strong man who was famous for his warlike deeds, and said, "You will not drive away the monster by merely looking at him; we must be in earnest here, but I see that you have all turned into women, and not one of you dares to encounter the animal." He ordered them to give him some armor, had a sword and spear brought, and armed himself. All praised his courage, though many feared for his life. The two barn doors were opened, and they saw the owl, which in the meantime had perched herself on the middle of a great crossbeam. He had a ladder brought, and when he raised it, and made ready to climb up, they all cried out to him that he was to bear himself bravely, and commended him to St. George, who slew the dragon.

When he had just got to the top, and the owl perceived that he had designs on her, and was also bewildered by the crowd and the shouting, and knew not how to escape, she rolled her eyes, ruffled her feathers, flapped her wings, snapped her beak, and cried, "Tuwhit, tuwhoo," in a harsh voice. "Strike home! strike home!" screamed the crowd outside to the valiant hero.

"Anyone who was standing where I am standing," answered he, "would not cry, 'Strike home!'" He certainly did plant his foot one rung higher on the ladder, but then he began to tremble, and half-fainting, went back again.

And now there was no one left who dared to put himself in such danger. "The monster," said they, "has poisoned and mortally wounded the very strongest man among us, by snapping at him and just breathing on him! Are we, too, to risk our lives?" They took counsel as to what they ought to do to prevent the whole town being destroyed. For a long time everything seemed to be of no use, but at length the mayor found an expedient.

"My opinion," said he, "is that we ought, out of the common purse, to pay for this barn, and whatever corn, straw, or hay it contains, and thus indemnify the owner, and then burn down the whole building, and the terrible beast with it. Thus no one will have to endanger his life. This is no time for thinking of expense, and niggardliness would be ill applied." All agreed with him. So they set fire to the barn at all four corners, and with it the owl was miserably burned. Let anyone who will not believe it, go there and inquire for himself.

75. *The Moon*

In days gone by there was a land where the nights were always dark, and the sky spread over it like a black cloth, for there the moon never rose, and no star shone in the obscurity. At the creation of the world, the light at night had been sufficient. Three young fellows once went out of this country on a traveling expedition, and arrived in another kingdom, where, in the evening when the sun had disappeared behind the mountains, a shining globe was placed on an oak tree, which shed a soft light far and wide. By means of this, everything could very well be seen and distinguished, even though it was not so brilliant as the sun. The travelers stopped and asked a countryman, who was driving past with his cart, what kind of a light that was. "That is the moon," answered he. "Our mayor bought it for three thalers, and fastened it to the oak tree. He has to pour oil into it daily, and to keep it clean, so that it may always burn clearly. He receives a thaler a week from us for doing it."

When the countryman had driven away, one of them said, "We could make some use of this lamp, we have an oak tree at home, which is just as big as this, and we could hang it on that. What a pleasure it would be not to have to feel about at night in the darkness!"

"I'll tell you what we'll do," said the second; "we will fetch a cart and horses and carry away the moon. The people here may buy themselves another."

"I'm a good climber," said the third, "I will bring it down." The fourth brought a cart and horses, and the third climbed the tree, bored a hole in the moon, passed a rope through it, and let it down. When the shining ball lay in the cart, they covered it over with a cloth, that no one might observe the theft. They conveyed it safely into their own country, and placed it on a high oak. Old and young rejoiced when the new lamp let its light shine over the whole land, and bedrooms and sitting rooms were filled with it. The dwarfs came forth from their caves in the rocks, and the tiny elves in their little red coats danced in rings on the meadows.

The four took care that the moon was provided with oil, cleaned the wick, and received their weekly thaler, but they became old men, and when one of them grew ill, and saw that he was about to die, he appointed that one quarter of the moon, should, as his property, be laid in the grave with him. When he died, the mayor climbed up the tree, and cut off a quarter with the hedge shears, and this was placed in his coffin. The light of the moon decreased, but still not visibly. When the second died, the second quarter was buried with him, and the light diminished. It grew weaker still after the death of the third, who likewise took his part of it away with him; and when the fourth was borne to his grave, the old state of darkness recommenced, and whenever the people went out at night without their lanterns they knocked their heads together.

When, however, the pieces of the moon had united themselves together again in the world below, where darkness had always prevailed, it came to pass that the dead became restless and awoke from their sleep. They were astonished when they were able to see again; the moonlight was quite sufficient for them, for their eyes had become so weak that they could not have borne the brilliance of the sun. They rose up and were merry, and fell into their former ways of living. Some of them went to the play and to dance, others hastened to the public houses, where they asked for wine, got drunk, brawled, quarreled, and at last took up cudgels, and belabored each other. The noise became greater and greater, and at last reached even to heaven.

Saint Peter who guards the gate of heaven thought the lower world had broken out in revolt and gathered together the heavenly troops, which are to drive back the Evil One when he and his associates storm the abode of the blessed. As these, however, did not come, he got on his horse and rode through the gate of heaven, down into the world below. There he reduced the dead to subjection, bade them lie down in their graves again, took the moon away with him, and hung it up in heaven.

76. *The Duration of Life*

When God had created the world and was about to fix the length of each creature's life, the ass came and asked, "Lord, how long shall I live?"

"Thirty years," replied God; "does that content you?"

"Ah, Lord," answered the ass, "that is a long time. Think of my painful existence! To carry heavy burdens from morning to night, to drag sacks of corn to the mill, that others may eat bread, to be cheered and refreshed with nothing but blows and kicks. Relieve me of a portion of this long time."

Then God had pity on him and relieved him of eighteen years. The ass went away comforted, and the dog appeared. "How long would you like to live?" said God to him. "Thirty years are too many for the ass, but you will be satisfied with that."

"Lord," answered the dog, "is that your will? Consider how I shall have to run, my feet will never hold out so long, and when I have once lost my voice for barking, and my teeth for biting, what will be left for me to do but run from one corner to another and growl?" God saw that he was right, and released him from twelve years of life.

Then came the monkey. "You will certainly live thirty years willingly?" said the Lord to him. "You have no need to work as the ass and the dog have to do, and will always enjoy yourself."

"Ah! Lord," he answered, "it may seem as if that were the case, but it is quite different. When it rains porridge I have no spoon. I am always to play merry pranks, and make faces that force people to laugh, and if they give me an apple, and I bite into it, why, it is sour! How often sadness hides itself behind mirth! I shall never be able to hold out for thirty years." God was gracious and took off ten.

At last man appeared, joyous, healthy and vigorous, and begged God to appoint his time for him. "Thirty years shall you live," said the Lord. "Is that enough for you?"

"What a short time," cried man, "when I have built my house and my fire burns on my own hearth; when I have planted trees that blossom and bear fruit, and am just intending to enjoy my life, I am to die! O Lord, lengthen my time."

"I will add to it the ass's eighteen years," said God.

"That is not enough," replied the man.

"You shall also have the dog's twelve years."

"Still too little!"

"Well, then," said God, "I will give you the monkey's ten years also, but more you shall not have." The man went away, but was not satisfied.

So man lives seventy years. The first thirty are his human years, which are soon gone; then is he healthy, merry, works with pleasure, and is glad of his life. Then follow the ass's eighteen years, when one burden after another is laid on him, he has to carry the corn that feeds others, and blows and kicks are the reward of his faithful services. Then come the dog's twelve years, when he lies in the corner, and growls and has no longer any teeth to bite with, and when this time is over the monkey's ten years form the end. Then man is weak-headed and foolish, does silly things, and becomes the jest of the children.

77. Death's Messengers

In ancient times a giant was once traveling on a great highway, when suddenly an unknown man sprang up before him, and said, "Halt, not one step farther!"

"What!" cried the giant. "A creature whom I can crush between my fingers, wants to block my way? Who are you that you dare to speak so boldly?"

"I am Death," answered the other. "No one resists me, and you also must obey my commands."

But the giant refused, and began to struggle with Death. It was a long, violent battle, at last the giant got the upper hand, and struck Death down with his fist, so that he dropped by a stone. The giant went his way, and Death lay there conquered, and so weak that he could not get up again. "What will be done now," said he, "if I stay lying here in a corner? No one will die in the world, and it will get so full of people that they won't have room to stand beside each other."

In the meantime a young man came along the road, who was strong and healthy, singing a song, and glancing around on every side. When he saw the half-fainting one, he went compassionately to him, raised him up, poured a strengthening draft out of his flask for him, and waited till he came around. "Do you know," said the stranger, while he was getting up, "who I am, and who it is whom you have helped on his legs again?"

"No," answered the youth, "I do not know you."

"I am Death," said he. "I spare no one, and can make no exception with you, but that you may see that I am grateful, I promise you that I will not fall on you unexpectedly, but will send my messengers to you before I come and take you away."

"Well," said the youth, "it is something gained that I shall know when you come, and at any rate be safe from you for so long." Then he went on his way, and was lighthearted, and enjoyed himself, and lived without thought.

But youth and health did not last long, soon came sicknesses and sorrows, which tormented him by day, and took away his rest by night. "Die, I shall not," said he to himself, "for Death will send his messengers before that, but I do wish these wretched days of sickness were over." As soon as he felt himself well again he began once more to live merrily. Then one day someone tapped him on the shoulder.

He looked around, and Death stood behind him, and said, "Follow me, the hour of your departure from this world has come."

"What," replied the man, "will you break your word? Did you not promise me that you would send your messengers to me before coming yourself? I have seen none!"

"Silence!" answered Death. "Have I not sent one messenger to you after another? Did not fever come and smite you, and shake you, and cast you down? Has dizziness not bewildered your head? Has not gout twitched you in all your limbs? Did not your ears sing? Did not toothache bite into your cheeks? Was it not dark before your eyes? And besides all that, has not my own brother Sleep reminded you every night of me? Did you not lie by night as if you were already dead?" The man could make no answer; he yielded to his fate, and went away with Death.

78. Master Pfriem
(Master Cobbler's Awl)

Master Pfriem was a short, thin, but lively man, who never rested a moment. His face, of which his turned-up nose was the only prominent feature, was marked with smallpox and pale as death, his hair was gray and shaggy, his eyes small, but they glanced perpetually about on all sides. He saw everything, criticized everything, knew everything best, and was always in the right. When he went into the streets, he moved his arms about as if he were rowing; and once he struck the pail of a girl, who was carrying water, so high in the air that he himself was wetted all over by it. "Stupid thing," cried he to her, while he was shaking himself, "could you not see that I was coming behind you?"

By trade he was a shoemaker, and when he worked he pulled his thread out with such force that he drove his fist into everyone who did not keep far enough off. No apprentice stayed more than a month with him, for he had always some fault to find with the very best work. At one time it was that the stitches were not even, at another that one shoe was too long, or one heel higher than the other, or the leather not cut large enough. "Wait," said he to his apprentice, "I will soon show you how we make skins soft," and he brought a strap and gave him a couple of strokes across the back. He called them all sluggards.

He himself did not turn much work out of his hands, for he never sat still for a quarter of an hour. If his wife got up very early in the morning and lighted the fire, he jumped out of bed, and ran barefooted into the kitchen, crying, "Will you burn my house down for me? That is a fire one could roast an ox by! Does wood cost nothing?" If the servants were standing by their washtubs and laughing, and telling each other all they knew, he scolded them, and said, "There stand the geese cackling, and forgetting their work, to gossip! And why fresh soap? Disgraceful extravagance and shameful idleness into the bargain! They want to save their hands, and not rub the things properly!" And out he would run and knock a pail full of soap and water over, so that the whole kitchen was flooded. Someone was building a new house, so he hurried to the window to look on. "There, they are using that red sandstone again that never dries!" cried he. "No one will ever be healthy in that house! And just look how badly the fellows are laying the stones! Besides, the mortar is good for nothing! It ought to have gravel in it, not sand. I shall live to see that house tumble down on the people who are in it." He sat down, put a couple of stitches in, and then jumped up again, unfastened his leather apron, and cried, "I will just go out, and appeal to those men's consciences."

He stumbled on the carpenters. "What's this?" cried he. "You are not working by the line! Do you expect the beams to be straight? One wrong will put all wrong." He snatched an ax out of a carpenter's hand and wanted to show him how he ought to cut; but as a cart loaded with clay came by, he threw the ax away, and hastened to the peasant who was walking by the side of it: "You are not in your right mind," said he. "Who yokes young horses to a heavily laden cart? The poor beasts will die on the spot." The peasant did not give him an answer, and Pfriem in a rage ran back into his workshop. When he was setting himself to work again, the apprentice reached him a shoe. "Well, what's that again?" screamed he. "Haven't I told you you ought not to cut shoes so broad? Who would buy a shoe like this, which is hardly anything else but a flounder? I insist on my orders being followed exactly."

"Master," answered the apprentice, "you may easily be quite right about the shoe being a bad one, but it is the one that you yourself cut out, and yourself set to work at. When you jumped up a while since, you knocked it off the table, and I have only just picked it up. An angel from heaven, however, would never make you believe that."

One night Master Pfriem dreamed he was dead, and on his way to heaven. When he got there, he knocked loudly at the door. "I wonder," said he to himself, "that they have no knocker on the door—one knocks one's knuckles sore." The apostle Peter opened the door, and wanted to see who demanded admission so noisily. "Ah, it's you, Master Pfriem," said he, "well, I'll let you in, but I warn you that you must give up that habit of yours, and find fault with nothing you see in heaven, or you may fare ill."

"You might have spared your warning," answered Pfriem. "I know already what is seemly, and here, God be thanked, everything is perfect, and there is nothing to blame as there is on Earth." So he went in, and walked up and down the wide expanses of heaven. He looked around him, to the left and to the right, but sometimes shook his head, or muttered something to himself. Then he saw two angels who were carrying away a beam. It was the beam that someone had had in his own eye while he was looking for the splinter in the eye of another. They did not, however, carry the beam lengthways, but obliquely. "Did anyone ever see such a piece of stupidity?" thought Master Pfriem; but he said nothing, and seemed satisfied with it. "It comes to the same thing after all, whichever way they carry the beam, straight or crooked, if they only get along with it, and truly I do not see them knock against anything."

Soon after this he saw two angels who were drawing water out of a well into a bucket, but at the same time he observed that the bucket was full of holes, and that the water was running out of it on every side. They were watering the earth with rain. "Hang it," he exclaimed; but happily recollected himself, and thought, "Perhaps it is only a pastime. If it is an amusement, then it seems they can do useless things of this kind even here in heaven, where people, as I have already noticed, do nothing but idle about."

He went farther and saw a cart that had stuck fast in a deep hole. "It's no wonder," said he to the man who stood by it; "who would load so unreasonably? What have you there?"

"Good wishes," replied the man, "I could not go along the right way with it, but still I have pushed it safely up here, and they won't leave me sticking here." In fact an angel did come and harnessed two horses to it.

"That's quite right," thought Pfriem, "but two horses won't get that cart out, it must at least have four to it." Another angel came and brought two more horses; she did not, however, harness them in front of it, but behind. That was too much for Master Pfriem. "Clumsy creature," he burst out with, "what are you doing there? Has anyone ever since the world began seen a cart drawn in that way? But you, in your conceited arrogance, think that you know everything best." He was going to say more, but one of the inhabitants of heaven seized him by the throat and pushed him forth with irresistible strength. Beneath the gateway Master Pfriem turned his head around to take one more look at the cart, and saw that it was being raised into the air by four winged horses.

At this moment Master Pfriem awoke. "Things are certainly arranged in heaven otherwise than they are on earth," said he to himself, "and that excuses much; but who can see horses harnessed both behind and before with patience; to be sure they had wings, but who could know that? It is, besides, great folly to fix a pair of wings to a horse that has four legs to run with already! But I must get up, or else they will make nothing but mistakes for me in my house. It is a lucky thing for me though, that I am not really dead."

79. *The Goose Girl at the Well*

There was once upon a time a very old woman, who lived with her flock of geese in a desolate place among the mountains, and had a little house there. The house was surrounded by a large forest, and every morning the old woman took her crutch and hobbled into it. There, however, the dame was quite active, more so than anyone would have thought, considering her age, and collected grass for her geese, picked all the wild fruit she could reach, and carried everything home on her back. Anyone would have thought that the heavy load would have weighed her to the ground, but she always brought it safely home. If anyone met her, she greeted him quite courteously. "Good day, dear countryman, it is a fine day. Ah! you wonder that I should drag grass about, but everyone must take his burden on his back."

Nevertheless, people did not like to meet her if they could help it, and took by preference a roundabout way, and when a father with his boys passed her, he whispered to them, "Beware of the old woman. She has claws beneath her gloves; she is a witch."

One morning, a handsome young man was going through the forest. The sun shone bright, the birds sang, a cool breeze crept through the leaves, and he was full of joy and gladness. He had as yet met no one, when he suddenly perceived the old witch kneeling on the ground cutting grass with a sickle. She had already wrapped a whole load into her cloth, and near it stood two baskets, which were filled with wild apples and pears. "But, good little mother," said he, "how can you carry all that away?"

"I must carry it, dear sir," answered she. "Rich folk's children have no need to do such things, but with the peasant folk the saying goes, don't look behind you, you will only see how crooked your back is!"

"Will you help me?" she said, as he remained standing by her. "You have a straight back and young legs still, it would be a trifle to you. Besides, my house is not so very far from here, it stands there on the heath behind the hill. How soon you would bound up there."

The young man took compassion on the old woman. "My father is certainly no peasant," replied he, "but a rich count; nevertheless, that you may see that it is not only peasants who can carry things, I will take your bundle."

"If you will try it," said she, "I shall be very glad. You will certainly have to walk for an hour, but what's that to you? Only you must carry the apples and pears as well." It now seemed to the young man just a little serious, when he heard of an hour's walk, but the old woman would not let him off, packed the bundle on his back, and hung the two baskets on his arm. "See, it is quite light," said she.

"No, it is not light," answered the count, and made a rueful face. "Verily, the bundle weighs as heavily as if it were full of cobblestones, and the apples and pears are as heavy as lead! I can scarcely breathe." He had a mind to put everything down again, but the old woman would not allow it.

"Just look," said she mockingly, "the young gentleman will not carry what I, an old woman, have so often dragged along. You are ready with fine words, but when it comes time to be earnest, you want to take to your heels. Why are you standing loitering there?" she continued. "Step out. No one will take the bundle off again."

As long as he walked on level ground, it was still bearable, but when they came to the hill and had to climb, and the stones rolled down under his feet as if they were alive, it was beyond his strength. The drops of perspiration stood on his forehead, and ran, hot and cold, down his back. "Dame," said he, "I can go no farther. I want to rest a little."

"Not here," answered the old woman. "When we have arrived at our journey's end, you can rest; but now you must go forward. Who knows what good it may do you?"

"Old woman, you are becoming shameless!" said the count, and tried to throw off the bundle, but he labored in vain; it stuck as fast to his back as if it grew there. He turned and twisted, but he could not get rid of it. The old woman laughed at this, and sprang about quite delighted on her crutch.

"Don't get angry, dear sir," said she, "you are growing as red in the face as a turkey-cock! Carry your bundle patiently. I will give you a good present when we get home."

What could he do? He was obliged to submit to his fate, and crawl along patiently behind the old woman. She seemed to grow more and more nimble, and his burden still heavier. All at once she made a spring, jumped onto the bundle and seated herself on the top of it; and however withered she might be, she was yet heavier than the stoutest country lass. The youth's knees trembled, but when he did not go on, the old woman hit him about the legs with a switch and with stinging nettles. Groaning continually, he climbed the mountain, and at length reached the old woman's house, when he was just about to drop.

When the geese perceived the old woman, they flapped their wings, stretched out their necks, ran to meet her, cackling all the while. Behind the flock walked, stick in hand, an old wench, strong and big, but ugly as night. "Good mother," said she to the old woman, "has anything happened to you, you have stayed away so long?"

"By no means, my dear daughter," answered she. "I have met with nothing bad, but, on the contrary, with this kind gentleman, who has carried my burden for me; only think, he even took me on his back when I was tired. The way, too, has not seemed long to us; we have been merry, and have been cracking jokes with each other all the time." At last the old woman slid down, took the bundle off the young man's back, and the baskets from his arm, looked at him quite kindly, and said, "Now seat yourself on the bench before the door, and rest. You have fairly earned your wages, and they shall not be wanting." Then she said to the goose girl, "Go into the house, my dear daughter, it is not becoming for you to be alone with a young gentleman; one must not pour oil onto the fire, he might fall in love with you."

The count knew not whether to laugh or to cry. "Such a sweetheart as that," thought he, "could not touch my heart, even if she were thirty years younger." In the meantime the old woman stroked and fondled her geese as if they were children, and then went into the house with her daughter. The youth lay down on the bench, under a wild apple tree. The air was warm and mild; on all sides stretched a green meadow, which was set with cowslips, wild thyme, and a thousand other flowers; through the middle of it rippled a clear brook on which the sun sparkled, and the white geese went walking backward and forward, or paddled in the water. "It is quite delightful here," said he, "but I am so tired that I cannot keep my eyes open; I will sleep a little. If only a gust of wind does not come and blow my legs off my body, for they are as rotten as tinder."

When he had slept a little while, the old woman came and shook him till he awoke. "Sit up," said she, "you cannot stay here; I have certainly treated you harshly, still it has not cost you your life. Of money and land you have no need, here is something else for you." Thereupon she thrust a little book into his hand, which was cut out of a single emerald.

"Take great care of it," said she, "it will bring you good fortune." The count sprang up, and as he felt that he was quite fresh, and had recovered his vigor, he thanked the old woman for her present, and set off without even once looking back at the "beautiful' daughter. When he was already some way off, he still heard in the distance the noisy cry of the geese.

For three days the count had to wander in the wilderness before he could find his way out. He then reached a large town, and as no one knew him, he was led into the royal palace, where the King and Queen were sitting on their throne. The count fell on one knee, drew the emerald book out of his pocket, and laid it at the Queen's feet. She bade him rise and hand her the little book. Hardly, however, had she opened it, and looked inside, than she fell as if dead to the ground. The count was seized by the King's servants, and was being led to prison, when the Queen opened her eyes, and ordered them to release him, and everyone was to go out, as she wished to speak with him in private.

When the Queen was alone, she began to weep bitterly, and said, "Of what use to me are the splendors and honors with which I am surrounded; every morning I awake in pain and sorrow. I had three daughters, the youngest of whom was so beautiful that the whole world looked on her as a wonder. She was as white as snow, as rosy as apple blossom, and her hair as radiant as sunbeams. When she cried, it was not tears that fell from her eyes, but pearls and jewels. When she was fifteen years old, the King summoned all three sisters to come before his throne. You should have seen how all the people gazed when the youngest entered, it was just as if the sun were rising! Then the King spoke, 'My daughters, I know not when my last day may arrive; I will today decide what each shall receive at my death. You all love me, but the one of you who loves me best, shall fare the best.' Each of them said she loved him best. 'Can you not express to me,' said the King, 'how much you do love me, and thus I shall see what you mean?' The eldest spoke. 'I love my father as dearly as the sweetest sugar.' The second, 'I love my father as dearly as my prettiest dress.' But the youngest was silent. Then the father said, 'And you, my dearest child, how much do you love me?' 'I do not know, and can compare my love with nothing.' But her father insisted that she should name something. So she said at last, 'The best food does not please me without salt, therefore I love my father like salt.' When the King heard that, he fell into a passion, and said, 'If you love me like salt, your love shall also be repaid you with salt.' Then he divided the kingdom between the two elder, but caused a sack of salt to be bound on the back of the youngest, and two servants had to lead her forth into the wild forest. We all begged and prayed for her," said the Queen, "but the King's anger was not to be appeased. How she cried when she had to leave us! The whole road was strewn with the pearls that flowed from her eyes. The King soon afterward repented of his great severity, and had the whole forest searched for the poor child, but no one could find her. When I think that the wild beasts have devoured her, I know not how to contain myself for sorrow; many a time I console myself with the hope that she is still alive, and may have hidden herself in a cave, or has found shelter with compassionate people. But picture to yourself, when I opened your little emerald book, a pearl lay inside, of exactly the same kind as those that used to fall from my daughter's eyes; and then you can also imagine how the sight of it stirred my heart. You must tell me how you came by that pearl."

The count told her that he had received it from the old woman in the forest, who had appeared very strange to him, and must be a witch, but he had neither seen nor heard anything of the Queen's child. The King and the Queen resolved to seek out the old woman. They thought that there where the pearl had been, they would obtain news of their daughter.

The old woman was sitting in that lonely place at her spinning wheel, spinning. It was already dusk, and a log that was burning on the hearth gave a scanty light. All at once there was a noise outside, the geese were coming home from the pasture, and uttering their hoarse cries. Soon afterward the daughter also entered. But the old woman scarcely thanked her, and only shook her head a little. The daughter sat down beside her, took her spinning wheel, and twisted the threads as nimbly as a young girl. Thus they both sat for two hours, and never exchanged a word. At last something rustled at the window, and two fiery eyes peered in. It was an old night owl, which cried, "Uhu!" three times.

The old woman looked up just a little, then she said, "Now, my little daughter, it is time for you to go out and do your work." She rose and went out, and where did she go? Over the meadows ever onward into the valley. At last she came to a well, with three old oak trees standing beside it; meanwhile the moon had risen large and round over the mountain, and it was so light that one could have found a needle. She removed a skin that covered her face, then bent down to the well, and began to wash herself. When she had finished, she dipped the skin also in the water, and then laid it on the meadow, so that it should bleach in the moonlight, and dry again. But how the maiden was changed! Such a change as that was never seen before! When the gray mask fell off, her golden hair broke forth like sunbeams, and spread about like a mantle over her whole form. Her eyes shone out as brightly as the stars in heaven, and her cheeks bloomed a soft red like apple blossom.

But the fair maiden was sad. She sat down and wept bitterly. One tear after another forced itself out of her eyes, and rolled through her long hair to the ground. There she sat, and would have remained sitting a long time, if there had not been a rustling and cracking in the boughs of the neighboring tree. She sprang up like a deer that has been overtaken by the shot of the hunter. Just then the moon was obscured by a dark cloud, and in an instant the maiden had put on the old skin and vanished, like a light blown out by the wind.

She ran back home, trembling like an aspen leaf. The old woman was standing on the threshold, and the girl was about to relate what had befallen her, but the old woman laughed kindly, and said, "I already know all." She led her into the room and lighted a new log. She did not, however, sit down to her spinning again, but fetched a broom and began to sweep and scour. "All must be clean and sweet," she said to the girl.

"But, mother," said the maiden, "why do you begin work at so late an hour? What do you expect?"

"Do you know then what time it is?" asked the old woman.

"Not yet midnight," answered the maiden, "but already past eleven o'clock."

"Do you not remember," continued the old woman, "that it is three years today since you came to me? Your time is up, we can no longer remain together."

The girl was terrified, and said, "Alas! dear mother, will you cast me off? Where shall I go? I have no friends, and no home to which I can go. I have always done as you bade me, and you have always been satisfied with me; do not send me away."

The old woman would not tell the maiden what lay before her. "My stay here is over," she said to her, "but when I depart, house and parlor must be clean: therefore do not hinder me in my work. Have no care for yourself, you shall find a roof to shelter you, and the wages that I will give you shall also content you."

"But tell me what is about to happen," the maiden continued to entreat.

"I tell you again, do not hinder me in my work. Do not say a word more, go to your chamber, take the skin off your face, and put on the silken gown that you had on when you came to me, and then wait in your chamber until I call you."

But I must once more tell of the King and Queen, who had journeyed forth with the count in order to seek out the old woman in the wilderness. The count had strayed away from them in the wood by night, and had to walk onward alone. Next day it seemed to him that he was on the right track. He still went forward, until darkness came on, then he climbed a tree, intending to pass the night there, for he feared that he might lose his way. When the moon illuminated the surrounding country he perceived a figure coming down the mountain. She had no stick in her hand, but yet he could see that it was the goose girl, whom he had seen before in the house of the old woman. "Oho," cried he, "there she comes, and once I get hold of one of the witches, the other shall not escape me!" But how astonished he was, when she went to the well, took off the skin and washed herself, when her golden hair fell down all about her, and she was more beautiful than anyone whom he had ever seen in the whole world. He hardly dared to breathe, but stretched his head as far forward through the leaves as he dared, and stared at her. Either he bent over too far, or whatever the cause might be, the bough suddenly cracked, and that very moment the maiden slipped into the skin, sprang away like a deer, and as the moon was suddenly covered, disappeared from his eyes.

Hardly had she disappeared, before the count descended from the tree, and hastened after her with nimble steps. He had not been gone long before he saw, in the twilight, two figures coming over the meadow. It was the King and Queen, who had perceived from a distance the light shining in the old woman's little house, and were going to it. The count told them what wonderful things he had seen by the well, and they did not doubt that it had been their lost daughter. They walked onward full of joy, and soon came to the little house. The geese were sitting all around it, and had thrust their heads under their wings and were sleeping, and not one of them moved.

The King and Queen looked in at the window; the old woman was sitting there quite quietly spinning, nodding her head and never looking around. The room was perfectly clean, as if the little mist men, who carry no dust on their feet, lived there. Their daughter, however, they did not see. They gazed at all this for a long time, at last they took heart, and knocked softly at the window. The old woman appeared to have been expecting them; she rose, and called out quite kindly, "Come in—I know you already." When they had entered the room, the old woman said, "You might have spared yourself the long walk, if you had not three years ago unjustly driven away your child, who is so good and lovable. No harm has come to her; for three years she has had to tend the geese; with them she has learned no evil, but has preserved her purity of heart. You, however, have been sufficiently punished by the misery in which you have lived." Then she went to the chamber and called, "Come out, my little daughter." Thereupon the door opened, and the princess stepped out in her silken garments, with her golden hair and her shining eyes, and it was as if an angel from heaven had entered.

She went up to her father and mother, fell on their necks and kissed them; there was no help for it, they all had to weep for joy. The young count stood near them, and when she perceived him she became as red in the face as a moss rose, she herself did not know why. The King said, "My dear child, I have given away my kingdom, what shall I give you?"

"She needs nothing," said the old woman. "I give her the tears that she has wept on your account; they are precious pearls, finer than those that are found in the sea, and worth more than your whole kingdom, and I give her my little house as payment for her services." When the old woman had said that, she disappeared from their sight. The walls rattled a little, and when the King and Queen looked around, the little house had changed into a splendid palace, a royal table had been spread, and the servants were running here and there.

The story goes still further, but my grandmother, who related it to me, had partly lost her memory, and had forgotten the rest. I shall always believe that the beautiful princess married the count, and that they remained together in the palace, and lived there in all happiness so long as God willed it. Whether the snow-white geese, which were kept near the little hut, were verily young maidens (no one need take offense,) whom the old woman had taken under her protection, and whether they now received their human form again, and stayed as handmaids to the young Queen, I do not exactly know, but I suspect it. This much is certain, that the old woman was no witch, as people thought, but a wise woman, who meant well. Very likely it was she who, at the princess's birth, gave her the gift of weeping pearls instead of tears. That does not happen nowadays, or else the poor would soon become rich.

80. *Eve's Various Children*

When Adam and Eve were driven out of Paradise, they were compelled to build a house for themselves on unfruitful ground, and eat their bread only by the sweat of their brow. Adam dug up the land, and Eve span. Every year Eve brought a child into the world; but the children were unlike each other, some pretty, and some ugly. After a considerable time had gone by, God sent an angel to them, to announce that he was coming to inspect their household. Eve, delighted that the Lord should be so gracious, cleaned her house diligently, decked it with flowers, and strewed reeds on the floor. Then she brought in her children, but only the beautiful ones. She washed and bathed them, combed their hair, put clean raiment on them, and cautioned them to conduct themselves decorously and modestly in the presence of the Lord. They were to bow down before him civilly, hold out their hands, and to answer his questions modestly and sensibly. The ugly children were, however, not to let themselves be seen. One hid himself beneath the hay, another under the roof, a third in the straw, the fourth in the stove, the fifth in the cellar, the sixth under a tub, the seventh beneath the wine cask, the eighth under an old fur cloak, the ninth and tenth beneath the cloth out of which she always made their clothes, and the eleventh and twelfth under the leather out of which she cut their shoes.

She had scarcely got ready, before there was a knock at the door. Adam looked through a chink, and saw that it was the Lord. Adam opened the door respectfully, and the Heavenly Father entered. There, in a row, stood the pretty children, and bowed before him, held out their hands, and knelt down. The Lord, however, began to bless them, laid his hands on the first, and said, "You shall be a powerful king;" and to the second, "You a prince;" to the third, "You a count;" to the fourth, "You a knight;" to the fifth, "You a nobleman;" to the sixth, "You a town citizen;" to the seventh, "You a merchant;" to the eighth, "You a learned man." He bestowed upon them also all his richest blessings.

When Eve saw that the Lord was so mild and gracious, she thought, "I will bring out my ill-favored children also, it may be that he will bestow his blessing on them likewise." So she ran and brought them out of the hay, the straw, the stove, and wherever else she had concealed them. Then came the whole coarse, dirty, shabby, sooty band.

The Lord smiled, looked at them all, and said, "I will bless these also." He laid his hands on the first, and said to him, "You shall be a peasant;" to the second, "You a fisherman;" to the third, "You a smith;" to the fourth, "You a tanner;" to the fifth, "You a weaver;" to the sixth, "You a shoemaker;" to the seventh, "You a tailor;" to the eighth, "You a potter;" to the ninth, "You a waggoner;" to the tenth, "You a sailor;" to the eleventh, "You an errand boy," to the twelfth, "You a kitchen boy all the days of your life."

When Eve had heard all this she said, "Lord, how unequally you divide your gifts! After all they are all of them my children, whom I have brought into the world, your favors should be given to all alike."

But God answered, "Eve, you do not understand. It is right and necessary that the entire world should be supplied from your children; if they were all princes and lords, who would grow corn, thresh it, grind and bake it? Who would be blacksmiths, weavers, carpenters, masons, laborers, tailors and seamstresses? Each shall have his own place, so that one shall support the other, and all shall be fed like the limbs of one body."

Then Eve answered, "Ah, Lord, forgive me, I was too quick in speaking to you. Have your divine will with my children."

81. *The Nix of the Millpond*

There was once upon a time a miller who lived with his wife in great contentment. They had money and land, and their prosperity increased year by year more and more. But ill luck comes like a thief in the night, as their wealth had increased so did it again decrease, year by year, and at last the miller could hardly call the mill in which he lived, his own. He was in great distress, and when he lay down after his day's work, found no rest, but tossed about in his bed, full of care. One morning he rose before daybreak and went out into the open air, thinking that perhaps there his heart might become lighter. As he was stepping over the mill dam the first sunbeam was just breaking forth, and he heard a rippling sound in the pond. He turned around and perceived a beautiful woman, rising slowly out of the water. Her long hair, which she was holding off her shoulders with her soft hands, fell down on both sides, and covered her white body. He soon saw that she was the Nix of the millpond, and in his fright did not know whether he should run away or stay where he was.

But the nix made her sweet voice heard, called him by his name, and asked him why he was so sad. The miller was at first struck dumb, but when he heard her speak so kindly, he took heart, and told her how he had formerly lived in wealth and happiness, but that now he was so poor that he did not know what to do. "Be easy," answered the nix, "I will make you richer and happier than you have ever been before, only you must promise to give me the young thing which has just been born in your house."

"What else can that be," thought the miller, "but a young puppy or kitten?" and he promised her what she desired. The nix descended into the water again, and he hurried back to his mill, consoled and in good spirits. He had not yet reached it, when the serving maid came out of the house, and cried to him to rejoice, for his wife had given birth to a little boy. The miller stood as if struck by lightning; he saw very well that the cunning nix had been aware of it, and had cheated him.

Hanging his head, he went up to his wife's bedside and when she said, "Why do you not rejoice over the fine boy?" he told her what had befallen him, and what kind of a promise he had given to the nix. "Of what use to me are riches and prosperity?" he added, "if I am to lose my child; but what can I do?"

Even the relations, who had come there to wish them joy, did not know what to say. In the meantime prosperity again returned to the miller's house. All that he undertook succeeded, it was as if presses and coffers filled themselves of their own accord, and as if money multiplied nightly in the cupboards. It was not long before his wealth was greater than it had ever been before. But he could not rejoice over it untroubled, for the bargain that he had made with the nix tormented his soul. Whenever he passed the millpond, he feared she might ascend and remind him of his debt. He never let the boy himself go near the water. "Beware," he said to him, "if you do but touch the water, a hand will rise, seize you, and draw you down."

But as year after year went by and the nix did not show herself again, the miller began to feel at ease. The boy grew up to be a youth and was apprenticed to a hunter. When he had learned everything, and had become an excellent hunter, the lord of the village took him into his service. In the village lived a beautiful and true-hearted maiden, who pleased the hunter, and when his master perceived that, he gave him a little house, the two were married, lived peacefully and happily, and loved each other with all their hearts.

One day the hunter was chasing a deer; and when the animal turned aside from the forest into the open country, he pursued it and at last shot it. He did not notice that he was now in the neighborhood of the dangerous millpond, and went, after he had disemboweled the stag, to the water, in order to wash his bloodstained hands. Scarcely, however, had he dipped them in than the nix ascended, smilingly wound her dripping arms around him, and drew him quickly down under the waves, which closed over him. When it was evening, and the hunter did not return home, his wife became alarmed. She went out to seek him, and as he had often told her that he had to be on his guard against the snares of the nix, and dared not venture into the neighborhood of the millpond, she already suspected what had happened. She hastened to the water, and when she found his hunting pouch lying on the shore, she could no longer have any doubt of the misfortune. Lamenting her sorrow, and wringing her hands, she called on her beloved by name, but in vain. She hurried across to the other side of the pond, and called him anew; she reviled the nix with harsh words, but no answer followed.

The surface of the water remained calm, only the crescent moon stared steadily back at her. The poor woman did not leave the pond. With hasty steps, she paced around and around it, without resting a moment, sometimes in silence, sometimes uttering a loud cry, sometimes softly sobbing.

At last her strength came to an end, she sank down to the ground and fell into a heavy sleep. Presently a dream took possession of her. She was anxiously climbing upward between great masses of rock; thorns and briars caught her feet, the rain beat in her face, and the wind tossed her long hair about. When she had reached the summit, quite a different sight presented itself to her; the sky was blue, the air soft, the ground sloped gently downwards, and on a green meadow, gay with flowers of every color, stood a pretty cottage. She went up to it and opened the door; there sat an old woman with white hair, who beckoned to her kindly.

At that very moment, the poor woman awoke, day had already dawned, and she at once resolved to act in accordance with her dream. She laboriously climbed the mountain; everything was exactly as she had seen it in the night. The old woman received her kindly, and pointed out a chair on which she might sit. "You must have met with a misfortune," she said, "since you have sought out my lonely cottage." With tears, the woman related what had befallen her. "Be comforted," said the old woman, "I will help you. Here is a golden comb for you. Wait till the full moon has risen, then go to the millpond, seat yourself on the shore, and comb your long black hair with this comb. When you are done, lay it down on the bank, and you will see what will happen." The woman returned home, but the time till the full moon came, passed slowly. At last the shining disc appeared in the heavens, then she went out to the millpond, sat down and combed her long black hair with the golden comb, and when she had finished, she laid it down at the water's edge. It was not long before there was a movement in the depths, a wave rose, rolled to the shore, and bore the comb away with it. In not more than the time necessary for the comb to sink to the bottom, the surface of the water parted, and the head of the hunter arose. He did not speak, but looked at his wife with sorrowful glances. At the same instant, a second wave came rushing up, and covered the man's head. All had vanished, the millpond lay peaceful as before, and nothing but the face of the full moon shone on it. Full of sorrow, the woman went back, but again the dream showed her the cottage of the old woman.

Next morning she again set out and complained of her woes to the wise woman. The old woman gave her a golden flute, and said, "Wait till the full moon comes again, then take this flute; play a beautiful tune on it, and when you have finished, lay it on the sand; then you will see what will happen." The wife did as the old woman told her. No sooner was the flute lying on the sand than there was a stirring in the depths, and a wave rushed up and bore the flute away with it. Immediately afterward the water parted, and not only the head of the man, but half of his body also arose. He stretched out his arms longingly toward her, but a second wave came up, covered him, and drew him down again.

"Alas, what does it profit me?" said the unhappy woman, "that I should see my beloved, only to lose him again!" Despair filled her heart anew, but the dream led her a third time to the house of the old woman.

She set out, and the wise woman gave her a golden spinning wheel, consoled her and said, "All is not yet fulfilled, wait until the time of the full moon, then take the spinning wheel, seat yourself on the shore, and spin the spool full, and when you have done that, place the spinning wheel near the water, and you will see what will happen." The woman obeyed all she said exactly; as soon as the full moon showed itself, she carried the golden spinning wheel to the shore, and span industriously until the flax came to an end, and the spool was quite filled with the threads. No sooner was the wheel standing on the shore than there was a more violent movement than before in the depths of the pond, and a mighty wave rushed up, and bore the wheel away with it. Immediately the head and the whole body of the man rose into the air, in a waterspout. He quickly sprang to the shore, caught his wife by the hand and fled. But they had scarcely gone a very little distance, when the whole pond rose with a frightful roar, and streamed out over the open country. The fugitives already saw death before their eyes, when the woman in her terror implored the help of the old woman, and in an instant they were transformed, she into a toad, he into a frog. The flood that had overtaken them could not destroy them, but it tore them apart and carried them far away.

When the water had dispersed and they both touched dry land again, they regained their human form, but neither knew where the other was; they found themselves among strange people, who did not know their native land. High mountains and deep valleys lay between them. In order to keep themselves alive, they were both obliged to tend sheep. For many long years they drove their flocks through field and forest and were full of sorrow and longing. When spring had once more broken forth on the earth, they both went out one day with their flocks, and as chance would have it, they drew near each other. They met in a valley, but did not recognize each other; yet they rejoiced that they were no longer so lonely. Each day they drove their flocks to the same place; they did not speak much, but they felt comforted.

One evening when the full moon was shining in the sky, and the sheep were already at rest, the shepherd pulled the flute out of his pocket, and played on it a beautiful but sorrowful tune. When he had finished he saw that the shepherdess was weeping bitterly. "Why are you weeping?" he asked.

"Alas," answered she, "thus shone the full moon when I played this tune on the flute for the last time, and the head of my beloved rose out of the water." He looked at her, and it seemed as if a veil fell from his eyes, and he recognized his dear wife, and when she looked at him and the moon shone in his face, she knew him also. They embraced and kissed each other, and no one need ask if they were happy.

82. *The Little Folks' Presents*

A tailor and a goldsmith were traveling together, and one evening when the sun had sunk behind the mountains, they heard the sound of distant music, which became more and more distinct. It sounded strange, but so pleasant that they forgot all their weariness and stepped quickly onward. The moon had already arisen when they reached a hill on which they saw a crowd of little men and women, who had taken each other's hands, and were whirling around in the dance with the greatest pleasure and delight.

They sang to it most charmingly, and that was the music which the travelers had heard. In the middle of them sat an old man who was rather taller than the rest. He wore a multicolored coat, and his iron-grey beard hung down over his breast. The two remained standing full of astonishment, and watched the dance. The old man made a sign that they should enter, and the little folks willingly opened their circle. The goldsmith, who had a hump, and like all hunchbacks was brave enough, stepped in; the tailor felt a little afraid at first, and held back, but when he saw how merrily all was going, he plucked up his courage, and followed. The circle closed again directly, and the little folks went on singing and dancing with the wildest leaps. The old man, however, took a large knife that hung to his girdle, whetted it, and when it was sufficiently sharpened, he looked around at the strangers. They were terrified, but they had not much time for reflection, for the old man seized the goldsmith and with the greatest speed, shaved the hair of his head clean off, and then the same thing happened to the tailor. But their fear left them when, after he had finished his work, the old man clapped them both on the shoulder in a friendly manner, as much as to say, they had behaved well to let all that be done to them willingly, and without any struggle. He pointed with his finger to a heap of coals that lay at one side, and signified to the travelers by his gestures that they were to fill their pockets with them. Both of them obeyed, although they did not know of what use the coals would be to them, and then they went on their way to seek a shelter for the night. When they had got into the valley, the clock of the neighboring monastery struck twelve, and the song ceased. In a moment all had vanished, and the hill lay in solitude in the moonlight.

The two travelers found an inn, and covered themselves up on their straw beds with their coats, but in their weariness forgot to take the coals out of them before doing so. A heavy weight on their limbs awakened them earlier than usual. They felt in the pockets, and could not believe their eyes when they saw that they were not filled with coals, but with pure gold; happily, too, the hair of their heads and beards was there again as thick as ever.

They had now become rich folks, but the goldsmith, who, in accordance with his greedy disposition, had filled his pockets better, was twice as rich as the tailor. A greedy man, even if he has much, still wishes to have more, so the goldsmith proposed to the tailor that they should wait another day, and go out again in the evening in order to bring back still greater treasures from the old man on the hill. The tailor refused, and said, "I have enough and am content; now I shall be a master, and marry my dear object (for so he called his sweetheart), and I am a happy man." But he stayed another day to please him.

In the evening the goldsmith hung a couple of bags over his shoulders that he might be able to stow away a great deal, and took the road to the hill. He found, as on the night before, the little folks at their singing and dancing, and the old man again shaved him clean, and signaled to him to take some coal away with him. He was not slow about sticking as much into his bags as would go, went back quite delighted, and covered himself over with his coat. "Even if the gold does weigh heavily," said he, "I will gladly bear that," and at last he fell asleep with the sweet anticipation of waking in the morning an enormously rich man.

When he opened his eyes, he got up in haste to examine his pockets, but how amazed he was when he drew nothing out of them but black coals, and that however often he put his hands in them it was the same. "The gold I got the night before is still there for me," thought he, and went and brought it out, but how shocked he was when he saw that it likewise had again turned into coal. He smacked his forehead with his dusty black hand, and then he felt that his whole head was bald and smooth, as was also the place where his beard should have been. But his misfortunes were not yet over; he now saw for the first time that in addition to the hump on his back, a second, just as large, had grown in front on his breast. Then he recognized the punishment of his greediness, and began to weep aloud.

The good tailor, who was wakened by this, comforted the unhappy fellow as well as he could, and said, "You have been my comrade in my traveling time; you shall stay with me and share in my wealth." He kept his word, but the poor goldsmith was obliged to carry the two humps as long as he lived, and to cover his bald head with a cap.

83. *The Giant and the Tailor*

A certain tailor who was great at boasting but ill at doing, took it into his head to go abroad for a while, and look about the world. As soon as he could manage it, he left his workshop, and wandered on his way, over hill and dale, sometimes here, sometimes there, but ever on and on.

Once when he was out he perceived in the blue distance a steep hill, and behind it a tower reaching to the clouds, which rose up out of a wild dark forest. "Thunder and lightning," cried the tailor, "what is that?" and as he was strongly goaded by curiosity, he went boldly toward it.

But what made the tailor open his eyes and mouth when he came near it, was to see that the tower had legs, and leapt in one bound over the steep hill, and was now standing as an all-powerful giant before him.

"What do you want here, you tiny fly's leg?" cried the giant, with a voice as if it were thundering on every side.

The tailor whimpered, "I want just to look about and see if I can earn a bit of bread for myself, in this forest."

"If that is what you are after," said the giant, "you may have a place with me."

"If it must be, why not? What wages shall I receive?"

"You shall hear what wages you shall have. Every year three hundred and sixty-five days, and when it is leap year, one more into the bargain. Does that suit you?"

"All right," replied the tailor, and thought, in his own mind, "a man must cut his coat according to his cloth; I will try to get away as fast as I can."

At this the giant said to him, "Go, little ragamuffin, and fetch me a jug of water."

"Had I not better bring the well itself at once, and the spring too?" asked the boaster, and went with the pitcher to the water.

"What! The well and the spring too," grumbled the giant into his beard, for he was rather clownish and stupid, and began to be afraid. "That knave is not a fool, he has a wizard in his body. Be on your guard, old Hans, this is no servant for you."

When the tailor had brought the water, the giant bade him go into the forest, and cut a couple of blocks of wood and bring them back.

"Why not the whole forest, at once, with one stroke. The whole forest, young and old, with all that is there, both rough and smooth?" asked the little tailor, and went to cut the wood.

"What! The whole forest, young and old, with all that is there, both rough and smooth, and the well and its spring too," growled the credulous giant into his beard, and was still more terrified. "The knave can do much more than bake apples, and has a wizard in his body. Be on your guard, old Hans, this is no servant for you!"

When the tailor had brought the wood, the giant commanded him to shoot two or three wild boars for supper. "Why not rather a thousand at one shot, and bring them all here?" inquired the ostentatious tailor.

"What!" cried the timid giant in great terror; "let well alone tonight, and lie down to rest."

The giant was so terribly alarmed that he could not close an eye all night long for thinking what would be the best way to get rid of this accursed sorcerer of a servant. Time brings counsel. Next morning the giant and the tailor went to a marsh, around which stood a number of willow trees. Then said the giant, "Listen, tailor, seat yourself on one of the willow branches, I long of all things to see if you are big enough to bend it down." All at once the tailor was sitting on it, holding his breath, and making himself so heavy that the bough bent down. When, however, he was compelled to draw breath, it flung him (for unfortunately he had not put his flatiron in his pocket) so high into the air that he never was seen again, and this to the great delight of the giant. If the tailor has not fallen down again, he must be hovering about in the air.

84. *The Nail*

A merchant had done good business at the fair; he had sold his wares, and lined his money bags with gold and silver. Then he wanted to travel homeward, and be in his own house before nightfall. So he packed his trunk with the money on his horse, and rode away.

At noon he rested in a town, and when he wanted to go farther the stable boy brought out his horse and said, "A nail is wanting, sir, in the shoe of its left hind foot."

"Let it be wanting," answered the merchant; "the shoe will certainly stay on for the six miles I have still to go. I am in a hurry."

In the afternoon, when he once more alighted and had his horse fed, the stable boy went into the room to him and said, "Sir, a shoe is missing from your horse's left hind foot. Shall I take him to the blacksmith?"

"Let it still be wanting," answered the man; "the horse can very well hold out for the couple of miles that remain. I am in haste."

He rode forth, but before long the horse began to limp. It had not limped long before it began to stumble, and it had not stumbled long before it fell down and broke its leg. The merchant was forced to leave the horse where it was, and unbuckle the trunk, take it on his back, and go home on foot. And there he did not arrive until quite late at night. "And that unlucky nail," said he to himself, "has caused all this disaster."

Hasten slowly.

85. *The Poor Boy in the Grave*

There was once a poor shepherd boy whose father and mother were dead, and he was placed by the authorities in the house of a rich man, who was to feed him and bring him up. The man and his wife had, however, bad hearts, and were greedy and anxious about their riches, and vexed whenever anyone put a morsel of their bread in his mouth. The poor young fellow might do what he liked, he got little to eat, but only so many blows the more.

One day he had to watch a hen and her chickens, but she ran through a hedge with them, and a hawk darted down instantly, and carried her off through the air. The boy called, "Thief! Thief! Rascal!" with all the strength of his body. But what good did that do? The hawk did not bring its prey back again.

The man heard the noise, and ran to the spot, and as soon as he saw that his hen was gone, he fell in a rage, and gave the boy such a beating that he could not stir for two days. Then he had to take care of the chickens without the hen, but now his difficulty was greater, for one ran here and the other there. He thought he was doing a very wise thing when he tied them all together with a string, because then the hawk would not be able to steal any of them away from him. But he was very much mistaken. After two days, worn out with running about and hunger, he fell asleep; the bird of prey came, and seized one of the chickens, and as the others were tied fast to it, it carried them all off together, perched itself on a tree, and devoured them. The farmer was just coming home, and when he saw the misfortune, he got angry and beat the boy so unmercifully that he was forced to lie in bed for several days.

When he was on his legs again, the farmer said to him, "You are too stupid for me, I cannot make a herdsman of you, you must go as errand boy." Then he sent him to the judge, to whom he was to carry a basketful of grapes, and he gave him a letter as well.

On the way hunger and thirst tormented the unhappy boy so violently that he ate two of the bunches of grapes. He took the basket to the judge, but when the judge had read the letter, and counted the bunches he said, "Two clusters are wanting." The boy confessed quite honestly that, driven by hunger and thirst, he had devoured the two that were wanting. The judge wrote a letter to the farmer, and asked for the same number of grapes again. These also the boy had to take to him with a letter.

As he again was so extremely hungry and thirsty, he could not help it, and again ate two bunches. But first he took the letter out of the basket, put it under a stone and seated himself on it in order that the letter might not see and betray him. The judge, however, again made him give an explanation about the missing bunches. "Ah," said the boy, "how have you learned that? The letter could not know about it, for I put it under a stone before I did it." The judge could not help laughing at the boy's simplicity, and sent the man a letter in which he cautioned him to keep the poor boy better, and not let him want for meat and drink, and also that he was to teach him what was right and what was wrong.

"I will soon show you the difference," said the hard man. "If you will eat, you must work, and if you do anything wrong, you shall be quite sufficiently taught by blows."

The next day he set him a hard task. He was to chop two bundles of straw for food for the horses, and then the man threatened: "In five hours," said he, "I shall be back again, and if the straw is not cut to chaff by that time, I will beat you until you cannot move a limb." The farmer went with his wife and the servant to the yearly fair, and left nothing behind for the boy but a small bit of bread.

The boy seated himself on the bench, and began to work with all his might. As he got warm over it he put his little coat off and threw it on the straw. In his terror lest he should not get done in time he kept constantly cutting, and in his haste, without noticing it, he chopped his little coat as well as the straw. He became aware of the misfortune too late; there was no repairing it. "Ah," cried he, "now all is over for me! The wicked man did not threaten me for nothing; if he comes back and sees what I have done, he will kill me. Rather than that I will take my own life."

The boy had once heard the farmer's wife say, "I have a pot with poison in it under my bed." She, however, had only said that to keep away greedy people, for there was honey in it. The boy crept under the bed, brought out the pot, and ate all that was in it.

"I do not know," said he. "Folks say death is bitter, but it tastes very sweet to me. It is no wonder that the farmer's wife has so often longed for death." He seated himself in a little chair, and was prepared to die. But instead of becoming weaker he felt himself strengthened by the nourishing food. "It cannot have been poison," thought he, "but the farmer once said there was a small bottle of poison for flies in the box in which he keeps his clothes; that, no doubt, will be the true poison, and bring death to me." It was, however, not poison for flies, but Hungarian wine. The boy got out the bottle, and emptied it.

"This death tastes sweet too," said he, but shortly after when the wine began to mount into his brain and stupefy him, he thought his end was drawing near. "I feel that I must die," said he. "I will go away to the churchyard, and seek a grave." He staggered out, reached the churchyard, and laid himself in a newly dug grave. He lost his senses more and more. In the neighborhood was an inn where a wedding was being held; when he heard the music, he fancied he was already in Paradise, until at length he lost all consciousness. The poor boy never awoke again; the heat of the strong wine and the cold night-dew deprived him of life, and he remained in the grave in which he had laid himself.

When the farmer heard the news of the boy's death he was terrified, and afraid of being brought to justice indeed, his distress took such a powerful hold of him that he fell fainting to the ground. His wife, who was standing on the hearth with a pan of hot fat, ran to him to help him. But the flames darted against the pan, the whole house caught fire, in a few hours it lay in ashes, and the rest of the years they had to live they passed in poverty and misery, tormented by the pangs of conscience.

86. *The True Bride*

There was once on a time a girl who was young and beautiful, but she had lost her mother when she was quite a child, and her stepmother did all she could to make the girl's life wretched. Whenever this woman gave her anything to do, she worked at it tirelessly, and did everything that lay in her power. Still she could not touch the heart of the wicked woman by that; she was never satisfied; it was never enough. The harder the girl worked, the more work was put upon her, and all that the woman thought of was how to weigh her down with still heavier burdens, and make her life still more miserable.

One day she said to her, "Here are twelve pounds of feathers, which you must strip, and if they are not done this evening, you may expect a good beating. Do you imagine you are to idle away the whole day?" The poor girl sat down to the work, but tears ran down her cheeks as she did so, for she saw plainly enough that it was quite impossible to finish the work in one day. Whenever she had a little heap of feathers lying before her, and she sighed or clasped her hands together in her anguish, they flew away, and she had to pick them out again, and begin her work anew.

Then she put her elbows on the table, laid her face in her two hands, and cried, "Is there no one, then, on God's earth to have pity on me?"

Then she heard a low voice that said, "Be comforted, my child, I have come to help you." The maiden looked up, and an old woman was by her side. She took the girl kindly by the hand, and said, "Only tell me what is troubling you."

Since she spoke so kindly, the girl told her of her miserable life, and how one burden after another was laid upon her, and she never could get to the end of the work that was given to her. "If I have not done these feathers by this evening, my stepmother will beat me; she has threatened she will, and I know she keeps her word."

Her tears began to flow again, but the good old woman said, "Do not be afraid, my child; rest a while, and in the meantime I will look to your work." The girl lay down on her bed, and soon fell asleep. The old woman seated herself at the table with the feathers, and how they did fly off the quills, which she scarcely touched with her withered hands! The twelve pounds were soon finished, and when the girl awoke, great snow-white heaps were lying, piled up, and everything in the room was neatly cleared away, but the old woman had vanished. The maiden thanked God, and sat still till evening came, when the stepmother came in and marveled to see the work completed.

"Just look, you awkward creature," said she, "what can be done when people are industrious; and why could you not set about something else? There you sit with your hands crossed." When she went out she said, "The creature is worth more than her salt. I must give her some work that is still harder."

Next morning she called the girl, and said, "There is a spoon for you; with that you must empty out for me the great pond that is beside the garden, and if it is not done by night, you know what will happen." The girl took the spoon, and saw that it was full of holes; but even if it had not been, she never could have emptied the pond with it. She set to work at once, knelt down by the water, into which her tears were falling, and began to empty it.

But the good old woman appeared again, and when she learned the cause of her grief, she said, "Be of good cheer, my child. Go into the thicket and lie down and sleep; I will soon do your work."

As soon as the old woman was alone, she barely touched the pond, and a vapor rose up on high from the water, and mingled itself with the clouds. Gradually the pond was emptied, and when the maiden awoke before sunset and came there, she saw nothing but the fishes that were struggling in the mud. She went to her stepmother, and showed her that the work was done. "It ought to have been done long before this," said she, and grew white with anger, but she meditated something new.

On the third morning she said to the girl, "You must build me a castle on the plain there, and it must be ready by the evening."

The maiden was dismayed, and said, "How can I complete such a great work?"

"I will endure no opposition," screamed the stepmother. "If you can empty a pond with a spoon that is full of holes, you can build a castle too. I will take possession of it this very day, and if anything is wanting, even if it be the most trifling thing in the kitchen or cellar, you know what lies before you!" She drove the girl out, and when she entered the valley, the rocks were there, piled up one above the other, and all her strength would not have enabled her even to move the very smallest of them. She sat down and wept, and still she hoped the old woman would help her.

The old woman was not long in coming; she comforted her and said, "Lie down there in the shade and sleep, and I will soon build the castle for you. If it would be a pleasure to you, you can live in it yourself." When the maiden had gone away, the old woman touched the gray rocks. They began to rise, and immediately moved together as if giants had built the walls; and on these the building arose, and it seemed as if countless hands were working invisibly, and placing one stone upon another. There was a dull heavy noise from the ground; pillars arose of their own accord on high, and placed themselves in order near each other. The tiles laid themselves in order on the roof, and when noon came, the great weathervane was already turning itself on the summit of the tower, like a golden figure of the Virgin with fluttering garments. The inside of the castle was being finished while evening was drawing near. How the old woman managed it, I know not; but the walls of the rooms were hung with silk and velvet, embroidered chairs were there, and richly ornamented armchairs by marble tables; crystal chandeliers hung down from the ceilings, and mirrored themselves in the smooth pavement; green parrots were there in gilt cages, and so were strange birds that sang most beautifully, and there was on all sides as much magnificence as if a king were going to live there.

The sun was just setting when the girl awoke, and the brightness of a thousand lights flashed in her face. She hurried to the castle, and entered by the open door. The steps were spread with red cloth, and the golden balustrade beset with flowering trees. When she saw the splendor of the apartment, she stood as if turned to stone. Who knows how long she might have stood there if she had not remembered the stepmother? "Alas!" she said to herself, "if she could but be satisfied at last, and would give up making my life a misery to me." The girl went and told her that the castle was ready.

"I will move into it at once," said she, and rose from her seat. When they entered the castle, she was forced to hold her hand before her eyes, the brilliancy of everything was so dazzling. "You see," said she to the girl, "how easy it has been for you to do this; I ought to have given you something harder." She went through all the rooms, and examined every corner to see if anything was wanting or defective; but she could discover nothing. "Now we will go down below," said she, looking at the girl with malicious eyes. "The kitchen and the cellar still have to be examined, and if you have forgotten anything you shall not escape your punishment." But the fire was burning on the hearth, and the meat was cooking in the pans, the tongs and shovel were leaning against the wall, and the shining brazen utensils all arranged in sight. Nothing was wanting, not even a coal box and water pail. "Which is the way to the cellar?" she cried. "If that is not abundantly filled, it shall go ill with you." She herself raised up the trapdoor and descended; but she had hardly made two steps before the heavy trapdoor, which was only laid back, fell down. The girl heard a scream, lifted up the door very quickly to go to her aid, but she had fallen down, and the girl found her lying lifeless at the bottom.

And now the magnificent castle belonged to the girl alone. She at first did not know how to reconcile herself to her good fortune. Beautiful dresses were hanging in the wardrobes, the chests were filled with gold or silver, or with pearls and jewels, and she never felt a desire that she was not able to gratify. And soon the fame of the beauty and riches of the maiden went over all the world. Wooers presented themselves daily, but none pleased her. At length the son of the King came and he knew how to touch her heart, and she betrothed herself to him. In the garden of the castle was a lime tree, under which they were one day sitting together, when he said to her, "I will go home and obtain my father's consent to our marriage. I entreat you to wait for me here under this lime tree, I shall be back with you in a few hours."

The maiden kissed him on his left cheek, and said, "Keep true to me, and never let anyone else kiss you on this cheek. I will wait here under the lime tree until you return."

The maid stayed beneath the lime tree until sunset, but he did not return. She sat three days from morning till evening, waiting for him, but in vain. As he still was not there by the fourth day, she said, "Some accident has assuredly befallen him. I will go out and seek him, and will not come back until I have found him." She packed up three of her most beautiful dresses, one embroidered with bright stars, the second with silver moons, the third with golden suns, tied up a handful of jewels in her handkerchief, and set out. She inquired everywhere for her betrothed, but no one had seen him; no one knew anything about him. Far and wide did she wander through the world, but she found him not. At last she hired herself to a farmer as a cowherd, and buried her dresses and jewels beneath a stone.

And now she lived as a herdswoman, guarded her herd, and was very sad and full of longing for her beloved one; she had a little calf that she taught to know her, and fed it out of her own hand, and when she said,

> "Little calf, little calf, kneel by my side,
> And do not forget your shepherd-maid,
> As the prince forgot his betrothed bride,
> Who waited for him 'neath the lime tree's shade."

The little calf knelt down, and she stroked it.

And when she had lived for a couple of years alone and full of grief, a report was spread over all the land that the King's daughter was about to celebrate her marriage. The road to the town passed through the village where the maiden was living, and it came to pass that once when the maiden was driving out her herd, her bridegroom traveled by. He was sitting proudly on his horse, and never looked around, but when she saw him she recognized her beloved, and it was just as if a sharp knife had pierced her heart. "Alas!" said she, "I believed him true to me, but he has forgotten me."

Next day he again came along the road. When he was near her she said to the little calf,

> "Little calf, little calf, kneel by my side,
> And do not forget your shepherd-maid,
> As the prince forgot his betrothed bride,
> Who waited for him 'neath the lime tree's shade."

When he was aware of the voice, he looked down and reined in his horse. He looked into the girl's face, and then put his hands before his eyes as if he were trying to remember something, but he soon rode onward and was out of sight. "Alas!" said she, "he no longer knows me," and her grief was ever greater.

Soon after this a great festival three days long was to be held at the King's court, and the whole country was invited to it.

"Now I will try my last chance," thought the maiden, and when evening came she went to the stone under which she had buried her treasures. She took out the dress with the golden suns, put it on, and adorned herself with the jewels. She let down her hair, which she had concealed under a handkerchief, and it fell down in long curls about her, and thus she went into the town, and in the darkness was observed by no one. When she entered the brightly-lighted hall, everyone started back in amazement, but no one knew who she was. The King's son went to meet her, but he did not recognize her. He led her out to dance, and was so enchanted with her beauty, that he thought no more of the other bride. When the feast was over, she vanished in the crowd, and hastened before daybreak to the village, where she once more put on her shepherdess's dress.

Next evening she took out the dress with the silver moons, and put a half-moon made of precious stones in her hair. When she appeared at the festival, all eyes were turned upon her, but the King's son hastened to meet her, and filled with love for her, danced with her alone, and no longer so much as glanced at anyone else. Before she went away she was forced to promise him to come again to the festival on the last evening.

When she appeared for the third time, she wore the star dress, which sparkled at every step she took, and her hair ribbon and girdle were starred with jewels. The prince had already been waiting for her for a long time, and forced his way up to her. "Do but tell who you are," said he, "I feel just as if I had already known you a long time."

"Do you not know what I did when you left me?" Then she stepped up to him, and kissed him on his left cheek, and in a moment it was as if scales fell from his eyes, and he recognized the true bride.

"Come," said he to her, "here I stay no longer," gave her his hand, and led her down to the carriage. The horses hurried away to the magic castle as if the wind had been harnessed to the carriage. The illuminated windows already shone in the distance. When they drove past the lime tree, countless fireflies were swarming about it. It shook its branches, and sent forth their fragrance. On the steps flowers were blooming, and the room echoed with the song of strange birds, but in the hall the entire court was assembled, and the priest was waiting to marry the bridegroom to the true bride.

87. *The Hare and the Hedgehog*

This story, my dear young folks, seems to be false, but it really is true, for my grandfather, from whom I have it, used always, when relating it, to say complacently, "It must be true, my son, or else no one could tell it to you." The story is as follows. One Sunday morning about harvesttime, just as the buckwheat was in bloom, the sun was shining brightly in heaven, the east wind was blowing warmly over the stubble fields, the larks were singing in the air, the bees buzzing among the buckwheat, the people were all going in their Sunday clothes to church, and all creatures were happy, and the hedgehog was happy too.

The hedgehog, however, was standing by his door with his arms folded, enjoying the morning breezes, and slowly trilling a little song to himself, which was neither better nor worse than the songs that hedgehogs are in the habit of singing on a blessed Sunday morning. While he was thus singing half aloud to himself, it suddenly occurred to him that, while his wife was washing and drying the children, he might very well take a walk into the field, and see how his turnips were going on. The turnips were, in fact, close beside his house, and he and his family were accustomed to eating them, for which reason he looked upon them as his own. No sooner said than done. The hedgehog shut the door behind him, and took the path to the field. He had not gone very far from home, and was just turning around the sloebush that stands there outside the field, to go up into the turnip field, when he observed the hare who had gone out on business of the same kind, namely, to visit his cabbages.

When the hedgehog caught sight of the hare, he bade him a friendly good morning. But the hare, who was in his own way a distinguished gentleman, and frightfully haughty, did not return the hedgehog's greeting, but said to him, assuming at the same time a very contemptuous manner, "How do you happen to be running about here in the field so early in the morning?"

"I am taking a walk," said the hedgehog.

"A walk!" said the hare, with a smile. "It seems to me that you might use your legs for a better purpose."

This answer made the hedgehog furiously angry, for he can bear anything but an attack on his legs, just because they are crooked by nature. So now the hedgehog said to the hare, "You seem to imagine that you can do more with your legs than I with mine."

"That is just what I do think," said the hare.

"That can be put to the test," said the hedgehog. "I wager that if we run a race, I will outstrip you."

"That is ridiculous! You with your short legs!" said the hare. "But for my part I am willing, if you have such a monstrous fancy for it. What shall we wager?"

"A golden louis d'or and a bottle of brandy," said the hedgehog.

"Done," said the hare. "Shake hands on it, and then we may as well come off at once."

"Nay," said the hedgehog, "there is no such great hurry! I am still fasting, I will go home first, and have a little breakfast. In half an hour I will be back again at this place."

Then the hedgehog departed, for the hare was quite satisfied with this. On his way the hedgehog thought to himself, "The hare relies on his long legs, but I will contrive to get the better of him. He may be a great man, but he is a very silly fellow, and he shall pay for what he has said." So when the hedgehog reached home, he said to his wife, "Wife, dress yourself quickly, you must go out to the field with me."

"What is going on, then?" said his wife.

"I have made a wager with the hare, for a gold louis d'or and a bottle of brandy. I am to run a race with him, and you must be present."

"Good heavens, husband," the wife now cried, "are you not right in your mind, have you completely lost your wits? What can make you want to run a race with the hare?"

"Hold your tongue, woman," said the hedgehog, "that is my affair. Don't begin to discuss things that are matters for men. Be off, dress yourself, and come with me." What could the hedgehog's wife do? She was forced to obey him, whether she liked it or not.

So when they had set out on their way together, the hedgehog said to his wife, "Now pay attention to what I am going to say. Look, I will make the long field our racecourse. The hare shall run in one furrow, and I in another, and we will begin to run from the top. Now all that you have to do is to place yourself here below in the furrow, and when the hare arrives at the end of the furrow, on the other side of you, you must cry out to him, 'I am here already!'"

Then they reached the field, and the hedgehog showed his wife her place, and then walked up the field. When he reached the top, the hare was already there. "Shall we start?" said the hare.

"Certainly," said the hedgehog.

"Then both at once." So saying, each placed himself in his own furrow. The hare counted, "Once, twice, thrice, and away!" and went off like a whirlwind down the field. The hedgehog, however, only ran about three paces, and then he stooped down in the furrow, and stayed quietly where he was.

When the hare therefore arrived in full career at the lower end of the field, the hedgehog's wife met him with the cry, "I am here already!"

The hare was shocked and wondered not a little, he thought no other than that it was the hedgehog himself who was calling to him, for the hedgehog's wife looked just like her husband. The hare, however, thought to himself, "That has not been done fairly," and cried, "It must be run again, let us have it again." And once more he went off like the wind in a storm, so that he seemed to fly. But the hedgehog's wife stayed quietly in her place.

So when the hare reached the top of the field, the hedgehog himself cried out to him, "I am here already."

The hare, however, quite beside himself with anger, cried, "It must be run again, we must have it again."

"All right," answered the hedgehog, "for my part we'll run as often as you choose."

So the hare ran seventy-three times more, and the hedgehog always held out against him, and every time the hare reached either the top or the bottom, either the hedgehog or his wife said, "I am here already."

At the seventy-fourth time, however, the hare could no longer reach the end. In the middle of the field he fell to the ground, blood streamed out of his mouth, and he lay dead on the spot. But the hedgehog took the louis d'or which he had won and the bottle of brandy, called his wife out of the furrow, and both went home together in great delight, and if they are not dead, they are living there still.

This is how it happened that the hedgehog made the hare run races with him on the Buxtehuder heath till he died, and since that time no hare has ever had any fancy for running races with a Buxtehuder hedgehog.

The moral of this story, however, is, firstly, that no one, however great he may be, should permit himself to jest at anyone beneath him, even if he is only a hedgehog. And, secondly, it teaches, that when a man marries, he should take a wife in his own position, who looks just as he himself looks. So whoever is a hedgehog let him see to it that his wife is a hedgehog also, and so forth.

88. *The Spindle, the Shuttle, and the Needle*

There was once a girl whose father and mother died while she was still a little child. All alone, in a small house at the end of the village, dwelt her godmother, who supported herself by spinning, weaving, and sewing. The old woman took the forlorn child to live with her, kept her to her work, and educated her in all that is good. When the girl was fifteen years old, the old woman became ill, called the child to her bedside, and said, "Dear daughter, I feel my end drawing near. I leave you the little house, which will protect you from wind and weather, and my spindle, shuttle, and needle, with which you can earn your bread." Then she laid her hands on the girl's head, blessed her, and said, "Only preserve the love of God in your heart, and all will go well with you."

Thereupon she closed her eyes, and when she was laid in the earth, the maiden followed the coffin, weeping bitterly, and paid her the last mark of respect. And now the maiden lived quite alone in the little house, and was industrious, and span, wove, and sewed, and the blessing of the good old woman was on all that she did. It seemed as if the flax in the room increased of its own accord, and whenever she wove a piece of cloth or carpet, or had made a shirt, she at once found a buyer who paid her amply for it, so that she was in want of nothing, and even had something to share with others.

About this time, the son of the King was traveling about the country looking for a bride. He was not to choose a poor one, and did not want to have a rich one. So he said, "She shall be my wife who is the poorest, and at the same time the richest." When he came to the village where the maiden dwelt, he inquired, as he did wherever he went, who was the richest and also the poorest girl in the place? They first named the richest; the poorest, they said, was the girl who lived in the small house quite at the end of the village. The rich girl was sitting in all her splendor before the door of her house, and when the prince approached her, she got up, went to meet him, and made him a low curtsy. He looked at her, said nothing, and rode on.

When he came to the house of the poor girl, she was not standing at the door, but sitting in her little room. He stopped his horse, and saw through the window, on which the bright sun was shining, the girl sitting at her spinning wheel, busily spinning. She looked up, and when she saw that the prince was looking in, she blushed all over her face, let her eyes fall, and went on spinning. I do not know whether, just at that moment, the thread was quite even; but she went on spinning until the King's son had ridden away again. Then she went to the window, opened it, and said, "It is so warm in this room!" but she still looked after him as long as she could distinguish the white feathers in his hat. Then she sat down to work again in her own room and went on with her spinning, and a saying, which the old woman had often repeated when she was sitting at her work, came into her mind, and she sang these words to herself—

> "Spindle, my spindle, haste, haste you away,
> And here to my house bring the wooer, I
> pray."

And what do you think happened? The spindle sprang out of her hand in an instant, and out of the door, and when, in her astonishment, she got up and looked after it, she saw that it was dancing out merrily into the open country, and drawing a shining golden thread after it. Before long, it had entirely vanished from her sight. As she now had no spindle, the girl took the weaver's shuttle in her hand, sat down to her loom, and began to weave.

The spindle, however, danced continually onward, and just as the thread came to an end, reached the prince. "What do I see?" he cried; "the spindle certainly wants to show me the way!" and turned his horse about, and rode back with the golden thread.

The girl was, however, sitting at her work singing,

> "Shuttle, my shuttle, weave well this day,
> And guide the wooer to me, I pray."

Immediately the shuttle sprang out of her hand and out through the door. Before the threshold, however, it began to weave a carpet that was more beautiful than the eyes of man had ever yet beheld. Lilies and roses blossomed on both sides of it, and on a golden ground in the center green branches ascended, under which bounded hares and rabbits, stags and deer stretched their heads in between them, brightly-colored birds were sitting in the branches above; they lacked nothing but the gift of song. The shuttle leapt here and there, and everything seemed to grow of its own accord.

As the shuttle had run away, the girl sat down to sew. She held the needle in her hand and sang,

> "Needle, my needle, sharp-pointed and fine,
> Prepare for a wooer this house of mine."

Then the needle leapt out of her fingers, and flew everywhere about the room as quick as lightning. It was just as if invisible spirits were working; they covered tables and benches with green cloth in an instant, and the chairs with velvet, and hung the windows with silken curtains. Hardly had the needle put in the last stitch than the maiden saw through the window the white feathers of the prince, whom the spindle had brought there by the golden thread. He alighted, stepped over the carpet into the house, and when he entered the room, there stood the maiden in her poor garments, but she shone out from within them like a rose surrounded by leaves. "You are the poorest and also the richest," said he to her. "Come with me, you shall be my bride." She did not speak, but she gave him her hand. Then he gave her a kiss, led her forth, lifted her onto his horse, and took her to the royal castle, where the wedding was solemnized with great rejoicings. The spindle, shuttle, and needle were preserved in the treasure chamber, and held in great honor.

89. *The Peasant and the Devil*

There was once on a time a farsighted, crafty peasant whose tricks were much talked about. The best story is, however, how he once got hold of the Devil, and made a fool of him. The peasant had one day been working in his field, and as twilight had set in, was making ready for the journey home, when he saw a heap of burning coals in the middle of his field, and when, full of astonishment, he went up to it, a little black devil was sitting on the live coals. "You do indeed sit upon a treasure!" said the peasant.

"Yes, in truth," replied the Devil, "on a treasure which contains more gold and silver than you have ever seen in your life!"

"The treasure lies in my field and belongs to me," said the peasant.

"It is yours," answered the Devil, "if you will for two years give me the half of everything your field produces. Money I have enough of, but I have a desire for the fruits of the earth."

The peasant agreed to the bargain. "In order, however, that no dispute may arise about the division," said he, "everything that is above ground shall belong to you, and what is under the earth to me." The Devil was quite satisfied with that, but the cunning peasant had sown turnips.

Now when the time for harvest came, the Devil appeared and wanted to take away his crop; but he found nothing but the yellow withered leaves, while the peasant, full of delight, was digging up his turnips. "You have had the best of it for once," said the Devil, "but the next time that won't do. What grows above ground shall be yours, and what is under it, mine."

"I am willing," replied the peasant; but when the time came to sow, he did not again sow turnips, but wheat. The grain became ripe, and the peasant went into the field and cut the full stalks down to the ground. When the Devil came, he found nothing but the stubble, and went away in a fury down into a cleft in the rocks. "That is the way to cheat the Devil," said the peasant, and went and fetched away the treasure.

90. *The Crumbs on the Table*

A countryman one day said to his little puppies, "Come into the parlor and enjoy yourselves, and pick up the bread crumbs on the table; your mistress has gone out to pay some visits."

Then the little dogs said, "No, no, we will not go. If the mistress gets to know it, she will beat us."

The countryman said, "She will know nothing about it. Do come; after all, she never gives you anything good."

Then the little dogs again said, "Nay, nay, we must let it alone; we must not go." But the countryman let them have no peace until at last they went, and got on the table, and ate up the bread crumbs with all their might.

But at that very moment the mistress came, and seized the stick in great haste, and beat them and treated them very harshly. And when they were outside the house, the little dogs said to the countryman, "Do, do, do, do, do you see?"

Then the countryman laughed and said, "Didn't, didn't, didn't you expect it?" So they just had to run away.

91. *The Mongoose*

There was once upon a time a princess, who, high under the battlements in her castle, had an apartment with twelve windows, which looked out in every possible direction, and when she climbed up to it and looked around her, she could inspect her whole kingdom. When she looked out of the first, her sight was more keen than that of any other human being; from the second she could see still better, from the third more distinctly still, and so it went on, until the twelfth, from which she saw everything above the earth and under the earth, and nothing at all could be kept secret from her. Moreover, as she was haughty, and would be subject to no one, but wished to keep the dominion for herself alone, she caused it to be proclaimed that no one should ever be her husband who could not conceal himself from her so effectually, that it should be quite impossible for her to find him. He who tried this, however, and was discovered by her, was to have his head struck off, and stuck on a post. Ninety-seven posts with the heads of dead men were already standing before the castle, and no one had come forward for a long time. The princess was delighted, and thought to herself, "Now I shall be free as long as I live."

Then three brothers appeared before her, and announced to her that they were desirous of trying their luck. The eldest believed he would be quite safe if he crept into a lime pit, but she saw him from the first window, made him come out, and had his head cut off. The second crept into the cellar of the palace, but she perceived him also from the first window, and his fate was sealed. His head was placed on the ninety-ninth post. Then the youngest came to her and entreated her to give him a day for consideration, and also to be so gracious as to overlook it if she should happen to discover him twice, but if he failed the third time, he would look on his life as over. As he was so handsome, and begged so earnestly, she said, "Yes, I will grant you that, but you will not succeed."

Next day he meditated for a long time how he should hide himself, but all in vain. Then he seized his gun and went out hunting. He saw a raven, took a good aim at him, and was just going to fire, when the bird cried, "Don't shoot; I will make it worth your while."

He put his gun down, went on, and came to a lake where he surprised a large fish that had come up from the depths below to the surface of the water. When he had aimed at it, the fish cried, "Don't shoot, and I will make it worth your while."

He allowed it to dive down again, went onward, and met a fox that was lame. He fired and missed it, and the fox cried, "You had much better come here and draw the thorn out of my foot for me." He did this; but then he wanted to kill the fox and skin it. The fox said, "Stop, and I will make it worth your while." The youth let him go, and then as it was evening, returned home.

Next day he was to hide himself; but however much he puzzled his brains over it, he did not know where. He went into the forest to the raven and said, "I let you live on, so now tell me where I am to hide myself, so that the King's daughter shall not see me."

The raven hung his head and thought it over for a long time. At length he croaked, "I have it." He fetched an egg out of his nest, cut it into two parts, and shut the youth inside it; then made it whole again, and seated himself on it.

When the King's daughter went to the first window she could not discover him, nor could she from the others, and she began to be uneasy, but from the eleventh she saw him. She ordered the raven to be shot, and the egg to be brought and broken, and the youth was forced to come out. She said, "For once you are excused, but if you do not do better than this, you are lost!"

Next day he went to the lake, called the fish to him and said, "I allowed you to live, now tell me where to hide myself so that the King's daughter may not see me."

The fish thought for a while, and at last cried, "I have it! I will shut you up in my stomach." He swallowed him, and went down to the bottom of the lake.

The King's daughter looked through her windows, and even from the eleventh did not see him, and was alarmed; but at length from the twelfth she saw him. She ordered the fish to be caught and killed, and then the youth appeared. Everyone can imagine what a state of mind he was in. She said, "Twice you are forgiven, but be sure that your head will be set on the hundredth post."

On the last day, he went with a heavy heart into the country, and met the fox. "You know how to find all kinds of hiding places," said he; "I let you live, now advise me where I shall hide myself so that the King's daughter shall not discover me."

"That's a hard task," answered the fox, looking very thoughtful. At length he cried, "I have it!" and went with him to a spring, dipped himself in it, and came out as a market stall-keeper, and dealer in animals. The youth had to dip himself in the water also, and was changed into a small mongoose. The merchant went into the town, and showed the pretty little animal, and many persons gathered together to see it.

At length the King's daughter came likewise, and as she liked it very much, she bought it, and gave the merchant a good deal of money for it. Before he gave it over to her, he said to it, "When the King's daughter goes to the window, creep quickly under the braids of her hair." And now the time arrived when she was to search for him. She went to one window after another in turn, from the first to the eleventh, and did not see him. When she did not see him from the twelfth either, she was full of anxiety and anger, and shut it down with such violence that the glass in every window shivered into a thousand pieces, and the whole castle shook.

She went back and felt the mongoose beneath the braids of her hair. Then she seized it, and threw it on the ground exclaiming, "Away with you, get out of my sight!" It ran to the merchant, and both of them hurried to the spring, in which they plunged, and received back their true forms.

The youth thanked the fox, and said, "The raven and the fish are idiots compared with you; you know the right tune to play, there is no denying that!"

The youth went straight to the palace. The princess was already expecting him, and accommodated herself to her destiny. The wedding was solemnized, and now he was King, and lord of all the kingdom. He never told her where he had concealed himself for the third time, and who had helped him, so she believed that he had done everything by his own skill, and she had a great respect for him, for she thought to herself, "He is able to do more than I."

92. *The Master Thief*

One day an old man and his wife were sitting in front of a miserable house resting a while from their work. Suddenly a splendid carriage with four black horses came driving up, and a richly-dressed man descended from it. The peasant stood up, went to the great man, and asked what he wanted, and in what way he could be useful to him? The stranger stretched out his hand to the old man, and said, "I want nothing but to enjoy for once a country dish; cook me some potatoes, in the way you always have them, and then I will sit down at your table and eat them with pleasure."

The peasant smiled and said, "You are a count or a prince, or perhaps even a duke; noble gentlemen often have such fancies, but you shall have your wish." The wife went into the kitchen, and began to wash and rub the potatoes, and to make them into balls, as they are eaten by the country folks.

While she was busy with this work, the peasant said to the stranger, "Come into my garden with me for a while, I have something to do there still." He had dug some holes in the garden, and now wanted to plant some trees in them.

"Have you no children," asked the stranger, "who could help you with your work?"

"No," answered the peasant, "I had a son, it is true, but it is long since he went out into the world. He was a ne'er-do-well; sharp, and knowing, but he would learn nothing and was full of bad tricks. At last he ran away from me, and since then I have heard nothing of him."

The old man took a young tree, put it in a hole, drove in a post beside it, and when he had shoveled in some earth and had trampled it firmly down, he tied the stem of the tree above, below, and in the middle, fast to the post by a rope of straw. "But tell me," said the stranger, "why you don't tie that crooked knotted tree, which is lying in the corner there, bent down almost to the ground, to a post also that it may grow straight, as well as these?"

The old man smiled and said, "Sir, you speak according to your knowledge, it is easy to see that you are not familiar with gardening. That tree there is old, and misshapen, no one can make it straight now.

Trees must be trained while they are young."

"That is how it was with your son," said the stranger. "If you had trained him while he was still young, he would not have run away; now he too must have grown hard and misshapen."

"Truly it is a long time since he went away," replied the old man. "He must have changed."

"Would you know him again if he were to come to you?" asked the stranger.

"Hardly by his face," replied the peasant, "but he has a mark about him, a birthmark on his shoulder, that looks like a bean." When he had said that the stranger pulled off his coat, bared his shoulder, and showed the peasant the bean. "Good God!" cried the old man, "You are really my son!" and love for his child stirred in his heart. "But," he added, "how can you be my son, if you have become a great lord who lives in wealth and luxury? How have you contrived to do that?"

"Ah, father," answered the son, "the young tree was bound to no post and has grown crooked, now it is too old, it will never be straight again. How have I got all that? I have become a thief, but do not be alarmed, I am a master thief. For me there are neither locks nor bolts, whatever I desire is mine. Do not imagine that I steal like a common thief, I only take some of the superfluity of the rich. Poor people are safe, I would rather give to them than take anything from them. It is the same with anything that I can have without trouble, cunning and dexterity, I never touch it."

"Alas, my son," said the father, "it still does not please me, a thief is still a thief. I tell you it will end badly."

He took him to his mother, and when she heard that was her son, she wept for joy, but when he told her that he had become a master thief, two streams flowed down over her face. At length she said, "Even if he has become a thief, he is still my son, and my eyes have beheld him once more."

They sat down to table, and once again he ate with his parents the wretched food that he had not eaten for so long. The father said, "If our Lord, the count up there in the castle, learns who you are, and what trade you follow, he will not take you in his arms and cradle you in them as he did when he held you at the font, but will cause you to swing from the gallows."

"Be easy, father, he will do me no harm, for I understand my trade.

I will go to him myself this very day." When evening drew near, the master thief seated himself in his carriage, and drove to the castle. The count received him civilly, for he took him for a distinguished man. When, however, the stranger made himself known, the count turned pale and was quite silent for some time.

At length he said, "You are my godson, and on that account mercy shall take the place of justice, and I will deal leniently with you. Since you pride yourself on being a master thief, I will put your art to the proof, but if you do not stand the test, you must marry the ropemaker's daughter, and the croaking of the raven must be your music on the occasion."

"Lord count," answered the master thief, "Think of three things, as difficult as you like, and if I do not perform your tasks, do with me what you will."

The count reflected for some minutes, and then said, "Well, then, in the first place, you shall steal the horse I keep for my own riding, out of the stable, in the next, you shall steal the sheet from beneath the bodies of my wife and myself when we are asleep, without our observing it, and the wedding ring of my wife as well; thirdly and lastly, you shall steal away out of the church, the parson and clerk. Mark what I am saying, for your life depends on it."

The master thief went to the nearest town; there he bought the clothes of an old peasant woman, and put them on. Then he stained his face brown, and painted wrinkles on it as well, so that no one could have recognized him. Then he filled a small cask with old Hungary wine in which was mixed a powerful sleeping potion. He put the cask in a basket, which he took on his back, and walked with slow and tottering steps to the count's castle. It was already dark when he arrived. He sat down on a stone in the courtyard and began to cough, like an asthmatic old woman, and to rub his hands as if he were cold.

In front of the door of the stable some soldiers were lying around a fire; one of them observed the woman, and called out to her, "Come nearer, old mother, and warm yourself beside us. After all, you have no bed for the night, and must take one where you can find it." The old woman tottered up to them, begged them to lift the basket from her back, and sat down beside them at the fire.

"What have you got in your little cask, old lady?" asked one.

"A good mouthful of wine," she answered. "I live by trade, for money and fair words I am quite ready to let you have a glass."

"Let us have it here, then," said the soldier, and when he had tasted one glass he said, "When wine is good, I like another glass," and had another poured out for himself, and the rest followed his example.

"Hello, comrades," cried one of them to those who were in the stable, "here is an old goody who has wine that is as old as herself; take a drink, it will warm your stomachs far better than our fire."

The old woman carried her cask into the stable. One of the soldiers had seated himself on the saddled riding horse, another held its bridle in his hand, a third had laid hold of its tail. She poured out as much as they wanted until the spring ran dry. It was not long before the bridle fell from the hand of the one, and he fell down and began to snore, the other left hold of the tail, lay down and snored still louder. The one who was sitting in the saddle, did remain sitting, but bent his head almost down to the horse's neck, and slept and blew with his mouth like the bellows of a forge. The soldiers outside had already been asleep for a long time, and were lying on the ground motionless, as if dead.

When the master thief saw that he had succeeded, he gave the first a rope in his hand instead of the bridle, and the other who had been holding the tail, a wisp of straw, but what was he to do with the one who was sitting on the horse's back? He did not want to throw him down, for he might have awakened and have uttered a cry. He had a good idea; he unbuckled the girths of the saddle, tied a couple of ropes that were hanging to a ring on the wall fast to the saddle, and drew the sleeping rider up into the air on it, then he twisted the rope around the posts, and made it fast. He soon released the horse from the chain, but if he had ridden over the stony pavement of the yard they would have heard the noise in the castle. So he wrapped the horse's hoofs in old rags, led him carefully out, leapt upon him, and galloped off.

When day broke, the master galloped to the castle on the stolen horse. The count had just got up, and was looking out of the window. "Good morning, Sir Count," he cried to him, "here is the horse, which I have got safely out of the stable! Just look, how beautifully your soldiers are lying there sleeping; and if you will but go into the stable, you will see how comfortable your watchers have made it for themselves."

The count could not help laughing, then he said, "For once you have succeeded, but things won't go so well the second time, and I warn you that if you come before me as a thief, I will handle you as I would a thief."

When the countess went to bed that night, she closed her hand with the wedding ring tightly together, and the count said, "All the doors are locked and bolted, I will keep awake and wait for the thief, but if he gets in by the window, I will shoot him."

The master thief, however, went in the dark to the gallows, cut a poor sinner who was hanging there down from the halter, and carried him on his back to the castle. Then he set a ladder up to the bedroom, put the dead body on his shoulders, and began to climb up. When he had got so high that the head of the dead man showed at the window, the count, who was watching in his bed, fired a pistol at him, and immediately the master let the poor sinner fall down, and hid himself in one corner. The night was sufficiently lighted by the moon, for the master to see distinctly how the count got out of the window onto the ladder, came down, carried the dead body into the garden, and began to dig a hole in which to lay it. "Now," thought the thief, "the favorable moment has come," stole nimbly out of his corner, and climbed up the ladder straight into the countess's bedroom.

"Dear wife," he began in the count's voice, "the thief is dead, but, after all, he is my godson, and has been more of a scapegoat than a villain. I will not put him to open shame; besides, I am sorry for the parents. I will bury him myself before daybreak, in the garden that the thing may not be known, so give me the sheet, I will wrap up the body in it, and bury him as a dog buries things by scratching." The countess gave him the sheet. "I tell you what," continued the thief, "I have a fit of magnanimity on me, give me the ring too—the unhappy man risked his life for it, so he may take it with him into his grave." She would not gainsay the count, and although she did it unwillingly she drew the ring from her finger, and gave it to him. The thief made off with both these things, and reached home safely before the count in the garden had finished his work of burying.

What a long face the count did make when the master came next morning, and brought him the sheet and the ring. "Are you a wizard?" said he. "Who has fetched you out of the grave in which I myself laid you, and brought you to life again?"

"You did not bury me," said the thief, "but the poor sinner on the gallows," and he told him exactly how everything had happened, and the count was forced to own to him that he was a clever, crafty thief.

"But you have not reached the end yet," he added, "you have still to perform the third task, and if you do not succeed in that, all is of no use." The master smiled and returned no answer.

When night had fallen he went with a long sack on his back, a bundle under his arms, and a lantern in his hand to the village church. In the sack he had some crabs, and in the bundle short wax candles. He sat down in the churchyard, took out a crab, and stuck a wax candle on his back. Then he lighted the little light, put the crab on the ground, and let it creep about. He took a second out of the sack, and treated it in the same way, and so on until the last was out of the sack. Then he put on a long black garment that looked like a monk's cowl, and stuck a gray beard on his chin. When at last he was quite unrecognizable, he took the sack in which the crabs had been, went into the church, and ascended the pulpit. The clock in the tower was just striking twelve; when the last stroke had sounded, he cried with a loud and piercing voice, "Listen, sinful men, the end of all things has come! The last day is at hand! Listen! Listen! Whoever wishes to go to heaven with me must creep into the sack. I am Peter, who opens and shuts the gate of heaven. Behold how the dead outside there in the churchyard, are wandering about collecting their bones. Come, come, and creep into the sack; the world is about to be destroyed!"

The cry echoed through the whole village. The parson and clerk who lived nearest to the church, heard it first, and when they saw the lights that were moving about the churchyard, they observed that something unusual was going on, and went into the church. They listened to the sermon for a while, and then the clerk nudged the parson and said, "It would not be amiss if we were to use the opportunity together, and before the dawning of the last day, find an easy way of getting to heaven."

"To tell the truth," answered the parson, "that is what I myself have been thinking, so if you are inclined, we will set out on our way."

"Yes," answered the clerk, "but you, the pastor, have the precedence, I will follow." So the parson went first, and ascended the pulpit where the master opened his sack. The parson crept in first, and then the clerk. The master immediately tied up the sack tightly, seized it by the middle, and dragged it down the pulpit steps, and whenever the heads of the two fools bumped against the steps, he cried, "We are going over the mountains." Then he drew them through the village in the same way, and when they were passing through puddles, he cried, "Now we are going through wet clouds." And when at last he was dragging them up the steps of the castle, he cried, "Now we are on the steps of heaven, and will soon be in the outer court." When he had got to the top, he pushed the sack into the pigeon house, and when the pigeons fluttered about, he said, "Hear how glad the angels are, and how they are flapping their wings!" Then he bolted the door upon them, and went away.

Next morning he went to the count, and told him that he had performed the third task also, and had carried the parson and clerk out of the church. "Where have you left them?" asked the lord.

"They are lying upstairs in a sack in the pigeon house, and imagine that they are in heaven."

The count went up himself, and convinced himself that the master had told the truth. When he had delivered the parson and clerk from their captivity, he said, "You are an arch-thief, and have won your wager. For once you escape with a whole skin, but see that you leave my land, for if ever you set foot on it again, you may count on your elevation to the gallows." The arch-thief took leave of his parents, once more went forth into the wide world, and no one has ever heard of him since.

93. *The Drummer*

A young drummer went out quite alone one evening into the country, and came to a lake on the shore of which he perceived three pieces of white linen lying. "What fine linen," said he, and put one piece in his pocket. He returned home, thought no more of what he had found, and went to bed.

Just as he was going to sleep, it seemed to him as if someone was saying his name. He listened, and was aware of a soft voice that cried to him, "Drummer, drummer, wake up!"

As it was a dark night he could see no one, but it appeared to him that a figure was hovering about his bed. "What do you want?" he asked.

"Give me back my dress," answered the voice, "that you took away from me last evening by the lake."

"You shall have it back again," said the drummer, "if you will tell me who you are."

"Ah," replied the voice, "I am the daughter of a mighty King; but I have fallen into the power of a witch, and am shut up on the glass mountain. I have to bathe in the lake every day with my two sisters, but I cannot fly back again without my dress. My sisters have gone away, but I have been forced to stay behind. I entreat you to give me my dress back."

"Be easy, poor child," said the drummer. "I will willingly give it back to you." He took it out of his pocket, and reached it to her in the dark. She snatched it in haste, and wanted to go away with it. "Stop a moment, perhaps I can help you."

"You can only help me by ascending the glass mountain, and freeing me from the power of the witch. But you cannot come to the glass mountain, and indeed if you were quite close to it you could not ascend it."

"When I want to do a thing I always can do it," said the drummer; "I am sorry for you, and have no fear of anything. But I do not know the way that leads to the glass mountain."

"The road goes through the great forest, in which the man-eaters live," she answered, "and more than that, I dare not tell you." And then he heard her wings quiver, as she flew away.

By daybreak the drummer arose, buckled on his drum, and went without fear straight into the forest. After he had walked for a while without seeing any giants, he thought to himself, "I must wake up the sluggards," and he hung his drum before him, and beat such a reveille that the birds flew out of the trees with loud cries.

It was not long before a giant who had been lying sleeping among the grass, rose up, and was as tall as a fir tree. "Wretch!" cried he; "what are you drumming here for, and waking me out of my best sleep?"

"I am drumming," he replied, "because I want to show the way to many thousands who are following me."

"What do they want in my forest?" demanded the giant.

"They want to put an end to you, and cleanse the forest of such a monster as you are!"

"Oho!" said the giant, "I will trample you all to death like so many ants."

"Do you think you can do anything against us?" said the drummer; "if you stoop to take hold of one, he will jump away and hide himself; but when you are lying down and sleeping, they will come forth from every thicket, and creep up to you. Every one of them has a hammer of steel in his belt, and with that they will beat in your skull."

The giant grew angry and thought, "If I meddle with the crafty folk, it might turn out badly for me. I can strangle wolves and bears, but I cannot protect myself from these earth-worms." He said, "Listen, little fellow, go back again, and I will promise you that for the future I will leave you and your comrades in peace, and if there is anything else you wish for, tell me, for I am quite willing to do something to please you."

"You have long legs," said the drummer, "and can run quicker than I; carry me to the glass mountain, and I will give my followers a signal to go back, and they shall leave you in peace this time."

"Come here, worm," said the giant; "seat yourself on my shoulder, I will carry you where you wish to be." The giant lifted him up, and the drummer began to beat his drum up aloft to his heart's delight. The giant thought, "That is the signal for the other people to turn back."

After a while, a second giant was standing in the road, who took the drummer from the first, and stuck him in his buttonhole. The drummer laid hold of the button, which was as large as a dish, held on by it, and looked merrily around. Then they came to a third giant, who took him out of the buttonhole, and set him on the rim of his hat. Then the drummer walked backward and forward up above, and looked over the trees, and when he perceived a mountain in the blue distance, he thought, "That must be the glass mountain," and so it was. The giant only made two steps more, and they reached the foot of the mountain, where the giant put him down. The drummer demanded to be put on the summit of the glass mountain, but the giant shook his head, growled something in his beard, and went back into the forest.

And now the poor drummer was standing before the mountain, which was as high as if three mountains were piled on each other, and at the same time as smooth as a looking glass, and did not know how to get up it. He began to climb, but that was useless, for he always slipped back again. "If one was a bird now," thought he; but what was the good of wishing, no wings grew for him.

While he was standing thus, not knowing what to do, he saw, not far from him, two men who were struggling fiercely together. He went up to them and saw that they were disputing about a saddle, which was lying on the ground before them, and which both of them wanted to have. "What fools you are," said he, "to quarrel about a saddle, when you have not a horse for it!"

"The saddle is worth fighting about," answered one of the men; "whoever sits on it, and wishes himself in any place, even if it should be the very end of the earth, gets there the instant he has uttered the wish. The saddle belongs to us in common. It is my turn to ride on it, but that other man will not let me do it."

"I will soon decide the quarrel," said the drummer, and he went to a short distance and stuck a white rod in the ground. Then he came back and said, "Now run to the goal, and whoever gets there first, shall ride first." Both put themselves into a trot; but hardly had they gone a couple of steps before the drummer swung himself on the saddle, wished himself on the glass mountain, and before anyone could turn around, he was there.

On the top of the mountain was a plain; there stood an old stone house, and in front of the house lay a great fishpond, but behind it was a dark forest. He saw neither men nor animals, everything was quiet; only the wind rustled among the trees, and the clouds moved by quite close above his head. He went to the door and knocked. When he had knocked for the third time, an old woman with a brown face and red eyes opened the door. She had spectacles on her long nose, and looked sharply at him; then she asked what he wanted. "Entrance, food, and a bed for the night," replied the drummer.

"That you shall have," said the old woman, "if you will perform three services in return."

"Why not?" he answered, "I am not afraid of any kind of work, however hard it may be." The old woman let him go in, and gave him some food and a good bed at night.

The next morning when he had had his sleep out, she took a thimble from her wrinkled finger, reached it to the drummer, and said, "Go to work now, and empty out the pond with this thimble; but you must have it done before night, and must have sought out all the fishes that are in the water and laid them side by side, according to their kind and size."

"That is strange work," said the drummer, but he went to the pond, and began to empty it. He bailed the whole morning; but what can anyone do to a great lake with a thimble, even if he were to bail for a thousand years?

When it was noon, he thought, "It is all useless, and whether I work or not it will come to the same thing." So he gave it up and sat down.

Then came a maiden out of the house who set a little basket with food before him, and said, "What ails you, that you sit so sadly here?"

He looked at her, and saw that she was wondrously beautiful. "Ah," said he, "I cannot finish the first piece of work, how will it be with the others? I came forth to seek a King's daughter who is said to dwell here, but I have not found her, and I will go farther."

"Stay here," said the maiden, "I will help you out of your difficulty. You are tired, lay your head in my lap, and sleep. When you awake again, your work will be done." The drummer did not need to be told that twice. As soon as his eyes were shut, she turned a wishing ring and said, "Rise, water. Fishes, come out." Instantly the water rose on high like a white mist, and moved away with the other clouds, and the fishes sprang on the shore and laid themselves side by side each according to his size and kind.

When the drummer awoke, he saw with amazement that all was done. But the maiden said, "One of the fish is not lying with those of its own kind, but quite alone; when the old woman comes tonight and sees that all she demanded has been done, she will ask you, 'What is this fish lying alone for?' Then throw the fish in her face, and say, 'This one shall be for you, old witch.'"

In the evening the witch came, and when she had put this question, he threw the fish in her face. She behaved as if she did not notice it, and said nothing, but looked at him with malicious eyes. Next morning she said, "Yesterday it was too easy for you, I must give you harder work. Today you must hew down the whole of the forest, split the wood into logs, and pile them up, and everything must be finished by the evening." She gave him an ax, a mallet, and two wedges. But the ax was made of lead, and the mallet and wedges were of tin. When he began to cut, the edge of the ax turned back, and the mallet and wedges were beaten out of shape.

He did not know how to manage, but at midday the maiden came once more with his dinner and comforted him. "Lay your head on my lap," said she, "and sleep; when you awake, your work will be done." She turned her wishing ring, and in an instant the whole forest fell down with a crash, the wood split, and arranged itself in heaps, and it seemed just as if unseen giants were finishing the work.

When he awoke, the maiden said, "Do you see that the wood is piled up and arranged, one bough alone remains; but when the old woman comes this evening and asks you about that bough, give her a blow with it, and say, 'That is for you, you witch.'"

The old woman came, "There you see how easy the work was!" said she; "but for whom have you left that bough, which is lying there still?"

"For you, you witch," he replied, and gave her a blow with it.

But she pretended not to feel it, laughed scornfully, and said, "Early tomorrow morning you shall arrange all the wood in one heap, set fire to it, and burn it." He rose at break of day, and began to pick up the wood, but how can a single man get a whole forest together? The work made no progress.

The maiden, however, did not desert him in his need. She brought him his food at noon, and when he had eaten, he laid his head on her lap, and went to sleep. When he awoke, the entire pile of wood was burning in one enormous flame, which stretched its tongues out into the sky. "Listen to me," said the maiden, "when the witch comes, she will give you all kinds of orders; do whatever she asks you without fear, and then she will not be able to get the better of you, but if you are afraid, the fire will lay hold of you, and consume you. At last when you have done everything, seize her with both your hands, and throw her into the middle of the fire."

The maiden departed, and the old woman came sneaking up to him. "Oh, I am cold," said she, "but that is a fire that burns; it warms my old bones for me, and does me good! But there is a log lying there that won't burn, bring it out for me. When you have done that, you are free, and may go where you like. Come; go in with a good will."

The drummer did not reflect long; he sprang into the middle of the flames, but they did not hurt him, and could not even singe a hair of his head. He carried the log out, and laid it down. Hardly, however, had the wood touched the earth than it was transformed, and the beautiful maiden who had helped him in his need stood before him, and by the silken and shining golden garments that she wore, he knew right well that she was the King's daughter.

But the old woman laughed venomously, and said, "You think you have her safe, but you have not got her yet!" Just as she was about to fall on the maiden and take her away, the youth seized the old woman with both his hands, raised her up on high, and threw her into the jaws of the fire, which closed over her as if it were delighted that an old witch was to be burned.

Then the King's daughter looked at the drummer, and when she saw that he was a handsome youth and remembered how he had risked his life to deliver her, she gave him her hand, and said, "You have ventured everything for my sake, but I also will do everything for yours. Promise to be true to me, and you shall be my husband. We shall not want for riches, we shall have enough with what the witch has gathered together here." She led him into the house, where there were chests and coffers crammed with the old woman's treasures. The maiden left the gold and silver where it was, and took only the precious stones.

She would not stay any longer on the glass mountain, so the drummer said to her, "Seat yourself by me on my saddle, and then we will fly down like birds."

"I do not like the old saddle," said she. "I need only turn my wishing ring and we shall be at home."

"Very well, then," answered the drummer. "Then wish us in front of the town gate." In the twinkling of an eye they were there, but the drummer said, "I will just go to my parents and tell them the news. Wait for me outside here, I shall soon be back."

"Ah," said the King's daughter, "I beg you to be careful. On your arrival do not kiss your parents on the right cheek, or else you will forget everything, and I shall stay behind here outside, alone and deserted."

"How can I forget you?" said he, and promised her to come back very soon, and gave his hand upon it.

When he went into his father's house, he had changed so much that no one knew who he was, for the three days that he had passed on the glass mountain had been three years. Then he made himself known, and his parents fell on his neck with joy, and his heart was so moved that he forgot what the maiden had said, and kissed them on both cheeks. But when he had given them the kiss on the right cheek, every thought of the King's daughter vanished from him. He emptied out his pockets, and laid handfuls of the largest jewels on the table. The parents had not the least idea what to do with the riches. Then the father built a magnificent castle all surrounded by gardens, woods, and meadows as if a prince were going to live in it, and when it was ready, the mother said, "I have found a maiden for you, and the wedding shall be in three days." The son was content to do as his parents desired.

The poor King's daughter had stood for a long time outside the town waiting for the return of the young man. When evening came, she said, "He must certainly have kissed his parents on the right cheek, and has forgotten me."

Her heart was full of sorrow, she wished herself into a solitary little hut in a forest, and would not return to her father's court. Every evening she went into the town and passed the young man's house; he often saw her, but he no longer knew her. At length she heard the people saying, "The wedding will take place tomorrow."

Then she said, "I will try to see if I can win his heart back."

On the first day of the wedding ceremonies, she turned her wishing ring, and said, "A dress as bright as the sun." Instantly the dress lay before her, and it was as bright as if it had been woven of real sunbeams.

When all the guests were assembled, she entered the hall. Everyone was amazed at the beautiful dress, and the bride most of all, and as pretty dresses were the things she had most delight in, she went to the stranger and asked if she would sell it to her. "Not for money," she answered, "but if I may pass the first night outside the door of the room where your betrothed sleeps, I will give it up to you." The bride could not overcome her desire and consented, but she mixed a sleeping potion with the wine her betrothed took at night, which made him fall into a deep sleep. When all had become quiet, the King's daughter crouched down by the door of the bedroom, opened it just a little, and cried,

> "Drummer, drummer, I pray you hear!
> Have you forgotten you held me dear?
> That on the glass mountain we sat hour by
> hour?
> That I rescued your life from the witch's
> power?
> Did you not pledge your troth to me?
> Drummer, drummer, listen to me!"

But it was all in vain, the drummer did not awake, and when morning dawned, the King's daughter was forced to go back again as she came. On the second evening she turned her wishing ring and said, "A dress as silvery as the moon." When she appeared at the feast in the dress, which was as soft as moonbeams, it again excited the desire of the bride, and the King's daughter gave it to her for permission to pass the second night also, outside the door of the bedroom. Then in the stillness of the night, she cried,

> "Drummer, drummer, I pray you hear!
> Have you forgotten you held me dear?
> That on the glass mountain we sat hour by
> hour?
> That I rescued your life from the witch's
> power?
> Did you not pledge your troth to me?
> Drummer, drummer, listen to me!"

But the drummer, who was stupefied with the sleeping potion, could not be aroused. Sadly next morning she went back to her hut in the forest. But the people in the house had heard the lamentation of the stranger maiden, and told the bridegroom about it. They told him also that it was impossible that he could hear anything of it, because the maiden he was going to marry had poured a sleeping potion into his wine.

On the third evening, the King's daughter turned her wishing ring, and said, "A dress glittering like the stars."

When she showed herself at the feast, the bride was quite beside herself with the splendor of the dress, which far surpassed the others, and she said, "I must, and will have it."

The maiden gave it as she had given the others for permission to spend the night outside the bridegroom's door. The bridegroom, however, did not drink the wine that was handed to him before he went to bed, but poured it behind the bed, and when everything was quiet, he heard a sweet voice that called to him,

> "Drummer, drummer, I pray you hear!
> Have you forgotten you held me dear?
> That on the glass mountain we sat hour by hour?
> That I rescued your life from the witch's power?
> Did you not pledge your troth to me?
> Drummer, drummer, listen to me!"

Suddenly, his memory returned to him. "Ah," cried he, "how can I have acted so unfaithfully; but the kiss that in the joy of my heart I gave my parents, on the right cheek, that is to blame for it all, that is what stupefied me!" He sprang up, took the King's daughter by the hand, and led her to his parents' bed. "This is my true bride," said he; "if I marry the other, I shall do a great wrong." The parents, when they heard how everything had happened, gave their consent. Then the lights in the hall were lighted again, drums and trumpets were brought, friends and relations were invited to come, and the real wedding was solemnized with great rejoicing. The first bride received the beautiful dresses as a compensation, and declared herself satisfied.

94. *The Ear of Corn*

In former times, when God himself still walked the earth, the fruitfulness of the soil was much greater than it is now; then the ears of corn did not bear fifty or sixty, but four or five hundred. Then the corn grew from the bottom to the very top of the stalk, and according to the length of the stalk was the length of the ear. Men however are so made, that when they are too well off they no longer value the blessings that come from God, but grow indifferent and careless. One day a woman was passing by a cornfield when her little child, who was running beside her, fell into a puddle, and dirtied her frock. At this the mother tore up a handful of the beautiful ears of corn, and cleaned the frock with them.

When the Lord, who just then came by, saw that, he was angry, and said, "Henceforth shall the stalks of corn bear no more ears; men are no longer worthy of heavenly gifts." The bystanders who heard this were terrified, and fell on their knees and prayed that he would still leave something on the stalks, even if the people were undeserving of it, for the sake of the innocent birds that would otherwise have to starve. The Lord, who foresaw their suffering, had pity on them, and granted the request. So the ears were left as they now grow.

95. *The Grave Mound*

A rich farmer was one day standing in his yard inspecting his fields and gardens. The corn was growing up vigorously and the fruit trees were heavily laden with fruit. The grain of the year before still lay in such immense heaps on the floors that the rafters could hardly bear it. Then he went into the stable, where there were well-fed oxen, fat cows, and horses bright as a looking glass. At length he went back into his sitting room, and cast a glance at the iron chest in which his money lay.

While he was thus standing surveying his riches, all at once there was a loud knock close by him. The knock was not at the door of his room, but at the door of his heart. It opened, and he heard a voice, which said to him, "Have you done good to your family with it? Have you considered the necessities of the poor? Have you shared your bread with the hungry? Have you been contented with what you have, or did you always desire to have more?"

The heart was not slow in answering, "I have been hard and pitiless, and have never shown any kindness to my own family. If a beggar came, I turned away my eyes from him. I have not troubled myself about God, but have thought only of increasing my wealth. If everything that the sky covers had been mine, I should still not have had enough."

When he was aware of this answer he was greatly alarmed, his knees began to tremble, and he was forced to sit down.

Then there was another knock, but the knock was at the door of his room. It was his neighbor, a poor man who had a number of children whom he could no longer satisfy with food. "I know," thought the poor man, "that my neighbor is rich, but he is as hard as he is rich. I don't believe he will help me, but my children are crying for bread, so I will venture it." He said to the rich man, "You do not readily give away anything that is yours, but I stand here like one who feels the water rising above his head. My children are starving, lend me four measures of corn."

The rich man looked at him long, and then the first sunbeam of mercy began to melt away a drop of the ice of greediness. "I will not lend you four measures," he answered, "but I will make you a present of eight, but you must fulfill one condition."

"What am I to do?" said the poor man.

"When I am dead, you shall watch for three nights by my grave." The peasant was disturbed in his mind at this request, but in the need in which he was, he would have consented to anything; he accepted, therefore, and carried the corn home with him.

It seemed as if the rich man had foreseen what was about to happen, for when three days had gone by, he suddenly dropped down dead. No one knew exactly how it came to pass, but no one grieved for him. When he was buried, the poor man remembered his promise; he would willingly have been released from it, but he thought, "After all, he acted kindly by me. I have fed my hungry children with his corn, and even if that were not the case, where I have once given my promise I must keep it."

At nightfall he went into the churchyard, and seated himself on the grave mound. Everything was quiet, only the moon appeared above the grave, and frequently an owl flew past and uttered her melancholy cry. When the sun rose, the poor man took himself in safety to his home, and in the same manner the second night passed quietly by. On the evening of the third day he felt a strange uneasiness, it seemed to him that something was about to happen. When he went out he saw, by the churchyard wall, a man whom he had never seen before. He was no longer young, had scars on his face, and his eyes looked sharply and eagerly around. He was entirely covered with an old cloak, and nothing was visible but his great riding boots. "What are you looking for here?" the peasant asked. "Are you not afraid of the lonely churchyard?"

"I am looking for nothing," he answered, "and I am afraid of nothing! I am like the youngster who went forth to learn how to shiver, and had his labor for his pains, but got the King's daughter to wed and great wealth with her, only I have remained poor. I am nothing but a paid-off soldier, and I mean to pass the night here, because I have no other shelter."

"If you are without fear," said the peasant, "stay with me, and help me to watch that grave there."

"To keep watch is a soldier's business," he replied. "Whatever we fall in with here, whether it be good or bad, we will share it between us." The peasant agreed to this, and they seated themselves on the grave together.

All was quiet until midnight, when suddenly a shrill whistling was heard in the air, and the two watchers perceived the Evil One standing bodily before them. "Be off, you ragamuffins!" cried he to them. "The man who lies in that grave belongs to me; I want to take him, and if you don't go away I will wring your necks!"

"Lord of the red feather," said the soldier, "you are not my captain, I have no need to obey you, and I have not yet learned how to fear. Go away, we shall stay sitting here."

The Devil thought to himself, "Money is the best thing with which to get hold of these two vagabonds." So he began to play a softer tune, and asked quite kindly, if they would not accept a bag of money, and go home with it?

"That is worth listening to," answered the soldier, "but one bag of gold won't serve us, if you will give as much as will go into one of my boots, we will quit the field for you and go away."

"I have not so much as that about me," said the Devil, "but I will fetch it. In the neighboring town lives a money changer who is a good friend of mine, and will readily advance it to me."

When the Devil had vanished the soldier took his left boot off, and said, "We will soon pull a trick on the charcoal burner, just give me your knife, comrade." He cut the sole off the boot, and put it in the high grass near the grave on the edge of a hole that was half overgrown. "That will do," said he; "now the chimney sweep may come."

They both sat down and waited, and it was not long before the Devil returned with a small bag of gold in his hand. "Just pour it in," said the soldier, raising up the boot a little, "but that won't be enough."

The Black One shook out all that was in the bag; the gold fell through, and the boot remained empty. "Stupid Devil," cried the soldier, "it won't do! Didn't I say so at once? Go back again, and bring more." The Devil shook his head, went, and in an hour's time came with a much larger bag under his arm. "Now pour it in," cried the soldier, "but I doubt the boot will be full." The gold clinked as it fell, but the boot remained empty.

The Devil looked in himself with his burning eyes, and convinced himself of the truth. "You have shamefully big calves to your legs!" cried he, and made a wry face.

"Did you think," replied the soldier, "that I had a cloven foot like you? Since when have you been so stingy? See that you get more gold together, or our bargain will come to nothing!" The Wicked One went off again. This time he stayed away longer, and when at length he appeared he was panting under the weight of a sack that lay on his shoulders. He emptied it into the boot, which was just as far from being filled as before. He became furious, and was just going to tear the boot out of the soldier's hands, but at that moment the first ray of the rising sun broke forth from the sky, and the Evil Spirit fled away with loud shrieks. The poor soul was saved.

The peasant wished to divide the gold, but the soldier said, "Give what falls to my lot to the poor, I will come with you to your cottage, and together we will live in rest and peace on what remains, as long as God is pleased to permit."

96. *Old Rinkrank*

There was once upon a time a King who had a daughter, and he caused a glass mountain to be made, and said that whoever could cross to the other side of it without falling should have his daughter as wife. Then there was one who loved the King's daughter, and he asked the King if he might have her. "Yes," said the King; "if you can cross the mountain without falling, you shall have her." And the princess said she would go over it with him, and would hold him if he were about to fall.

So they set out together to go over it, and when they were halfway up the princess slipped and fell, and the glass mountain opened and shut her up inside it, and her betrothed could not see where she had gone, for the mountain closed immediately. Then he wept and lamented much, and the King was miserable too, and had the mountain broken open where she had been lost, and thought he would be able to get her out again, but they could not find the place into which she had fallen. Meanwhile the King's daughter had fallen quite deep down into the earth into a great cave. An old fellow with a very long gray beard came to meet her, and told her that if she would be his servant and do everything he bade her, she might live, if not he would kill her. So she did all he bade her. In the mornings he took his ladder out of his pocket, and set it up against the mountain and climbed to the top by its help, and then he drew up the ladder after him. The princess had to cook his dinner, make his bed, and do all his work, and when he came home again he always brought with him a heap of gold and silver.

When she had lived with him for many years, and had grown quite old, he called her Mother Mansrot, and she had to call him Old Rinkrank. Then once when he was out, and she had made his bed and washed his dishes, she shut the doors and windows all fast, and there was one little window through which the light shone in, and this she left open. When Old Rinkrank came home, he knocked at his door, and cried, "Mother Mansrot, open the door for me."

"No," said she, "Old Rinkrank, I will not open the door for you." Then he said,

> "Here stand I, poor Rinkrank,
> On my seventeen long shanks,
> On my weary, worn-out foot,
> Wash my dishes, Mother Mansrot."

"I have washed your dishes already," said she. Then again he said,

> "Here stand I, poor Rinkrank,
> On my seventeen long shanks,
> On my weary, worn-out foot,
> Make me my bed, Mother Mansrot."

"I have made your bed already," said she. Then again he said,

> "Here stand I, poor Rinkrank,
> On my seventeen long shanks,
> On my weary, worn-out foot,
> Open the door, Mother Mansrot."

Then he ran all around his house, and saw that the little window was open, and thought, "I will look in and see what she can be about, and why she will not open the door for me." He tried to peep in, but could not get his head through because of his long beard. So he first put his beard through the open window, but just as he had got it through, Mother Mansrot came by and pulled the window down with a cord that she had tied to it, and his beard was shut fast in it. Then he began to cry most piteously, for it hurt him very much, and to entreat her to release him again. But she said not until he gave her the ladder with which he ascended the mountain. Then, whether he wanted to or not, he had to tell her where the ladder was. And she fastened a very long ribbon to the window, and then she set up the ladder, and ascended the mountain, and when she was at the top of it she opened the window.

She went to her father, and told him all that had happened to her. The King rejoiced greatly, and her betrothed was still there, and they went and dug up the mountain, and found Old Rinkrank inside it with all his gold and silver. Then the King had Old Rinkrank put to death, and took all his gold and silver. The princess married her betrothed, and lived right happily in great magnificence and joy.

97. *The Crystal Ball*

There was once an enchantress, who had three sons who loved each other as brothers, but the old woman did not trust them, and thought they wanted to steal her power from her. So she changed the eldest into an eagle, which was forced to dwell in the rocky mountains, and was often seen sweeping in great circles in the sky. The second, she changed into a whale, which lived in the deep sea, and all that was seen of it was that it sometimes spouted up a great jet of water in the air. Each of them bore his human form for only two hours daily. The third son, who was afraid she might change him into a raging wild beast, a bear perhaps, or a wolf, went secretly away.

He had heard that a King's daughter who was bewitched, was imprisoned in the Castle of the Golden Sun, and was waiting for deliverance. Those, however, who tried to free her risked their lives; twenty-three youths had already died a miserable death, and now only one other might make the attempt, after which no more must come. And as his heart was without fear, he had the idea of seeking out the Castle of the Golden Sun. He had already traveled about for a long time without being able to find it, when he came by chance into a great forest, and did not know the way out of it. All at once he saw in the distance two giants, who made a sign to him with their hands, and when he came to them they said, "We are quarreling about a cap, and which of us it is to belong to, and as we are equally strong, neither of us can get the better of the other. The small men are cleverer than we are, so we will leave the decision to you."

"How can you dispute about an old cap?" said the youth.

"You do not know what properties it has! It is a wishing cap; whoever puts it on, can wish himself away wherever he likes, and in an instant he will be there."

"Give me the cap," said the youth, "I will go a short distance off, and when I call you, you must run a race, and the cap shall belong to the one who gets first to me." He put it on and went away, and thought of the King's daughter, forgot the giants, and walked continually onward.

At length he sighed from the very bottom of his heart, and cried, "Ah, if I were but at the Castle of the Golden Sun," and hardly had the words passed his lips than he was standing on a high mountain before the gate of the castle.

He entered and went through all the rooms, until in the last he found the King's daughter. But how shocked he was when he saw her. She had an ashen-gray face full of wrinkles, bleary eyes, and red hair. "Are you the King's daughter, whose beauty the whole world praises?" cried he.

"Ah," she answered, "this is not my form; human eyes can only see me in this state of ugliness, but that you may know what I am like, look in the mirror, it does not let itself be misled. It will show you my image as it is in truth." She gave him the mirror in his hand, and he saw in it the likeness of the most beautiful maiden on earth, and saw, too, how the tears were rolling down her cheeks with grief.

Then said he, "How can you be set free? I fear no danger."

She said, "He who gets the crystal ball, and holds it before the enchanter, will destroy his power with it, and I shall resume my true shape. Ah," she added, "so many have already gone to meet death for this, and you are so young; I grieve that you should encounter such great danger."

"Nothing can keep me from doing it," said he, "but tell me what I must do."

"You shall know everything," said the King's daughter; "when you descend the mountain on which the castle stands, a wild bull will stand below by a spring, and you must fight with it, and if you have the luck to kill it, a fiery bird will spring out of it, which bears in its body a burning egg, and in the egg the crystal ball lies like a yolk. The bird will not, however, let the egg fall until forced to do so, and if it falls on the ground, it will flame up and burn everything that is near, and melt even ice itself, and with it the crystal ball, and then all your trouble will have been in vain."

The youth went down to the spring, where the bull snorted and bellowed at him. After a long struggle he plunged his sword in the animal's body, and it fell down. Instantly a fiery bird arose from it, and was about to fly away, but the young man's brother, the eagle, who was passing between the clouds, swooped down, hunted it away to the sea, and struck it with his beak until, in its extremity, it let the egg fall. The egg did not, however, fall into the sea, but on a fisherman's hut that stood on the shore and the hut began at once to smoke and was about to break out in flames. Then arose in the sea waves as high as a house, they streamed over the hut, and subdued the fire. The other brother, the whale, had come swimming to them, and had driven the water up on high. When the fire was extinguished, the youth sought for the egg and happily found it; it was not yet melted, but the shell was broken by being so suddenly cooled with the water, and he could take out the crystal ball unhurt.

When the youth went to the enchanter and held it before him, the latter said, "My power is destroyed, and from this time forth you are the King of the Castle of the Golden Sun. With this you can likewise give back to your brothers their human form." Then the youth hastened to the King's daughter, and when he entered the room, she was standing there in the full splendor of her beauty, and joyfully they exchanged rings with each other.

98. *Maid Maleen*

There was once a King who had a son who asked in marriage the daughter of a mighty King; she was called Maid Maleen, and was very beautiful. As her father wished to give her to another, the prince was rejected; but as they both loved each other with all their hearts, they would not give each other up, and Maid Maleen said to her father, "I can and will take no other for my husband."

Then the King flew into a passion, and ordered a dark tower to be built, into which no ray of sunlight or moonlight should enter. When it was finished, he said, "In that you shall be imprisoned for seven years, and then I will come and see if your perverse spirit is broken." Meat and drink for the seven years were carried into the tower, and then she and her waiting maid were led into it and walled up, and thus cut off from the sky and from the earth. There they sat in the darkness, and knew not when day or night began. The King's son often went around and around the tower, and called their names, but no sound from outside pierced through the thick walls. What else could they do but lament and complain?

Meanwhile the time passed, and by the diminution of the food and drink they knew that the seven years were coming to an end. They thought the moment of their deliverance had come; but no stroke of the hammer was heard, no stone fell out of the wall, and it seemed to Maid Maleen that her father had forgotten her. As they only had food for a short time longer, and saw a miserable death awaiting them, Maid Maleen said, "We must try our last chance, and see if we can break through the wall." She took the bread knife, and picked and bored at the mortar of a stone, and when she was tired, the waiting maid took her turn. With great labor they succeeded in getting out one stone, and then a second, and a third, and when three days were over the first ray of light fell on their darkness, and at last the opening was so large that they could look out. The sky was blue, and a fresh breeze played on their faces; but how melancholy everything looked all around! Her father's castle lay in ruins, the town and the villages were, so far as could be seen, destroyed by fire, the fields far and wide laid to waste, and no human being was visible. When the opening in the wall was large enough for them to slip through, the waiting maid sprang down first, and then Maid Maleen followed. But where were they to go? The enemy had ravaged the whole kingdom, driven away the King, and slain all the inhabitants. They wandered forth to seek another country, but nowhere did they find a shelter, or a human being to give them a mouthful of bread, and their need was so great that they were forced to appease their hunger with nettles. When, after long journeying, they came into another country, they tried to get work everywhere; but wherever they knocked they were turned away, and no one would have pity on them. At last they arrived in a large city and went to the royal palace. There also they were ordered to go away, but at last the cook said that they might stay in the kitchen and be kitchen maids.

The son of the King in whose kingdom they were, was, however, the very man who had been betrothed to Maid Maleen. His father had chosen another bride for him, whose face was as ugly as her heart was wicked. The wedding was fixed, and the maiden had already arrived; but because of her great ugliness, however, she shut herself in her room, and allowed no one to see her, and Maid Maleen had to take her meals from the kitchen. When the day came for the bride and the bridegroom to go to church, she was ashamed of her ugliness, and afraid that if she showed herself in the streets, she would be mocked and laughed at by the people. Then said she to Maid Maleen, "A great piece of luck has befallen you. I have sprained my foot, and cannot well walk through the streets; you shall put on my wedding clothes and take my place; a greater honor than that you cannot have!"

Maid Maleen, however, refused it, and said, "I wish for no honor that is not suitable for me."

It was in vain, too, that the bride offered her gold. At last she said angrily, "If you do not obey me, it shall cost you your life. I have but to speak the word, and your head will lie at your feet." Then she was forced to obey, and put on the bride's magnificent clothes and all her jewels.

When she entered the royal hall, everyone was amazed at her great beauty, and the King said to his son, "This is the bride whom I have chosen for you, and whom you must lead to church."

The bridegroom was astonished, and thought, "She is like my Maid Maleen, and I should believe that it was she herself, but she has long been shut up in the tower, or dead." He took her by the hand and led her to church. On the way was a nettle bush, and she said,

> "Oh, nettle bush,
> Little nettle bush,
> What do you here alone?
> I have known the time
> When I ate you unboiled,
> When I ate you unroasted."

"What are you saying?" asked the King's son.

"Nothing," she replied, "I was only thinking of Maid Maleen." He was surprised that she knew about her, but kept silence. When they came to the foot-plank into the churchyard, she said,

> "Footbridge, do not break,
> I am not the true bride."

"What are you saying there?" asked the King's son.

"Nothing," she replied, "I was only thinking of Maid Maleen."

"Do you know Maid Maleen?"

"No," she answered, "how should I know her; I have only heard of her." When they came to the church door, she said once more,

> "Church door, break not,
> I am not the true bride."

"What are you saying there?" asked he.

"Ah," she answered, "I was only thinking of Maid Maleen." Then he took out a precious chain, put it around her neck, and fastened the clasp. Thereupon they entered the church, and the priest joined their hands together before the altar, and married them. He led her home, but she did not speak a single word the whole way. When they got back to the royal palace, she hurried into the bride's chamber, put off the magnificent clothes and the jewels, dressed herself in her gray gown, and kept nothing but the jewel on her neck, which she had received from the bridegroom.

When the night came, and the bride was to be led into the prince's apartment, she let her veil fall over her face, that he might not observe the deception. As soon as everyone had gone away, he said to her, "What did you say to the nettle bush that was growing by the wayside?"

"To which nettle bush?" asked she; "I don't talk to nettle bushes."

"If you did not do it, then you are not the true bride," said he. So she thought to herself, and said,

> "I must go out unto my maid,
> Who keeps my thoughts for me."

She went out and sought Maid Maleen. "Girl, what have you been saying to the nettle?"

"I said nothing but,

> "Oh, nettle bush,
> Little nettle bush,
> What do you here alone?
> I have known the time
> When I ate you unboiled,
> When I ate you unroasted."

The bride ran back into the chamber, and said, "I know now what I said to the nettle," and she repeated the words that she had just heard.

"But what did you say to the footbridge when we went over it?" asked the King's son.

"To the footbridge?" she answered. "I don't talk to footbridges."

"Then you are not the true bride."

She again said,

> "I must go out unto my maid,
> Who keeps my thoughts for me,"

and ran out and found Maid Maleen. "Girl, what did you say to the footbridge?"

"I said nothing but,

> "Footbridge, do not break,
> I am not the true bride."

"That costs you your life!" cried the bride, but she hurried into the room, and said, "I know now what I said to the footbridge," and she repeated the words.

"But what did you say to the church door?"

"To the church door?" she replied; "I don't talk to church doors."

"Then you are not the true bride."

She went out and found Maid Maleen, and said, "Girl, what did you say to the church door?"

"I said nothing but,

> "Church door, break not,
> I am not the true bride."

"That will break your neck for you!" cried the bride, and flew into a terrible passion, but she hastened back into the room, and said, "I know now what I said to the church door," and she repeated the words.

"But where have you the jewel that I gave you at the church door?"

"What jewel?" she answered; "you did not give me any jewel."

"I myself put it around your neck, and I myself fastened it; if you do not know that, you are not the true bride." He drew the veil from her face, and when he saw her immeasurable ugliness, he sprang back terrified, and said, "How did you get here? Who are you?"

"I am your betrothed bride, but because I feared lest the people should mock me when they saw me out of doors, I commanded the kitchen maid to dress herself in my clothes, and to go to church instead of me."

"Where is the girl?" said he; "I want to see her, go and bring her here." She went out and told the servants that the kitchen maid was an impostor, and that they must take her out into the courtyard and strike off her head. The servants laid hold of Maid Maleen and wanted to drag her out, but she screamed so loudly for help, that the King's son heard her voice, hurried out of his chamber and ordered them to set the maiden free instantly. Lights were brought, and then he saw on her neck the gold chain that he had given her at the church door.

"You are the true bride," said he, "who went with me to the church; come with me now to my room." When they were both alone, he said, "On the way to church you did name Maid Maleen, who was my betrothed bride; if I could believe it possible, I should think she was standing before me. You are like her in every respect."

She answered, "I am Maid Maleen, who for your sake was imprisoned seven years in the darkness, who suffered hunger and thirst, and has lived so long in want and poverty. Today, however, the sun is shining on me once more. I was married to you in the church, and I am your lawful wife." Then they kissed each other, and were happy all the days of their lives. The false bride was rewarded for what she had done by having her head cut off.

The tower in which Maid Maleen had been imprisoned remained standing for a long time, and when the children passed by it they sang,

"Kling, klang, gloria.
Who sits within this tower?
A King's daughter, she sits within,
A sight of her I cannot win,
The wall, it will not break,
The stone cannot be pierced.
Little Hans, with your coat so gay,
Follow me, follow me, fast as you may."

99. *The Boots of Buffalo Leather*

A soldier who is afraid of nothing, troubles himself about nothing. One of this kind had received his discharge, and as he had learned no trade and could earn nothing, he traveled about and begged alms of kind people. He had an old waterproof cloak on his back, and a pair of riding boots of buffalo leather that were still left to him. One day he was walking he knew not where, straight out into the open country, and at length came to a forest. He did not know where he was, but saw sitting on the trunk of a tree, which had been cut down, a man who was well dressed and wore a green hunting coat. The soldier shook hands with him, sat down on the grass by his side, and stretched out his legs. "I see you have good boots on, which are well polished," said he to the hunter; "but if you had to travel about as I have, they would not last long. Look at mine, they are of buffalo leather, and have been worn for a long time, but in them I can go through thick and thin." After a while the soldier got up and said, "I can stay no longer, hunger drives me onward; but, Brother Brightboots, where does this road lead to?"

"I don't know that myself," answered the hunter, "I have lost my way in the forest."

"Then you are in the same plight as I," said the soldier; "birds of a feather flock together, let us remain together, and seek our way." The hunter smiled a little, and they walked on further and further, until night fell.

"We do not get out of the forest," said the soldier, "but there in the distance I see a light shining, which will help us to find something to eat." They found a stone house, knocked at the door, and an old woman opened it. "We are looking for quarters for the night," said the soldier, "and some lining for our stomachs, for mine is as empty as an old knapsack."

"You cannot stay here," answered the old woman; "this is a robbers' house, and you would do wisely to get away before they come home, or you will be lost."

"It won't be so bad as that," answered the soldier. "I have not had a mouthful for two days, and whether I am murdered here or die of hunger in the forest is all the same to me. I shall go in." The hunter would not follow, but the soldier drew him in with him by the sleeve. "Come, my dear brother, we shall not come to an end so quickly as that!"

The old woman had pity on them and said, "Creep in here behind the stove, and if they leave anything, I will give it to you on the sly when they are asleep." Scarcely were they in the corner before twelve robbers came bursting in, seated themselves at the table, which was already laid, and vehemently demanded some food. The old woman brought in some great dishes of roast meat, and the robbers enjoyed that thoroughly.

When the smell of the food ascended the nostrils of the soldier, he said to the hunter, "I cannot hold out any longer, I shall seat myself at the table, and eat with them."

"You will bring us to destruction," said the hunter, and held him back by the arm. But the soldier began to cough loudly.

When the robbers heard that, they threw away their knives and forks, leapt up, and discovered the two who were behind the stove. "Aha, gentlemen, are you in the corner?" cried they. "What are you doing here? Have you been sent as spies? Wait a while, and you shall learn how to fly on a dry bough."

"But do be civil," said the soldier, "I am hungry, give me something to eat, and then you can do what you like with me."

The robbers were astonished, and the captain said, "I see that you have no fear; well, you shall have some food, but after that you must die."

"We shall see," said the soldier, and seated himself at the table, and began to cut away valiantly at the roast meat. "Brother Brightboots, come and eat," cried he to the hunter; "you must be as hungry as I am, and cannot have better roast meat at home," but the hunter would not eat.

The robbers looked at the soldier in astonishment, and said, "The rascal uses no ceremony."

After a while he said, "I have had enough food, now get me something good to drink."

The captain was in the mood to humor him in this also, and called to the old woman, "Bring a bottle out of the cellar, and make it the best."

The soldier drew the cork out with a loud noise, and then went with the bottle to the hunter and said, "Pay attention, brother, and you shall see something that will surprise you; I am now going to drink the health of the whole clan." Then he brandished the bottle over the heads of the robbers, and cried, "Long life to you all, but with your mouths open and your right hands lifted up," and then he drank a hearty gulp. Scarcely were the words said than they all sat motionless as if made of stone, and their mouths were open and their right hands stretched up in the air.

The hunter said to the soldier, "I see that you are acquainted with tricks of another kind, but now come and let us go home."

"Oho, my dear brother, but that would be marching away far too soon; we have conquered the enemy, and must first take the booty. Those men there are sitting fast, and are opening their mouths with astonishment, but they will not be allowed to move until I permit them. Come, eat and drink."

The old woman had to bring another bottle of the best wine, and the soldier would not stir until he had eaten enough to last for three days. At last when day came, he said, "Now it is time to strike our tents, and that our march may be a short one, the old woman shall show us the nearest way to the town." When they had arrived there, he went to his old comrades, and said, "Out in the forest I have found a nest full of gallows' birds, come with me and we will take it."

The soldier led them, and said to the hunter, "You must go back again with me to see how they shake when we seize them by the feet." He placed the men around about the robbers, and then he took the bottle, drank a mouthful, brandished it above them, and cried, "Live again." Instantly they all regained the power of movement, but were thrown down and bound hand and foot with cords. Then the soldier ordered them to be thrown into a cart as if they had been so many sacks, and said, "Now drive them straight to prison." The hunter, however, took one of the men aside and gave him another commission besides.

"Brother Brightboots," said the soldier, "we have safely routed the enemy and been well fed, now we will quietly walk behind them as if we were stragglers!" When they approached the town, the soldier saw a crowd of people pouring through the gate of the town who were raising loud cries of joy, and waving green boughs in the air. Then he saw that the entire royal bodyguard was coming up. "What can this mean?" said he to the hunter.

"Do you not know?" he replied, "that the King has for a long time been absent from his kingdom, and that today he is returning, and everyone is going to meet him."

"But where is the King?" said the soldier. "I do not see him."

"Here he is," answered the hunter. "I am the King, and have announced my arrival." Then he opened his hunting coat, and his royal garments were visible. The soldier was alarmed, and fell on his knees and begged him to forgive him for having in his ignorance treated him as an equal, and spoken to him by such a name. But the King shook hands with him, and said, "You are a brave soldier, and have saved my life. You shall never again be in want, I will take care of you. And if you would ever like to eat a piece of roast meat, as good as that in the robbers' house, come to the royal kitchen. But if you would drink to health, you must first ask my permission."

100. The Golden Key

I n the winter time, when deep snow lay on the ground, a poor boy was forced to go out on a sled to fetch wood. When he had gathered it together, and packed it, he wished, as he was so frozen with cold, not to go home at once, but to light a fire and warm himself a little. So he scraped away the snow, and as he was thus clearing the ground, he found a tiny, gold key. Hereupon he thought that where the key was, the lock must be also, and dug in the ground and found an iron chest. "If the key does but fit it!" thought he; "no doubt there are precious things in that little box." He searched, but no keyhole was there. At last he discovered one, but so small that it was hardly visible. He tried it, and the key fitted it exactly. Then he turned it once around, and now we must wait until he has quite unlocked it and opened the lid, and then we shall learn what wonderful things were lying in that box.

CHILDREN'S LEGENDS

LEGEND 1.

St. Joseph in the Forest

There was once on a time a mother who had three daughters, the eldest of whom was rude and wicked, the second much better, although she had her faults, but the youngest was a pious, good child. The mother was, however, so strange, that it was just the eldest daughter whom she most loved, and she could not bear the youngest. On this account, she often sent the poor girl out into the great forest in order to get rid of her, for she thought she would lose herself and never come back again. But the guardian angel that every good child has did not forsake her, but always brought her into the right path again. Once, however, the guardian angel behaved as if he were not there, and the child could not find her way out of the forest again. She walked on constantly until evening came, and then she saw a tiny light burning in the distance, ran up to it at once, and came to a little hut. She knocked, the door opened, and she came to a second door, where she knocked again. An old man, who had a snow-white beard and looked venerable, opened it for her; and he was no other than St. Joseph. He said quite kindly, "Come, dear child, seat yourself on my little chair by the fire, and warm yourself; I will fetch you clear water if you are thirsty; but here in the forest, I have nothing for you to eat but a couple of little roots, which you must first scrape and boil."

St. Joseph gave her the roots. The girl scraped them clean, then she brought a piece of pancake and the bread that her mother had given her to take with her, mixed all together in a pan, and cooked herself a thick soup. When it was ready, St. Joseph said, "I am so hungry; give me some of your food." The child was quite willing, and gave him more than she kept for herself, but God's blessing was with her, so that she was satisfied.

When they had eaten, St. Joseph said, "Now we will go to bed; I have, however, only one bed, lay yourself in it. I will lie on the ground on the straw."

"No," answered she, "stay in your own bed, the straw is soft enough for me." St. Joseph, however, took the child in his arms, and carried her into the little bed, and there she said her prayers, and fell asleep.

Next morning when she awoke, she wanted to say good morning to St. Joseph, but she did not see him. Then she got up and looked for him, but could not find him anywhere; at last she perceived, behind the door, a bag with money so heavy that she could just carry it, and on it was written that it was for the child who had slept there that night. She took the bag, bounded away with it, and got safely to her mother, and as she gave her mother all the money, she could not help being satisfied with her.

The next day, the second child also took a fancy to go into the forest. Her mother gave her a much larger piece of pancake and bread. It happened with her just as with the first child. In the evening she came to St. Joseph's little hut, who gave her roots for a thick soup. When it was ready, he likewise said to her, "I am so hungry, give me some of your food."

Then the child said, "You may have your share." Afterward, when St. Joseph offered her his bed and wanted to lie on the straw, she replied, "No, lie down in the bed, there is plenty of room for both of us." St. Joseph took her in his arms and put her in the bed, and laid himself on the straw.

In the morning when the child awoke and looked for St. Joseph, he had vanished, but behind the door she found a little sack of money that was about as long as a hand, and on it was written that it was for the child who had slept there last night. So she took the little bag and ran home with it, and took it to her mother, but she secretly kept two pieces for herself.

The eldest daughter had by this time grown curious, and the next morning also insisted on going out into the forest. Her mother gave her pancakes to take with her—as many as she wanted, and bread and cheese as well. In the evening she found St. Joseph in his little hut, just as the two others had found him. When the soup was ready and St. Joseph said, "I am so hungry, give me some of your food," the girl answered, "Wait until I am satisfied; then if there is anything left you shall have it." She ate, however, nearly the whole of it, and St. Joseph had to scrape the dish.

Afterward, the good old man offered her his bed, and wanted to lie on the straw. She took it without making any opposition, laid herself down in the little bed, and left the hard straw to the white-haired man. Next morning when she awoke, St. Joseph was not to be found, but she did not trouble herself about that. She looked behind the door for a moneybag. She fancied something was lying on the ground, but as she could not very well distinguish what it was, she stooped down, and examined it closely, but it remained hanging to her nose, and when she got up again, she saw, to her horror, that it was a second nose, which was hanging fast to her own. Then she began to scream and howl, but that did no good; she was forced to see it always on her nose, for it stretched out so far. Then she ran out and screamed without stopping till she met St. Joseph, at whose feet she fell and begged until, out of pity, he took the nose off her again, and even gave her two pennies. When she got home, her mother was standing before the door, and asked, "What have you had given to you?"

Then she lied and said, "A great bag of money, but I have lost it on the way."

"Lost it!" cried the mother, "oh, but we will soon find it again," and took her by the hand, and wanted to seek it with her. At first she began to cry, and did not wish to go, but at last she went. On the way, however, so many lizards and snakes broke loose on both of them, that they did not know how to save themselves. At last they bit the wicked child to death, and they bit the mother in the foot, because she had not brought her up better.

LEGEND 2.

The Twelve Apostles

Three hundred years before the birth of the Lord Christ, there lived a mother who had twelve sons, but was so poor and needy that she no longer knew how she was to keep them alive at all. She prayed to God daily that he would grant that all her sons might be on the earth with the promised Redeemer. When her necessity became still greater she sent one of them after the other out into the world to seek bread for her. The eldest was called Peter, and he went out and had already walked a long way, a whole day's journey, when he came into a great forest. He sought for a way out, but could find none, and went farther and farther astray, and at the same time felt such great hunger that he could scarcely stand. At length he became so weak that he was forced to lie down, and he believed death to be at hand. Suddenly there stood beside him a small boy who shone with brightness, and was as beautiful and kind as an angel. The child clapped his little hands together, until Peter was forced to look up and saw him. Then the child said, "Why are you sitting there in such trouble?"

"Alas!" answered Peter, "I am going about the world seeking bread, that I may yet see the dear Savior who is promised, that is my greatest desire."

The child said, "Come with me, and your wish shall be fulfilled." He took poor Peter by the hand, and led him between some cliffs to a great cavern. When they entered it, everything was shining with gold, silver, and crystal, and in the middle of it twelve cradles were standing side by side. Then said the little angel, "Lie down in the first, and sleep a while, I will rock you." Peter did so, and the angel sang to him and rocked him until he was asleep. And when he was asleep, the second brother came also, guided there by his guardian angel, and he was rocked to sleep like the first, and thus came the others, one after the other, until all twelve lay there sleeping in the golden cradles. They slept, however, three hundred years, until the night when the Savior of the world was born. Then they awoke, and were with him on earth, and were called the twelve apostles.

LEGEND 3.

The Rose

There was once a poor woman who had two children. The youngest had to go every day into the forest to fetch wood. Once when she had gone a long way to seek it, a little child, who was quite strong, came and helped her industriously to pick up the wood and carry it home, and then before a moment had passed the strange child disappeared. The child told her mother this, but at first she would not believe it. At length she brought a rose home, and told her mother that the beautiful child had given her this rose, and had told her that when it was in full bloom, he would return. The mother put the rose in water. One morning her child could not get out of bed. The mother went to the bed and found her dead, but she lay looking very happy. On the same morning, the rose was in full bloom.

LEGEND 4.

Poverty and Humility Lead to Heaven

There was once a King's son who went out into the world, and he was full of thought and sadness. He looked at the sky, which was so beautifully pure and blue, then he sighed, and said, "How well must all be with one up there in heaven!" Then he saw a poor gray-haired man who was coming along the road toward him, and he spoke to him, and asked, "How can I get to heaven?"

The man answered, "By poverty and humility. Put on my ragged clothes, wander about the world for seven years, and get to know what misery is, take no money, but if you are hungry ask compassionate hearts for a bit of bread; in this way you will reach heaven."

Then the King's son took off his magnificent coat, and wore in its place the beggar's garment, went out into the wide world, and suffered great misery. He took nothing but a little food, said nothing, but prayed to the Lord to take him into his heaven. When the seven years were over, he returned to his father's palace, but no one recognized him. He said to the servants, "Go and tell my parents that I have come back again." But the servants did not believe it, and laughed and left him standing there. Then said he, "Go and tell it to my brothers that they may come down, for I should so like to see them again." The servants would not do that either, but at last one of them went, and told it to the King's children, but these did not believe it, and did not trouble themselves about it.

Then he wrote a letter to his mother, and described to her all his misery, but he did not say that he was her son. So, out of pity, the Queen had a place under the stairs assigned to him, and food taken to him daily by two servants. But one of them was ill-natured and said, "Why should the beggar have the good food?" and kept it for himself, or gave it to the dogs, and took the weak, wasted-away beggar nothing but water; the other, however, was honest, and took the beggar what was sent to him. It was little, but he could live on it for a while, and all the time he was quite patient, but he grew continually weaker. As, however, his illness increased, he desired to receive the last sacrament. When the host was being elevated down below, all the bells in the town and neighborhood began to ring. After Mass the priest went to the poor man under the stairs, and there he lay dead. In one hand he had a rose, in the other a lily, and beside him was a paper on which was written his history.

When he was buried, a rose grew on one side of his grave, and a lily on the other.

LEGEND 5.

God's Food

There were once upon a time two sisters, one of whom had no children and was rich, and the other had five and was a widow, and so poor that she no longer had food enough to satisfy herself and her children. In her need, therefore, she went to her sister, and said, "My children and I are suffering the greatest hunger; you are rich, give me a mouthful of bread."

The very rich sister was as hard as a stone, and said, "I myself have nothing in the house," and drove away the poor creature with harsh words. After some time the husband of the rich sister came home, and was just going to cut himself a piece of bread, but when he made the first cut into the loaf, out flowed red blood. When the woman saw that she was terrified and told him what had occurred. He hurried away to help the widow and her children, but when he entered her room, he found her praying. She had her two youngest children in her arms, and the three eldest were lying dead.

He offered her food, but she answered, "For earthly food we have no longer any desire. God has already satisfied the hunger of three of us, and he will listen to our supplications likewise." Scarcely had she uttered these words than the two little ones drew their last breath, whereupon her heart broke, and she sank down dead.

LEGEND 6.

The Three Green Twigs

There was once on a time a hermit who lived in a forest at the foot of a mountain, and passed his time in prayer and good works, and every evening he carried, to the glory of God, two pails of water up the mountain. Many a beast drank of it, and many a plant was refreshed by it, for on the heights above, a strong wind blew continually, which dried the air and the ground, and the wild birds that dread mankind wheel about there, and with their sharp eyes search for a drink. And because the hermit was so pious, an angel of God, visible to his eyes, went up with him, counted his steps, and when the work was completed, brought him his food, just as the ravens by God's command had fed the prophet. When the hermit in his piety had already reached a great age, it happened that he once saw from afar a poor sinner being taken to the gallows. He said carelessly to himself, "There, that one is getting his deserts!"

In the evening, when he was carrying the water up the mountain, the angel who usually accompanied him did not appear, and also brought him no food. Then he was terrified, and searched his heart, and tried to think how he could have sinned, as God was so angry, but he did not discover it. Then he neither ate nor drank, threw himself down on the ground, and prayed day and night. And as he was one day thus bitterly weeping in the forest, he heard a little bird singing beautifully and delightfully, and then he was still more troubled and said, "How joyously you sing, the Lord is not angry with you. Ah, if you could but tell me how I can have offended him, that I might do penance, and then my heart also would be glad again."

Then the bird began to speak and said, "You have done injustice, in that you have condemned a poor sinner who was being led to the gallows, and for that the Lord is angry with you. He alone sits in judgment. However, if you will do penance and repent your sins, he will forgive you." Then the angel stood beside him with a dry branch in his hand and said, "You shall carry this dry branch until three green twigs sprout out of it, but at night when you will sleep, you shall lay it under your head. You shall beg your bread from door to door, and not stay more than one night in the same house. That is the penance that the Lord lays on you."

Then the hermit took the piece of wood, and went back into the world, which he had not seen for so long. He ate and drank nothing but what was given him at the doors; many petitions were, however, not listened to, and many doors remained shut to him, so that he often did not get a crumb of bread.

Once when he had gone from door to door from morning till night, and no one had given him anything, and no one would shelter him for the night, he went forth into a forest, and at last found a cave that someone had made, and an old woman was sitting in it. Then said he, "Good woman, keep me with you in your house for this night;" but she said, "No, I dare not, even if I wished. I have three sons who are wicked and wild, if they come home from their robbing expedition, and find you, they would kill us both."

The hermit said, "Let me stay, they will do no injury either to you or to me," and the woman was compassionate, and let herself be persuaded. Then the man lay down beneath the stairs, and put the bit of wood under his head. When the old woman saw him do that, she asked the reason of it, at which he told her that he carried the bit of wood about with him for a penance, and used it at night for a pillow, and that he had offended the Lord, because, when he had seen a poor sinner on the way to the gallows, he had said he was getting his deserts.

Then the woman began to weep and cried, "If the Lord thus punishes one single word, how will it fare with my sons when they appear before him in judgment?"

At midnight the robbers came home and blustered and stormed. They made a fire, and when it had lighted up the cave and they saw a man lying under the stairs, they fell in a rage and cried to their mother, "Who is the man? Have we not forbidden anyone whatsoever to be taken in?"

Then said the mother, "Let him alone, it is a poor sinner who is atoning for his crime."

The robbers asked, "What has he done?" To him they cried, "Old man, tell us your sins."

The old man raised himself and told them how he, by one single word, had so sinned that God was angry with him, and how he was now expiating this crime. The robbers were so powerfully touched in their hearts by this story, that they were shocked with their life up to this time, reflected, and began with hearty repentance to do penance for it. The hermit, after he had converted the three sinners, lay down to sleep again under the stairs. In the morning, however, they found him dead, and out of the dry wood on which his head lay, three green twigs had grown up on high. Thus the Lord had once more received him into his favor.

LEGEND 7.

Our Lady's Little Glass

Once upon a time a waggoner's cart that was heavily laden with wine had stuck so fast that in spite of all that he could do, he could not get it to move again. Then it chanced that Our Lady just happened to come by that way, and when she perceived the poor man's distress, she said to him, "I am tired and thirsty, give me a glass of wine, and I will set your cart free for you."

"Willingly," answered the waggoner, "but I have no glass in which I can give you the wine."

Then Our Lady plucked a little white flower with red stripes, called field bindweed, which looks very like a glass, and gave it to the waggoner. He filled it with wine, and then Our Lady drank it, and in the same instant the cart was set free, and the waggoner could drive onward. The little flower is still always called Our Lady's Little Glass.

LEGEND 8.

The Aged Mother

In a large town there was an old woman who sat in the evening alone in her room thinking how she had lost first her husband, then both her children, then one by one all her relations, and at length, that very day, her last friend, and now she was quite alone and desolate. She was very sad at heart, and heaviest of all her losses to her was that of her sons; and in her pain she blamed God for it. She was still sitting lost in thought, when all at once she heard the bells ringing for early prayer. She was surprised that she had thus in her sorrow watched through the whole night, and lighted her lantern and went to church. It was already lighted up when she arrived, but not as it usually was with wax candles, but with a dim light. It was also crowded already with people, and all the seats were filled; and when the old woman got to her usual place it also was not empty, but the whole bench was entirely full. And when she looked at the people, they were none other than her dead relations who were sitting there in their old-fashioned garments, but with pale faces. They neither spoke nor sang; but a soft humming and whispering was heard all over the church.

Then an aunt of hers stood up, stepped forward, and said to the poor old woman, "Look there beside the altar, and you will see your sons." The old woman looked there, and saw her two children, one hanging on the gallows, the other bound to the wheel. Then said the aunt, "You see, this is how it would have been with them if they had lived, and if the good God had not taken them to himself when they were innocent children." The old woman went trembling home, and on her knees thanked God for having dealt with her more kindly than she had been able to understand, and on the third day she lay down and died.

LEGEND 9.

The Heavenly Wedding

A poor peasant boy one day heard the priest say in church that whoever desired to enter into the kingdom of heaven must always go straight onward. So he set out, and walked continually straight onward over hill and valley without ever turning aside. At length his way led him into a great town, and into the middle of a church, where just at that time God's service was being performed. Now when he beheld all the magnificence of this, he thought he had reached heaven, sat down, and rejoiced with his whole heart.

When the service was over, and the clerk bade him go out, he replied, "No, I will not go out again, I am glad to be in heaven at last."

So the clerk went to the priest, and told him that there was a child in the church who would not go out again, because he believed he was in heaven. The priest said, "If he believes that, we will leave him inside." So he went to him, and asked if he had any inclination to work.

"Yes," the little fellow replied, "I am accustomed to work, but I will not go out of heaven again." So he stayed in the church, and when he saw how the people came and knelt and prayed to Our Lady with the blessed child Jesus that was carved in wood, he thought, "That is the good God," and said, "Dear God, how thin you are! The people must certainly let you starve; but every day I will give you half my dinner." From this time forth, he every day took half his dinner to the image, and the image began to enjoy the food. When a few weeks had gone by, people remarked that the image was growing larger and stout and strong, and wondered much. The priest also could not understand it, but stayed in the church, and followed the little boy about, and then he saw how he shared his food with the Virgin Mary, and how she accepted it.

After some time the boy became ill, and for eight days could not leave his bed; but as soon as he could get up again, the first thing he did was to take his food to Our Lady. The priest followed him, and heard him say, "Dear God, do not take it amiss that I have not brought you anything for such a long time, for I have been ill and could not get up."

Then the image answered him and said, "I have seen your good will, and that is enough for me. Next Sunday you shall go with me to the wedding." The boy rejoiced at this, and repeated it to the priest, who begged him to go and ask the image if he, too, might be permitted to go. "No," answered the image, "you alone." The priest wished to prepare him first, and give him the holy communion and the child was willing, and next Sunday, when the host came to him, he fell down and died, and was at the eternal wedding.

LEGEND 10

The Haƺel Branch

One afternoon the Christ Child had laid himself in his cradle and had fallen asleep. Then his mother came to him, looked at him full of gladness, and said, "Have you laid yourself down to sleep, my child? Sleep sweetly, and in the meantime I will go into the wood, and fetch you a handful of strawberries, for I know that you will be pleased with them when you awake." In the wood outside, she found a spot with the most beautiful strawberries; but as she was stooping down to gather one, an adder sprang up out of the grass. She was alarmed, left the strawberries where they were, and hastened away. The adder darted after her; but Our Lady, as you can readily understand, knew what it was best to do. She hid herself behind a hazel bush, and stood there until the adder had crept away again. Then she gathered the strawberries, and as she set out on her way home she said, "As the hazel bush has been my protection this time, it shall in future protect others also." Therefore, from the most remote times, a green hazel branch has been the safest protection against adders, snakes, and everything else that creeps on the earth.